DISCARDED

THE BEST FROM
FANTASY AND
SCIENCE FICTION
Nineteenth Series

THE BEST FROM
FANTASY AND
SCIENCE FICTION
Nineteenth Series

EDITED BY
Edward L. Ferman

DOUBLEDAY & COMPANY, INC., GARDEN CITY, NEW YORK

*All of the characters in this book
are fictitious, and any resemblance
to actual persons, living or dead,
is purely coincidental.*

ACKNOWLEDGMENTS

The editor hereby makes grateful acknowledgment to the following authors and authors' representatives for giving permission to reprint the material in this volume:

Robin Scott Wilson for *Gone Fishin'*

Virginia Kidd for *Selectra Six-ten* by Avram Davidson

Robert P. Mills Ltd. for *Longtooth* by Edgar Pangborn and *An Adventure in the Yolla Bolly Middle Eel Wilderness* by Vance Aandahl

Scott Meredith Literary Agency, Inc. for *Sundance* by Robert Silverberg and *Dream Patrol* by Charles W. Runyon

Robert Lantz-Candida Donadio Agency for *The Brief, Swinging Career of Dan and Judy Smythe* by Carter Wilson

Henry Morrison for *Calliope and Gherkin and the Yankee Doodle Thing* by Evelyn E. Smith

Barry N. Malzberg for *Notes Just Prior to the Fall*

Ron Goulart for *Confessions*

Larry Niven for *Get a Horse!*

Theodore Sturgeon for *The Man Who Learned Loving*

Harold Matson Co. for *Litterbug* by Tony Morphett and *Starting From Scratch* by Robert Sheckley

Bruce McAllister for *Benji's Pencil*

Gahan Wilson for the cartoons

94382

CONTENTS

GONE FISHIN'   Robin Scott Wilson   11

SELECTRA SIX-TEN   Avram Davidson   29

LONGTOOTH   Edgar Pangborn   37

SUNDANCE   Robert Silverberg   77

THE BRIEF, SWINGING CAREER OF DAN
    AND JUDY SMYTHE   Carter Wilson   95

DREAM PATROL   Charles W. Runyon   103

CALLIOPE AND GHERKIN AND THE
    YANKEE DOODLE THING   Evelyn E. Smith   119

NOTES JUST PRIOR TO THE FALL   Barry N. Malzberg   161

CONFESSIONS   Ron Goulart   175

GET A HORSE!   Larry Niven   195

THE MAN WHO LEARNED LOVING   Theodore Sturgeon   213

LITTERBUG   Tony Morphett   223

AN ADVENTURE IN THE YOLLA BOLLY MIDDLE
    EEL WILDERNESS   Vance Aandahl   245

STARTING FROM SCRATCH   Robert Sheckley   267

BENJI'S PENCIL   Bruce McAllister   273

            SIX CARTOONS by Gahan Wilson

AFTERWORD   Edward L. Ferman   285

CONTENTS

THE BEST FROM
FANTASY AND
SCIENCE FICTION
Nineteenth Series

Mr. Wilson (who was at one time employed by a cloak-and-dagger outfit) offers a suspense filled account of a telepathic spy—one of "ours"—and what happens when a U.S. agent trys to move him from Moscow to Washington.

GONE FISHIN'

by Robin Scott Wilson

They had briefed me in Washington just before I took off for Frankfurt, but it had been pretty sketchy; you don't need to know much about a case to perform escort courier duty. I knew only that this boy—Kurt Johnston—was some kind of mental freak; other than that there was just the standard info: physical description, date and place of birth, security clearance. He was black enough, God knows. Darker than my own *cafe au lait* which, before black became beautiful, was a source of secretive pride but open embarrassment to my mother, who used Royal Creme Pomade to straighten my sister Kitty's hair and sang a lot about Jesus while she ironed. "Honkie bastard" was what our neighbor, a fat, evil-smelling lady named Mrs. Beamis called me when she came over one night to bitch about me messing around with her Sadie. But that was way back in the late forties, when I was just old enough to wander out of the grits-and-grease smell and into trouble on U Street NE in Our Nation's Capital, before I was old enough to wander all the way out.

He made me think a little of Lena Horne, for whom I used to have the hots in the way you did toward movie stars back in the days when movies were lasciviously chaste and not pornographic, when they didn't show people screwing and you could look at a beautiful woman and—since no one else was having her—imagine you were; back when "Stormy Weather" was the only black and white you could see in living color, and Sidney Poitier hadn't come to dinner yet, and Lela White hadn't yet been seduced by Dustin Hoffman or whatever his name was.

Same pinched, almost semitic features, as if Haile Selassie had scattered his maker's image through the land, fathering Lena and grandfathering this boy; straight little nose: she could flare a nostril like nobody's business when she inhaled dramatically about four bars into "Bill Bailey," and I'd get shaky sitting there in the balcony of the Grand thinking about me and Lena and listening to the sibilant whispers of "shee-it, man" chorusing around me in the dark, which I guess gives you a good idea of how old I am.

And he wore his hair in a full Afro, pretty much the way Petey had after his first semester at Princeton, after he stopped answering our letters and—I guess—went Panther. But there was nothing of Petey's wiry build about this boy, this Kurt Johnston. When he stood up for the introduction, stiffly, German style, he stuck up out of the ground a good half a foot above my five foot eight, and there was lots of muscle under his bulging, too-tight German schoolboy's jacket. Difficult to believe he was only fourteen.

"*Sehr Angenehm*, Mister Bronstein," he said, acknowledging our introduction with formulary precision, bowing slightly, almost clicking his heels.

"*Freut mich sehr*," I said, unconsciously adopting the nigger-who-made-it-good stiffness toward another, unknown black man. It went with the German. "*Aber sprichst du kein englisch?*" I used the familiar *du* form because I knew he was only fourteen. Without the briefing, I would have used the formal *Sie*: so adult did he look; so much power did he seem to radiate.

"Yes, sir," he said a little haltingly, in a voice that still cracked a bit. "I am speaking the English very well."

Even after fifteen years off and on in European operations, I am still a little startled when I meet a black man whose native tongue is German. But of course there are many thousands of them after thirty-five years of American troops in the *Bundesrepublik*. They are the progeny of black soldiers who have suddenly found they are members of a minority so small that it becomes less a disadvantage than simply a curiosity; who have played out the big black stud bull animalistic image their white comrades have established for them, who have screwed white girls or the mulatto daughters of their predecessors-in-arms because there are no other girls, because there is still some status in screwing white, because they buy the myth and play the role a dominant culture has assigned them, because there still are not enough Lena Hornes to go around for all the little black boys in balconies who stiffen up watching the latest white sex-goddess and whisper "shee-it, mother!" to one another in the sticky popcorn dark.

Still, it is startling. But who am I to be surprised at ethnic oddities? A black man with a Jewish name who started out as a showcase negro in 1960 and played the system the right, cautious, uptight way and made it big in twenty years of government service; a good establishment-nigger who for most of that time did not think of himself as a Tom, so far had he wandered from the grease-and-grits; a not very black man who never heard that ancient phrase, "to cross over," without a pang and whose occasional, crushing, obliterating sense of guilt was maybe a little bit requited by a son who died of a cerebral hemorrhage induced by a night-stick. In Chicago, twelve years ago, they called them "batons," as if the fuzz—no, that was Petey's word—as if the police used them to conduct the chorus of chanting militants, *andante con moto*, in "Hell no, we won't go!" I guess Petey and the others were still chanting it eleven years later at Princeton. But, my God! Whatever I thought I was then, I never thought I was a New Jersey State Policeman!

Yes. Well. There in the Air Force ready room of the Rhine-Main air terminal just outside Frankfurt, walled about with chipped blue-gray plywood, fall-leaf littered with squashed paper coffee cups cradling drowned brown cigarette butts, Ed Gary completed the introduction and said to me, "Well, Peter, he's your package now. You wanted temporary courier duty, and you got yourself a real piss-cutter this time."

I nodded. I'd known Ed a long time, since we'd learned the business together at the Berlin Wall. He would never say or even think "some of my best friends . . ." but for him it was true. "You want to fill me in?" I said.

Ed beckoned me over toward the curtained windows, away from the two men and the boy they were protecting. Except for the

five of us, the ready room was deserted, cleared of its usual crowd
of transiting servicemen.

When we were out of earshot, Ed said, "This is a rough one.
Have you been briefed on COKEBOTTLE?"

The word—a code name—rang a bell. "Yes, I think so. When
I was Chief in Copenhagen a couple of years ago, there was
something about digging through school psychologists' records all
over the place, some kind of computer analysis to find . . . what
was it? Some kind of special mental attributes?"

"Telepaths."

"Telepaths!" I was genuinely surprised. I hadn't known all that
much about COKEBOTTLE. There had, obviously, been no need
for me to know. "I didn't know *that!*"

"Yeah. In '77 the Psycho-Medical staff came up with a special
requirements list, and the Outfit ran a massive search everywhere
they could in the West. From what they tell me, they had a
pretty good idea what to look for from studies of certain cases of
juvenile catatonia, and what they wanted to find was a kid who
looked like he might have the characteristics of a latent telepath,
but hadn't developed it to a point where it would get to him.
That was COKEBOTTLE."

"Um," I said, beginning to understand. "I remember the search,
or at least the little piece of it in Denmark in '78. I don't think
they found much of anything there. I thought at the time it
was pretty much of a boondoggle."

"Well, it wasn't. They didn't find anything in Denmark or the
U.S. or much of anywhere except here in Germany." He nodded
toward the boy seated across the room reading a *Micky Maus*
comic book. "Maybe it was because he was the only black kid
in the *Kinderheim*. Got used to being different before the talent
hit him. . . . Right, Kurt?" Ed's voice was barely audible to me,
but the boy looked up, smiled, and nodded.

"You mean he's a telepath?" I couldn't suppress the astonishment
in my voice, although I usually come on pretty cool. It is part
of my schtik. "He can read minds?" Ed nodded and the boy
nodded as if they were strung to a single puppeteer. "Come on

now," I said. "You must be kidding me." Of course, I didn't really disbelieve Ed at all; elaborate practical jokes are not part of life in the Outfit. But still I had to show disbelief; it is part of human nature to solicit more information by expressing doubt. Think of the folks who learned aerodynamics by saying: "What? Two bicycle mechanics from Dayton, Ohio, have built a machine that flies? Horseshit!"

"Yeah, I know," said Ed. He flicked his eyes in Kurt's direction. The boy rose, carefully laid his comic book open on the settee, and walked across the room to join us. The two men started to follow him, but Ed waved them back. They had no need to know. Out loud, Ed said, "Do you mind a little demonstration, Kurt? You know how it is with new ones."

"No. I do not mind, Mr. Gary."

I thought: what a splendid-looking boy he is. How strange it would be if the successor to Homo sapiens should be the result of racial intermarriage on a new, broad scale. What a blow it would be to the racists—both kinds—if somehow the massive mixing of genes should produce a whole new race with the beauty and strength of this boy. And maybe a new kind of mind. . . .

The boy said, "Thank you, Mr. Bronstein. I try to keep healthy, I exercise with *die Hantel*—uh—barbells? But please do not think me to be some freak or new thing. My father was an American, like you. My mother was a German, I think *eine Mulattin wie Sie*. There are other boys like me in other—uh—*Kinderheim*, but think they do not understand the *thinking*. And—uh—*Rassenhass* . . ." He was stuck for the word and looked questioningly at me.

"Race hatred. Racism."

". . . *Ja* . . . race hatred will always be here no matter what is happening, no?"

"Yes. Of course."

"But," he added a little shyly, "I am happy that you are not one, not a—uh—racist."

I thought: my God, he really can read minds! There are things there he should not see. I felt embarrassed, like a kid surprised in a locked bathroom.

The boy smiled broadly. "Do not worry, Mr. Bronstein. I do not pry. Only things that are now, up on top, when you think. Other things are very hard for me and very unpleasant."

"Here," said Ed, handing me a newspaper. "Read something to yourself from this and you'll see why the Outfit has been interested in Kurt and what he's been able to do for us. Okay, Kurt?"

The boy nodded and I began to read silently. It was a copy of that day's Paris edition of *The New York Times*. As I read, Kurt spoke rapidly, much more rapidly than his English conversation: "Richmond, 14 April 1980 (AP). Black Co-op Party Chairman Enoch Jarvis announced today a broad new range of economic sanctions against consumer-oriented businesses, including specific corporations in publishing, chemicals, transportation, and the ailing automotive industry. The BCP, now under investigation by a Federal Grand Jury, has in recent months. . . ." I stopped reading and Kurt fell silent.

"Okay," I said. "I'm convinced." And then I realized and whistled. Kurt smiled before I said, "The perfect espionage agent! He can read anybody's secret files anywhere, as long as someone else is reading them!"

"Not quite anywhere," said Ed. "We had to teach him Russian, for instance. And his range is only a couple of dozen miles."

"Then you must have had him in . . . ?"

"Moscow. Right. For over a year. In an embassy apartment six kilometers from the Gorky Street KGB headquarters. We cleaned them out before they tumbled to it."

"How'd they find out?"

"We don't know. They've been doing a lot of research in ESP too. Maybe they've got their own Kurt. We don't know. All we know is that they are committing everything they've got to get hold of Kurt, or kill him. We've lost three men just moving him this far."

I looked at the boy with sympathy, my right hand moving automatically to the clip on my waistband and the .38 Police Special nestled there. "Are you frightened, Kurt?"

"Yes, sir. But when I come to America, everything will be all right." I looked at Ed and tried to suppress the thought. "Yes," said Kurt. "I know that not everything in America will be good. But there I will not be so different. There are others of my color. It will be harder for them to find me."

Standing there in the oddly deserted ready room, I remembered Petey's statement one evening the previous summer, just before he returned to Princeton for the last time. We had maintained a polite, low-key debate all summer, I not so much disagreeing with his growing militancy as acting as a sounding board for his ideas. That evening, on the back steps of the house in McLean, he had said, "But, dad, nobody ever got anything without a struggle, and it's these little local actions that give us the experience for the big ones."

"Okay," I had said. "But what else do they accomplish? And look at the risk."

He had stood up then and pointed to the stars just breaking into light. "Like stars, or fish in the ocean, dad. The Man sees us that way. To the Man, we all look alike. We are only twelve percent, and we need leaders, right? The danger is when we all look alike to each other. Guys like me are learning how to be the different ones, the leaders."

"Yes," I had said, unable to keep the sad cynicism out of my voice. "And guys like Huey Newton and Martin Luther King and Fred Hampton and Malcolm X and George Maxwell—dead men don't make very effective leaders."

Petey had shrugged and given me a look I wish to God I'd never seen. "Neither," he said, "do GS-16s in the government." It had been one of those futile, wounding, incoherent conversations that I guess all fathers have with their college-age sons.

But Kurt was right, of course. A little cosmetic work by the Outfit's specialists, a new identity, submergence in a heterogeneous population: To the Man, we all look alike. I admired the boy's courage. Aloud, I said, "Right, son. We'll make it all right." Why, I wondered, had I said "son"?

Kurt smiled at me with the look lonely boys have. There was something between us that we both knew. Maybe it was just race. Maybe it was something more. For the first time, I consciously

communicated to him without verbalizing. *You know, don't you.
About Petey and the Princeton riot. About Mary and me, about
the guilt and feeling lost. Why I'm working as a courier instead
of a country chief. The distraction of keeping on the move, and
Mary keeping busy in the Black Co-op movement, trying to pay
the bill for twenty years of noninvolvement; and I am pulling
further and further back into myself trying to understand if "Black
American" is a contradiction in terms and losing, every day, losing
a little more of identification with. . . . But why do I need to
confess to a fourteen-year-old boy?*

"Yes," said Kurt, his smile gone. "I understand. There is a
gap." Ed looked from one of us to the other, suddenly outside.
There was a prolonged silence. "I think you better get going,
Peter," he said.

I swam back up from the painful depths of introspection and
gave my head a quick little nervous shake of impatience. "Right.
What have you laid on?"

"Well, we think you are okay here so far. We've got positive control on the airfield. General Conners has got the 3745th APs all
over the place, and there's an MP detachment from Heidelberg
spread out around the perimeter."

I nodded. "Are we flying MATS?"

"No. We're sending a decoy out to the MATS 747. You're going
commercial superson. There's a Pan Am flight direct to Dulles. The
KGB won't be expecting that."

"Sort of the purloined letter bit, hey?"

"That's the idea." Ed looked at his watch. "The decoy will be
moving out now." He parted the curtain on the window overlooking
the flight line. Down on the field, a blue Air Force Mercedes was
drawing up to the side of the MATS 747. Two men got out, one a
tall, burly negro, the other a shorter black man. They moved hurriedly up the boarding ramp and the aircraft door swung shut behind
them. Almost instantly, the massive old plane began to move out
the taxi strip toward the downwind end of the runway. I turned
away from the window. "Come on, Kurt. If there're any KGB
heavies around, they'll be making a play for the MATS plane.
Let's get going."

Ed said, "Go directly to the Pan Am boarding gate and mingle with the other passengers. We'll have the whole area covered." He handed me our tickets, and Kurt and I left the ready room, walked through the Air Force administrative spaces, and entered the main passenger terminal. The loading area for our flight was crowded; the Boeing superson carries just over three hundred people in both classes. I stuck close to Kurt as we filed through the gate and walked with the hurrying crowd to our plane. Out at the end of the field, I could see the big MATS plane turning to start its takeoff run. Suddenly there was a black plume of smoke and a few seconds later the sound of an explosion reached our ears. The 747 burst into flame and skidded off the runway and slewed violently in the grass, one giant wing dropping and crumpled. Fire sirens screamed and men rushed to vehicles.

"Rockets!" shouted Ed, who was just behind us in the crowd. "They got it with rockets!" We kept on going, across the ramp and up the stairs and into the interior of the superson. Ed stayed behind at the foot of the steps, his eyes busy on the crowd, his pistol half drawn. A few people who had preceded us into the plane and had seen the explosion out the starboard windows rose from their seats, scrabbled coats and packages from the overhead rack, and headed back toward the door, their taste for flying suddenly gone. There was considerable confusion in the aisles.

I got Kurt into a seat and stood out of the aisle watching everyone who came aboard. Kurt looked up at me. "Mr. Bronstein, there is a man. He has a gun. Under his raincoat. It is black . . ."

I had my pistol out and was firing before the man with the black raincoat draped over his arm was able to get off a shot. He fell backward through the door and into the passengers behind him. Someone in the tower must have given the pilot the word. The door slammed shut on the confused and screaming group at the head of the steps, and a moment later the plane began to move. The pilot swung the aircraft through ninety degrees and fed full power to the engines. The taxiway was clear and long enough, and the pilot took off directly, using it as a substitute runway. We were airborne in seconds and there was no rocket fire.

By the time we had reached cruising altitude, the hostesses had most of the passengers quieted down. They were a white-faced bunch, following us with their eyes as we went forward to the cockpit. I wanted to talk to the captain. Judging from the magnitude and desperation of the KGB effort at Rhine-Main, we could anticipate something almost as desperate at Dulles when we landed three hours later. Espionage agents—professionals—taking pot shots at each other in dark alleys is one thing; a suicidal rocket attack on a passenger aircraft is something else again. God knew what they would have waiting for us at Dulles; it didn't occur to me then that we had anything else to worry about. All I could think of was that it was essential that the crew be persuaded to land at some other airport, somewhere where the KGB could not be expecting us.

Kurt was round-eyed with a boy's excitement, full of questions about the aircraft, most of which I could not answer. He seemed blithely unconcerned about the attempts on his life. When I thought that, hustling him forward up the aisle, he shrugged and said, "There is nothing I can do about it." And then, without drawing breath, he said, "How high are we, Mr. Bronstein? How fast does the airplane fly? How many passengers will it carry? How long does it last, this flight? Is this a bigger airplane than the Concorde? I have ridden once upon a Concorde. From Moscow to Rome once I have ridden upon an Illyushin. But they are not so big I think and not so fast as this Boeing."

Up forward, I turned Kurt and his questions over to the first officer and sat with the captain at the navigator's bench. He was a middle-aged man named Greyson, and he was worried. "I don't know what this is all about, Mr. Bronstein," he said, "but I've got almost two hundred passengers back there and I don't want any more trouble."

I explained the situation to him as well as I could, leaving out the intelligence aspects of it. "So you see, we can expect similar difficulties at Dulles."

Greyson nodded. "All right, I'll radio for clearance at Baltimore Friendship."

"No. No radio. They'll have you on radar anyway. I want you to call for emergency landing clearance as soon as you get in the

Friendship pattern. I don't want any radio until you're just ready to land."

Greyson shook his head. "I don't know. I'm in enough trouble already with that hairy takeoff at Rhine-Main. . . ."

"Don't worry, Captain. My organization will square it with the FAA and your company."

"You got that much clout?"

I showed him the little card in my billfold, the one with the Presidential seal. He nodded and shrugged. "You got that much clout."

The third officer, who was minding the store, shouted, "Captain! We got aircraft approaching! Radar shows them bearing zero one zero and closing at 1300."

The captain took three quick strides to the left-hand seat, slipped his earphones on, and said to me, "Bronstein! These KGB people wouldn't go after a flag aircraft in the middle of the Atlantic, would they?"

I said, "I don't know. They may be desperate enough to try anything." Kurt, who had been standing behind the first officer, said, "They're—uh—*freundlich*, Mr. Bronstein. They come from some place in Iceland."

The captain turned in his seat and looked curiously at Kurt. "How do you know, young man?"

Kurt looked at me questioningly. "He just knows," I said.

Simmons, the third officer, said, "Radar shows them at five miles. They've turned parallel to us. They ought to be visual." It was a clear, bright afternoon above the cloud-decked Atlantic. I peered out through the navigator's window. Off to the south, three specks raced along with us. I couldn't make out the type, but Simmons, who had binoculars, could. "The kid's right. They're F-115s."

The navigator had resumed his position behind me to monitor the radar at his desk. "Three more!" he said. "Coming up fast at one one zero!"

"They are Russians," said Kurt. "They have orders to *ubivaht*—uh—*zerstoren*—this aircraft!" There was no fear in the boy's voice. Only great excitement.

I translated: "Destroy!"

"Give me full power, Al!" shouted the captain, and the flight engineer got busy at his console. The F-115s wheeled out in front of us and zipped back past us to the east and the threat there.

Kurt said, "It is getting dim to me; the distance. . . . But one of them has died. A Russian. Another is not dead yet, but he thinks only of his mother, and he is *ohnmachtige*—un—unconscious."

"Probably passed out in a high-G turn," said Greyson. "They must be dogfighting." There was just the slightest sound of envy in his voice. Kurt looked up at him. "I would like someday to hear about your forty-eight missions in Korea, sir."

I was suddenly struck with how completely we all accepted Kurt's power. I had not hesitated to shoot the man with the raincoat draped over his arm. Greyson accepted Kurt's interpretation of the events behind us—now many miles—without really questioning it. Such was the boy's presence, his obvious calm control. A drama was being acted out behind us, maybe fifty miles or so, in the clear April sky. I hoped only that it would stay behind us.

The captain called for a fuel report and ordered cruise power again. Simmons reported another flight of three aircraft entering escort pattern with us. Kurt confirmed that they were friendly. "They are from some place called Argentina. One of the pilots is very angry because he had to miss something. He calls it a 'heavy date' in his head, and. . . ." He broke off in fourteen-year-old confusion. "I do not entirely understand."

Laughter is a good cathartic, and the tension in the cockpit diminished. Greyson surrendered the left-hand seat to the first officer and joined me once again at the navigator's bench. "I got to hand it to you, Bronstein. Your people seem to have thought of everything. It's good to see those 115s out there."

"Yeah. I don't think either of us knows just how valuable your cargo is this trip." And then it struck me just how valuable this boy was. What power! Not only could he clean out the files of the Gorky Street KGB headquarters, he could handle tactical situations with calm and intelligence. No one engaged in conflict of any sort could stand against an operational intelligence system such as Kurt, single-handed—or should one say single-minded?—represented. No wonder the Sovs were willing to do anything to see the end of him.

Do anything? Land-based rocket attack. Mig-27 air attack. What else lay in their arsenal? MIRVs? Targeting would be a problem and they wouldn't dare use nukes. Kurt wasn't worth *that* much to them. That left. . . .

"Kurt!" The sound of my own voice startled me. "How did you detect the hostile aircraft?"

He was startled too and a little at a loss to answer properly. It was like asking someone how he smells onions. "Why—uh—why, when the man said he saw aircraft on the radar, I thought about the aircraft, in that direction, and I heard . . . no . . . *verstand* . . . what they were doing. I—uh—"

"Okay, Kurt. That's all right." There was obviously no word for what he did. "But now, think down. Down to the sea and under the sea. A small room. Many dials and gauges. A man in a submarine —*ein Unterseeboot. Siehst du was?*"

There was a moment of dead silence, only the buzzing hum of the autopilot as it corrected for the weight of a passenger walking aft to the toilet. Then: "Yes! Mr. Bronstein, yes! There is something down. A green room with many, many lights and dials. Like this, only bigger." He waved his arm around the cockpit. "And a man. He is counting backward in Russian, *vo'sem, sem, shest, pyat.* . . ."

"Yeah, Greyson!" I shouted. "A submarine! They're counting down! Surface-to-air!"

Greyson was back in his seat before I had finished. "Seatbelts!" he shouted. "Full power!" He twisted his head to glance at me. "We're at 45,000 feet, Bronstein. How much time from launch?"

I did some quick calculations, trying to recall the characteristics of the SAM's we knew were deployed on the Z-class nuclears that cruised the North Atlantic. "Seventeen or eighteen seconds at most."

"*Dva, adin*—uh—*feur!* He pushed a button, this man, and said 'fire'!" Kurt's excitement confused his tongue.

"Hang on!" said Greyson, and I was thrown hard against the bulkhead as he kicked hard left rudder. Kurt tumbled back against me, and I put an arm around his shoulders in instinctual protectiveness, even though—at fourteen—he outweighed me by twenty pounds. He did not shrink from my embrace. There was a moment of crushing weight and then a lightening and then the horizon out-

side the windows straightened again. There was a noiseless blast a
mile or so off to port and the plane jumped like a car crossing railroad tracks.

Kurt stirred in my arms and pulled himself erect. "They count
again," he said. There was a look of real joy on his face, a look
Petey used to have at baseball games. He was enjoying the whole
thing as only a fourteen-year-old could. Me, I was so scared I
feared for continuing sphincter control. "*Desyat, devyat, vosem . . .*"
counted Kurt in Russian.

"Gimme full power again!" There was sudden acceleration and
another tight, climbing turn. Again, I was crushed to the deck with
Kurt, a tight fetal ball, curled against me. Like a kid who has lit the
fuse to the biggest cherry bomb he could find and waits, full of
pleasurable anticipation, for the neighborhood, the city, the state,
the world to explode. I wondered how the passengers were taking it
back aft. We straightened out on our original course. Another sound-
less blast shook the aircraft from two miles away.

"What's the range of those goddamn SAMs, Bronstein?"

"Fifty miles, max."

"Okay. We ought to be clear unless there's another sub ahead of
us." He looked questioningly at Kurt, who shook his head. There
was just the slightest look of disappointment in his fine, coffee
features. "All right, Al," said the captain. "Let's drop back to cruise."

A stewardess came in through the cockpit door, and Greyson met
her anxious look with words of reassurance. "Tell the passengers we
were evading a thunderhead."

"At 45,000 feet?"

"They won't know the difference. Tell them we are all clear now.
Tell them we'll be landing in about forty-five minutes and that because of weather at Dulles, we'll have to land at Friendship."

"Hold it," I said. "Don't tell them that. Don't mention it to
anybody." The stewardess looked at me and then at Greyson. He
nodded. "Do like the man says, honey."

The rest of the flight went without incident. No more Migs, no
more submarines. Kurt continued his interrogation of the first
officer, his enthusiasm for the details of the aircraft unabated. Only
now and then did he pause a few seconds as if he were listening

for something. I subsided into the jump seat behind Greyson and thought about the reception to come, about what the Outfit could do to protect this boy, about the years ahead of him guarded everywhere, a secret weapon, property of the state. He would be America's secret weapon, all right. With him, everything was open to us, anything was possible. We had something better than the ultimate source of knowledge about everybody's ultimate weapon. It saddened me, somehow.

When we were in the landing pattern over Baltimore, Greyson called for and was granted emergency landing clearance, and I put in a call to headquarters, redirecting whatever escort they had arranged to Friendship. The plane landed, and Greyson taxied up to the ramp. The passengers debarked, but Kurt and I stayed behind, waiting for the escort to come for us.

They had done an elaborate job. A heavily armored semitrailer and six-place cab was waiting for us. There were enough armed men to guard Fort Knox. As soon as we were in the truck cab, I asked Joe D'Amore if all the fuss wouldn't attract too much attention.

"Sure. It might. But I think we've got it whipped." He slid back a hatchway in the rear of the cab as we pulled out onto the Baltimore-Washington turnpike. "You and the boy can go back into the trailer through here." Back in the gloom was a battered '74 Buick. "As soon as we reach a blind pull-off on the parkway, we'll drop you off in the car. If there's any KGB around and they want to follow the truck the rest of the night, fine. You won't be in it."

I nodded. It was the purloined letter business again. Kurt and I scrambled back through the hatch and got into the Buick. The Outfit had been thorough, as usual. There were even some old cane poles sticking out through the rear windows. What could be less suspicious, less worth the attention of the most dangerous espionage agency in the world than two black men cruising through the soft April evening along the Baltimore-Washington turnpike, going fishing?

They all look alike, don't they?

Just south of the AEC turnoff there is a pulloff. We had the Buick out of the semi and were bowling down the turnpike alone within thirty seconds. I took a tortuous course through Silver Springs and then over on the Circumferential to Bethesda, where I drove up one street and down another, checking for a tail.

There was nothing, although a Bethesda police car followed us for a while, until they were sure we were leaving their jurisdiction. We were home free. Now all I had to do was to drive over into Virginia to the Outfit. There, I would be relieved of my charge, and Kurt would begin his new life.

But something was bothering me. A whole lot of things, a year, twenty years, a lifetime of things were suddenly bothering me. I pulled off the Circumferential and drove up the narrow road into the seclusion of Potomac Park. We were safe enough there. And inconspicuous. Two black men with fishing poles. I stopped, and in the fading twilight, I turned to face the young man beside me. He looked at me, sweetly calm, trusting. "Kurt," I said. "You are a very powerful human being."

He grinned. "Yes, I know." There wasn't a shred of arrogance in his voice.

"What do you want to do with your power?"

He waggled his head in uncertainty. "I am not sure. I want to do things, good things. I want to do things for my—people."

"America, you mean? Your country?"

"Yes. So far."

"And do you see America and Mr. Gary and me and the government as all the same thing?"

Kurt waited a while before he answered me, his fine features glazed by the diminishing light. In profile, the resemblance to Lena Horne was striking, although there was nothing the least feminine about his face. "No. Not really the same thing," he answered with some hesitation. "You and Mr. Gary and the government are all *part* of America, but it is perhaps something more." He hesitated again and then added, his manner more firm, his words more forceful: "I think I want to help America be what it should be, maybe not what it wants to be. Do you understand? I am not sure of the words. . . ."

"I understand. And that's what I wanted to know. But there is maybe something more." I hesitated in an odd embarrassment, my thoughts ahead of my tongue, braver.

"I understand," he said when I paused. "About your son Petey and the gap and why you are confused about what it is to be a Negro in this country in this time. I understand, and, yes, I would be flattered to be considered so by you. But perhaps your wife, perhaps she might feel differently about me. . . ."

"Ha!" I said explosively, suddenly sure of myself, suddenly aware of who I was, sliding the old Buick into motion again with an exuberant jerk. "There is a kind of telepathy between married folks, too, son. You'll see. Mary will be. . . ." I was overcome with emotion. I drove down to the Circumferential again and headed south toward Richmond. At the first pulloff in Virginia, I stopped to use the telephone.

When I returned, Kurt looked at me expectantly. "Don't worry, son," I said. "Everything's fine. Mary will meet us in Richmond. She is very happy. She will call the right people, and they will arrange things for us."

"And the people you work for? And Mr. Gary and the others? What will they think?"

"Mr. Gary, at least, will understand, I think. I will not want them to think you have been captured by the Soviets. I will send them a telegram in the next few days. I will write: 'Angeln gegangen.'"

"Ah," said Kurt, struggling to translate into the idiomatic English he would need. "That means 'gone fishing. . . .'"

For reasons which will quickly become obvious, this manuscript has been reproduced exactly as received. It is a fantastic story of retribution that you are about to read, as chilling as anything in the history of "editorial correspondence" (letters about money, if you've ever wondered).

SELECTRA SIX-TEN

by Avram Davidson

His Honor the Ed., F&SF
Dear Ed:
Well, whilst sorry that you didn't feel BELINDA
BEESWAX didn't exactly and immediately leap up
and wrap her warm, white (or, in this case, <u>cold</u>)
arms around you, so to speak, nevertheless I am
bound to admit that your suggestions for its
revision don't altogether seem difficult or
unreasonable. Though, mind you, it is against my
moral principles to admi this to any editor. Even
you. However. This once. I'll do, I think I shd
be able to do the rewrites quite soonly, and whip
them off to you with the speed of light. At
least, the speed of whatever dim light it is
which filters through the window of our local
Post Office and its 87,000 friendly branches
throughout the country.
By the way, excuse absence of mrag, or even
marger Oh you would would you. Take that. And
THAT. AND THSTHATHAT. har har, he laughed
harshly. The lack of m a r g i n s. There. I have
just gotten a new typewriter, viz an Selectra
Six-Ten, with Automated Carriage
Return
Return

Return
hahahaHA! I can't resist it, just impress the tab
and without sweat or indeed evidence of labor of
any swort, or sort, whatsoever,
ZING.
RETURN! You will excsuse me, won't you? There I
knew you would. A wild lad, Master Edward, I sez
to the Gaffer, I sez, but lor blesse zur its just
hanimal sperrits, at art h's a good lad, I sez.
WELL. Enough of this lollygagging ansd skylarking
Ferman. I am a WORKING WORITER and so to business.
Although, mind ewe, with this Device it seems
more like play. It hums and clicks and buzzes
whilst I am congor even cog cog cog got it now?
gooood. cogitating. very helpful to thought.
Soothing. So. WHERE we was. Yus. BELINDA BEESWAX.
Soonly. I haven't forgotten that advance I got
six years ago when ny wife had the grout. Anxious
to please. (Tugs forelock. Exit, pursued by a
Your Seruant to Command,
Avram

Eddy dear;
I mean, of course, Mr Ferman Sir. Or is it now
Squire Ferman, with you off in the moors and
crags of Cornwall Connecticut. Sounds very
Jamaica Inn, Daphne Du Maurieresque. I can see
you on wild and stormy nights, muffled to your
purple ears in your cloak and shawl, going out on
the rocky headlands with False Lights to decoy
the Fall River Line vessels, or even the Late
After-Theater Special of the New York, New Haven,
and Hartburn, onto the Rocks. And the angry rocks
they gored her sides /Like the horns of an angry
bull. Zounds they don't indite Poerty like that
anymore. I mean, I don't have to tell you, ethn
ethic pride, all very well, _en_thic? e t h n i c,

there, THAT wasn't hard, was it deary? Noooo. Now
you can ahve a piece of treacle. Where was I. I
mean, my grandfather was a was a, well,
acttually, no, he WAS n 't a Big Rabbi In The Old
Country, he drove a laundry wagon in Yonkers,
N.Y., but what Imeantosayis: "Over the rocks and
the foaming brine/They burned the wreck of the
Palatine "—can ALAN GUINZBURG write poetry like
that? No. Fair is fair,
Zippetty-ping. Kerriage Return. Automatic.
Whheee! After all Ed I have known you a very long
time, that time your old girl friend, the one you
hired to read Manuscripts, you remember? Nuf sed.
And I know you have only my own welfare at heart.
Right? Right. So you wouldn't be angry when I
explain that Igot the idea, whilst triping on my
new tripewriter, that if I carried out your nifty
kean suggestions for the rewrite of my BELINDA
BEESWAX story, that would drolly enough convert
it into a Crime Story, as well as F and SF. Just
for the fun of it, then, I couldn't resist
sharyimg or even s h a r i n g, my amusement at
this droll conceit with Santiago Ap Popkin, the
editor over at QUENTIN QUEELEY's MYSTERY MUSEUM.
But evidentially I wasn't as clear in my
explanations as I should have been. Fingers just
ran away with themselves, laughing and giggling
over their shoulders (well, knuckles. be
pedantic), down the pike. ANYhow, Caligula Fitz-
Bumpkin somehow misunderstood. He is not, I mean
we must simply Face these things, and Seneca Mac
Zipnick is just NOT/ very bright. He, do you know
what simpleton did? this will hand yez a real
alugh, *Ed:
Guy sent a check. Thought I was offering the

---

* or "laugh", as some have it.—Ibid.

story to <u>him</u>. Boob. A doltish fellowe,
Constantine O'Kaplan. But, well, Ed, put yourself
in my position. Could I embarass the boy? Bring a
blush to those downy cheeks? Nohohohoho.
Well Ed it's just one of those things that we
have to face as we go through life: and the fact
that QQMM happens to pay four or is it five times
what F&SF pays, has got simply nothing to do with
it. Avile canard, and that's that.
However, I have not forgotten that advance the
time I was in Debtors Prison. And I will, I <u>will</u>,
promise you now NOW, I''l sit down at my merry
chuckling Selectra Six-Ten, and write you a real
sockdaol sok?dolager of a Science Fiction story.
VISCIOUS TERRESTRIAL BIPED xxxxxxxxxxxxxx
XXXXXXXXXX ZZZZZZZzzzznnngfhfghhhBZZZ blurtle
blep ha ha, well, perhaps not quite along
<u>those</u> lines. Zo. So
"Forgiven"?
Thine ever so
Avram

Dear Ed:
Well, you mehk me sheahme, mahn, the way you have
forgiven me for that peculiar contretemps anent
BELINDA BEESWAX's going to the QUENTIN QUEELEY's
MYSTERY MUSEUM people instead. That yuck, Gerardo
A Klutskas. Anyway, I have really been sticking to
my last, tappetty-tapp. "Tap". ZWWWWEEPPP! Cling.
It's a veritable psychodrama of Semi-Outer Space.
XXXXXXXXXnnnnnggggg llullrp prurp plup ZZZZBBGGGgnn
INTELLIGENT NONCHITINOUS BIPED ATTEND ATTEND ATTEND
ATTEND haha it's always fun and games with this new
Selectra Six-Ten, clicketty-cluch, <u>hmble-hmble</u>-
<u>hmble-hmble</u>. Just you should drip by you the mouth,
so enclosed is a couple pp of the first darft.
draught. drocht Spell it can't, not for sour owl

stools, but leave us remember the circumstances
under which it grew to maturity. More to be piddled
than centered. You like, huh? Huh? Huh . Thass whut
I thought. XXXxxZZZZzzzzxxxxngngngn clurkle cluhnkle
NOCHITINOUS BIFRU BIFURCATE ATTEND ATTEND ATTEND.
Agreat line, hey? Arrests you with its like
remorseless sweep, doesn't it? Well well,
back to the saline cavern
Love and kisses,
Avram

Dear ED:
See, I knew you would enjoy LOADSTAR EXPRESS.
Even the first draft gripped you like ursus
somethingorothera, din't it? Yes. True, it was
rather rough. Amorphous, as you might say. But I
was going to take care of that anyway. Yesyes I
had that rough spot, pp 3-to-4 well in mind.
I admit that I hsdn't a hadn't exactly planned to do
it the way you tentatively suggest. But. Since you
do. It would be as well that way as any other.
Blush, chuckle. Not exactly what one would formerly
have considered for the pp of a family, or even
a Family Magazine. Tempura o mores, what? However.
WHY N T? XXXXXxxxx==== ZZZZZzzzz bgbgbgbngngngn
bluggabluggablugga TATATA TA TA AT ATT AT ATTEND
ATTEND ATTEND TERRESTRIOUS BIFURCATE NONCHERIDER-
MATIC XXXNN FASCIST AGGRESSIVE BIPED goddam Must
quit reading alla them student Undrground Wellhung
Classified Revolt Papers. To work work WORK toil
"With fingers weary and worn, with eyelids heavy
and red/ Awoman sat in unwomanly rags, mumbling a
crust of bread." Can Laurence Ferlinghetti write
lines like that? Can Richard Gumbeiner? It is to
laugh. Anon, sir, anon. We Never Forget. Advances
advanced to us in our hour od Need, earned eternal
gratichude. clicketty-clunck.
Industrously, Avram

Dear Edward:
WowWowWOW! WOW-WOW/WOWW'. ! gotcha at alst)) Ignore.
Confused by Joy. BUNNYBOY. B U N N Y B O Y, hippetty
goddam HOP, B*U*N*N*N*Y*B*O*Y* M*A*G*A*Z*I*N*E*.
You got that? Educational & Literary Compendium?
With the big tzitzkas? Tha-hats the one. Bunnyboy
Magazine has bumped a burst of bold, gumped a
gurse of XXXXXXX xHa xHa xHa bgnbgn of gold,
dumped a purse of gold in my lap. I kid y ou not.
NOT NOT. "Not." He adumbrated hilarriously.
EXPLOITIVE DIOXIDIFEROUS BIPEDS ah cummon now,
cumMON. Shhest, I hardly know what to say, and this
Selectra Six-Ten, elecrtified wit and terror, never
but never a case of The DULL LINE LABOURS, AND
THE WHEEL TURNS SLOW, goes faster than my MIND, my
mind is BLOWN, out through both ears, walls all
plastered with brain tissue.
Carriage return. When in doubt. Carstairs Macanley,
formerly of Midland Review, to which I sold,
years ago—but you don't want to hear about that,
anyway he is now and has been for some time past
Fiction Editor of Bunnyboy . So whilst making with
the clicketty-clack and addressing the MS of
LOADSTAR EXPRESS, I H happened to be thinking of
him, and just for kicks, you know, Ed,I mean, YOU.
Know me. Ed. Just abig, overgrown kid. So just for
k.i.c.k.s., I absentmindedly addressed it to him.
Laughed like a son of a gun' when I found out what
I'd done. And had already stamped the manila!
"Well . . ." (I figured) "I'll send it to good old
Ed at F&SF soons as Carstairs Macanley returns it.
Just to let him see what I'm doing these days.
Ed, you have never wished me nothing but good, Ed,
from the very first day we met, Ed, and I know that
the last thing on your pure, sweet mind, i would be
that I return the money to Bunyboy, and, besides, I
am almost 100% sure it's already in type: and we

could hardly expect them to yank it. You're a pro
yourself, Ed. But don't think for aminute, Eddy,
that I've got abig head and/or have forgotten that
advance you so, well, <u>tenderly</u> is really the only—
And, Ed, any time you're out on the West Coast,
just any time at <u>all</u>, night or day, give me a ring,
and we'll go out for dinner somewhere. "A Hot bird
and a cold bottle", eh Ed? Hows that b grabg bgrarg
XXXxx TREACHEROUS BgN BgN bGN TERCH XXXXX zzZZZ bgn
bgn bgn TREACHEROUS AMBULATORY TERRESTRIAL AGGRES-
SIVE BIPED ATTEND ATTNEDNA Attn bgna bgn cluck.
Please excuse my high spirits, my head is just
buzzing and clicking right now, Inever SAW such a
C*E*C*K* in my L I F E L I F E in my life. Hey, Ed,
I could offer to rewrite the story for <u>Bunnyboy</u>
leaving out the parts you suggested, but I don't
think it would be right to deprive you of the
pleasure of seiing them in print. Wait for the
story. I"ll do you something else sometime.
Right now I'm going out and buy the biggest can of
typewriter cleaning fluid anybody ever saw WE
EXSALIVATE ON YOUR PROFFERED BRIBES EXPLOITIVE
TERCHEOROSE TERRESTRIAL BIPED AGGRESSIVE NONCHERO-
DERMATOID BIPED LANDING YOUR PLANETARY-RAPING PROBE
MODULEWS ON THE SACRED CHITIN OF OUR MOTHER-
WORLD FASCISTICLY TERMED "MOOM" XXXZZZZBGN BGN BGN
BGN BGN BGN IGNORING OUR JUST LONG-REPRESSED PLEAS
FOR YOUR ATTEND ATTE ND ATTEnD OHmigod
ed oh ed my god i i oh
e
d
e
d
o
bgna bgna bgna bgna bgna bgna bgna bgna bgna bgna
bpur bpur bpur bpur bpur bpur bpur bpur bpur BURP

Edgar Pangborn will be remembered by long-time readers for his fine stories about Davy ("The Golden Horn," "A War of No Consequence"), which were later combined into a novel called DAVY. *Mr. Pangborn lives in Woodstock, New York, the pleasant country town that went through a temporary derangement as a result of the now famous mammoth rock festival. His latest story takes place in the country, in Maine, and it concerns something frightening that did not belong in the peaceful woods.*

LONGTOOTH

by Edgar Pangborn

My word is good. How can I prove it? Born in Darkfield, wasn't I? Stayed away thirty more years after college, but when I returned I was still Ben Dane, one of the Darkfield Danes, Judge Marcus Dane's eldest. And they knew my word was good. My wife died and I sickened of all cities; then my bachelor brother Sam died too, who'd lived all his life here in Darkfield, running his one-man law office over in Lohman—our nearest metropolis, pop. 6437. A fast coronary at fifty; I had loved him. Helen gone, then Sam—I wound up my unimportances and came home, inheriting Sam's housekeeper Adelaide Simmons, her grim stability and celestial cooking. Nostalgia for Maine is a serious matter, late in life: I had to yield. I expected a gradual drift into my childless old age playing correspondence chess, translating a few of the classics. I thought I could take for granted the continued respect of my neighbors. I say my word is good.

I will remember again that middle of March a few years ago, the snow skimming out of an afternoon sky as dirty as the bottom of an old aluminum pot. Harp Ryder's back road had been plowed since the last snowfall; I supposed Bolt-Bucket could make the mile and a half in to his farm and out again before we got caught. Harp had asked me to get him a book if I was making a trip to Boston, any goddamn book that told about Eskimos, and I had one for him, De

Poncins' *Kabloona*. I saw the midget devils of white running crazy down a huge slope of wind, and recalled hearing at the Darkfield News Bureau, otherwise Cleve's General Store, somebody mentioning a forecast of the worst blizzard in forty years. Joe Cleve, who won't permit a radio in the store because it pesters his ulcers, inquired of his Grand Inquisitor who dwells ten yards behind your right shoulder: "Why's it always got to be the worst in so-and-so many years, that going to help anybody?" The Bureau was still analyzing this difficult inquiry when I left, with my cigarettes and as much as I could remember of Adelaide's grocery list after leaving it on the dining table. It wasn't yet three when I turned in on Harp's back road, and a gust slammed at Bolt-Bucket like death with a shovel.

I tried to win momentum for the rise to the high ground, swerved to avoid an idiot rabbit and hit instead a patch of snow-hidden melt-and-freeze, skidding to a full stop from which nothing would extract me but a tow.

I was fifty-seven that year, my wind bad from too much smoking and my heart (I now know) no stronger than Sam's. I quit cursing —gradually, to avoid sudden actions—and tucked *Kabloona* under my parka. I would walk the remaining mile to Ryder's, stay just to leave the book, say hello, and phone for a tow; then, since Harp never owned a car and never would, I could walk back and meet the truck.

If Leda Ryder knew how to drive, it didn't matter much after she married Harp. They farmed it, back in there, in almost the manner of Harp's ancestors of Jefferson's time. Harp did keep his two hundred laying hens by methods that were considered modern before the poor wretches got condemned to batteries, but his other enterprises came closer to antiquity. In his big kitchen garden he let one small patch of weeds fool themselves for an inch or two, so he'd have it to work at; they survived nowhere else. A few cows, a team, four acres for market crops, and a small dog Droopy, whose grandmother had made it somehow with a dachshund. Droopy's only menace in obese old age was a wheezing bark. The Ryders must have grown nearly all vital necessities except chewing tobacco and once in a while a new dress for Leda. Harp could snub the 20th Century, and I doubt if Leda was consulted about it in spite of his obsessive devotion for her. She was almost thirty years younger, and yes, he should not have married her. Other side up just as scratchy; she should not have married him, but she did.

Harp was a dinosaur perhaps, but I grew up with him, he a year the younger. We swam, fished, helled around together. And when I returned to Darkfield growing old, he was one of the few who acted glad to see me, so far as you can trust what you read in a face like a granite promontory. Maybe twice a week Harp Ryder smiled.

I pushed on up the ridge, and noticed a going-and-coming set of wide tire-tracks already blurred with snow. That would be the egg-truck I had passed a quarter-hour since on the main road. Whenever the west wind at my back lulled, I could swing around and enjoy one of my favorite prospects of birch and hemlock lowland. From Ryder's Ridge there's no sign of Darkfield two miles southwest except one church spire. On clear days you glimpse Bald Mountain and his two big brothers, more than twenty miles west of us.

The snow was thickening. It brought relief and pleasure to see the black shingles of Harp's barn and the roof of his Cape Codder. Foreshortened, so that it looked snug against the barn; actually house and barn were connected by a two-story shed fifteen feet wide and forty feet long—woodshed below, hen-loft above. The Ryders' sunrise-facing bedroom window was set only three feet above the eaves of that shed roof. They truly went to bed with the chickens. I shouted, for Harp was about to close the big shed door. He held it for me. I ran, and the storm ran after me. The west wind was bouncing off the barn; eddies howled at us. The temperature had tumbled ten degrees since I left Darkfield. The thermometer by the shed door read 15 degrees, and I knew I'd been a damn fool. As I helped Harp fight the shed door closed, I thought I heard Leda, crying.

A swift confused impression. The wind was exploring new ranges of passion, the big door squawked, and Harp was asking: "Ca' break down?" I do still think I heard Leda wail. If so, it ended as we got the door latched and Harp drew a newly fitted two-by-four bar across it. I couldn't understand that: the old latch was surely proof against any wind short of a hurricane.

"Bolt-Bucket never breaks down. Ought to get one, Harp—lots of company. All she did was go in the ditch."

"You might see her again come spring." His hens were scratching overhead, not yet scared by the storm. Harp's eyes were small gray glitters of trouble. "Ben, you figure a man's getting old at fifty-six?"

"No." My bones (getting old) ached for the warmth of his kitchen-dining-living-everything room, not for sad philosophy. "Use your phone, okay?"

"If the wires ain't down," he said, not moving, a man beaten on by other storms. "Them loafers didn't cut none of the overhang branches all summer. I told 'em of course, I told 'em how it would be . . . I meant, Ben, old enough to get dumb fancies?" My face may have told him I thought he was brooding about himself with a young wife. He frowned, annoyed that I hadn't taken his meaning. "I meant, *seeing* things. Things that can't be so, but—"

"We can all do some of that at any age, Harp."

That remark was a stupid brush-off, a stone for bread, because I was cold, impatient, wanted in. Harp had always a tense one-way sensitivity. His face chilled. "Well, come in, warm up. Leda ain't feeling too good. Getting a cold or something."

When she came downstairs and made me welcome, her eyes were reddened. I don't think the wind made that noise. Droopy waddled from her basket behind the stove to snuff my feet and give me my usual low passing mark.

Leda never had it easy there, young and passionate with scant mental resources. She was twenty-eight that year, looking tall because she carried her firm body handsomely. Some of the sullenness in her big mouth and lucid gray eyes was sexual challenge, some pure discontent. I liked Leda; her nature was not one for animosity or meanness. Before her marriage the Darkfield News Bureau used to declare with its customary scrupulous fairness that Leda had been covered by every goddamn thing in pants within thirty miles. For once the Bureau may have spoken a grain of truth in the malice, for Leda did have the smoldering power that draws men without word or gesture. After her abrupt marriage to Harp—Sam told me all this; I wasn't living in Darkfield then and hadn't met her—the garbage-gossip went hastily underground: enraging Harp Ryder was never healthy.

The phone wires weren't down, yet. While I waited for the garage to answer, Harp said, "Ben, I can't let you walk back in that. Stay over, huh?"

I didn't want to. It meant extra work and inconvenience for Leda, and I was ancient enough to crave my known safe burrow. But I felt Harp wanted me to stay for his own sake. I asked Jim Short at the garage to go ahead with Bolt-Bucket if I wasn't there to meet him. Jim roared: "Know what it's doing right now?"

"Little spit of snow, looks like."

"Jesus!" He covered the mouthpiece imperfectly. I heard his enthusiastic voice ring through cold-iron echoes: "Hey, old Ben's got that thing into the ditch again! Ain't that something . . . ? Listen, Ben, I can't make no promises. Got both tow trucks out already. You better stop over and praise the Lord you got that far."

"Okay," I said. "It wasn't much of a ditch."

Leda fed us coffee. She kept glancing toward the landing at the foot of the stairs where a night-darkness already prevailed. A closed-in stairway slanted down at a never-used front door; beyond that landing was the other ground floor room-parlor, spare, guest room—where I would sleep. I don't know what Leda expected to encounter in that shadow. Once when a chunk of firewood made an odd noise in the range, her lips clamped shut on a scream.

The coffee warmed me. By that time the weather left no loophole for argument. Not yet 3:30, but west and north were lost in furious black. Through the hissing white flood I could just see the front of the barn forty feet away. "Nobody's going no place into that," Harp said. His little house shuddered, enforcing the words. "Leda, you don't look too brisk. Get you some rest."

"I better see to the spare room for Ben."

Neither spoke with much tenderness, but it glowed openly in him when she turned her back. Then some other need bent his granite face out of its normal seams. His whole gaunt body leaning forward tried to help him talk. "You wouldn't figure me for a man'd go off his rocker?" he asked.

"Of course not. What's biting, Harp?"

"There's something in the woods, got no right to be there." To me that came as a letdown of relief: I would not have to listen to another's marriage problems. "I wish, b' Jesus Christ, it would hit somebody else once, so I could say what I know and not be laughed at all to hell. I *ain't* one for dumb fancies."

You walked on eggs, with Harp. He might decide any minute that *I* was laughing. "Tell me," I said. "If anything's out there now it must feel a mite chilly."

"Ayah." He went to the north window, looking out where we knew the road lay under white confusion. Harp's land sloped down the other side of the road to the edge of mighty evergreen forest. Katahdin stands more than fifty miles north and a little east of us. We live in a withering, shrink-world, but you could still set out from Harp's farm and, except for the occasional country road and the rivers—not many large ones—you could stay in deep forest all the way to the tundra, or Alaska. Harp said, "This kind of weather is when it comes."

He sank into his beat-up kitchen armchair and reached for *Ka-bloona*. He had barely glanced at the book while Leda was with us. "Funny name."

"Kabloona's an Eskimo word for white man."

"He done these pictures . . . ? Be they good, Ben?"

"I like 'em. Photographs in the back."

"Oh." He turned the pages hastily for those, but studied only the ones that showed the strong Eskimo faces, and his interest faded. Whatever he wanted was not here. "These people, be they—civilized?"

"In their own way, sure."

"Ayah, this guy looks like he could find his way in the woods."

"Likely the one thing he couldn't do, Harp. They never see a tree unless they come south, and they hate to do that. Anything below the Arctic is too warm."

"That a fact . . . ? Well, it's a nice book. How much was it?" I'd found it second-hand; he paid me to the exact penny. "I'll be glad to read it." He never would. It would end up on the shelf in the parlor with the Bible, an old almanac, a Longfellow, until some day this place went up for auction and nobody remembered Harp's way of living.

"What's this all about, Harp?"

"Oh . . . I was hearing things in the woods, back last summer. I'd

think, fox, then I'd know it wasn't. Make your hair stand right on
end. Lost a cow, last August, from the north pasture acrosst the rud.
Section of board fence tore out. I mean, Ben, the two top boards
was *pulled out from the nail holes*. No hammer marks."

"Bear?"

"Only track I found looked like bear except too small. You know a
bear wouldn't *pull* it out, Ben."

"Cow slamming into it, panicked by something?"

He remained patient with me. "Ben, would I build a cow-pasture
fence nailing the cross-pieces from the outside? Cow hit it with all
her weight she might bust it, sure. And kill herself doing it, be blood
and hair all over the split boards, and she'd be there, not a mile and
a half away into the woods. Happened during a big thunderstorm.
I figured it had to be somebody with a spite ag'inst me, maybe
some son of a bitch wanting the prop'ty, trying to scare me off
that's lived here all my life and my family before me. But that don't
make sense. I found the cow a week later, what was left. Way into
the woods. The head and the bones. Hide tore up and flang
around. Any *person* dressing off a beef, he'll cut whatever he wants
and take off with it. He don't sit down and chaw the meat off the
bones, b' Jesus Christ. He don't tear the thighbone out of the
joint . . . All right, maybe bear. But no bear did that job on that
fence and then driv old Nell a mile and a half into the woods to
kill her. Nice little Jersey, clever's a kitten. Leda used to make over
her, like she don't usually do with the stock . . . I've looked plenty
in the woods since then, never turned up anything. Once and again
I did smell something. Fishy, like bear-smell but—*different*."

"But Harp, with snow on the ground—"

"Now you'll really call me crazy. When the weather is clear, I
ain't once found his prints. I hear him then, at night, but I go out
by daylight where I think the sound was, there's no trail. Just the
usual snow tracks. I know. He lives in the trees and don't come
down except when it's storming, I got to believe that? Because then
he does come, Ben, when the weather's like now, like right now.
And old Ned and Jerry out in the stable go wild, and sometimes we
hear his noise under the window. I shine my flashlight through the
glass—never catch sight of him. I go out with the ten-gauge if there's

any light to see by, and there's prints around the house—holes filling
up with snow. By morning there'll be maybe some marks left, and
they'll lead off to the north woods, but under the trees you won't
find it. So he gets up in the branches and travels that away? . . .
Just once I have seen him, Ben. Last October. I better tell you one
other thing first. A day or so after I found what was left of old Nell,
I lost six roaster chickens. I made over a couple box stalls, maybe
you remember, so the birds could be out on range and roost in the
barn at night. Good doors, and I always locked 'em. Two in the
morning, Ned and Jerry go crazy. I got out through the barn into the
stable, and they was spooked, Ned trying to kick his way out. I got
'em quiet, looked all over the stable—loft, harness room, everywhere.
Not a thing. Dead quiet night, no moon. It had to be something the
horses smelled. I come back into the barn, and found one of the
chicken-pen doors open—*tore* out from the lock. Chicken thief
would bring along something to pry with—wouldn't he be a Christly
idjut if he didn't . . . ? Took six birds, six nice eight-pound roasters,
and left the heads on the floor—bitten off."

"Harp—some lunatic. People *can* go insane that way. There are
old stories—"

"Been trying to believe that. Would a man live the winter out
there? Twenty below zero?"

"Maybe a cave—animal skins."

"I've boarded up the whole back of the barn. Done the same with
the hen-loft windows—two-by-fours with four-inch spikes driv slant-
wise. They be twelve feet off the ground, and he ain't come for 'em,
not yet . . . So after that happened I sent for Sheriff Robart.
Son of a bitch happens to live in Darkfield, you'd think he might've
took an interest."

"Do any good?"

Harp laughed. He did that by holding my stare, making no sound,
moving no muscle except a disturbance at the eye corners. A New
England art; maybe it came over on the *Mayflower*. "Robart he
come by, after a while. I showed him that door. I showed him them
chicken heads. Told him how I'd been spending my nights out there
on my ass, with the ten-gauge." Harp rose to unload tobacco juice
into the range fire; he has a theory it purifies the air. "Ben,

I might've showed him them chicken heads a shade close to his nose. By the time he got here, see, they wasn't all that fresh. He made out he'd look around and let me know. Mid-September. Ain't seen him since."

"Might've figured he wouldn't be welcome?"

"Why, he'd be welcome as shit on a tablecloth."

"You spoke of—seeing it, Harp?"

"Could call it seeing . . . All right. It was during them Indian summer days—remember? Like June except them pretty colors, smell of windfalls—God, I like that, I like October. I'd gone down to the slope acrosst the rud where I mended my fence after losing old Nell. Just leaning there, guess I was tired. Late afternoon, sky pinking up. You know how the fence cuts acrosst the slope to my east wood lot. I've let the bushes grow free—lot of elder, other stuff the birds come for. I was looking down toward that little break between the north woods and my wood lot, where a bit of old growed-up pasture shows through. Pretty spot. Painter fella come by a few years ago and done a picture of it, said the place looked like a coro, dunno what the hell that is, he didn't say."

I pushed at his brown study. "You saw it there?"

"No. Off to my right in them elder bushes. Fifty feet from me, I guess. By God I didn't turn my head. I got it with the tail of my eye and turned the other way as if I meant to walk back to the rud. Made like busy with something in the grass, come wandering back to the fence some nearer. He stayed for me, a brownish patch in them bushes by the big yellow birch. Near the height of a man. No gun with me, not even a stick . . . Big shoulders, couldn't see his goddamn feet. He don't stand more'n five feet tall. His hands, if he's got real ones, hung out of my sight in a tangle of elder bushes. He's got brown fur, Ben, reddy-brown fur all over him. His face too, his head, his big thick neck. There's a shine to fur in sunlight, you can't be mistook. So—I did look at him direct. Tried to act like I still didn't see him, but he knowed. He melted back and got the birch between him and me. Not a sound." And then Harp was listening for Leda upstairs. He went on softly: "Ayah, I ran back for a gun, and searched the woods, for all the good it did me. You'll want to know about his face. I ain't told Leda all this part. See, she's scared, I don't want to make it no worse, I just said it was some animal that snuck off before I could see it good. A big face, Ben. Head real human except it sticks out too much around the jaw. Not much nose—open spots in the fur. Ben, the—the *teeth!* I seen his mouth drop open and he pulled up one side of his lip to show me them stabbing things. I've seen as big as that on a full-growed bear. That's what I'll hear, I ever try to tell this. They'll say I seen a bear. Now I shot my first bear when I was sixteen and Pa took me over toward Jackman. I've got me one maybe every other year since then. I know 'em, all their ways. But that's what I'll hear if I tell the story."

I am a frustrated naturalist, loaded with assorted facts. I know there aren't any monkeys or apes that could stand our winters except maybe the harmless Himalayan langur. No such beast as Harp described lived anywhere on the planet. It didn't help. Harp was honest; he was rational; he wanted reasonable explanation as much as I did. Harp wasn't the village atheist for nothing. I said, "I guess you will, Harp. People mostly won't take the—unusual."

"Maybe you'll hear him tonight, Ben."

Leda came downstairs, and heard part of that. "He's been telling you, Ben. What do you think?"

"I don't know what to think."

"Led', I thought, if I imitate that noise for him—"

"No!" She had brought some mending and was about to sit down with it, but froze as if threatened by attack. "I couldn't stand it, Harp. And—it might bring them."

"Them?" Harp chuckled uneasily. "I don't guess I could do it that good he'd come for it."

"Don't *do* it, Harp!"

"All right, hon." Her eyes were closed, her head drooping back. "Don't git nerved up so."

I started wondering whether a man still seeming sane could dream up such a horror for the unconscious purpose of tormenting a woman too young for him, a woman he could never imagine he owned. If he told her a fox bark wasn't right for a fox, she'd believe him. I said, "We shouldn't talk about it if it upsets her."

He glanced at me like a man floating up from under water. Leda

said in a small, aching voice: "I wish to God we could move
to Boston."

The granite face closed in defensiveness. "Led', we been over all
that. Nothing is going to drive me off of my land. I got no time for
the city at my age. What the Jesus would I do? Night watchman?
Sweep out somebody's back room, b' Jesus Christ? Savings'd be
gone in no time. We been all over it. We ain't moving nowhere."

"I could find work." For Harp of course that was the worst
thing she could have said. She probably knew it from his stricken
silence. She said clumsily, "I forgot something upstairs." She
snatched up her mending and she was gone.

We talked no more of it the rest of the day. I followed through the
milking and other chores, lending a hand where I could, and we
made everything as secure as we could against storm and other
enemies. The long-toothed furry thing was the spectral guest at dinner, but we cut him, on Leda's account, or so we pretended. Supper
would have been awkward anyway. They weren't in the habit of
putting up guests, and Leda was a rather deadly cook because she
cared nothing about it. A Darkfield girl, I suppose she had the usual
20th-Century mishmash of television dreams until some impulse
or maybe false signs of pregnancy tricked her into marrying a man
out of the 19th. We had venison treated like beef and overdone
vegetables. I don't like venison even when it's treated right.

At six Harp turned on his battery radio and sat stone-faced
through the day's bad news and the weather forecast—"a blizzard
which may prove the worst in 42 years. Since 3:00 PM, 18 inches
have fallen at Bangor, 21 at Boston. Precipitation is not expected to
end until tomorrow. Winds will increase during the night with gusts
up to 70 miles per hour." Harp shut it off, with finality. On other
evenings I had spent there he let Leda play it after supper only kind
of soft, so there had been a continuous muted bleat and blatter all
evening. Tonight Harp meant to listen for other sounds. Leda washed
the dishes, said an early good night, and fled upstairs.

Harp didn't talk, except as politeness obliged him to answer some
blah of mine. We sat and listened to the snow and the lunatic wind.
An hour of it was enough for me; I said I was beat and wanted to
turn in early. Harp saw me to my bed in the parlor and placed a new

chunk of rock maple in the pot-bellied stove. He produced a difficult
granite smile, maybe using up his allowance for the week, and
pulled out a bottle from a cabinet that had stood for many
years below a parlor print—George Washington, I think, concluding
a treaty with some offbeat sufferer from hepatitis who may have
been General Cornwallis if the latter had two left feet. The bottle
contained a brand of rye that Harp sincerely believed to be drink-
able, having charred his gullet forty-odd years trying to prove it.
While my throat healed Harp said, "Shouldn't 've bothered you with
all this crap, Ben. Hope it ain't going to spoil your sleep." He got me
his spare flashlight, then let me be, and closed the door.

I heard him drop back into his kitchen armchair. Under too many
covers, lamp out, I heard the cruel whisper of the snow. The stove
muttered, a friend, making me a cocoon of living heat in a waste of
outer cold. Later I heard Leda at the head of the stairs, her voice
timid, tired, and sweet with invitation: "You comin' up to bed,
Harp?" The stairs creaked under him. Their door closed; presently
she cried out in that desired pain that is brief release from trouble.

I remembered something Adelaide Simmons had told me about
this house, where I had not gone upstairs since Harp and I were boys.
Adeladie, one of the very few women in Darkfield who never spoke
unkindly of Leda, said that the tiny west room across from Harp's
and Leda's bedroom was fixed up for a nursery, and Harp wouldn't
allow anything in there but baby furniture. Had been so since they
were married seven years before.

Another hour dragged on, in my exasperations of sleeplessness.
Then I heard Longtooth.

The noise came from the west side, beyond the snow-hidden
vegetable garden. When it snatched me from the edge of sleep, I
tried to think it was a fox barking, the ringing, metallic shriek the
little red beast can belch dragon-like from his throat. But wide
awake, I knew it had been much deeper, chestier. Horned owl?—
no. A sound that belonged to ancient times when men relied on
chipped stone weapons and had full reason to fear the dark.

The cracks in the stove gave me firelight for groping back into my
clothes. The wind had not calmed at all. I stumbled to the west
window, buttoning up, and found it a white blank. Snow had drifted
above the lower sash. On tiptoe I could just see over it. A light ap-

peared, dimly illuminating the snowfield beyond. That would be
coming from a lamp in the Ryders' bedroom, shining through the
nursery room and so out, weak and diffused, into the blizzard chaos.
Yaaarrhh!

Now it had drawn horribly near. From the north windows of the
parlor I saw black nothing. Harp squeaked down to my door.
"'Wake, Ben?"

"Yes. Come look at the west window."

He had left no night light burning in the kitchen, and only a scant
glow came down to the landing from the bedroom. He murmured
behind me, "Ayah, snow's up some. Must be over three foot on the
level by now."

Yaaarrhh!

The voice had shouted on the south side, the blinder side of the
house, overlooked only by one kitchen window and a small one in
the pantry where the hand pump stood. The view from the pantry
window was mostly blocked by a great maple that overtopped the
house. I heard the wind shrilling across the tree's winter bones.

"Ben, you want to git your boots on? Up to you—can't ask it. I
might have to go out." Harp spoke in an undertone as if the beast
might understand him through the tight walls.

"Of course." I got into my knee boots and caught up my parka as
I followed him into the kitchen. A .30-caliber rifle and his heavy
shotgun hung on deerhorn over the door to the woodshed. He found
them in the dark.

What courage I possessed that night came from being shamed
into action, from fearing to show a poor face to an old friend in
trouble. I went through the Normandy invasion. I have camped out
alone, when I was younger and healthier, and slept nicely. But that
noise of Longtooth stole courage. It ached along the channel of
the spine.

I had the spare flashlight, but knew Harp didn't want me to use
it here. I could make out the furniture, and Harp reaching for the
gun rack. He already had on his boots, fur cap, and mackinaw.
"You take this'n," he said, and put the ten-gauge in my hands.
"Both barrels loaded. Ain't my way to do that, ain't right, but since
this thing started—"

Yaaarrhh!

"Where's he got to now?" Harp was by the south window. "Round this side?"

"I thought so . . . Where's Droopy?"

Harp chuckled thinly. "Poor little shit! She come upstairs at the first sound of him and went under the bed. I told Led' to stay upstairs. She'd want a light down here. Wouldn't make sense."

Then, apparently from the east side of the hen-loft and high, booming off some resonating surface: *Yaaarrhh!*

"He can't! Jesus, that's twelve foot off the ground!" But Harp plunged out into the shed, and I followed. "Keep your light on the floor, Ben." He ran up the narrow stairway. "Don't shine it on the birds, they'll act up."

So far the chickens, stupid and virtually blind in the dark, were making only a peevish tut-tutting of alarm. But something was clinging to the outside of the barricaded east window, snarling, chattering teeth, pounding on the two-by-fours. With a fist?—it sounded like nothing else. Harp snapped, "Get your light on the window!" And he fired through the glass.

We heard no outcry. Any noise outside was covered by the storm and the squawks of the hens scandalized by the shot. The glass was dirty from their continual disturbance of the litter; I couldn't see through it. The bullet had drilled the pane without shattering it, and passed between the two-by-fours, but the beast could have dropped before he fired. "I got to go out there. You stay, Ben." Back in the kitchen he exchanged rifle for shotgun. "Might not have no chance to aim. You remember this piece, don't y'?—eight in the clip."

"I remember it."

"Good. Keep your ears open." Harp ran out through the door that gave on a small paved area by the woodshed. To get around under the east loft window he would have to push through the snow behind the barn, since he had blocked all the rear openings. He could have circled the house instead, but only by bucking the west wind and fighting deeper drifts. I saw his big shadow melt out of sight.

Leda's voice quavered down to me: "He—get it?"

"Don't know. He's gone to see. Sit tight . . ."

I heard that infernal bark once again before Harp returned, and again it sounded high off the ground; it must have come from the big maple. And then moments later—I was still trying to pierce the dark, watching for Harp—a vast smash of broken glass and wood, and the violent bang of the door upstairs. One small wheezing shriek cut short, and one scream such as no human being should ever hear. I can still hear it.

I think I lost some seconds in shock. Then I was groping up the narrow stairway, clumsy with the rifle and flashlight. Wind roared at the opening of the kitchen door, and Harp was crowding past me, thrusting me aside. But I was close behind him when he flung the bedroom door open. The blast from the broken window that had slammed the door had also blown out the lamp. But our flashlights said at once that Leda was not there. Nothing was, nothing living.

Droopy lay in a mess of glass splinters and broken window sash, dead from a crushed neck—something had stamped on her. The bedspread had been pulled almost to the window—maybe Leda's hand had clenched on it. I saw blood on some of the glass fragments, and on the splintered sash, a patch of reddish fur.

Harp ran back downstairs. I lingered a few seconds. The arrow of fear was deep in me, but at the moment it made me numb. My light touched up an ugly photograph on the wall, Harp's mother at fifty or so, petrified and acid-faced before the camera, a puritan deity with shallow, haunted eyes. I remembered her.

Harp had kicked over the traces when his father died, and quit going to church. Mrs. Ryder "disowned" him. The farm was his; she left him with it and went to live with a widowed sister in Lohman, and died soon, unreconciled. Harp lived on as a bachelor, crank, recluse, until his strange marriage in his fifties. Now here was Ma still watchful, pucker-faced, unforgiving. In my dullness of shock I thought: Oh, they probably always made love with the lights out.

But now Leda wasn't there.

I hurried after Harp, who had left the kitchen door to bang in the wind. I got out there with rifle and flashlight, and over across the road I saw his torch. No other light, just his small gleam and mine.

I knew as soon as I had forced myself beyond the corner of the house and into the fantastic embrace of the storm that I could never make it. The west wind ground needles into my face. The snow was up beyond the middle of my thighs. With weak lungs and maybe an imperfect heart, I could do nothing out here except die quickly to no purpose. In a moment Harp would be starting down the slope of the woods. His trail was already disappearing under my beam. I drove myself a little further, and an instant's lull in the storm allowed me to shout: "Harp! I can't follow!"

He heard. He cupped his mouth and yelled back: "Don't try! Git back to the house! Telephone!" I waved to acknowledge the message and struggled back.

I only just made it. Inside the kitchen doorway I fell flat, gun and flashlight clattering off somewhere, and there I stayed until I won back enough breath to keep myself living. My face and hands were ice-blocks, then fires. While I worked at the task of getting air into my body, one thought continued, an inner necessity: *There must be a rational cause. I do not abandon the rational cause.* At length I hauled myself up and stumbled to the telephone. The line was dead.

I found the flashlight and reeled upstairs with it. I stepped past poor Droopy's body and over the broken glass to look through the window space. I could see that snow had been pushed off the shed roof near the bedroom window; the house sheltered that area from the full drive of the west wind, so some evidence remained. I guessed that whatever came must have jumped to the house roof from the maple, then down to the shed roof and then hurled itself through the closed window without regard for it as an obstacle. Losing a little blood and a little fur.

I glanced around and could not find that fur now. Wind must have pushed it out of sight. I forced the door shut. Downstairs, I lit the table lamps in kitchen and parlor. Harp might need those beacons—if he came back. I refreshed the fires, and gave myself a dose of Harp's horrible whisky. It was nearly one in the morning. If he never came back?

It might be days before they could plow out the road. When the storm let up I could use Harp's snowshoes, maybe . . .

Harp came back, at 1:20, bent and staggering. He let me support him to the armchair. When he could speak he said, "No trail. No trail." He took the bottle from my hands and pulled on it. "Christ Jesus! What can I do? Ben . . . ? I got to go to the village, get help. If they got any help to give."

"Do you have an extra pair of snowshoes?"

He stared toward me, battling confusion. "Hah? No, I ain't. Better you stay anyhow. I'll bring yours from your house if you want, if I can git there." He drank again and slammed in the cork with the heel of his hand. "I'll leave you the ten-gauge."

He got his snowshoes from a closet. I persuaded him to wait for coffee. Haste could accomplish nothing now; we could not say to each other that we knew Leda was dead. When he was ready to go, I stepped outside with him into the mad wind. "Anything you want me to do before you get back?" He tried to think about it.

"I guess not, Ben . . . God, ain't I *lived* right? No, that don't make sense? God? That's a laugh." He swung away. Two or three great strides and the storm took him.

That was about two o'clock. For four hours I was alone in the house. Warmth returned, with the bedroom door closed and fires working hard. I carried the kitchen lamp into the parlor, and then huddled in the nearly total dark of the kitchen with my back to the wall, watching all the windows, the ten-gauge near my hand, but I did not expect a return of the beast, and there was none.

The night grew quieter, perhaps because the house was so drifted in that snow muted the sounds. I was cut off from the battle, buried alive.

Harp would get back. The seasons would follow their natural way, and somehow we would learn what had happened to Leda. I supposed the beast would have to be something in the human pattern—mad, deformed, gone wild, but still human.

After a time I wondered why we had heard no excitement in the stable. I forced myself to take up gun and flashlight and go look. I groped through the woodshed, big with the jumping shadows of Harp's cordwood, and into the barn. The cows were peacefully drowsing. In the center alley I dared to send my weak beam swooping and glimmering through the ghastly distances of the hayloft. Quiet, just quiet; natural rustling of mice. Then to the stable,

where Ned whickered and let me rub his brown cheek, and Jerry
rolled a humorous eye. I suppose no smell had reached them to touch
off panic, and perhaps they had heard the barking often enough so
that it no longer disturbed them. I went back to my post, and the
hours crawled along a ridge between the pits of terror and exhaustion. Maybe I slept.

No color of sunrise that day, but I felt paleness and change;
even a blizzard will not hide the fact of dayshine somewhere. I
breakfasted on bacon and eggs, fed the hens, forked down hay and
carried water for the cows and horses. The one cow in milk, a
jumpy Ayrshire, refused to concede that I meant to be useful. I'd
done no milking since I was a boy, the knack was gone from my
hands, and relief seemed less important to her than kicking over
the pail; she was getting more amusement than discomfort out of
it, so for the moment I let it go. I made myself busy-work shovel-
ing a clear space by the kitchen door. The wind was down, the snowfall persistent but almost peaceful. I pushed out beyond the house
and learned that the stuff was up over my hips.

Out of that, as I turned back, came Harp in his long, snowshoe
stride, and down the road three others. I recognized Sheriff Robart,
overfed but powerful; and Bill Hastings, wry and ageless, a cousin
of Harp's and one of his few friends; and last, Curt Davidson,
perhaps a friend to Sheriff Robart but certainly not to Harp.

I'd known Curt as a thickwitted loudmouth when he was a
kid; growing to man's years hadn't done much for him. And when
I saw him I thought, irrationally perhaps: Not good for our side.
A kind of absurdity, and yet Harp and I were joined against the
world simply because we had experienced together what others
were going to call impossible, were going to interpret in harsh, even
damnable ways; and no help for it.

I saw the white thin blur of the sun, the strength of it growing.
Nowhere in all the white expanse had the wind and the new snow
allowed us any mark of the visitation of the night.

The men reached my cleared space and shook off snow. I opened
the woodshed. Harp gave me one hopeless glance of inquiry and I
shook my head.

"Having a little trouble?" That was Robart, taking off his snow-shoes.

Harp ignored him. "I got to look after my chores." I told him I'd done it except for that damn cow. "Oh, Bess, ayah, she's nervy. I'll see to her." He gave me my snowshoes that he had strapped to his back. "Adelaide, she wanted to know about your groceries. Said I figured they was in the ca'."

"Good as an icebox," says Robart, real friendly.

Curt had to have his pleasures too. "Ben, you sure you got hold of old Bess by the right end, where the tits was?" Curt giggles at his own jokes, so nobody else is obliged to. Bill Hastings spat in the snow.

"Okay if I go in?" Robart asked. It wasn't a simple inquiry: he was present officially and meant to have it known. Harp looked him up and down.

"Nobody stopping you. Didn't bring you here to stand around, I suppose."

"Harp," said Robart pleasantly enough, "don't give me a hard time. You come tell me certain things has happened, I got to look into it is all." But Harp was already striding down the woodshed to the barn entrance. The others came into the house with me, and I put on water for fresh coffee. "Must be your ca' down the rud a piece, Ben? Heard you kind of went into a ditch. All's you can see now is a hump in the snow. Deep freeze might be good for her, likely you've tried everything else." But I wasn't feeling comic, and never had been on those terms with Robart. I grunted, and his face shed mirth as one slips off a sweater. "Okay, what's the score? Harp's gone and told me a story I couldn't feed to the dogs, so what about it? Where's Mrs. Ryder?"

Davidson giggled again. It's a nasty little sound to come out of all that beef. I don't think Robart had much enthusiasm for him either, but it seems he had sworn in the fellow as a deputy before they set out. "Yes, sir," said Curt, "that was *really* a story, that was."

"Where's Mrs. Ryder?"

"Not here," I told him. "We think she's dead."

He glowered, rubbing cold out of his hands. "Seen that window. Looks like the frame is smashed."

"Yes, from the outside. When Harp gets back you'd better look. I closed the door on that room and haven't opened it. There'll be more snow, but you'll see about what we saw when we got up there."

"Let's look right now," said Curt.

Bill Hastings said, "Curt, ain't you a mite busy for a dep'ty? Mr. Dane said when Harp gets back." Bill and I are friends; normally he wouldn't mister me. I think he was trying to give me some flavor of authority.

I acknowledged the alliance by asking: "You a deputy too, Bill?" Giving him an opportunity to spit in the stove, replace the lid gently, and reply: "Shit no."

Harp returned and carried the milk pail to the pantry. Then he was looking us over. "Bill, I got to try the woods again. You want to come along?"

"Sure, Harp. I didn't bring no gun."

"Take my ten-gauge."

"Curt here'll go along," said Robart. Real good man on snow-shoes. Interested in wild life."

Harp said, "That's funny, Robart. I guess that's the funniest thing I heard since Cutler's little girl fell under the tractor. You joining us too?"

"Fact is, Harp, I kind of pulled a muscle in my back coming up here. Not getting no younger neither. I believe I'll just look around here a little. Trust you got no objection? To me looking around a little?"

"Coffee's dripped," I said.

"Thing of it is, if I'd 've thought you had any objection, I'd 've been obliged to get me a warrant."

"Thanks, Ben." Harp gulped the coffee scalding. "Why, if looking around the house is the best you can do, Sher'f, I got no objection. Ben, I shouldn't be keeping you away from your affairs, but would you stay? Kind of keep him company? Not that I got much in the house, but still—you know—"

"I'll stay." I wished I could tell him to drop that manner; it only got him deeper in the mud.

Robart handed Davidson his gun belt and holster. "Better have it, Curt, so to be in style."

Harp and Bill were outside getting on their snowshoes; I half heard some remark of Harp's about the sheriff's aching back. They took off. The snow had almost ceased. They passed out of sight down the slope to the north, and Curt went plowing after them. Behind me Robart said, "You'd think Harp believed it himself."

"That's how it's to be? You make us both liars before you've even done any looking?"

"I got to try to make sense of it is all." I followed him up to the bedroom. It was cruelly cold. He touched Droopy's stiff corpse with his foot. "Hard to figure a man killing his own dog."

"We get nowhere with that kind of idea."

"Ben, you got to see this thing like it looks to other people. And keep out of my hair."

"That's what scares me, Jack. Something unreasonable did happen, and Harp and I were the only ones to experience it—except Mrs. Ryder."

"You claim you saw this—animal?"

"I didn't say that. I heard her scream. When we got upstairs this room was the way you see it." I looked around, and again couldn't find that scrap of fur, but I spoke of it, and I give Robart credit for searching. He shook out the bedspread and blankets, examined the floor and the closet. He studied the window space, leaned out for a look at the house wall and the shed roof. His big feet avoided the broken glass, and he squatted for a long gaze at the pieces of window sash. Then he bore down on me, all policeman personified, a massive, rather intelligent, conventionally honest man with no patience for imagination, no time for any fact not already in the books. "Piece of fur, huh?" He made it sound as if I'd described a Jabberwock with eyes of flame. "Okay, we're done up here." He motioned me downstairs—all policemen who'd ever faced a crowd's dangerous stupidity with their own.

As I retreated I said, "Hope you won't be too busy to have a chemist test the blood on that sash."

"We'll do that." He made move-along motions with his slab hands.

"Going to be a pleasure to do that little thing for you and your friend."

Then he searched the entire house, shed, barn, and stable. I had never before watched anyone on police business; I had to admire his zeal. I got involved in the farce of holding the flashlight for him while he rooted in the cellar. In the shed I suggested that if he wanted to restack twenty-odd cords of wood he'd better wait till Harp could help him; he wasn't amused. He wasn't happy in the barn loft either. Shifting tons of hay to find a hypothetical corpse was not a one-man job. I knew he was capable of returning with a crew and machinery to do exactly that. And by his lights it was what he ought to do. Then we were back in the kitchen, Robart giving himself a manicure with his jackknife, and I down to my last cigarette, almost the last of my endurance.

Robart was not unsubtle. I answered his questions as temperately as I could—even, for instance: "Wasn't you a mite sweet on Leda yourself?" I didn't answer any of them with flat silence; to do that right you need an accompanying act like spitting in the stove, and I'm not a chewer. From the north window he said: "Comin' back. It figures." They had been out a little over an hour.

Harp stood by the stove with me to warm his hands. He spoke as if alone with me: "No trail, Ben." What followed came in an undertone: "Ben, you told me about a friend of yours, scientist or something, professor—"

"Professor Malcolm?" I remembered mentioning him to Harp a long while before; I was astonished at his recalling it. Johnny Malcolm is a professor of biology who has avoided too much specialization. Not a really close friend. Harp was watching me out of a granite despair as if he had asked me to appeal to some higher court. I thought of another acquaintance in Boston too, whom I might consult—Dr. Kahn, a psychiatrist who had once seen my wife Helen through a difficult time . . .

"Harp," said Robart, "I got to ask you a couple, three things. I sent word to Dick Hammond to get that goddamned plow of his into this road as quick as he can. Believe he'll try. Whiles we wait on him, we might 's well talk. You know I don't like to get tough."

"Talk away," said Harp, "only Ben here he's got to get home without waiting on no Dick Hammond."

"That a fact, Ben?"

"Yes. I'll keep in touch."

"Do that," said Robart, dismissing me. As I left he was beginning a fresh manicure, and Harp waited rigidly for the ordeal to continue. I felt morbidly that I was abandoning him.

Still—corpus delicti—nothing much more would happen until Leda Ryder was found. Then if her body were found dead by violence, with no acceptable evidence of Longtooth's existence—well, what then?

I don't think Robart would have let me go if he'd known my first act would be to call Short's brother Mike and ask him to drive me in to Lohman where I could get a bus for Boston.

Johnny Malcolm said, "I can see this is distressing you, and you wouldn't lie to me. But, Ben, as biology it won't do. Ain't no such animile. You know that."

He wasn't being stuffy. We were having dinner at a quiet restaurant, and I had of course enjoyed the roast duckling too much. Johnny is a rock-ribbed beanpole who can eat like a walking famine with no regrets. "Suppose," I said, "just for argument and because it's not biologically inconceivable, that there's a basis for the Yeti legend."

"Not inconceivable. I'll give you that. So long as any poorly known corners of the world are left—the Himalayan uplands, jungles, tropic swamps, the tundra—legends will persist and some of them will have little gleams of truth. You know what I think about moon flights and all that?" He smiled; privately I was hearing Leda scream. "One of our strongest reasons for them, and for the biggest flights we'll make if we don't kill civilization first, is a hunt for new legends. We've used up our best ones, and that's dangerous."

"Why don't we look at the countries inside us?" But Johnny wasn't listening much.

"Men can't stand it not to have closed doors and a chance to push at them. Oh, about your Yeti—he might exist. Shaggy anthropoid able to endure severe cold, so rare and clever the explorers haven't tripped over him yet. Wouldn't have to be a carnivore to have big ugly canines—look at the baboons. But if he was active in a Himalayan winter, he'd have to be able to use meat, I think. Mind you, I don't believe any of this, but you can have it as a biological not-impossible. How'd he get to Maine?"

"Strayed? Tibet—Mongolia—Arctic ice."

"Maybe." Johnny had begun to enjoy the hypothesis as something to play with during dinner. Soon he was helping along the brute's passage across the continents, and having fun till I grumbled something about alternatives, extraterrestrials. He wouldn't buy that, and got cross. Still hearing Leda scream, I assured him I wasn't watching for little green men.

"Ben, how much do you know about this—Harp?"

"We grew up along different lines, but he's a friend. Dinosaur, if you like, but a friend."

"Hardshell Maine bachelor picks up dizzy young wife—"

"She's not dizzy. Wasn't. Sexy, but not dizzy."

"All right. Bachelor stewing in his own juices for years. Sure he didn't get up on that roof himself?"

"Nuts. Unless all my senses were more paralyzed than I think, there wasn't time."

"Unless they were more paralyzed than you think."

"Come off it! I'm not senile yet . . . What's he supposed to have done with her? Tossed her into the snow?"

"Mph," said Johnny, and finished his coffee. "All right. Some human freak with abnormal strength and the endurance to fossick around in a Maine blizzard stealing women. I liked the Yeti better. You say you suggested a madman to Ryder yourself. Pity if you had to come all the way here just so I could repeat your own guesswork. To make amends, want to take in a bawdy movie?"

"Love it."

The following day Dr. Kahn made time to see me at the end of the afternoon, so polite and patient that I felt certain I was keeping him from his dinner. He seemed undecided whether to be concerned with the traumas of Harp Ryder's history or those of mine. Mine were already somewhat known to him. "I wish you had time to talk all this out to me. You've given me a nice summary of what the physical events appear to have been, but—"

"Doctor," I said, "it *happened*. I heard the animal. The window *was* smashed—ask the sheriff. Leda Ryder did scream, and when Harp and I got up there together, the dog had been killed and Leda was gone."

"And yet, if it was all as clear as that, I wonder why you thought of consulting me at all, Ben. I wasn't there. I'm just a head-shrinker."

"I wanted . . . Is there any way a delusion could take hold of Harp *and* me, disturb our senses in the same way? Oh, just saying it makes it ridiculous."

Dr. Kahn smiled. "Let's say, difficult."

"Is it possible Harp could have killed her, thrown her out through the window of the *west* bedroom—the snow must have drifted six feet or higher on that side—and then my mind distorted my time sense? So I might've stood there in the dark kitchen all the time it went on, a matter of minutes instead of seconds? Then he jumped down by the shed roof, came back into the house the normal way while I was stumbling upstairs? Oh, hell."

Dr. Kahn had drawn a diagram of the house from my description, and peered at it with placid interest. "Benign" was a word Helen had used for him. He said, "Such a distortion of the time sense would be—unusual . . . Are you feeling guilty about anything?"

"About standing there and doing nothing? I can't seriously believe it was more than a few seconds. Anyway that would make Harp a monster out of a detective story. He's not that. How could he count on me to freeze in panic? Absurd. I'd 've heard the struggle, steps, the window of the west room going up. Could he have killed her and I known all about it at the time, even witnessed it, and then suffered amnesia for that one event?"

He still looked so patient I wished I hadn't come. "I won't say any trick of the mind is impossible, but I might call that one highly improbable. Academically, however, considering your emotional involvement—"

"I'm not emotionally involved!" I yelled that. He smiled, looking

much more interested. I laughed at myself. That was better than
poking him in the eye. "I'm upset, Doctor, because the whole thing
goes against reason. If you start out knowing nobody's going to believe you, it's all messed up before you open your mouth."

He nodded kindly. He's a good joe. I think he'd stopped listening
for what I didn't say long enough to hear a little of what I did say.
"You're not unstable, Ben. Don't worry about amnesia. The explanation, perhaps some human intruder, will turn out to be within
the human norm. The norm of possibility does include such things
as lycanthropic delusions, maniacal behavior, and so on. Your police
up there will carry on a good search for the poor woman. They won't
overlook that snowdrift. Don't underestimate them, and don't worry
about your own mind, Ben."

"Ever seen our Maine woods?"

"No, I go away to the Cape."

"Try it some time. Take a patch of it, say about fifty miles by
fifty, that's twenty-five hundred square miles. Drop some eager
policemen into it, tell 'em to hunt for something they never saw before and don't want to see, that doesn't want to be found."

"But if your beast is human, human beings leave traces. Bodies
aren't easy to hide, Ben."

"In those woods? A body taken by a carnivorous animal? Why
not?" Well, our minds didn't touch. I thanked him for his patience
and got up. "The maniac responsible," I said. "But whatever we call
him, Doctor, he was *there*."

Mike Short picked me up at the Lohman bus station, and told me
something of a ferment in Darkfield. I shouldn't have been surprised. "They're all scared, Mr. Dane. They want to hurt somebody." Mike is Jim Short's younger brother. He scrapes up a living
with his taxi service and occasional odd jobs at the garage. There's
a droop in his shaggy ringlets, and I believe thirty is staring him in
the face. "Like old Harp he wants to tell it like it happened and
nobody buys. That's sad, man. You been away what, three days?
The fuzz was pissed off. You better connect with Mister Sheriff
Robart like soon. He climbed all over my ass just for driving you
to the bus that day, like I should've known you shouldn't."

"I'll pacify him. They haven't found Mrs. Ryder?"

Mike spat out the car window, which was rolled down for the mild air. "Old Harp he never got such a job of snow-shoveling done in all his days. By the c'munity, for free. No, they won't find her." In that there was plenty of I-want-to-be-asked, and something more, a hint of the mythology of Mike's generation.

"So what's your opinion, Mike?"

He maneuvered a fresh cigarette against the stub of the last and drove on through tiresome silence. The road was winding between ridged mountains of plowed, rotting snow. I had the window down on my side too for the genial afternoon sun, and imagined a tang of spring. At last Mike said, "You prob'ly don't go along . . . Jim got your ca' out, by the way. It's at your place . . . Well, you'll hear 'em talking it all to pieces. Some claim Harp's telling the truth. Some say he killed her himself. They don't say how he made her disappear. Ain't heard any talk against you, Mr. Dane, nothing that counts. The sheriff's peeved, but that's just on account you took off without asking." His vague, large eyes watched the melting landscape, the ambiguous messages of spring. "Well, I think, like, a demon took her, Mr. Dane. She was one of his own, see? You got to remember, I knew that chick. Okay, you can say it ain't scientific, only there is a science to these things, I read a book about it. You can laugh if you want."

I wasn't laughing. It wasn't my first glimpse of the contemporary medievalism and won't be my last if I survive another year or two. I wasn't laughing, and I said nothing. Mike sat smoking, expertly driving his 20th-Century artifact while I suppose his thoughts were in the 17th, sniffing after the wonders of the invisible world, and I recalled what Johnny Malcolm had said about the need for legends. Mike and I had no more talk.

Adelaide Simmons was dourly glad to see me. From her I learned that the sheriff and state police had swarmed all over Harp's place and the surrounding countryside, and were still at it. Result, zero. Harp had repeatedly told our story and was refusing to tell it any more. "Does the chores and sets there drinking," she said, "or staring off. Was up to see him yesterday, Mr. Dane— felt I should. Couple days they didn't let him alone a minute, maybe now they've eased off some. He asked me real sharp, was you back yet. Well, I redd up his place, made some bread, least I could do."

When I told her I was going there, she prepared a basket, while I sat in the kitchen and listened. "Some say she busted that window herself, jumped down and run off in the snow, out of her mind. Any sense in that?"

"Nope."

"And some claim she deserted him. Earlier. Which'd make you a liar. And they say whichever way it was, Harp's made up this crazy story because he can't stand the truth." Her clever hands slapped sandwiches into shape. "They claim Harp got you to go along with it, they don't say how."

"Hypnotized me, likely. Adelaide, it all happened the way Harp told it. I heard the thing too. If Harp is ready for the squirrels, so am I."

She stared hard, and sighed. She likes to talk, but her mill often shuts off suddenly, because of a quality of hers which I find good as well as rare: I mean that when she has no more to say she doesn't go on talking.

I got up to Ryder's Ridge about suppertime. Bill Hastings was there. The road was plowed slick between the snow ridges, and I wondered how much of the litter of tracks and crumpled paper and spent cigarette packages had been left by sight-seers. Ground frost had not yet yielded to the mud season, which would soon make normal driving impossible for a few weeks. Bill let me in, with the look people wear for serious illness. But Harp heaved himself out of that armchair, not sick in body at least. "Ben, I heard him last night. Late."

"What direction?"

"North."

"You hear it, Bill?" I set down the basket.

My pint-size friend shook his head. "Wasn't here." I couldn't guess how much Bill accepted of the tale.

Harp said, "What's the basket?—oh. Obliged. Adelaide's a nice woman." But his mind was remote. "It was north, Ben, a long

way, but I think I know about where it would be. I wouldn't
've heard it except the night was so still, like everything had
quieted for me. You know, they been a-deviling me night and
day. Robart, state cops, mess of smart little buggers from the
papers. I couldn't sleep, I stepped outside like I was called. Why,
he might've been the other side of the stars, the sky so full of 'em
and nothing stirring. Cold . . . You went to Boston, Ben?"

"Yes. Waste of time. They want it to be something human,
anyhow something that fits the books."

Whittling, Bill said neutrally, "Always a man for the books
yourself, wasn't you, Ben?"

I had to agree. Harp asked, "Hadn't no ideas?"

"Just gave me back my own thoughts in their language. We
have to find it, Harp. Of course some wouldn't take it for true
even if you had photographs."

Harp said, "Photographs be goddamned."

"I guess you got to go," said Bill Hastings. "We been talking
about it, Ben. Maybe I'd feel the same if it was me . . . I
better be on my way or supper'll be cold and the old woman
raising hell-fire." He tossed his stick back in the woodbox.

"Bill," said Harp, "you won't mind feeding the stock couple,
three days?"

"I don't mind. Be up tomorrow."

"Do the same for you some time. I wouldn't want it mentioned
anyplace."

"Harp, you know me better'n that. See you, Ben."

"Snow's going fast," said Harp when Bill had driven off. "Be
in the woods a long time yet, though."

"You wouldn't start this late."

He was at the window, his lean bulk shutting off much light
from the time-seasoned kitchen where most of his indoor life
had been passed. "Morning, early. Tonight I got to listen."

"Be needing sleep, I'd think."

"I don't always get what I need," said Harp.

"I'll bring my snowshoes. About six? And my carbine—I'm best
with a gun I know."

He stared at me a while. "All right, Ben. You understand, though,
you might have to come back alone. I ain't coming back till I
get him, Ben. Not this time."

At sunup I found him with Ned and Jerry in the stable. He
had lived eight or ten years with that team. He gave Ned's
neck a final pat as he turned to me and took up our conversation
as if night had not intervened. "Not till I get him. Ben, I don't
want you drug into this ag'inst your inclination."

"Did you hear it again last night?"

"I heard it. North."

The sun was at the point of rising when we left on our snowshoes, like morning ghosts ourselves. Harp strode ahead down the
slope to the woods without haste, perhaps with some reluctance.
Near the trees he halted, gazing to his right where a red blaze
was burning the edge of the sky curtain; I scolded myself for
thinking that he was saying goodbye to the sun.

The snow was crusted, sometimes slippery even for our web
feet. We entered the woods along a tangle of tracks, including
the fat tire-marks of a snow-scooter. "Guy from Lohman," said
Harp. "Hired the goddamn thing out to the state cops and hisself
with it. Goes pootin' around all over hell, fit to scare everything
inside eight, ten miles." He cut himself a fresh plug to last the
morning. "I b'lieve the thing is a mite further off than that.
They'll be messing around again today." His fingers dug into my
arm. "See how it is, don't y'? They ain't looking for what we are.
Looking for a dead body to hang onto my neck. And if they
was to find her the way I found—the way I found—"

"Harp, you needn't borrow trouble."

"I know how they think," he said. "Was I to walk down the
road beyond Darkfield, they'd pick me up. They ain't got me in
shackles because they got no—no body, Ben. Nobody needs to
tell me about the law. They got to have a body. Only reason
they didn't leave a man here overnight, they figure I can't go
nowhere. They think a man couldn't travel in three, four foot
of snow . . . Ben, I mean to find that thing and shoot it down
. . . We better slant off thisaway."

He set out at a wide angle from those tracks, and we soon had them out of sight. On the firm crust our snowshoes left no mark. After a while we heard a grumble of motors far back, on the road. Harp chuckled viciously. "Bright and early like yesterday." He stared back the way we had come. "They'll never pick that up, without dogs. That son of a bitch Robart did talk about borrying a hound somewhere, to sniff Leda's clothes. More likely give 'em a sniff of mine, now."

We had already come so far that I didn't know the way back. Harp would know it. He could never be lost in any woods, but I have no mental compass such as his. So I followed him blindly, not trying to memorize our trail. It was a region of uniform old growth, mostly hemlock, no recent lumbering, few landmarks. The monotony wore down native patience to a numbness, and our snowshoes left no more impression than our thoughts.

An hour passed, or more; after that sound of motors faded. Now and then I heard the wind move peacefully overhead. Few bird calls, for most of our singers had not yet returned. "Been in this part before, Harp?"

"Not with snow on the ground, not lately." His voice was hushed and careful. "Summers. About a mile now, and the trees thin out some. Stretch of slash where they was taking out pine four, five years back and left everything a Christly pile of shit like they always do."

No, Harp wouldn't get lost here, but I was well lost, tired, sorry I had come. Would he turn back if I collapsed? I didn't think he could, now, for any reason. My pack with blanket roll and provisions had become infernal. He had said we ought to have enough for three or four days. Only a few years earlier I had carried heavier camping loads than this without trouble, but now I was blown, a stitch beginning in my side. My wrist watch said only nine o'clock.

The trees thinned out as he had promised, and here the land rose in a long slope to the north. I looked up across a tract of eight or ten acres where the devastation of stupid lumbering might be healed if the hurt region could be let alone for sixty years. The deep snow, blinding out here where only scrub growth interfered with the sunlight, covered the worst of the wreckage. "Good place for wild ras'berries," Harp said quietly. "Been time for 'em to grow back. Guess it was nearer seven years ago when they cut here and left this mess. Last summer I couldn't hardly find their logging road. Off to the left—"

He stopped, pointing with a slow arm to a blurred gray line that wandered up from the left to disappear over the rise of ground. The nearest part of that gray curve must have been four hundred feet away, and to my eyes it might have been a shadow cast by an irregularity of the snow surface; Harp knew better. Something had passed there, heavy enough to break the crust. "You want to rest a mite, Ben? Once over that rise I might not want to stop again."

I let myself down on the butt of an old log that lay tilted toward us, cut because it had happened to be in the way, left to rot because they happened to be taking pine. "Can you really make anything out of that?"

"Not enough," said Harp. "But it could be him." He did not sit by me but stood relaxed with his load, snowshoes spaced so he could spit between them. "About half a mile over that rise," he said, "there's a kind of gorge. Must've been a good brook, former times, still a stream along the bottom in summer. Tangle of elders and stuff. Couple, three caves in the bank at one spot. I guess it's three summers since I been there. Gloomy goddamn place. There was foxes into one of them caves. Natural caves, I b'lieve. I didn't go too near, not then."

I sat in the warming light, wondering whether there was any way I could talk to Harp about the beast—if it existed, if we weren't merely a pair of aging men with disordered minds. Any way to tell him the creature was important to the world outside our dim little village? That it ought somehow to be kept alive, not just shot down and shoveled aside? How could I say this to a man without science, who had lost his wife and also the trust of his fellow-men?

Take way that trust and you take away the world.

Could I ask him to shoot it in the legs, get it back alive? Why, to my own self, irrationally, that appeared wrong, horrible, as well as beyond our powers. Better if he shot to kill. Or if I did. So in the end I said nothing, but shrugged my pack into place and told him I was ready to go on.

With the crust uncertain under that stronger sunshine, we picked our way slowly up the rise, and when we came at length to that line of tracks, Harp said matter-of-factly, "Now you've seen his mark. It's him."

Sun and overnight freezing had worked on the trail. Harp estimated it had been made early the day before. But wherever the weight of Longtooth had broken through, the shape of his foot showed clearly down there in its pocket of snow, a foot the size of a man's but broader, shorter. The prints were spaced for the stride of a short-legged person. The arch of the foot was low, but the beast was not actually flat-footed. Beast or man. I said, "This is a man's print, Harp. Isn't it?"

He spoke without heat. "No. You're forgetting, Ben. I seen him."

"Anyhow there's only one."

He said slowly, "Only one set of tracks."

"What d' you mean?"

Harp shrugged. "It's heavy. He could've been carrying something. Keep your voice down. That crust yesterday, it would've held me without no web feet, but he went through, and he ain't as big as me." Harp checked his rifle and released the safety. "Half a mile to them caves. B'lieve that's where he is, Ben. Don't talk unless you got to, and take it slow."

I followed him. We topped the rise, encountering more of that lumberman's desolation on the other side. The trail crossed it, directly approaching a wall of undamaged trees that marked the limit of the cutting. Here forest took over once more, and where it began, Longtooth's trail ended. "Now you seen how it goes," Harp said. "Any place where he can travel above ground he does. He don't scramble up the trunks, seems like. Look here—he must've got aholt of that branch and swung hisself up. Knocked off some snow, but the wind knocks off so much too you can't tell nothing. See, Ben, he—he figures it out. He knows about trails. He'll have come down out of these trees far enough from where we are now so there ain't no chance of us seeing the place from here. Could be anywhere in a halfcircle, and draw it as big as you please."

"Thinking like a man."

"But he ain't a man," said Harp. "There's things he don't know. How a man feels, acts. I'm going on to them caves." From necessity, I followed him . . .

I ought to end this quickly. Prematurely I am an old man, incapacitated by the effects of a stroke and a damaged heart. I keep improving a little—sensible diet, no smoking, Adelaide's care. I expect several years of tolerable health on the way downhill. But I find, as Harp did, that it is even more crippling to lose the trust of others. I will write here once more, and not again, that my word is good.

It was noon when we reached the gorge. In that place some melancholy part of night must always remain. Down the center of the ravine between tangles of alder, water murmured under ice and rotting snow, which here and there had fallen in to reveal the dark brilliance. Harp did not enter the gorge itself but moved slowly through tree-cover along the left edge, eyes flickering for danger. I tried to imitate his caution. We went a hundred yards or more in that inching advance, maybe two hundred. I heard only the occasional wind of spring.

He turned to look at me, with a sickly triumph, a grimace of disgust and of justification, too. He touched his nose and then I got it also, a rankness from down ahead of us, a musky foulness with an ammoniacal tang and some smell of decay. Then on the other side of the gorge, off in the woods but not far, I heard Longtooth.

A bark, not loud. Throaty, like talk.

Harp suppressed an answering growl. He moved on until he could point down to a black cave-mouth on the opposite side. The breeze blew the stench across to us. Harp whispered, "See, he's got like a path. Jumps down to that flat rock, then to the cave. We'll see him in a minute." Yes, there were sounds in the brush. "You keep back." His left palm lightly stroked the underside of his rifle barrel.

So intent was he on the opening where Longtooth would appear, I may have been first to see the other who came then to the cave mouth and stared up at us with animal eyes. Longtooth had called again, a rather gentle sound. The woman wrapped in filthy hides may have been drawn by that call or by the noise of our approach.

Then Harp saw her.

He knew her. In spite of the tangled hair, scratched face, dirt, and the shapeless deer-pelt she clutched around herself against the cold, I am sure he knew her. I don't think she knew him, or me. An inner blindness, a look of a beast wholly centered on its own needs. I think human memories had drained away. She knew Longtooth was coming. I think she wanted his warmth and protection, but there were no words in the whimper she made before Harp's bullet took her between the eyes.

Longtooth shoved through the bushes. He dropped the rabbit he was carrying and jumped down to that flat rock snarling, glancing sidelong at the dead woman who was still twitching. If he understood the fact of death, he had no time for it. I saw the massive overdevelopment of thigh and leg muscles, their springy motions of preparation. The distance from the flat rock to the place where Harp stood must have been fifteen feet. One spear of sunlight touched him in that blue-green shade, touched his thick red fur and his fearful face.

Harp could have shot him. Twenty seconds for it, maybe more. But he flung his rifle aside and drew out his hunting knife, his own long tooth, and had it waiting when the enemy jumped.

So could I have shot him. No one needs to tell me I ought to have done so.

Longtooth launched himself, clawed fingers out, fangs exposed. I felt the meeting as if the impact had struck my own flesh. They tumbled roaring into the gorge, and I was cold, detached, an instrument for watching.

It ended soon. The heavy brownish teeth clenched in at the base of Harp's neck. He made no more motion except the thrust that sent his blade into Longtooth's left side. Then they were quiet in that embrace, quiet all three. I heard the water flowing under the ice.

I remember a roaring in my ears, and I was moving with slow care, one difficult step after another, along the lip of the gorge and through mighty corridors of white and green. With my hardwon detached amusement I supposed this might be the region where I had recently followed poor Harp Ryder to some destination or other, but not (I thought) one of those we talked about when we were boys. A band of iron had closed around my forehead, and breathing was an enterprise needing great effort and caution, in order not to worsen the indecent pain that clung as another band around my diaphragm. I leaned against a tree for thirty seconds or thirty minutes, I don't know where. I knew I mustn't take off my pack in spite of the pain, because it carried provisions for three days. I said once: "Ben, you are lost."

I had my carbine, a golden bough, staff of life, and I recall the shrewd management and planning that enabled me to send three shots into the air. Twice.

It seems I did not want to die, and so hung on the cliff-edge of death with a mad stubbornness. They tell me it could not have been the second day that I fired the second burst, the one that was heard and answered—because, they say a man can't suffer the kind of attack I was having and then survive a whole night of exposure. They say that when a search party reached me from Wyndham Village (18 miles from Darkfield), I made some garbled speech and fell flat on my face.

I woke immoblized, without power of speech or any motion except for a little life in my left hand, and for a long time memory was only a jarring of irrelevancies. When that cleared I still couldn't talk for another long deadly while. I recall someone saying with exasperated admiration that with cerebral hemorrhage on top of coronary infarction, I had no damn right to be alive; this was the first sound that gave me any pleasure. I remember recognizing Adelaide and being unable to thank her for her presence. None of this matters to the story, except the fact that for months I had no bridge of communication with the world; and yet I loved the world and did not want to leave it.

One can always ask: What will happen next?

Some time in what they said was June my memory was (I think) clear. I scrawled a little, with the nurse supporting the deadened part of my arm. But in response to what I wrote, the doctor, the nurses, Sheriff Robart, even Adelaide Simmons and Bill Hastings, looked—sympathetic. I was not believed. I am not believed now, in the most important part of what I wish I might say: that there are things in our world that we do not understand, and that this ignorance ought to generate humility. People find this obvious, bromidic—oh, they always have!—and therefore they do not listen, retaining the pride of their ignorance intact.

Remnants of the three bodies were found in late August, small thanks to my efforts, for I had no notion what compass direction we took after the cut-over area, and there are so many such areas of desolation I couldn't tell them where to look. Forest scavengers, including a pack of dogs, had found the bodies first. Water had moved them too, for the last of the big snow melted suddenly, and for a couple of days at least there must have been a small river raging through that gorge. The head of what they are calling the "lunatic" got rolled downstream, bashed against rocks, partly buried in silt. Dogs had chewed and scattered what they speak of as "the man's fur coat."

It will remain a lunatic in a fur coat, for they won't have it any other way. So far as I know, no scientist ever got a look at the wreckage, unless you glorify the coroner by that title. I believe he was a good vet before he got the job. When my speech was more or less regained, I was already through trying to talk about it. A statement of mine was read at the inquest— that was before I could talk or leave the hospital. At this ceremony society officially decided that Harper Harrison Ryder, of this township, shot to death his wife Leda and an individual, male, of unknown identity, while himself temporarily of unsound mind, and died of knife injuries received in a struggle with the said individual of unknown, and so forth.

I don't talk about it because that only makes people more sorry for me, to think a man's mind should fail so, and he not yet sixty.

I cannot even ask them: "What is truth?" They would only look more saddened, and I suppose shocked, and perhaps find reasons for not coming to see me again.

They are kind. They will do anything for me, except think about it.

"I don't like the looks of that, at all!"

*This story is about Tom Two Ribbons, a biologist-spaceman of Ameri-
can Indian descent, who is an uneasy member of an expedition that is
eliminating a "pest" on an alien planet. It has the strong plotting and
convincing background that you would expect from a Robert Silverberg
story; it also has a constantly shifting viewpoint which reflects the re-
actions of Tom and the other members of the expedition. Because of
the rhythm and reason behind each shift, the story is involving in the
best kind of way. It is probably something of a departure for Mr.
Silverberg; we think you'll agree that it is a successful and rewarding
one.*

SUNDANCE

by Robert Silverberg

Today you liquidated about 50,000 Eaters in Sector A, and now
you are spending an uneasy night. You and Herndon flew east
at dawn, with the green-gold sunrise at your backs, and sprayed
the neural pellets over a thousand hectares along the Forked River.
You flew on into the prairie beyond the river, where the Eaters
have already been wiped out, and had lunch sprawled on that
thick, soft carpet of grass where the first settlement is expected
to rise. Herndon picked some juiceflowers, and you enjoyed half
an hour of mild hallucinations. Then, as you headed toward the
copter to begin an afternoon of further pellet spraying, he said
suddenly, "Tom, how would you feel about this if it turned out
that the Eaters weren't just animal pests? That they were *people*,
say, with a language and rites and a history and all?"

You thought of how it had been for your own people.

"They aren't," you said.

"Suppose they were. Suppose the Eaters—"

"They aren't. Drop it."

Herndon has this streak of cruelty in him that leads him to
ask such questions. He goes for the vulnerabilities; it amuses him.

All night now his casual remark has echoed in your mind. Suppose the Eaters . . . Suppose the Eaters . . . Suppose . . . Suppose . . .

You sleep for a while, and dream, and in your dreams you swim through rivers of blood.

Foolishness. A feverish fantasy. You know how important it is to exterminate the Eaters fast, before the settlers get here. They're just animals, and not even harmless animals at that; ecology-wreckers is what they are, devourers of oxygen-liberating plants, and they have to go. A few have been saved for zoological study. The rest must be destroyed. Ritual extirpation of undesirable beings, the old, old story. But let's not complicate our job with moral qualms, you tell yourself. Let's not dream of rivers of blood.

The Eaters don't even *have* blood, none that could flow in rivers, anyway. What they have is, well, a kind of lymph that permeates every tissue and transmits nourishment along the inter-faces. Waste products go out the same way, osmotically. In terms of process, it's structurally analogous to your own kind of circulatory system, except there's no network of blood vessels hooked to a master pump. The life-stuff just oozes through their bodies, as though they were amoebas or sponges or some other low-phylum form. Yet they're definitely high-phylum in nervous system, di-gestive setup, limb-and-organ template, etc. Odd, you think. The thing about aliens is that they're alien, you tell yourself, not for the first time.

The beauty of their biology for you and your companions is that it lets you exterminate them so neatly.

You fly over the grazing grounds and drop the neural pellets. The Eaters find and ingest them. Within an hour the poison has reached all sectors of the body. Life ceases; a rapid breakdown of cellular matter follows, the Eater literally falling apart molecule by molecule the instant that nutrition is cut off; the lymph-like stuff works like acid; a universal lysis occurs; flesh and even the bones, which are cartilaginous, dissolve. In two hours, a puddle on the ground. In four, nothing at all left. Considering how many millions of Eaters you've scheduled for extermination here, it's sweet of the bodies to be self-disposing. Otherwise what a charnel house this world would become!

Suppose the Eaters . . .

Damn Herndon. You almost feel like getting a memory-editing in the morning. Scrape his stupid speculations out of your head. If you dared. If you dared.

In the morning he does not dare. Memory-editing frightens him; he will try to shake free of his new-found guilt without it. The Eaters, he explains to himself, are mindless herbivores, the unfortunate victims of human expansionism, but not really deserving of passionate defense. Their extermination is not tragic; it's just too bad. If Earthmen are to have this world, the Eaters must relinquish it. There's a difference, he tells himself, between the elimination of the Plains Indians from the American prairie in the nineteenth century and the destruction of the bison on that same prairie. One feels a little wistful about the slaughter of the thundering herds; one regrets the butchering of millions of the noble brown woolly beasts, yes. But one feels outrage, not mere wistful regret, at what was done to the Sioux. There's a difference. Reserve your passions for the proper cause.

He walks from his bubble at the edge of the camp toward the center of things. The flagstone path is moist and glistening. The morning fog has not yet lifted, and every tree is bowed, the long, notched leaves heavy with droplets of water. He pauses, crouching, to observe a spider-analog spinning its asymmetrical web. As he watches, a small amphibian, delicately shaded turquoise, glides as inconspicuously as possible over the mossy ground. Not inconspicuously enough; he gently lifts the little creature and puts it on the back of his hand. The gills flutter in anguish, and the amphibian's sides quiver. Slowly, cunningly, its color changes until it matches the coppery tone of the hand. The camouflage is excellent. He lowers his hand and the amphibian scurries into a puddle. He walks on.

He is forty years old, shorter than most of the other members of the expedition, with wide shoulders, a heavy chest, dark glossy hair, a blunt, spreading nose. He is a biologist. This is his third career, for he has failed as an anthropologist and as a developer of real estate. His name is Tom Two Ribbons. He has been married twice but has had no children. His great-grandfather died of alcoholism; his grandfather was addicted to hallucinogens; his father had compulsively visited cheap memory-editing parlors. Tom Two Ribbons is conscious that he is failing a family tradition, but he has not yet found his own mode of self-destruction.

In the main building he discovers Herndon, Julia, Ellen, Schwartz, Chang, Michaelson, and Nichols. They are eating breakfast; the others are already at work. Ellen rises and comes to him and kisses him. Her short soft yellow hair tickles his cheeks. "I love you," she whispers. She has spent the night in Michaelson's bubble. "I love you," he tells her, and draws a quick vertical line of affection between her small pale breasts. He winks at Michaelson, who nods, touches the tops of two fingers to his lips, and blows them a kiss. We are all good friends here, Tom Two Ribbons thinks.

"Who drops pellets today?" he asks.

"Mike and Chang," says Julia. "Sector C."

Schwartz says, "Eleven more days and we ought to have the whole peninsula clear. Then we can move inland."

"If our pellet supply holds up," Chang points out.

Herndon says, "Did you sleep well, Tom?"

"No," says Tom. He sits down and taps out his breakfast requisition. In the west, the fog is beginning to burn off the mountains. Something throbs in the back of his neck. He has been on this world nine weeks now, and in that time it has undergone its only change of season, shading from dry weather to foggy. The mists will remain for many months. Before the plains parch again, the Eaters will be gone and the settlers will begin to arrive. His food slides down the chute and he seizes it. Ellen sits beside him. She is a little more than half his age; this is her first voyage; she is their keeper of records, but she is also skilled at editing. "You look troubled," Ellen tells him. "Can I help you?"

"No. Thank you."

"I hate it when you get gloomy."

"It's a racial trait," says Tom Two Ribbons.

"I doubt that very much."

"The truth is that maybe my personality reconstruct is wearing thin. The trauma level was so close to the surface. I'm just a walking veneer, you know."

Ellen laughs prettily. She wears only a sprayon halfwrap. Her skin looks damp; she and Michaelson have had a swim at dawn. Tom Two Ribbons is thinking of asking her to marry him, when this job is over. He has not been married since the collapse of the real estate business. The therapist suggested divorce as part of the reconstruct. He sometimes wonders where Terry has gone and whom she lives with now. Ellen says, "You seem pretty stable to me, Tom."

"Thank you," he says. She is young. She does not know.

"If it's just a passing gloom I can edit it out in one quick snip."

"Thank you" he says. "No."

"I forgot. You don't like editing."

"My father—"

"Yes?"

"In fifty years he pared himself down to a thread," Tom Two Ribbons says. "He had his ancestors edited away, his whole heritage, his religion, his wife, his sons, finally his name. Then he sat and smiled all day. Thank you, no editing."

"Where are you working today?" Ellen asks.

"In the compound, running tests."

"Want company? I'm off all morning."

"Thank you, no," he says, too quickly. She looks hurt. He tries to remedy his unintended cruelty by touching her arm lightly and saying, "Maybe this afternoon, all right? I need to commune a while. Yes?"

"Yes," she says, and smiles, and shapes a kiss with her lips.

After breakfast he goes to the compound. It covers a thousand hectares east of the base; they have bordered it with neural-field projectors at intervals of eighty meters, and this is a sufficient fence to keep the captive population of two hundred Eaters from straying. When all the others have been exterminated, this study group will remain. At the southwest corner of the compound stands a lab bubble from which the experiments are run: metabolic, psychological, physiological, ecological. A stream crosses the compound diagonally. There is a low ridge of grassy hills at its eastern edge. Five distinct copses of tightly clustered knifeblade trees are separated by patches of dense savanna. Sheltered beneath the grass are the oxygen-plants, almost completely hidden except for the photosynthetic spikes that jut to heights of three or four meters at regular intervals, and for the lemon-colored respiratory bodies, chest high, that make the grassland sweet and dizzying with exhaled gases. Through the fields move the Eaters in a straggling herd, nibbling delicately at the respiratory bodies.

Tom Two Ribbons spies the herd beside the stream and goes toward it. He stumbles over an oxygen-plant hidden in the grass but deftly recovers his balance and, seizing the puckered orifice of the respiratory body, inhales deeply. His despair lifts. He approaches the Eaters. They are spherical, bulky, slow-moving creatures, covered by masses of coarse orange fur. Saucer-like eyes protrude above narrow rubbery lips. Their legs are thin and scaly, like a chicken's, and their arms are short and held close to their bodies. They regard him with bland lack of curiosity. "Good morning, brothers!" is the way he greets them this time, and he wonders why.

I noticed something strange today. Perhaps I simply sniffed too much oygen in the fields; maybe I was succumbing to a suggestion Herndon planted; or possibly it's the family masochism cropping out. But while I was observing the Eaters in the compound, it seemed to me, for the first time, that they were behaving intelligently, that they were functioning in a ritualized way.

I followed them around for three hours. During that time they uncovered half a dozen outcroppings of oxygen-plants. In each case they went through a stylized pattern of action before starting to munch. They:

Formed a straggly circle around the plants.

Looked toward the sun.

Looked toward their neighbors on left and right around the circle.

Made fuzzy neighing sounds *only* after having done the foregoing. Looked toward the sun again.

Moved in and ate.

If this wasn't a prayer of thanksgiving, a saying of grace, then what was it? And if they're advanced enough spiritually to say grace, are we not therefore committing genocide here? Do chimpanzees say grace? Christ, we wouldn't even wipe out chimps the way we're cleaning out the Eaters! Of course, chimps don't interfere with human crops, and some kind of coexistence would be possible, whereas Eaters and human agriculturalists simply can't function on the same planet. Nevertheless, there's a moral issue here. The liquidation effort is predicated on the assumption that the intelligence level of the Eaters is about on a par with that of oysters, or, at best, sheep. Our consciences stay clear because our poison is quick and painless and because the Eaters thoughtfully dissolve upon dying, sparing us the mess of incinerating millions of corpses. But if they pray—

I won't say anything to the others just yet. I want more evidence, hard, objective. Films, tapes, record cubes. Then we'll see. What if I can show that we're exterminating intelligent beings? My family knows a little about genocide, after all, having been on the receiving end just a few centuries back. I doubt that I could halt what's going on here. But at the very least I could withdraw from the operation. Head back to Earth and stir up public outcries.

I hope I'm imagining this.

I'm not imagining a thing. They gather in circles; they look to the sun; they neigh and pray. They're only balls of jelly on chicken-legs, but they give thanks for their food. Those big round eyes now seem to stare accusingly at me. Our tame herd here knows what's going on: that we have descended from the stars to eradicate their kind, and that they alone will be spared. They have no way of fighting back or even of communicating their displeasure, but they *know*. And hate us. Jesus, we have killed two million of them since we got here, and in a metaphorical way I'm stained with blood, and what will I do, what can I do?

I must move very carefully, or I'll end up drugged and edited.

I can't let myself seem like a crank, a quack, an agitator. I can't stand up and *denounce!* I have to find allies. Herndon, first. He surely is on to the truth; he's the one who nudged *me* to it, that day we dropped pellets. And I thought he was merely being vicious in his usual way!

I'll talk to him tonight.

He says, "I've been thinking about that suggestion you made. About the Eaters. Perhaps we haven't made sufficiently close psychological studies. I mean, if they really *are* intelligent—"

Herndon blinks. He is a tall man with glossy dark hair, a heavy beard, sharp cheekbones. "Who says they are, Tom?"

"You did. On the far side of the Forked River, you said—"

"It was just a speculative hypothesis. To make conversation."

"No, I think it was more than that. You really believed it."

Herndon looks troubled. "Tom, I don't know what you're trying to start, but don't start it. If I for a moment believed we were killing intelligent creatures, I'd run for an editor so fast I'd start an implosion wave."

"Why did you ask me that thing, then?" Tom Two Ribbons says.

"Idle chatter."

"Amusing yourself by kindling guilts in somebody else? You're a bastard, Herndon. I mean it."

"Well, look, Tom, if I had any idea that you'd get so worked up about a hypothetical suggestion—" Herndon shakes his head. "The Eaters aren't intelligent beings. Obviously. Otherwise we wouldn't be under orders to liquidate them."

"Obviously," says Tom Two Ribbons.

Ellen said, "No, I don't know what Tom's up to. But I'm pretty sure he needs a rest. It's only a year and a half since his personality reconstruct, and he had a pretty bad breakdown back then."

Michaelson consulted a chart. "He's refused three times in a row to make his pellet-dropping run. Claiming he can't take time away from his research. Hell, we can fill in for him, but it's the idea that he's ducking chores that bothers me."

"What kind of research is he doing?" Nichols wanted to know.

"Not biological," said Julia. "He's with the Eaters in the compound all the time, but I don't see him making any tests on them. He just watches them."

"And talks to them," Chang observed.

"And talks, yes," Julia said.

"About what?" Nichols asked.

"Who knows?"

Everyone looked at Ellen. "You're closest to him," Michaelson said. "Can't you bring him out of it?"

"I've got to know what he's in, first," Ellen said. "He isn't saying a thing."

You know that you must be very careful, for they outnumber you, and their concern for your mental welfare can be deadly. Already they realize you are disturbed, and Ellen has begun to probe for the source of the disturbance. Last night you lay in her arms and she questioned you, obliquely, skillfully, and you knew what she is trying to find out. When the moons appeared she suggested that you and she stroll in the compound, among the sleeping Eaters. You declined, but she sees that you have become involved with the creatures.

You have done probing of your own—subtly, you hope. And you are aware that you can do nothing to save the Eaters. An irrevocable commitment has been made. It is 1876 all over again; these are the bison, these are the Sioux, and they must be destroyed, for the railroad is on its way. If you speak out here, your friends will calm you and pacify you and edit you, for they do not see what you see. If you return to Earth to agitate, you will be mocked and recommended for another reconstruct. You can do nothing. You can do nothing.

You cannot save, but perhaps you can record.

Go out into the prairie. Live with the Eaters; make yourself their friend; learn their ways. Set it down, a full account of their culture, so that at least that much will not be lost. You know the techniques of field anthropology. As was done for your people in the old days, do now for the Eaters.

He finds Michaelson. "Can you spare me for a few weeks?" he asks.

"Spare you, Tom? What do you mean?"

"I've got some field studies to do. I'd like to leave the base and work with Eaters in the wild."

"What's wrong with the ones in the compound?"

"It's the last chance with wild ones, Mike. I've got to go."

"Alone, or with Ellen?"

"Alone."

Michaelson nods slowly. "All right, Tom. Whatever you want. Go. I won't hold you here."

I dance in the prairie under the green-gold sun. About me the Eaters gather. I am stripped; sweat makes my skin glisten; my heart pounds. I talk to them with my feet, and they understand.

They understand.

They have a language of soft sounds. They have a god. They know love and awe and rapture. They have rites. They have names. They have a history. Of all this I am convinced.

I dance on thick grass.

How can I reach them? With my feet, with my hands, with my grunts, with my sweat. They gather by the hundreds, by the thousands, and I dance. I must not stop. They cluster about me and make their sounds. I am a conduit for strange forces. My great-grandfather should see me now! Sitting on his porch in Wyoming, the firewater in his hand, his brain rotting—see me now, old one! See the dance of Tom Two Ribbons! I talk to these strange ones with my feet under a sun that is the wrong color. I dance. I dance.

"Listen to me," I say. "I am your friend, I alone, the only one you can trust. Trust me, talk to me, teach me. Let me preserve your ways, for soon the destruction will come."

I dance, and the sun climbs, and the Eaters murmur.

There is the chief. I dance toward him, back, toward, I bow, I point to the sun, I imagine the being that lives in that ball of flame, I imitate the sounds of these people, I kneel, I rise, I dance. Tom Two Ribbons dances for you.

I summon skills my ancestors forgot. I feel the power flowing in me. As they danced in the days of the bison, I dance now, beyond the Forked River.

I dance, and now the Eaters dance too. Slowly, uncertainly, they move toward me, they shift their weight, lift leg and leg, sway about. "Yes, like that!" I cry. "Dance!"

We dance together as the sun reaches noon height.

Now their eyes are no longer accusing. I see warmth and kinship. I am their brother, their redskinned tribesman, he who dances with them. No longer do they seem clumsy to me. There is a strange ponderous grace in their movements. They dance. They dance. They caper about me. Closer, closer, closer!

We move in holy frenzy.

They sing, now, a blurred hymn of joy. They throw forth their arms, unclench their little claws. In unison they shift weight, left foot forward, right, left, right. Dance, brothers, dance, dance, dance! They press against me. Their flesh quivers; their smell is a sweet one. They gently thrust me across the field, to a part of the meadow where the grass is deep and untrampled. Still dancing, we seek for the oxygen-plants, and find clumps of them beneath the grass, and they make their prayer and seize them with their awkward arms, separating the respiratory bodies from the photosynthetic spikes. The plants, in anguish, release floods of oxygen. My mind reels. I laugh and sing. The Eaters are nibbling the lemon-colored perforated globes, nibbling the stalks as well. They thrust their plants at me. It is a religious ceremony, I see. Take from us, eat with us, join with us, this is the body, this is the blood, take, eat, join. I bend forward and put a lemon-colored globe to my lips. I do not bite; I nibble, as they do, my teeth slicing away the skin of the globe. Juice spurts into my mouth, while oxygen drenches my nostrils. The Eaters sing hosannas. I should be in full paint for this, paint of my forefathers, feathers too, meeting their religion in the regalia of what should have been mine. Take, eat, join. The juice of the oxygen-plant flows in my veins. I embrace my brothers. I sing, and as my voice leaves my lips it becomes an arch that glistens like new steel, and I pitch my song lower, and the arch turns to tarnished silver. The Eaters crowd close. The scent of their bodies is fiery red to me. Their soft cries are puffs of steam. The sun is very warm; its rays are tiny jagged pings of puckered sound, close to the top of my range of hearing, plink! plink! plink! The thick grass hums to me, deep and rich, and the wind hurls points of flame along the prairie. I devour another oxygen-plant, and then a third. My brothers laugh and shout. They tell me of their gods, the god of warmth, the god of food, the god of pleasure, the god of death, the god of holiness, the god of wrongness, and the others. They recite for me the names of their kings, and I hear their voices as splashes of green mold on the clean sheet of the sky. They instruct me in their holy rites. I must remember this, I tell myself, for when it is gone it will never come again. I continue to dance. They continue to dance. The color of the hills becomes rough and coarse, like abrasive gas. Take, eat, join. Dance. They are so gentle!

I hear the drone of the copter, suddenly.

It hovers far overhead. I am unable to see who flies in it. "No," I scream. "Not here! Not these people! Listen to me! This is Tom Two Ribbons! Can't you hear me? I'm doing a field study here! You have no right—!"

My voice makes spirals of blue moss edged with red sparks. They drift upward and are scattered by the breeze.

I yell, I shout, I bellow. I dance and shake my fists. From the wings of the copter the jointed arms of the pellet-distributors unfold. The gleaming spigots extend and whirl. The neural pellets rain down into the meadow, each tracing a blazing track that lingers in the sky. The sound of the copter becomes a furry carpet stretching to the horizon, and my shrill voice is lost in it.

The Eaters drift away from me, seeking the pellets, scratching at the roots of the grass to find them. Still dancing, I leap into their midst, striking the pellets from their hands, hurling them into

the stream, crushing them to powder. The Eaters growl black
needles at me. They turn away and search for more pellets. The
copter turns and flies off, leaving a trail of dense oily sound.
My brothers are gobbling the pellets eagerly.

There is no way to prevent it.

Joy consumes them and they topple and lie still. Occasionally
a limb twitches; then even this stops. They begin to dissolve.
Thousands of them melt on the prairie, sinking into shapelessness,
losing their spherical forms, flattening, ebbing into the ground.
The bonds of the molecules will no longer hold. It is the twilight
of protoplasm. They perish. They vanish. For hours I walk the
prairie. Now I inhale oxygen; now I eat a lemon-colored globe.
Sunset begins with the ringing of leaden chimes. Black clouds
make brazen trumpet calls in the east and the deepening wind
is a swirl of coaly bristles. Silence comes. Night falls. I dance.
I am alone.

The copter comes again, and they find you, and you do not
resist as they gather you in. You are beyond bitterness. Quietly
you explain what you have done and what you have learned,
and why it is wrong to exterminate these people. You describe
the plant you have eaten and the way it affects your senses, and
as you talk of the blessed synesthesia, the texture of the wind and
the sound of the clouds and the timbre of the sunlight, they
nod and smile and tell you not to worry, that everything will be
all right soon, and they touch something cold to your forearm,
so cold that it is a whir and a buzz and the deintoxicant sinks
into your vein and soon the ecstasy drains away, leaving only
the exhaustion and the grief.

He says, "We never learn a thing, do we? We export all our
horrors to the stars. Wipe out the Armenians, wipe out the Jews,
wipe out the Tasmanians, wipe out the Indians, wipe out everyone
who's in the way, and then come out here and do the same
damned murderous thing. You weren't with me out there. You
didn't dance with them. You didn't see what a rich, complex
culture the Eaters have. Let me tell you about their tribal structure.

It's dense: seven levels of matrimonial relationships, to begin with, and an exogamy factor that requires—"

Softly Ellen says, "Tom, darling, nobody's going to harm the Eaters."

"And the religion," he goes on. "Nine gods, each one an aspect of *the* god. Holiness and wrongness both worshiped. They have hymns, prayers, a theology. And we, the emissaries of the god of wrongness—"

"We're not exterminating them," Michaelson says. "Won't you understand that, Tom? This is all a fantasy of yours. You've been under the influence of drugs, but now we're clearing you out. You'll be clean in a little while. You'll have perspective again."

"A fantasy?" he says bitterly. "A drug dream? I stood out in the prairie and saw you drop pellets. And I watched them die and melt away. I didn't dream that."

"How can we convince you?" Chang asks earnestly. "What will make you believe? Shall we fly over the Eater country with you and show you how many millions there are?"

"But how many millions have been destroyed?" he demands.

They insist that he is wrong. Ellen tells him again that no one has ever desired to harm the Eaters. "This is a scientific expedition, Tom. We're here to *study* them. It's a violation of all we stand for to injure intelligent lifeforms."

"You admit that they're intelligent?"

"Of course. That's never been in doubt."

"Then why drop the pellets?" he asks. "Why slaughter them?"

"None of that has happened, Tom," Ellen says. She takes his hand between her cool palms. "Believe us. Believe us."

He says bitterly, "If you want me to believe you, why don't you do the job properly? Get out the editing machine and go to work on me. You can't simply *talk* me into rejecting the evidence of my own eyes."

"You were under drugs all the time," Michaelson says.

"I've never taken drugs! Except for what I ate in the meadow, when I danced—and that came after I had watched the massacre going on for weeks and weeks. Are you saying that it's a retroactive delusion?"

"No, Tom," Schwartz says. "You've had this delusion all along. It's part of your therapy, your reconstruct. You came here programmed with it."

"Impossible," he says.

Ellen kisses his fevered forehead. "It was done to reconcile you to mankind, you see. You had this terrible resentment of the displacement of your people in the nineteenth century. You were unable to forgive the industrial society for scattering the Sioux, and you were terribly full of hate. Your therapist thought that if you could be made to participate in an imaginary modern extermination, if you could come to see it as a necessary operation, you'd be purged of your resentment and able to take your place in society as—"

He thrusts her away. "Don't talk idiocy! If you knew the first thing about reconstruct therapy, you'd realize that no reputable therapist could be so shallow. There are no one-to-one correlations in reconstructs. No, don't touch me. Keep away. Keep away."

He will not let them persuade him that this is merely a drugborn dream. It is no fantasy, he tells himself, and it is no therapy. He rises. He goes out. They do not follow him. He takes a copter and seeks his brothers.

Again I dance. The sun is much hotter today. The Eaters are more numerous. Today I wear paint, today I wear feathers. My body shines with my sweat. They dance with me, and they have a frenzy in them that I have never seen before. We pound the trampled meadow with our feet. We clutch for the sun with our hands. We sing, we shout, we cry. We will dance until we fall.

This is no fantasy. These people are real, and they are intelligent, and they are doomed. This I know.

We dance. Despite the doom, we dance.

My great-grandfather comes and dances with us. He too is real. His nose is like a hawk's, not blunt like mine, and he wears the big headdress, and his muscles are like cords under his brown skin. He sings, he shouts, he cries.

Others of my family join us.

We eat the oxygen-plants together. We embrace the Eaters. We know, all of us, what it is to be hunted.

The clouds make music and the wind takes on texture and the sun's warmth has color.

We dance. We dance. Our limbs know no weariness.

The sun grows and fills the whole sky, and I see no Eaters now, only my own people, my father's fathers across the centuries, thousands of gleaming skins, thousands of hawk's noses, and we eat the plants, and we find sharp sticks and thrust them into our flesh, and the sweet blood flows and dries in the blaze of the sun, and we dance, and we dance, and some of us fall from weariness, and we dance, and the prairie is a sea of bobbing headdresses, an ocean of feathers, and we dance, and my heart makes thunder, and my knees become water, and the sun's fire engulfs me, and I dance, and I fall, and I dance, and I fall, and I fall, and I fall.

Again they find you and bring you back. They give you the cool snout on your arm to take the oxygen-plant drug from your veins, and then they give you something else so you will rest. You rest and you are very calm. Ellen kisses you and you stroke her soft skin, and then the others come in and they talk to you, saying soothing things, but you do not listen, for you are searching for realities. It is not an easy search. It is like falling through many trapdoors, looking for the one room whose floor is not hinged. Everything that has happened on this planet is your therapy, you tell yourself, designed to reconcile an embittered aborigine to the white man's conquest; nothing is really being exterminated here. You reject that and fall through and realize that this must be the therapy of your friends; they carry the weight of accumulated centuries of guilts and have come here to shed that load, and you are here to ease them of their burden, to draw their sins into yourself and give them forgiveness. Again you fall through, and see that the Eaters are mere animals who threaten the ecology and must be removed; the culture you imagined for them is your hallucination, kindled out of old churnings. You try to withdraw your objections to this necessary extermination, but you fall through again and discover that there is no extermination except in your mind, which is troubled and disordered by your obsession with the crime against your ancestors, and you sit up, for you wish to apologize to these friends of yours, these innocent scientists whom you have called murderers. And you fall through.

Carter Wilson is 28, lives in Cambridge, is the author of two novels,
CRAZY FEBRUARY *and* I HAVE FOUGHT THE GOOD FIGHT, *and one book
for children,* ON FIRM ICE. *He writes: "In the past the spicy things I
did were: 1. attended Harvard, 2. did work in anthropology with Mayan
Indians. The last years I've taught writing at Stanford, Harvard
and Tufts and wrote and produced a documentary film about Mexico."
This was his first story for F&SF, and it is a small gem, a cautionary
tale that you might want to pass on to a friend who's been taking the
sexual revolution too seriously.*

THE BRIEF, SWINGING CAREER OF DAN AND JUDY SMYTHE

by Carter Wilson

In Cambridge where they came from, Dan and Judy Smythe
were known as a couple who got the lay of the land very quickly.
At the new university in the San Fernando Valley where Dan
had his appointment in Classics, they soon saw they were being
forced to choose up sides. Judy noticed that at parties the displaced
Easterners clung in dark cabalistic circles inside, damning the West
and trying to recreate a New Haven or New York of the mind.
The people who were willing to commit themselves to the new
life made their light, laughing conversations out on the flagstone
patios, admiring the hibiscus, the neon blue of the descending
evening, and themselves.

The patio people, Judy noted to Dan, had tenure or were about
to get it. The others not.

But Dan and Judy had many reasons for throwing themselves
into California life with such abandon. They were essentially
optimistic young people, in love with their young bodies and their
new prosperity and possessions, and just past the crest of their
first great, comfortable married love. Falling wholeheartedly into

California life extended their pleasure with each other beyond the period their affection might otherwise have had.

Judy's copy of Julia Child gathered dust, and her *Sunset Cookbook* got thumbed and thumbed, and bits of batter and goo appeared on many of its pages. Dan stood outside one night while the dinner guests tinkled away merrily behind him and noted he could now produce cooking coals on the hibachi in seventeen minutes flat. He found that he was childishly pleased with this skill, something back in Cambridge he would not have dreamed he might ever want. In his old life Dan had wanted most to write a relatively popular but deeply scholarly book on the images of decadence to be found in the Later Empire Poets. Now the book had moved down several spaces on Dan's list of dreams.

Their guests, Herbert and Angela Ingiless, were telling Judy that last year thirty-one people in the Valley died of illnesses attributed to smog. It was a story Dan and Judy had heard before and assiduously refused to believe.

"Brandy in the den," Dan announced. "It's an Old California Custom, which means we did it last year too."

The Ingilesses were good folk, of the kind who blossom when they at last find California. Herbert, slightly older, was a professor of African history. He had a passing interest in the Roman sites he had seen in Tunis and, hence, in what little Dan knew about Empire history. Angela was desirable and looked dissipation-prone. The Ingilesses had recently returned from a sabbatical in Kenya where, Angela said, they had collected many interesting things which the Smythes just *had* to come over and see.

For Christmas Judy gave Dan a subscription to an underground newspaper called *The Androgynous Valley*. "If you're going to be a *real* pornographer," she said, "you'll need those ads in the back."

"Oh come now," Dan said, "I may buy an erotic book from time to time, but who looks at them before bedtime? Who?"

"I'm just trying to share your hobbies," Judy said.

Though each read the classified ads assiduously and in secret, Dan and Judy of course never thought of answering any of them. For a while it merely pleased them to believe that in all the twinkling bungalows around them lurked pedophiliacs and Nikon-carrying voyeurs and worse.

One night when there were guests, in the dark Dan tripped over the damned hibachi, upsetting the red coals and spraining his ankle. The doctor said luckily he hadn't broken anything, that heat would reduce the swelling and a masseur might be a very good idea.

Dan asked if maybe Judy couldn't be shown how to massage his ankle, but the doctor shook his head and said no, he meant a real professional, and Dan decided to stick to a heating pad.

But when he got home after his evening seminar on Catullus and limped into the living room, he found a strange puritanically slim and wiry young man in rimless spectacles waiting to knead and pull the painfully knotted sinews and cords of his ankle. At first Dan was leery of even such a small intimacy (the young man had suggested music while he worked and had selected Josquin Desprez for the stereo), but by the time the half hour was up, Dan was rather daydreaming of those supple, hard hands soothing the rest of him.

The young man told Dan he should take more acid and then his body wouldn't get so uptight.

"Where did *he* come from?" Dan asked when the masseur had been paid and had zoomed off into the hazy dark in his VW.

"Alyosha? I got him for you through the paper," Judy said. "His ad was called 'No Kinks Too Great,' but he turned out to be the straightest of the ones I talked to."

Dan felt wonderment, as though Judy had been trafficking in forbidden commodities behind his back for years and years, and he was filled with admiration.

That spring they went to a group marathon symposium at a motel in Palm Springs where everyone, including the therapist, groped each other underwater in the well-heated motel pool. Judy had a good time and thought the weekend improved the quality of their relationship, though she was disappointed by the sensation of underwater touching, which was mild. When he realized Judy was the most desirable woman at the marathon, Dan was both happy and sad. They stopped short at trading partners, which some of the other couples, including the therapist and his wife, did.

One night Dan looked up and discovered his wife waiting coyly for him to get to something in *The Androgynous Valley*. She had gotten into the playful habit of marking with a red check items in papers and magazines and sex manuals which she thought might amuse him. When he found what she had checked now, Dan said, "It's bad Latin, at least."

"But it might be good fun."

"Do you think so?"

"I thought it would be right up your alley."

The red-checked item read: DUO SWINGENDUM. Classics-minded young hetero couple seeks likes for lively Roman feasting. Sincere only. Photo if you have. No joke. P.O. Box 288 AV.

"What do you think it would be like? Seriously, Dan."

"Togas improvised out of bedsheets, crushing grapes in each others' navels, that sort of thing," he said.

"Oh."

And he didn't hear another word about it—although he noticed the ad continued to run for the next two weeks—until Judy broke the news to him.

"Know who the Swinging Duo turn out to be?"

"No—Batman and Robin?"

"No—Herbert and Angela."

"No!" A man about to be considered for his permanent job, Dan thought. Risking it all at this stage of his career.

"Angela said she was so glad *we* answered. She had been meaning to have us for dinner for a long time anyway."

"But you didn't accept."

"Of course, silly."

"Oh." Dan thought of putting his foot down; he thought of Angela Ingiless in her blue-knit with the no-bra, and asked if they were supposed to bring anything and when it was to be.

The excitement of the new experience showed in the Ingilesses' flushed faces and maybe Dan thought, in theirs too. Herbert was wearing a corny laurel wreath around his head and a pink bedsheet. Predictable. Dan complimented Angela on her safety-pinned sari and tinkling gold bangles, and she, leading him through a house decorated in Zebra skins and ebony masks, said she wouldn't be wearing them for long.

"Can we do that without disturbing the neighbors?" Dan asked.

"Oh, yes. See—" They stood at the picture window and looked down on the sunken backyard and the blue, light-flooded pool. The entire area was enclosed by a board fence, perhaps twelve or fifteen feet high. "—Herbert and I were into sunbathing a long time since, so we're perfectly prepared," Angela said sweetly.

At the deep end of the pool a nude concrete lady unendingly spilled her vase into the water. "But let me show you something," Herbert said, and went galloping off to the shed where it seemed the heating unit and valves were housed. Almost as soon as Herbert disappeared into the shed there was a frightening clanking and a roar, and the water stopped trickling from the lady's vase and gushed from between her concrete thighs. Herbert reappeared guffawing and togaless.

In a trice Angela was out of her sari and into the water. Judy followed and Dan shucked off his clothes more slowly, careful to fold his socks inside his shoes for future reference.

"Emperor! Emperor!" Angela called from the shallow end. "How about some vino?"

"I'd say thumbs up to that," Herbert giggled and started plump-ended for the house.

Dan slunk crocodile-like into the pool, caught his unsuspecting wife from behind, and bit her earlobe.

"Me too, me too!" cried Angela, pushing through waist-high water to get to him. Judy didn't seem to mind when he kissed Angela and rubbed up against her.

"This is always such *fun*," Angela said. "I'll go get the deviled *usque* and the feasting can commence. *Usque*, 'eggs,' isn't that right, Danny?"

"Sure," he said, thinking, bad Latin but lovely breasts.

Angela went into the house and dried herself off, put on a bath-robe and joined Herbert at the picture window. He had already poured the wine and turned on the floodlights. Dan and Judy Smythe were embracing at the shallow end, rather forced about it. They seemed aware someone was watching them. The Ingilesses toasted each other in honeyed zinfandel.

"Where's Alexander?"

"I haven't let him out yet."

"Can I do it?"

"Of course, my dear."

Angela had never actually pressed the button herself before. When she did, she could hear a faint buzzing as the electric bolt on the shed sprang open.

Alexander took his time about coming out, probably the flood-lights bothered his great, hungry eyes.

When they saw him, Dan and Judy began at first very softly to call things like, Oh, my good God! and Jesus, dear gentle Jesus! and then louder, Judy, what have you gotten me into! and It's a prank, Dan, a prank! Herbert? Angela? Just stay in the water, Dan, he won't come in the water. They hate water. Oh, sweet Jesus!

Alexander prowled around the pool several times and then sat down to wait for it to finish draining. He shook his long silky mane and lapped at the water expectantly, as though to hurry things along.

"Well," Herbert said, "I wouldn't say thumbs up to them. Very poor show."

Dan and Judy were clutched against each other, sobbing now.

"No," Angela agreed, "thumbs down on them. Phooey on them, I say."

Only once had they seriously considered using the horsemeat they always kept ready. That was with a sweet little couple named Hinton. When the water got down to the Hintons' knees and Alexander crouched, the Hintons got religion all of a sudden and started loudly singing "Onward Christian Soldiers" in unison.

"Very well, Miss Apple—call my broker."

This strong and convincing story concerns one man in a lonely sentinel-ship, and what happens when he is exposed to an enemy hypnotic attack so effective that its illusions push to the edge of reality.

DREAM PATROL

by Charles W. Runyon

Harul stopped whimpering as I strapped him into the padded capsule. For one instant his eyes lost their gaze of terror, his loose lips firmed up. "Marsh, where did I lose it? How do I pick up the thread?"

"They'll tell you back at the base, old buddy. They'll put you back on the track." I swung the lid down over my ex-shipmate. "Be good, old buddy."

I set the clamps and watched the sealant ooze out and harden around the seams. Through the inspection port I saw Harul's eyes roll up under his brows; his mouth opened so wide I could see down the moist pink tunnel of his throat, but his scream was contained within the cylinder. I pressed the button which released a sedative gas into the capsule and watched his face collapse like a punctured basketball. I started the freezing circuit, stepped out of the airlock bubble, and spun the wheel on the hatch.

I pressed my thumb to the EJECT switch, and felt only an anticlimactic tremor as the capsule fired. A spear of light arrowed into the blackness of space, became a pinpoint, then winked out.

I was alone, four hundred million miles from the nearest flesh-and-blood human being, trapped in my own untenable reality. The woman was lounging on a sofa covered with green plush, wearing a loose burgundy gown. Her vivid flesh tones made the duroplast interior of my sentinel-ship seem as gray and abstract as a black- and-white photograph.

She closed her eyes and drew on a long cigarette, expelling a circlet of green smoke from her orange lips. "What now, soldier? Are you going to waste your life in this chunk of metal while the civilians back home take your jobs and your girls?"

I turned my back and dialed my supper, deliberately filling my mind with thoughts of medium-rare steak, mushroom gravy, mashed potatoes and red wine. It was all reconstituted from the same gray gruel in the nutrient tank, but it looked, tasted and smelled like the real thing. At least it did to me. I'd been in the service since I was twelve, and had forgotten the taste of natural food.

She watched over my shoulder as I ladled psuedo-gravy over my psuedo-potatoes. I caught the subtle witch hazel fragrance of her perfume and began telling myself what I'd told Harul when she'd first appeared in our sentinel-ship two weeks before.

"She's not real. She's a projection, a piece of Fen propaganda and nothing more."

I picked up my tray and turned, but she was standing between me and the fold-down table. She wore the uniform of a waitress in the Central Base Officers' Club: short blue skirt and blouse of silvery fabric, with a cleavage plunging down to the rose-ivory cup of her navel. She looked like a girl I'd tried unsuccessfully to date during my last furlough.

I considered walking around her, but my dignity recoiled from the picture of a six-foot-two-inch, twice-decorated space force lieutenant playing step-on-a-crack in the solitude of a sentinel-ship. I drew a deep breath and walked toward her, gazing into her large, gray-green eyes. She seemed to draw herself up into a defiant posture, and I wondered what it would do to my mind if I walked, splat! into those two pneumatic protuberances she wore so tantalizingly high on her chest. My head ached from the strain of subconscious combat. It was my will against . . . what? I didn't know.

When I was two steps away, she began to shimmer. I felt a sense of space being stretched painfully in all directions. Abruptly the whole universe shifted imperceptibly to the left, and the girl disappeared.

As I ate, I reflected that I was playing a dangerous game. If she'd refused to move, I'd have been forced to accept her as an objective reality. Harul had gone over the edge the night I found him caressing his pillow and crooning his wife's name. She'd been killed three years ago in the Fen raid on Solem. His little girl had been captured and put in a Fen fattening compound. Harul might have endured the thought of his child being the main course at a banquet attended by slaty, ten-foot arthropods, but when she climbed on his knee and asked to be trotted . . .

"I couldn't take it either," I said aloud, gazing at a black splash on the far bulkhead where Harul had tried to disperse his torturing visions with a blaster. If he'd taken time to set the weapon for a narrow beam, he'd have holed the ship and killed us both. I'd jettisoned all weapons after that incident. Knives, scissors and all pointed instruments had followed when Harul tried to slash his own throat with a ceremonial dagger. When he tried to hang himself with his own coveralls, I'd resolved never to sleep unless Harul was thoroughly sedated. Last night I'd awakened to find him at the controls, turning the ship toward Zone N. It's a ten-light-year strip of seared planets and empty space which constitutes no man's land, or no Fen's land, depending on which side you're on. All ships entering the zone are given the same treatment a mouse would get if he tried to tiptoe through a room full of hungry cats.

I'd had no alternative then but to send Harul back to base. Now I realized that taking care of him had been the major factor keeping me sane. I gathered up the cups and plates and fed them into the converter, where they'd be broken down into atoms and reconstituted at some future date as plates, food, clothing or anything else my quartermaster unit was programmed to synthesize. I dialed coffee and a cigarette and sat down at the table smoking, gazing with an impacted sourness at the twenty-foot hemisphere which composed my entire habitable universe.

Nothing could have been less stimulating to the human eye. All instruments, bunks, sanitary facilities and communications equipment were folded into the walls and concealed by smooth duroplast paneling. The panels were luminescent, giving the effect of being inside a transparent membrane enveloped by a vast incandescence. As in prison, the light was never off. The view-ports were round inkwells set into membrane, and did nothing to alleviate my growing illusion that I was an unhatched embryo in a gigantic egg.

Suddenly she was sitting across from me, her chin resting on her laced fingers. "Couldn't we have a candle?"

A candle appeared between us, shedding its soft glow on her lovely face. A small button nose made her eyes seem even larger than they actually were. I noticed that her upper front incisors were prominent in an interesting sort of way.

"And music?"

Violins wailed in the background. She rose and swayed, her shining walnut hair moving on her shoulders like a rich, heavy fabric. "Shall we dance?"

I threw my coffee cup into her smiling face. Her configuration winked out like a soap bubble, while the cup continued its arcing trajectory to the far bulkhead and shattered into mealy fragments. As I swept up the mess, I wondered what I'd have done if the cup had bounced off her nose. It was another of those mind-traps I kept setting for myself. It was wiser to take no notice of her.

A minute later she appeared on my bunk, lying on a bright orange bedspread and cuddling a pale mustard pillow. A golden tan covered her nude body and conveyed a hint of pale chocolate to the tips of her breasts.

I turned my back and dialed another cup of coffee, neglecting the preliminary step of first acquiring a cup. The scalding liquid spewed over my thumb and fingers. I did a dancing pirouette, clutching my hand against my stomach. The girl appeared in the control chair wearing a pair of transparent harem pants and a smile of quiet amusement.

"Know something, darling? You'll be sucking your own toes before they get around to sending a replacement."

I framed a supercilious reply to the effect that Egbert Yancy Marsh possessed mental resources beyond her feeble comprehension, then I realized she was probably right. I pulled out the code-sender and punched out an A-7 priority, aware that I was leaving myself open for a reprimand. The only messages which rated A-class priorities were those involving imminent physical death, invasion, or capture of a Fen ship.

The clearance light flashed, and I tapped out the message: *Under intense hypno-attack. Request immediate relief.*

A half-hour passed while I sat staring at the black message-screen. I could hear her moving about the ship, but I refused to look at her. Then the glowing letters danced across the screen: *Contact medical secretariat, subheading psychiatric unit, priority P-2.*

I cursed silently at the priority rating. It meant that I had to use the subspace etheric voice transmitter, which would have been like someone five hundred years ago using Pony Express when he had a telephone on his desk.

I took down the microphone and drew a deep breath. "This is Marsh two-three-five-two-nine-seven, Sentinel. A forty-seven. Attention medical secretariat, subheading psychiatric unit, subject intensified hypnotic warfare."

I paused to catch my breath while the machine hummed, waiting for my next words to activate the tape. As soon as the entire message was recorded, it would be condensed into a shrill blip! and flashed to base. It would be retarded, transcribed on coded tape, monitored and sent to the department concerned. From there it would be carried from one desk to another until it reached someone who couldn't pass it on. The process sometimes took several days.

I cleared my throat. "Okay, whoever you are, you must be an expert on this subject. I had to send my shipmate back, and I need a new one, quick. I'm alone on the edge of Zone N, and there's a girl here who'd like nothing better than to see me run for it." I became aware of her long fingernails tapping the communications console. "She looks like a waitress I met in the officer's club lounge at base. I'm wondering if the Fens haven't found a way of actually projecting images into our ships. If this girl has been captured, that would account for it, and for the fact that my shipmate kept seeing his wife and kid. Her name is . . ."

She leaned down and whispered in my ear. "Rose, darling. Rose Marie, and I love you." She unbuttoned her blouse and slid her hand under the shoulder strap. I closed my eyes.

"Her name is Rose Marie, and she's getting realer by the hour. Give it the emergency treatment. Marsh two-three-five-two-nine-seven, out."

I pressed the SEND button, then went to the monitor screens and checked out each one of my forty traps. Their detectors swept ten million miles in all directions thirty times each second. If they encountered anything, they clamped it in a stasis field and flashed a signal to my ship. Sometimes the Fens jammed the signals, so I had to check the traps visually once a day. I hoped I'd caught a drone bomb, which would mean going out and detonating it personally. A Fen scout would've been even better. I could've spent a full day freezing, tagging and sending it back to base.

Today all traps were empty, fueled, and working perfectly.

I got out the chess board and set up a problem. A delicate white hand slid over my shoulder and moved the white bishop into a position flanking the black knight. It was exactly the move I'd decided on. Well, why not let her—?

I came to my senses and raked all the chessmen onto the floor.

I hooked up a 3-D projector and settled back to watch a pastoral adventure which had been filmed on my home planet, Zporan, before it was concreted over as a staging area for the third invasion fleet. I watched the jewel-like figures cavort inside the box until the heroine was captured by a mava-beast. Peering from the slimy reptilian coils was a familiar face framed in walnut hair. I hit the turn-off switch, dropped a sleep-tab, and stretched out on my bunk.

I dreamed she visited me during my sleep. I awoke with the vague mingling of guilt and secret glee which always follows a night of wild debauchery. A long, walnut-brown hair lay on my pillow. I reached out to touch it and the hair disappeared—but not before my senses registered a distinct impression of solidity.

At breakfast she sat across from me reading the paper while I spooned up my reconstituted oatmeal. I felt guilty for not offering her at least a piece of toast. I tried to build a mental wall against her presence, but she kept rustling the paper.

"It's going to be a long war," she said conversationally. "Imagine me in three thousand other sentinel-ships, not to mention the big attack fleets. Can a man fight when a beautiful woman keeps popping up in front of his gun?"

At that point the S-set buzzed. I leaped for the switch like a drowning man grabbing a rope, then had to stand tugging my earlobe while the tape oozed out of the retarder. I hooked it to the speaker, and a deep, well-modulated voice began speaking with a false camaraderie which puckered my nerves.

"Hi, Marsh, this is Basil Underhof, psych unit. Sorry to report there'll be a delay in getting you a new shipmate. All available men are trying to stem the Sector Q breakthrough. As far as this new hypnotic gimmick is concerned, it heightens your suggestibility to a fantastic degree but projects no actual image. You supply the image yourself. Whatever it says or does represents your own thoughts although there seems to be a strong push toward fantasies of a suicidal nature. Captain Yakov chewed halfway through his right wrist under the impression that his arm was a python trying to strangle him, so consider yourself lucky you drew a girl. I visited her in the club, by the way. She doesn't remember you, but sends regards. All the advice I can offer is to remember that your tour's up in six months, think happy thoughts and examine any unusual event closely. Our research boys are digging into this thing, and I'll let you know what they turn up. Underhof, four-seven-six-nine-two, out."

The tape went flappety-flap and whirred to a stop. The girl leaned against the bulkhead and smiled. "I wonder what Underhof would do if you flew back to base and dropped a bomb on the psych unit?"

My thoughts, I said to myself. Damn right they were my thoughts. I jerked down the microphone and growled, "Listen, Underhof, six months may seem like nothing to a base commando, but six more days with this witch, and I'll bite my own jugular vein in two. I need help and I need it quick. How do I turn her off?"

After I sent the message, I checked out my traps again, hoping I'd snagged at least a meteorite. I'd have had to check it out personally, because you never knew what kind of camouflage the Fens would dream up.

Each of my forty monitors gave me the same black stare.

I decided to start a journal, recalling the happy days of my youth.

It went fine for a couple of hours, then I noticed that she was stand-ing on the ceiling. Both her hair and skirt hung toward her feet in total defiance of the ship's artificial gravity.

"Did you ever stop to consider," she said, "that *you* might be the illusion, and *I* might be real?"

It seemed only fair to consider her side of the question. I pon-dered it for about thirty seconds before I realized it was a shortcut to madness. I swallowed a double sleeping potion and went to bed. She woke me up to ask for a drink of water, and I was standing at the spigot before I realized that I was the one who was thirsty. I drank the water and went back to bed.

The next day she didn't talk at all, and my nerves coiled up like springs. She leered at me when I used the sanitary facilities, pursed her lips in sympathy when I bumped my shin, wrinkled her nose as she read my jottings in the journal.

That night I woke up to find her soft form stretched out beside me. I felt the warmth of her body, and smelled the hot, sugary sweetness of her sweat. I cast back into my dream and remembered making love to her. Desire was still with me, and I told myself the game was up anyway since I could feel and smell her, so why not just finish what I'd started?

With a howl of dismay I leaped out of bed. I spent the next five hours playing solitaire, but I had to quit when she started turning the cards face up. I returned to my old stand-by, the journal, and fell asleep with my head resting on the open pages.

During the next two days she never left the front rank of my consciousness. She developed a technique of ignoring my presence, while manifesting her own in a dozen subtle ways. She must have taken twenty showers. She'd sit before a mirror arranging her hair, combing it out, and then rearranging it in a different style. She'd riffle through the pages of books, reading from back to front. She had a habit of humming tunelessly and tapping her foot at the same time, but to a totally different rhythm.

Finally I found myself sitting in the control chair, thinking how easy it would be to head the ship into the N-Zone and tie down the accelerator button. I heard her calm reasoning voice behind me:

"Maybe it wouldn't be a bad idea. I've heard the Fens are offering amnesty and a planetary section to every trooper who comes across."

That was too much. I turned and hurled a cushion at her. Then I tore off the chair arm and charged her, swinging it over my head. She ran behind a potted palm which had somehow found its way into the spacecraft. I kicked it aside and saw her peering out from behind a hulking brute whom I recognized as my drill sergeant from basic training.

A still voice inside me said, *You've slipped over the edge, Marsh.* Another still voice said, *So what?* I plunged through the drill sergeant and seized her hair, but it turned to smoke and blew away. I saw her outside the spaceport looking in, wagging her fingers in her ears. I hammered on the port until the chair arm came apart, then I fell on the deck and hammered with my fist until my muscles froze into a leaden cramp.

The buzz of the S-set saved my sanity. I jumped up and turned it on.

"Underhof here, Marsh. Sorry I'm late. Took yesterday off to go skiing with your waitress. Well, down to business. Turning her off. Hmmm. Suppose you killed the hypnotic image, that is, acted out the girl's death in a convincing manner? I recall someone trying that. There was some unpleasant side effect, but I can't remember what it was. Of course, you have to accept her existence before you can believe in her death. Then you'd have to keep on believing you've killed her, otherwise she'll show up again. I doubt that it'll work, but it'll give you something to do. Keep your chin up, everybody here at headquarters is pulling hard for you boys in the field. This is Underhof, four-seven-six-nine-two, out."

Could I believe in her? I could, to the limit of my senses. A part of me would continue to doubt her reality, as it was always doubting reality itself, snickering secretly at my strident endeavors to prove my own existence.

That night she visited me in a sheer black nightie. I removed it gently from her warm body, twisted it into a tight spiral, and looped it around her neck. Her eyes bulged and her tongue lolled out. She gasped, "I'm real, please don't—!"

When she was dead I dismembered her with a knife I'd overlooked when I jettisoned all deadly weapons. Her blood ran all over the deck. My shoes made sticky adhesive sounds as I walked around, cutting the parts of her body up into little pieces. Then I cut the little pieces up into littler pieces, stacked the whole bloody mess in the airlock and flushed it into space.

Her remains floated around the ship for two days. Now and then a finger or a kidney would drift past the viewport. When I couldn't bear it any longer, I moved the ship. I thought of the last pathetic words she'd spoken, and I told myself:

"You murdered her, Marsh. She was only trying to keep you company, and you killed her. You're a dirty bastard."

I wished I'd kept a souvenir, a swatch of her dress, a lock of her hair, an eyeball. I was like a bereaved lover, listening for her footsteps, remembering the dimple in her cheek, the way her hips rotated while she brushed her teeth. I couldn't eat, I didn't sleep. I thought of Captain Yakov, and made an effort to gnaw through the artery in my wrist, but my teeth had been weakened by too many years of reconstituted food. I tried hanging from an overhead conduit and dropping on my head. I only bounced in the half-G gravity and got a muscle spasm in my neck which immobilized me for an hour. I discovered how hard it was to damage yourself in a ship padded for sudden course changes. There were no sharp corners or projecting buttons, all was rounded and resilient, even the dial covers were made of transparent plastic which crumbled instead of shattering. I tried getting a fish bone caught in my throat, but the reconstituted nutrient melted to paste.

The surest way of effecting my own demise remained the simplest. I opened the control panel, headed the ship into the lethal midnight of the N-Zone, and held my thumb above the accelerator button.

Ding! A bell announced the arrival of a capsule.

I watched it warm up in the airlock, sparkling with the condensation of space-frost. I waited, then went in. Through the inspection plate I saw the familiar face framed in walnut-brown hair. My mind shattered into a thousand fragments, each one containing its own incoherent thought:

She's real this time. No she isn't, you created her with your mind. *You conceited ass, you really believe you could create a seven-foot cylinder of duroplast crackling with cold and coruscating with brilliance, bearing the official seal of the space force?* Why not? It's no harder than believing, that a waitress from the officers' club lounge would arrive in a freeze-capsule.

I had reached the point of deciding to smash the face-plate and shoot her back into space when the shipping tag caught my eye:

CONTENTS: ONE FROZEN ENLISTED PERSON
Rigomundo, R. M.
124921 Female
Rank: Cpl.
Assignment: Sentinel N-47

I felt a humble gratitude for the benevolent omniscience of the Space Secretariat. If Underhof had been present, I would have kissed him. I pressed the de-freeze button and waited. When the time was up, I lifted her from the capsule and carried her into the ship. I lay her on my bunk and savored the reality of her presence. Her hair had golden highlights I hadn't noticed before.

Her breath quickened as she approached consciousness. To make her comfortable, I removed her white freeze-suit. Beneath it she wore a blue one-piece tunic reaching to midthigh. Her right sleeve held her insignia of rank, and her left carried the sunburst emblem of the Space Secretariat. On her right breast pocket was embroidered: COMPANION.

She opened her eyes and looked at me. "I remember, you always ordered some weird drink."

I grinned. "Gatroxip. It's the native beer of my home planet."

"You asked me to go moonsailing."

"And you quoted the regulation against fraternizing."

"XR–428–22–6389." She smiled and the dimples in her cheeks were deeper than I remembered.

I decided a cup of coffee would ease our relationship. As I opened the food-panel, I said, "I suppose that word on your pocket represents the psych department's answer to the hypno-war."

"Lieutenant, you are looking at a member of the first graduating class of the Galactic Space Force Corps of Companions." She swung her feet to the deck and walked over beside me. "That's my job, by the way." She took the cups from my hand and held them under the spigot. "You use cream or sugar?"

"Neither one." My face broke into another grin as I watched her carry the cups to the table. She was pleasantly shy and self-conscious, not one of those brisk, efficient women who make a man feel like a six-thumbed ape.

She sat down across from me and flicked the hair off her shoulders with the back of her hand. "I'll also need to know such things as how you like your eggs. Shirts with or without starch. There's no hurry. I'll be your companion for the remainder of your tour."

I wanted to jump up and dance, but I kept my voice casual. "Have you noticed we have no facilities for segregation of sexes as provided by regulation XR–428–22–6389?"

At that point I couldn't help breaking into a grin so lascivious that a bright pink flush climbed above the collar of her tunic. She took a folded paper from her pocket and held it out to me, her lips set in a taut line.

"I hope this doesn't spoil your fun."

The document revealed that the commanding general, on behalf of the Fleet Secretary, did ". . . hereby declare that a state of marriage exists between the following personnel, (Cpl) Rose Marie Rigomundo and (Lt) Egbert Marsh, til death do them part, unless otherwise specified. Specifications: None."

I folded the paper. Despite its tone of official fiat, the marriage produced an air of mystery, veiled shadows, and delights yet to be revealed. I saw that she was looking at me with concern.

"It's . . . standard procedure to make it effective only until the end of the tour, but . . . I insisted. I grew up in an old-fashioned family." Her chin jutted. "If you'll turn your back, I'll get ready for bed."

It would have been crude to refuse, since I was assured of a complete revelation, eventually. I turned my face to the black ovoid of the viewport. It was not my plan to see her nude image reflected

there, but I accepted it as a well-deserved fringe benefit of chivalry.
I contemplated her muscular full-calved legs and wondered if they'd
turn flabby during the enforced idleness of ship duty.

"I guess you'll miss your skiing," I said, watching the white veil of
her nightdress drop over her head.

She frowned in my direction. "What makes you think I ski?"

Confused words filled my mouth like dry popcorn. "Why . . .
ah, your legs, I guess."

She gave them a quick over-the-shoulder inspection. "These are
waitress legs. I don't ski."

"But . . . Underhof said he took you skiing!" I turned, hearing
the echo of my voice as though I were alone in the room. I seemed
to be standing on a taut membrane which shimmered and trembled
beneath my feet.

"Underhof?" She frowned. "Who's he?"

"He's . . ." I had to lick my dry lips. "He's in the psych department. You went skiing with him."

She walked over and slid her arms around my neck. "He just said
that to impress you. I never dated those psychs. They're too conceited."

I'd forgotten how soft women are, how perfectly adapted to men.
I pressed my lips to her warm neck and thought of the test I'd per-
formed on the other girl. It was a test I couldn't win. If Rose Marie
failed, she'd be gone. If she passed the test, she'd also be gone, and
in a gory, gruesome manner.

"You . . . you're not a fantasy?" I begged to be convinced.

"Darling, if I were fantasy, would we be standing here discussing
it? Wouldn't we be doing what you want to do?"

It was flawless feminine logic, but I perceived the flaw. The brain
which had created belief in one woman in order to dispose of her,
could create belief in another in order to get her back. And if my
belief required the support of freeze-capsules, uniforms, and official
marriage orders, then those items would be included in my belief.

I began to realize what Underhof meant about unpleasant side
effects. Disbelief in reality was no different than belief in illusion;
my thoughts spun in Hamlet-like circles until, with a shout of frus-

tration, I picked her up and carried her to my bunk, growling like a maddened mava-beast.

Next morning I lay musing on my pillow: "Sometimes you have to lose your mind in order to keep your sanity."

"What does that mean, darling?"

I pressed my nose into the musty veil of her hair. "What are we having for breakfast?"

"Flapjacks, syrup, scrambled eggs, smoked sausage, orange juice and coffee. How does that sound?"

"It sounds . . . exactly like the breakfast I had in mind." I laughed.

And laughed.

And—

Laughed?

"I'm afraid this simulator test indicates Commodore Brent would be a poor choice for the lunar expedition."

Many of Evelyn E. Smith's past contributions to F&SF were notable for a sure-handed light touch, the kind of barbed, but basically "white" humor that seems in short supply these days. We had not heard from Miss Smith in some years, and it was a happy day when we received this hilarious tale of two youngsters in darkest adolescence and their confrontations with the middle-class, the middle-aged and other aliens.

CALLIOPE AND GHERKIN AND THE YANKEE DOODLE THING

by Evelyn E. Smith

Although, unlike the young David Copperfield, I lay no claim to a personal experience of events which took place in a time before I was even conceived of, the happenings which ultimately led to my appearance upon this plane and planet have been recounted to me so often and with such detail by all having any connection with an event not even my mother could describe as blessed that I feel far better qualified to tell it like it was, so to speak, than either the prime participants or their well-meaning, thus doubly-culpable, manipulators. My story—no, not yet my story, the story of those two star-uncrossed nonlovers who sponsored my birth might be given an arbitrary beginning upon the afternoon that Gherkin, having quitted his picket line and concluded his college day, walked into the Bobbery Shop, a preoccupied expression upon his amorphous adolescent countenance. This abstraction went unheeded by Calliope, for she was big with news and anxious to deliver herself; therefore, even though her first question, "Where the hell did you disappear to Friday night?" might appear on the surface to express a kindly concern, it was mere rhetoric; for, as he opened his mouth to tell of the strange and wondrous things that had befallen him upon the Friday night in question, she proceeded to burble of her own insignificant adventurings.

"I got tired waiting around for you to show, so I went up to

Mattie's pad all by myself, and, guess what, we got busted—or almost, anyway! We'd just lit up when the fuzz appeared and hauled us all down to headquarters . . . very non-violently," she added, regretful, for she knew the mere fact of near or even total arrest without dynamic confrontation was insufficient to qualify her as a bona fide activist. "Then they found out the grass they'd collected at Mattie's was nothing but catnip, and it seems there's no law against smoking that *yet*, so they gave us the boot. Without carfare or anything!" She frowned. "But do you think that's what we've been getting high on all along at Mattie's, just plain, old-fashioned *Nepeta Cataria*?"

"Well, cats get high on the stuff," Gherkin said, still very preoccupied, almost intense, if anybody'd had the decency to notice, "so why not people? Speaking of cats—"

"But the prices Mattie was charging! For stuff you could get in the five and dime. And she seemed so humanistic, you know what I mean, I'd never have figured her for a fink. Worst part is now I won't have any place for next Friday; 'tisn't easy to find a nice respectable pothouse these days."

At this point she recognized Gherkin as not merely audience cum wailing wall but as an individual with sufficient self-identity to suffer along with her . . . and serve him right for standing her up! She continued on a note of melancholy glee, "Which means you won't have anywhere for next Friday either, unless you've found yourself another place where I don't happen to be welcome—in which case all you've got to do is say the word. I'm not one to make a scene where I'm not wanted."

"If you'll shut up and give me a chance. . . . I *did* find a new place. That's why I wasn't at Mattie's. I was on a trip." He was smug because this had been the real thing; over the weekend he had found the key that unlocked the universe. "I went up and all the way and it was like—" he paused for the *mot juste* "—it was like wow. And they said I could come again next week and bring a friend so—" His gesture of invitation was almost courtly.

Calliope was impressed, gratified, frightened. "You mean . . . like acid? Golly gee, but that can be dangerous. I mean like I know the establishment is always trying to put down everything really meaningful, but I happen to have it on good authority from a bio major that this bit is straight. The stuff can mess up your chromosomes, you know what I mean, and when you have kids they freak out or something—"

"It wasn't acid! Think I don't know better than that? It was something else, something new to—well—something new. Guaranteed absolutely harmless, the cat said, no undesirable aftereffects, no addiction, no nothing."

How could he be so credulous; how *dared* he be so credulous, and flaunt his overprivileged innocence in her face? "Are you that simple, man? You think they're going to come right out and tell you like each trip you take you blow a little piece of mind en route? Let me tell you that is not the kind of pitch to attract customers. By the way, just how much loot did they stick you for?"

He hesitated, finally admitted, "Not a cent. They said they were doing this as—well—a public service. . . ."

"Oh, boy-ee!" Calliope's face was disgusted, her voice was disgusted, even the way she stabbed her spoon into the glob of pistachio ice-cream was disgusted. "You swallowed that? Nobody's ever told you about the birds and the beastlies? This has all the stink of a commercial operation. Sure, you get it free the first time, very cheap the second, maybe even the third. Then, when you're hooked and on your knees screaming, they start to put on the screws. That's the system, baby."

"But these cats aren't part of the system. They come from outside the system." He stopped, then said, sounding very lame as he got stood up against the communications wall, "They're different."

"You're different. I'm different. But there can't be any more different than that. Black, white, male, female, weren't those differences enough for anyone?"

"What does it matter!" he said impatiently. "They were beautiful; the whole thing was beautiful."

But the thing hadn't begun beautiful. In fact it had begun pretty ugly, and he'd thought, insofar as he was still capable of thinking after it had started, that it was going to be one of those bad trips you hear about but never expect to happen to stable, chemically balanced you. She asked exactly how he had taken the stuff, but he couldn't remember; he just knew he hadn't swallowed or smoked it, nor had he been given an injection. "Maybe it was like some kind of gas. I remember smelling something funny halfway over, but they told me it was fresh air which I didn't recognize because I'd never had a chance to smell any before."

Whatever it was that had been administered to him, it had made him sick, really physically sick, first like just a bad case of seasickness, then worse and worse, radiating from the pit of his stomach all the way out to his extremities until his fingers and his head were all qualmy and quivering; then slowly, inexorably, he'd begun to turn inside out, little by agonizing little. It was like he was standing off somewhere at a distance seeing—no, not exactly seeing, *observing* his own eversion. His guts crawled all over him snakelike and squeezed, tighter and tighter, compressing what was left of him into a small dark ball with the brain huddled inside shrieking with terror until it shrank into nothingness and he blanked into infinity.

When consciousness came back, he found he had been . . . reassembled, not merely in another place but another *where*. "Like another world, kind of."

"You mean like Oz, Never-Never Land, Back of the Looking Glass, that sort of thing?"

He hesitated, finally said, "Yeh," as if that was easier than trying to give it a name himself. He did try to break it down into details; he'd been able to see colors that weren't part of the spectrum he knew . . . heard sounds that were—well—he hadn't the words to describe them but the ugly part was over, finished, dissolved; from then on it was all beauty.

Since he seemed to be going into free fall—the stuff obviously was not without aftereffects no matter what he'd been *told*—she asked who or what had been in this simplistic dream universe along with him, not because she was interested (she'd heard better hallucinations) but because she wanted to bring him back to whatever was currently passing for reality. After a pause, he finally said they were people—"sort of." And, among them one special person. In short, a girl. But—there he went again—different from all the other

girls he had ever known, really different. In the first place, she'd
been green.

"You really are uptight about this color thing, aren't you, baby?
Black and white aren't enough for you the way they are for most
folks; you've got to have green too!"

"Everybody there—everybody who *belonged* there, lived there—
was green," he said, very defensive. "I don't mean their skins were
actually green—"

"Well, that's a relief; we have enough chromatic problems—"

"I mean they had green fur, so I wouldn't know what color their
skins were."

"Your out-of-this-world chick was covered with hair like a gorilla?
A green gorilla? Well, I must say that certainly *is* different!"

Gherkin was annoyed. "She wasn't like a gorilla at all. Her fur was
soft and delicate like fuzz—" Calliope made face and he smiled
grudgingly and amended that to "—like down or velvet."

"I s'pose she had a tail, too."

"Well, sure, that was what made it so beautiful. I mean, you
have no idea how groovy a tail can be when you—" he stopped.

"You mean to say you made out with this green-tailed person?"

He didn't speak, but from the obscenely rhapsodic expression on
his face she could tell he had and that it had been a good scene.
"Hell, Callie," he burst out, "she was only in my mind so what does
it matter? I've had dreams like that before."

But the way he talked, the way he looked, he'd never before,
dreaming or waking, dug anybody like that green chick. Not that
he'd had much experience with the sex-experience; and Calliope,
to her embarrassment, none at all. But, even though virgin by
circumstance, she knew she could be groovier than any green girl,
groovier than any girl in the whole universe as soon as she got clued
in on what it was all about. Sometimes she thought the reason
Gherkin'd never tried for a physical interaction with her was because he was leery of breaking in a beginner, and sometimes she wondered if maybe he had some kind of sexual hang-up (she had theories
on that subject), but most times she felt no matter how lib-
erated and humanistic and with it he was, the skin thing still bugged

him. If so, you could say maybe his hallucination about making it
with a furry green girl meant he was trying to overcome his own
unconscious rejection of her. But that was such a Psychology I way
of looking at things. No, the truth of the matter probably was he
thought of her as a soul brother.

From the way he smiled to himself she could tell that to him the
green girl was more than merely a fantasy projection with whom he
had spent an imaginary weekend. There could be a rational explanation. "Maybe while you were thinking green fluff you were actually
balling one of the chicks who was making the trip along with you."

"That's the funny thing; there wasn't anybody else making the
trip. Nobody I saw, anyway, 'cept the cats who set it up, and I have
an idea they didn't actually participate. More the cold, scientific
type."

She was glad to be given a value-reason for verbalizing her shock.
"But that's wrong. Taking a trip alone—that's sick, downright
perverted. Tripping's got to be a together thing or it's just another
cop-out, you know what I mean. And the greenies, the ones in your
mind, don't count."

As a matter of fact, he told her, after he'd arrived at . . . wherever it was; it'd had a name but he'd lost it somewhere on the way
back . . . he had seen other people around, in the distance, people of his own kind, unfurred, and, yes, yes, yes, black as well as
white. He really hadn't paid much attention. Who would look at human beings with their slick, ugly pink (or brown or black) plastic
skins when there were the softly furred green folk to be looked at,
girls like . . . dammit, he'd lost her name too . . . to be looked
at, loved . . . ? Of course, he snapped before Calliope had a chance,
he knew the human beings didn't count any more than the green
people when it came to the reality thing; they must have been in
the mind too. But it felt like a group experience so it was a good
scene.

No, she told him, it had been bad, no matter how good it looked,
because loneliness was the root of all evil, leading to alienation,
loss of identity, all kinds of hang-ups. The tribal instinct was the only
sound one man had, the only one that might, possibly, pull him

through. He told her to quit lecturing; she sounded like a mother and he already had enough mother.

"I tried to call you over the weekend," Callie said. "There were two concerts and a smash-in in Central Park I thought we might go to together, but nobody answered the phone over at your place."

And what would have happened if somebody other than Gherkin himself had answered, she wondered, never having had occasion to call him at home before, since mostly he had been wherever she was. She had never met his parents, nor had he met hers, because nobody introduced anybody to parents nowadays. You didn't let them in on anything that was real and decent; you kept them in their place while there was still a place for them. You didn't even tell them your real, personal, group-given names. Still, would both of them have conformed so rigorously to the tribal pattern if they and their parents had been other than they were?

Calliope's mother was a schoolteacher; her father worked for the Post Office. Both belonged to all the right causes, her mother being more involved because of her job—a teacher was expected to be militant if she knew what was good for her—but in their hearts neither was what their daughter would have considered truly committed. They had worked too hard to reach middle-class status to give it up lightly at the cry of "Uncle Tom," and, although they were hip enough not to come right out and say so, some of their best friends were white people, with whom they usually felt a little uncomfortable.

Both Mr. and Mrs. Fillmore had been born in Harlem before the press started calling it a "ghetto." "When I was a boy, people used the word *ghetto* to mean a place where Jews lived," Mr. Fillmore used to say, bewildered. "They even talked about a 'Gilded Ghetto' where rich Jews lived. How did it get to mean a black slum all of a sudden?"

"Mark my words, it's all that Sammy Davis, Jr.'s fault," said Mr. Fillmore's old Aunt Ada who, although an emigré from the South of half a century's standing, refused to be reconstructed. "What I say is I ain't got nothin' against Jews, but when you're born with one strike against you, why go out and ask for another?" And when her nephew pointed out that Sammy Davis, Jr. seemed to be doing all right in spite of both handicaps, she said, "Them Yids always look out for their own."

Callie had been born in Harlem, but now she and her parents lived in a towering modern middle-income housing project on the Upper West Side that was integrated, in the sense that any Negro who could afford the exorbitant rents and exacting references was welcome. But the Fillmores were beginning to find it less and less attractive. The walls were so thin you could hear everything that went on in the adjoining apartments, from the Spanish family with their bongos, to the Italians with their screaming quarrels. "And with everybody running water so much of the time," Mrs. Fillmore observed, "you'd think the kids would be cleaner." Another thing that bugged her was that every time she stuck her nose outside the apartment, walked in the hall or rode in the elevator, all the white tenants made a particular point of chatting with her. "When they wouldn't give each other the time of day. Don't they figure we could use some privacy too?"

Gherkin's family had been middle-class for so many generations he wasn't even self-conscious about it any more and, when needled, would say tolerantly, "After all it's the bourgeoisie who have always, wittingly or unwittingly, footed the bills for revolutions." The Rosenblums lived in an East Side cooperative that they'd owned for ages, so it wasn't like one of those very expensive new ones, still. . . . Yet that didn't embarrass him either; the only thing that seemed to bother him was the fact that his father was a dentist. He apparently thought there was something slightly shameful about this noble old profession.

Gherkin's mother didn't have a job. She'd been a model up until before her first child, Gherkin's older sister—now married to a successful L.A. podiatrist—was born, and had never gone back to work, since Dr. Rosenblum disapproved of women's working unless it was for some really important reason, like helping put their husbands through dental school. "Now Roz and I're both grown-up, Mom's active on a lot of committees and things," Gherkin said contemptuously, but Calliope didn't see anything wrong with that—or with a wife's not having to work either.

Gherkin didn't seem to mind that Callie had phoned him at home, but, then, even if he did, he'd be careful not to show it. So, probably would his parents even if they could tell about her from her voice. Liberals were sneaky that way. "I guess Mom and Dad must've been out mooning over that house they're buying in the West Seventies."

"In the West Seventies! How come they're not moving out to Long Island like all the other—uh—prosperous people?"

"They say leaving the city would be copping-out." And he and Callie laughed richly at the idea that parents could ever think *anything* they did could be other than a cop-out.

"Tell me about the house; is it a brownstone and are your folks turning it into apartments or are they going to occupy the whole thing themselves?"

"Who can afford to keep up a private house in New York these days, even on the West Side?" he said, blissfully unconscious of capitalistic overtones. "Also I understand there's a tax advantage if they make it over into two duplexes . . . with a little hole in the basement for some unfortunate troglodytes. They're—" he mimicked what was presumably his mother's voice, since there was no reason to suppose his father squeaked "—looking for a really congenial family to move into the other duplex. Guess they don't care who takes the basement as long as they're—" he met Callie's eye "—quiet."

"How many rooms are there and is there much of a garden and isn't it a pity that'll go with the basement apartment?"

Gherkin said he believed they were planning to run back stairs down from the first floor into the garden so that the basement dwellers should be deprived of all advantages. Aside from that, he didn't know anything about the house; what was more, he didn't care.

"Aren't you even a *little* bit curious?" Calliope was a nest-builder; she would have loved to see the house and discuss renovations and wallpaper patterns and help plan bathrooms. She wished that she had the courage to demand a confrontation with his mother, an introduction, anyway. . . . "How come *you* never answered the phone? Were you out all weekend too?"

"Haven't you listened to anything I've been telling you? I was off in—" he gave a little laugh "—Greenland."

"You mean you were there all weekend, not just Friday night?"

He looked at her puzzled and said he thought he'd made it clear the trip had lasted two days and three nights, the way it actually had been. For some milky reason it bothered her that everything else should have been so distorted and not time. Also, where had his body been all the time his body was out, just lying there where it was—someplace in Long Island, he said—in a stupor? Probably on a cold floor too. If he didn't blow his mind, he'd probably get pneumonia.

When he asked her flat out if she wanted to make the trip with him next weekend, she said no, but only for openers, because she knew in the end she would agree . . . curious to experience what he had experienced, but even more, afraid that if she refused he would take some other girl to share this thing, whatever it was, with him.

Then, after she'd said yes, all right, she'd go, stop rapping at her, he happened to mention real casual in passing, oh, by the way, the cat who headed up the operation had said he shouldn't bring anybody over eighteen. Didn't Gherkin realize what a sinister stipulation that was? Because even nowadays when it was common knowledge that each year after you hit twenty-one you died a little until by the time you reached thirty you weren't you any more, just a duffy (which was mostly what was wrong with the world today; the duffies were running it); still what with the laws being duffy laws, nobody who dealt with anything real made a deliberate effort to attract jailbait and add to his load.

"Sure they're not witches or like that looking for a bee-yo-ti-ful young virgin to sacrifice on the altar of their unspeakable lusts?"

He looked at her, doubtful, she saw, in spite of her quavering laugh, whether a joke was intended, wondering whether in the crannies of her mind she really believed in that kind of thing, dark voodoo traditions handed down from her barbaric forebears and such. It came to her then that maybe what had held him off her all these months was not that she was black (actually a kind of light brown, but to describe or think of oneself as anything but black was a cop-out these days, unless of course you were white) but that she wasn't primitive over and beyond the average sixteen-year-old female norm, thus destroying his entire white racist male preconception of what black girls, even high I.Q. literate types, were like; and she hoped that now it would be brought out into the open, so she could stomp on his ego a little, but he skidded lily-livered over the topic. "No reason to suppose nowadays that just because a girl is under eighteen she's still a virgin. Anyway, they didn't say bring a girl; they said bring a friend, no sex specified. They explained that man's creative powers are . . . uh . . . at their height when you're seventeen or eighteen, then they start declining. I guess maybe they meant the stuff wouldn't work as well in older people, so why waste it? Which makes sense."

Which was one of the things that worried her. So few things made sense nowadays that the rational was almost automatically suspect. Moreover, the vibrations she got from this whole thing were very bad. She tried to pin him down. "Just how did you find out about this pad?" It wasn't a pad, strictly speaking, he said. He'd called a number that appeared in an advertisement he'd read in the *Village Voice*, and she didn't find too much comfort in this, yet not enough on which to base a positive objection, as if, for instance, it had been the *East Village Other*.

"Exactly what did this ad say?"

"Oh, something like 'enterprising young individuals willing to travel who wanted to go on an unusual trip, all expenses paid.' They played it real cool."

"They sure did," she agreed, thinking of ways and means to get out of her promise.

In the days that followed she didn't see too much of Gherkin for, being a scholarship student and timorous about the privileges which she could not bring herself to consider as her just and proper due, she picketed only during study periods, choosing only the most genteel of the demonstrations to which to lend shy support . . . while Gherkin cut classes and accused the police of unnatural Oedipal relationships with the reckless abandon of one whose parents would, if he blew the finals, subsidize another semester; even, supposing the administration got up on its hind legs and dumped him, arrange for his transfer to another, less illiberal institution.

She felt guilty at not being able to commit herself totally to battling at his side in the academic arena; however, this onus at least was lifted from her at midweek when, after several vigorous redefinitions of principle, the campus demonstrations polarized along racial lines, white uptown, blacks down, while her own Ladies' Picket Line and Marching Society (so-called by its detractors) outside the cafeteria dissolved as the question of edible food on campus took on a picayune aspect against the weighty, even if undefined, or perhaps because undefined, issues that spurred the other demonstrators on.

Her heart leaped when a journalism student from the uptown campus brought word that the trouble there had escalated into a really kinetic confrontation between students and police, ending with the corrupt minions of the power structure *wantonly* attacking a group of peaceful, unarmed, soft-spoken youths, beating them with nightsticks, kicking them in their respective groins, and performing other typical acts of police brutality before dragging them into vans and taking them to the station where they were even now being submitted to unspeakable tortures. Although Calliope sincerely hoped Gherkin had not been injured, she would have rejoiced to have him briefly jugged, for, in short, long enough to make it impossible for them to start on their trip that Friday.

However, even allowing for the standard overstatement that was the only meaningful method for oppressed minorities to get their message through the biased barrier of the middle-class mass media, the whole tale proved to have but slight connection with the actual fact, which was that the police had mistakenly thrown the head of the mathematics department out of a window under the impression that he was president of the university. After a good laugh all round, the day's demonstration had broken up in a display of unusual student-police rapport. Gherkin was untrammeled, eager to keep their Friday afternoon tryst; and his eagerness, she knew, was not for her, but for that damned fur girl whom he expected to meet with again in the green pastures of his mind.

"But why do we have to stay the *whole* weekend?" Calliope asked mournfully as they got into the subway.

"I guess that's how long it takes to . . . uh . . . work. Or for us to come out of it." He looked apprehensive. "You did give your folks some kind of cover story, didn't you? I mean, they're not going to send out a search party or anything?"

"What do you think I am, a child? I told them I was staying over at Marjorie's, and, since they don't know Marjorie, they think everything's all sand and sweet potatoes. Only . . . well, I kind of hate to lie to them . . ." her voice getting very small at the end.

He looked stern. "Well, if they're so narrow-minded there's nothing you can do *but* lie to them. Fundamentally they're the ones who are to blame for forcing you into dishonesty. It's a black mark against them, not you."

White mark, pink mark, green mark . . . did he have to say *black*? "What did you tell your folks?" she asked. "Or are they above prying into your private life?"

He made a bubbling noise, a sound of contempt. "If they were they wouldn't be parents. I told them I was spending the weekend with some fellows upstate doing something manly like killing small animals. There wasn't any alternative. Until the family as a concept is either restructured or eliminated entirely, the only way to deal with parents is to lie to them."

But why bother to lie unless to keep from hurting their feelings, because he loved them? In which case was it the hypocrisy or the love that was the hang-up? From his quickness to accuse everyone with whom he differed of maternal incest, Callie had deduced that he had a complex, and she had already indulged in interesting speculations as to the possibility of the green girl's standing for his mother, in which case the fur and tail must have some deep significance which she couldn't quite put her finger on.

"Is green your mother's favorite color?" she asked.

"No," he said, "but it was her maiden name."

There, if that didn't prove something she didn't know what did.

They rode all the way to the end of the line in Queens, where the subway became an elevated, so they had to walk down stairs to leave, which gave her such a shot of the uncannies she felt as if she had already started on the trip; after all, what could be weirder than a subway up in the air! Then there was a bus that humped along for half an hour before disgorging them somewhere that looked like the middle of nowhere. From here, Gherkin said, they would take bicycles.

"*Bicycles!* You're putting me on. In the first place, where on Earth will we get bicycles? In the second—"

"They'll be behind that shed waiting for us." And so they were, two Schwinn Racers, leaning against the wall, very shiny and new looking and not a soul in sight. Must be a very honest neighborhood, she thought resentfully.

She hesitated before committing herself to the machine . . . fearful for her mind, her body, even her suddenly precious virginity. She had never ridden a bicycle before. She had never had any desire to ride a bicycle.

"Lucky you aren't wearing a skirt because they're both boy bicycles."

"You know I practically never wear a skirt."

"Well, what are you waiting for?"

No help for it; she mounted. "You sure you know the way there?" she asked, wobbling down the street more or less alongside him; luckily there was little traffic. "All we need to make it a real boss evening is to get lost out here in the wilderness."

"As a matter of fact, I don't know the way. These are homing bicycles."

"Oh, come off it. Enough's enough, you know what I mean? If you don't want to tell me your little secrets, okay, but don't pick a time when I'm in peril of life and limb to get cutesy." Still, funny thing, although she was pedalling furiously, she didn't seem fully in control. First she ascribed this to unfamiliarity with the machine. Then once, when Gherkin started turning a corner and she, absorbed in her own chatter, kept going in a relatively straight line, it seemed that her bicycle actually turned itself to follow him. But that was just imagination; probably her unconscious had been following Gherkin faithfully all along.

Bicycles and riders stopped in front of a large warehouse, the kind of blatantly nondescript building movie gangsters use as a front, and there was a cat sitting outside watching them, a real, pussy-type cat, a ginger tom, wearing a gold collar studded with green stones. It eyed them, then turned and trotted into the building; Calliope had the weirdest feeling that it had gone ahead to announce them.

By the time they'd propped the bicycles tidily against the brick warehouse wall, a man had come out to lead them in, a lithe, red-haired fellow with a pointed face and green eyes and skin so white it looked as if he had been presoaked in Clorox. He wore something that looked like a cross between a skin diver's gear and an astronaut's outfit in pearly form-fitting vinyl, very mod and probably very expensive. The whole setup inside looked expensive, sterile and functional to the point of ostentation and (Gherkin was right) much more like a laboratory than someone's pad. Too ridiculous for words if they'd fallen into the hands of a cliche, a mad scientist.

Calliope had intended to ask all kinds of questions, but somehow there she was being ushered into something sinisterly like a dentist's chair (a spillover from Gherkin's unconscious?) before she even had a chance to open her mouth. Pretty fast going—except that it didn't seem fast; it seemed more as if time had been slowed down for her while the cat was moving along at normal speed. Just the same you'd think there'd be some kind of formalities, an exchange of false names, something by way of transition if not convention. "But what *is* all this stuff?" she demanded, as the man fussed with dials and levers on a thing that looked like a computer or a giant control board, something terribly technological whatever it was.

"Surely your friend has told you?" He had a slight foreign accent.

"He talked but he didn't say anything really meaningful about the experience. He didn't—"

"I didn't understand it too well myself," Gherkin explained from a nearby . . . cubicle . . . sort of . . . where he was being installed in another dentist-type chair by a black-haired man wearing a black vinyl outfit with white sneakers. He had green eyes too, the same whiter-than-white skin.

"You thought it wisest to let him interpret his own experience," the red-haired one said. "Sound thinking, especially as your communications—"

"I'm not a—hey!" Calliope screamed. "You stop that, do you hear me, man? Nobody said anything 'bout being strapped down. I positively refuse to—"

"Believe me, it's necessary." The man snicked the buckles or whatever the fastenings actually were. "It lessens the initial discomfort of the trip. Otherwise you might be crushed."

"You let me out of here right away or I'll scream the place down—" she began. Then she saw he wasn't there—at least not near her. She could see him in another compartment strapping himself into a chair and so was the other cat, the black one with white paws, and it was funny because not only was the compartment outside her line of sight but the wall between was opaque; and it was then she realized that at some point along the line—she could see now what Gherkin had meant when he said he couldn't explain how the stuff had been administered—she had been started on her way into the trackless wilderness of her own mind. The whole building seemed to shudder; there was a distinct sensation of movement, a funny smell, and a force squashed down on her. The ginger cat hadn't been putting her on about being crushed. "If you just relax," he called over, "you'll find take-off easier. Try to breathe naturally."

But how could you breathe naturally when nothing else was natural, when you were being flattened into a flapjack while at the same time somebody'd started to play some of that awfully modern music which can give you a headache at the best of times, especially when you have to make like you enjoy it, but politeness is not called for at a moment when you are attempting to carry out your threat to scream your head off, knowing at the same time nobody outside is likely to hear you above the banging and screeching and whining, through the walls of time and space and apathy. Besides, those weren't her own screams vibrating in her head; they were Gherkin's. Probably he was turning inside out again and if we ever do get back from this lousy rotten trip she thought as something chopped her into mincemeat with long neat even strokes I'm going to turn him inside out for real.

Finally she whited out, and when she came to, she was in what looked to be that exact same other world Gherkin had been talking

about, and there was a fuzzy green chick staring at her in a mixture
of perplexity and amusement, though how Calliope knew this was
more than she could tell, because the other girl's face was completely
expressionless in human terms, she not being human by a long
shot, though definitely, enviably, mammalian. First Callie thought
this had to be the same green girl as Gherkin's; then she told herself, irritated, it couldn't possibly be. His was in his dream and this
was her dream. But why would she dream about a girl at all, especially a busty green gorilla girl? There she'd been wondering if
Gherkin had problems and look at what she herself dreamed about.

The green girl spoke. "Oh, gosh, golly, gee, somebody has goofed
but good!" Only her lips didn't move; she was talking and her lips
didn't move.

"Telepathy, that's how I come to understand you, isn't it?" Callie
asked alertly.

A girl seemed to smile except she didn't really and said, still
without moving her lips, "That's close enough, or as close as you
can get with your . . ." there was a mind blur that resolved itself
into "limited communication ability . . . point is there was a terrible mistake. Baby, you're not supposed to be making this scene
a-tall."

"Not even equal opportunity dreams these days," Callie muttered.

The green girl's eyes unmistakably widened. "But why should
color, of all the kooky things, hang us up? I admit you folks being all
naked and plucked-looking like that . . ." definite projection of
disgust ". . . is a little hard to take, but I guess you can't help the
way you look."

"Well, I wouldn't be naked if somebody hadn't swiped my
threads," Callie pointed out reasonably.

"They were taken off you in quarantine; you'll get them back at
checkout time. Necessary health precaution. Sorry you have to show
yourself all raw like that but rules are rules." She added musingly,
"Hard to think of an intelligent life form, even a primitive one,
without fur, or, at the very least, feathers, but the . . ." a thought
blur resolved itself into something like "Scouts . . . claim you have

an intellectual potential almost as good as ours. Tell me, was there some kind of disaster on your planet? An epidemic or a fire?"

"Not that I know of. We come like this."

"Of course you normally wear coverings to hide your deficiencies, so you can't be totally insensitive. Matter of fact it's those coverings of yours that started the whole mix-up. The Scouts said the different sexes of your species wore different kinds of threads and males had shorter crest fur. I told everybody the Scouts weren't as smart as they cracked themselves up to be, but everybody said we had to listen to them; they knew everything; they would save us." Her mind went "Tcha!"

"Well, straight types do do the different hair, different threads bit so I guess you could say it operates as a general rule. But it isn't the —what did you call them?—Scouts' fault; you can't expect foreigners to be on top of things when practically everybody over the age of twenty-five doesn't know what it's all about, you know what I mean?"

"We needed young people," the girl said after a moment of blankness. "The Scouts claimed your males are at their breeding best around seventeen or eighteen of your years; after that their fertility starts to decline, and fertility's what we're after."

Enlightenment came to Calliope with the eclat of a comic strip light bulb exploding in a balloon overhead. "Oh, then that's what you wanted studs for. As studs. I'm sorry I turned out to be the wrong sex."

"It certainly wasn't your fault," the girl said with equal politeness. "The Scouts should've been more careful."

"It must be pretty rough on you, feeling the way you do about us to have to—do you do it the same way? But of course you'd have to or the project would never have gotten off the ground in the first place."

"The idea is . . . nauseating. . . ." Only, the concept in her mind was much more so than nauseating; when these green folks tossed their cookies, looked as if they really went for broke. "But if it really is your only chance of keeping the race going, we'll just have to sacrifice ourselves."

This was total commitment, indeed! Callie studied the other girl, wondering whether she would be able to sink herself in the greater good if called upon to couple with an alopecic baboon. "But do you think it'll work out, honey? Even though science isn't my bag, I can see we're pretty drastically different. . . ."

"The Scouts've been dragging around any life forms they could find who were even remotely like us and laying them on our doorstep," the girl said despondently. "None of the likely-looking ones panned out and now they're really scraping barrel-bottom. You see, the trouble is our males seem to have lost their viability. There hasn't been a kid born in—oh. . . ."

The thought seemed to indicate a very long stretch of time, but then they lived a very long stretch of time, much longer than human beings. Still, they weren't anything like immortal and, until the Scouts arrived, all involved with taking up the superior species' burden, it looked as if the race were going to die out. The Scouts, as Callie had already gathered, were the cats who had started her and Gherkin on their trip. They were, the green girl said, a race of do-gooders, roving the galaxies, bringing aid and comfort to the lesser breeds, both within and without the law, and whether they wanted it or not. At first the green folk had been glad to see them, even hopeful, but by now a lot of them, present company included, present company particularly, were beginning to think race extinction might be preferable. "Specially if we did happen to mesh and the offspring turned out to look like—like some of the species they fetched in. Still, they did say our characteristics would be dominant, so it did seem worth a try. Just the same, it's all been so horrible, sometimes I think it's a nightmare; I'll wake up and find it never happened."

"But it is a—" Callie broke off, not wanting to hurt the illusion's feelings. "I know how you must feel," she said.

The girl seemed displeased. "Forgive me, but you couldn't possibly have the least *inkling* of how we feel. Oh, I'm sure you mean well, but you're so alien you wouldn't even begin to understand us, let alone identify. You have such an utterly different life experience."

Some people—some creatures—thought they were so special. But Calliope was not going to bicker with a creation of her own mind.

"Guess I might as well go back home since I don't seem to be playing any meaningful role here."

"'Fraid that's out of the question. Spaceship isn't scheduled to go back until . . . your Sunday night . . . looks as if you're stuck here for the weekend."

Spaceship! Callie thought . . . said . . . "Spaceship?" But this whole happening was only a dream, a hallucination, a trip—and, of course, the spaceship fitted in nicely with that part of it. Golly, I am immature; first a spaceship, next Santa Claus complete with reindeer.

The green one's inward-outward smile was more like a sneer. If she was as smart as she claimed, she'd know she wasn't real. But of course she wouldn't admit it; no one likes to admit he's been made up, especially by someone he despises.

"Long as you are our guest, you might as well see the sights . . ." although the phrase she actually projected was more like "encompass the ambience insofar as your limited faculties allow."

And she led Callie from the indeterminate quasi-subjective place where they had been holding their mental chat to somewhere definitely out-of-doors, only park-like storybook out-of-doors, only maybe that was the way Callie's "limited faculties" perceived it. The air had an odd, tangy quality to it. Maybe that was where Gherkin had got the original idea of fresh air. No, that had been—was—the smell of the drug cutting through the hallucination to remind her once again that it wasn't real . . . that the furred green youth who leaned morosely against a tree and plucked some kind of stringed instrument while he sang a sad song of some unrequited emotion that was definitely not love was also, regrettably, no more than a product of her imagination.

"Here's a little treat for you, meatball," the green girl mocked, her attitude a familiarity devoid of friendliness that to the Earth mind interpreted itself as marriage. "Seems there was a mistake in the shipment and our loss looks to be your gain."

Ignoring his fellow life form, the boy looked at Calliope. He had green fur, a tail, humanoid but quite inhuman features. He was the handsomest creature she had ever seen and for a moment she felt overwhelming shame at her bald state, seeing herself as she must seem to him—napless, naked, primitive, perhaps even bestial. Never before had she abased herself simply to please a male, but, as the tender emotion engulfed her—for the first time, she realized now—she forgot feminism in femininity and tried to look winsome and petlike.

Then the first mind surge reached her from him, longing and lingering, and she knew that he saw her as more than a mascot. The hallucination turned out to be a dream of a dream, as she lost all identity, black, human, female, and merged, submerged in his.

Or, as she told Gherkin later, "We grooved at first sight." He and she were in the subway now, starting to come out of the nebulous state in which their trip had left them, so spaced out they could barely remember either their arrival at the warehouse or their departure therefrom. Half in a dream, they had mounted their bicycles and a quarter in a dream they had got on the bus; now, in the IRT, they were coming back to full consciousness. "I never dug anyone the way I did him." The whole thing had been, as in Gherkin's own apt summation of his previous dream experience, "like wow." She gave a little, self-realizing laugh. "Course I know it was only a hallucination but it was really out of this world, you know what I mean." She snuggled against him, to make her point clearer. He didn't respond. And the old hang-ups that the dream had blotted out came inkling back. "What's bugging you? Afraid somebody'll lynch us for being mix instead of match?"

"Stop projecting your hostilities," he said absently. "What's dragging me is it's funny we should both've made the same vision scene."

"Well, I guess it's like mass hypnosis or the collective unconscious if you can mass or collect with only two. What I mean is you told me so much about your first time that it seemed like real, so I must've just psyched I was in the same place having the same experience . . . and maybe, even while we were hallucinating, we communicated somehow, so our minds crisscrossed and came back with the same scene, you know what I mean?"

"If it was my scene how come they didn't say anything to me about the race dying out and how they needed guys from here to give it a shot in the arm or wherever? They kept it from me, and you know why? They didn't want me to know I was being *used*, like a—a stallion," he finished, finding morbid pleasure in the noble concept of himself as a proud-maned Arabian steed.

She looked at him, incredulous. She grabbed his arm and shook him. "Gherkin, baby, you're falling out of your tree. The whole thing was a hallucination, spelled D-R-E-A-M. Nobody's been keeping anything from you; that was my own variation on your theme. The green people, the green place, they were just in our minds." And when his face stayed shut in resolute, mulish blankness—"Okay, if you insist it's got to make solid down-to-Earth sense, how come you were able to breathe their air, drink their water?"

"You mean you were dopey enough to drink the water without boiling it first? How could you be so careless, even in a dream? I made sure—" He stopped and then, thank God, he broke up and she relaxed thinking it's okay; it's all going to be okay.

"I guess maybe like a few gears did like slip out of place," he admitted as his laughter ebbed, "but they're back in line." He went on ruefully. "Guess I'm a little squeeged because I didn't dream about the same chick this time as I did last. It was another green girl. Looked like the first one and claimed she was the same, but I knew she wasn't. There was no communion; we didn't dig each other at all. Now why would I have dreamed a thing like that?"

She was taken aback, not realizing that he would know the difference right off or that it would have been so big and bad a difference. But what reality could stack up against a dream, she consoled herself. Would the actual Gherkin ever be able to hold a candle to the man of her dream? She tried to visualize green velvet features overflowing and encompassing Gherkin's pasty, pimply pubescent face. Difficult, but given time—especially if Gherkin could be persuaded to grow a beard; the whole concept of hair flowered into new meaning (besides, pubescent *did* mean hairy, didn't it?)— it could become less incongruous. He could, she could, they both could. . . .

She made her voice soft, gentle, croodling. "You thought you dreamed about a different girl because this time there really was a different girl—a real girl, to wit, me, you know what I mean?"

"No, I do not know what you mean!"

She forced herself not to snap back. "Look, I definitely made the sex scene with *somebody*. And who else was there except those cats, which I don't think. . . ."

He had to agree. "No, not the cats. They're . . . like inhuman."

"Definite duffy types."

He suggested feebly, "Maybe you just imagined you—"

"No doubt about that part of it. Believe me, I know. And it was like great." She looked at him fondly. "I'm only sorry I couldn't come up to your first trip."

He swallowed hard, gulping down what reason told him had to be fact, unless he wanted to accept the fact that he had really flipped. "If it did happen it was all balled up so it—my feelings have nothing to do with you personally. I mean, what I felt, what you felt, had nothing to do with objective reality, even if what happened had some basis of realism." He burst out, "But, for Pete's sake, if you're right then who did I make out with the first time? There wasn't any girl there with me."

Why tell him now that the original green girl had likely been a symbolic version of his beautiful ex-model mother? Save it for another, more hostile occasion. So all she said was, tactfully, "She must've been a real illusion; that's probably why she was so out-of-this-world good."

When they got back to their respective abodes that evening, their parents and the TV broadcasts were full of news, distorted as usual through having been filtered through the establishment viewpoint. There had been a really definitive confrontation on campus, with all classes suspended indefinitely pending the release of the dean, whom the Divinity School students were holding hostage until their prayers were answered. "Mind you, Janet," Mrs. Fillmore said, "I don't want you going anywhere near the campus until the police are called off, because you're especially vulnerable. They'll hit you when they'd never dare touch a white girl."

"They hit white girls, too, Mama; I've seen the bruises."

Her mother gave her a tolerant I-know-better-than-you look.

"You're not to join any picket lines, you hear? You're not even to stand around playing a supportive role. Participation in the total school experience is important, but not if it means there's any chance of my little girl getting hurt. You better spend the next few days in the public library doing some constructive studying."

But, once she knew there would be no classes, Calliope had other plans. Her commitments had been re-oriented in a direction more classic than either scholarship or political activism. She had telephoned Marjorie, the graduate student with whom she'd been supposedly spending the weekend to get the lowdown on what had actually happened; however, Marjorie was preoccupied with problems of her own and was taking this Heaven-sent opportunity to go to Puerto Rico for an abortion, as she had found herself in what seemed an especially sorry position for a Home Economics major. Although she'd be glad to have Calliope use her apartment while she was gone—and, indeed, after her return; group activities were not only more humanistic but meant there would always be somebody to remind you to keep from adding to the population problem—she warned her to be particularly careful not to get herself in the same predicament. But that was the one thing in the whole sex-experience of which Calliope had no fear. She had been hopefully taking the pill ever since her fifteenth birthday without having its efficacy tested even once.

She persuaded Gherkin to quit his picket line, and together they repaired to Marjorie's apartment to experience mutually conscious conjugation for the first time. It was, though neither wanted to admit it at first, no good. All the groove, all the wow had been in the drug, the gas, whatever it had been. It was everything; they were nothing . . . or so it seemed then. "No wonder they can afford to give it away free at the beginning," Callie mourned. "It would be awful easy to get strung up on it."

"Yeah," he said, "it sure would."

There was a dread in her—more than in him because, despite his glib prattle of drugs as a necessary part of the total human experience, he'd never had to live with junkies on every street-corner—that she might from now on never be able to re-achieve what in retrospect she recognized must have been that old soap-opera standby . . . ecstasy . . . without chemical assistance. And that was just about the worst scene of all. It meant you were crippled from the start. So, when Gherkin reasumed his academic responsibilities and joined the occupation forces by now in virtual charge of the uptown campus, she called upon Dave Kikipu, leader of the Junior African Militants and, like all the demonstration leaders, a big man on campus—athletes were absolutely nowhere these days—and, both black and white co-eds said, a Master of Sex as well as Science (the latter being the degree toward which he was working; he aimed to be a high-school teacher and help young minds to upshoot).

Since Calliope was a brand he had for some time desired to snatch from the burning—going steady with a white man being a mortal sin these days—he delegated power for an afternoon to a subordinate in order to come to the apartment to wrestle with Calliope's soul and whatever else needed wrestling with. "I'm glad to see you're gaining a sense of black identity and refusing to have anything to do with that racist white bastard," he said—nothing personal against Gherkin, of course, just a matter of princi-ple. After which they got down to the nitty gritty. Dave was older than Gherkin, more experienced than Gherkin, more accomplished than Gherkin would, perhaps, ever be. From him Calliope derived a considerable degree of what might have under different circum-stances been pleasure. But it was still not like wow; it would never, she knew now, be like wow unassisted by the cats, the Scouts, whatever you called those archfiends or demigods who stood between her and Abraham's bosom. "Now you know what Black Power is all about," he said when he left. But it was Green Power she craved.

She didn't care now if she blew her mind all over the Universe and eternally compromised her chromosomes; she had to have more of the stuff. She had trouble, though, persuading Gherkin to go out to the Island with her the next Friday afternoon. Finally he was badgered into admitting that since it was his first ex-perience he wanted to relive, not his second, he felt she would be a hindrance. By dint of coaxing plus whitemail she made him take her there, but, when they got to the end of the bus line and looked behind the shed—no bicycles.

"Maybe somebody else is using them," Gherkin said, and both remembered uneasily that at the end of the previous outing no invitation had been extended for a further trip . . . so far as they could recall. Yet, even if no longer welcome, they had to make one last push for Nirvana, so they rented wheels and for the next few days toured the borough of Queens and the neighboring county of Nassau, even extending their search to the border marches of Suffolk. Long Island is a big place, full of warehouses, but they never found the one they sought. As a last, desperate, almost ritual measure, they called the original telephone number through which Gherkin had made contact, but it was no longer, a recorded voice informed them, a working number. While the *Village Voice* said with hauteur that it couldn't possibly give out information about its paid advertisers.

From here on they lost contact with the rational and would have freaked out completely had they been able to. They tried everything they could get their hands on—pot (the real stuff this time), acid, speed, junk, and something the boys in the chem lab had whipped up during an all-night sit-in that was reported not only to bend minds but tie them in bowknots. Not only did all these potions fail to have the desired effect on them, they failed to have any effect at all. They would have thought they were being screwed again, as viz. the original catnip episode, but their companions—these were the standard guided tours, no more private blast-offs—exhibited all satisfactory signs of going off and away. In fact their own immunity was beginning to cause such comment they had to drop out of the drug scene entirely. "It's like those other trips had like inoculated us against anything else," Gherkin observed.

"Sounds like a great built-in commercial gimmick except where are they now to slice the bread?" She cast her eyes up to the heavens. "Come back, come back wherever you are, baby," she pleaded, "you got customers!"

"Don't be—" Gherkin began, stopped.

"Sacrilegious? Blasphemous? You pays your money and you takes your choice. If there is a choice."

"Don't be silly. I mean, that was what I was going to say: Don't be silly."

After the university library got itself blown up by a person or persons unknown (the students said deliberate police provocation but everyone knew the abolition of books had been a prime plank in several activist platforms), the administration finally terminated the spring term two weeks ahead of schedule. Both Gherkin and Calliope had jobs lined up for the summer; however, a week before Callie was to start in as office aide for one of her mother's causes, she woke up one morning and a little voice told her she was pregnant—and, when she went to the doctor, so she proved to be!

"But I thought girls didn't get pregnant any more these days!" Gherkin cried, when apprised of this development.

Whereupon Callie burst into tears, saying she was sorry, she guessed she was just a square and was going to have a square baby. But definitely a baby. She could show him the doctor's report and everything.

"Didn't you . . . take precautions?" He'd been under the impression women nowadays took them as casually as tranquillizers, and for pretty much the same reason.

"Sure I took pills! It must've been the same deal as the catnip. I got sold ersatz."

"Poor little thing," he said, suddenly very masculine and manly —after all in a month he was going to be eighteen, a responsible adult—"you need someone to take care of you." And, moved by the impulses of his ancient bourgeois heritage, he offered marriage which she, descendant of slaves, accepted immediately. She didn't bother to mention the interim episode, which didn't count, she assured herself, because the thing between Dave and herself had been purely mechanistic, not a real relationship. Besides, no chance at all Dave would marry her—marriage, he always declared, was a device the ruling classes had laid on their oppressed subjects —and right then in her panic all she wanted was a solid establishment-approved alliance.

Although the two were conscious of having violated no mean-ingful moral code, they were not sanguine about what would happen when they told their tradition-oriented parents what was on the agendum—which they did forthwith, as under the System, pregnancy, marriage, all the formalities of a corrupt society cost money and the subsidies might as well start at once. Things turned out worse even than anticipated. A lot of acrimonious rhetoric; then Mrs. Rosenblum got Callie aside and said not that she didn't *welcome* her as a daughter-in-law but didn't she think she was too young to take on the wife-mother role? If she wanted to—er—"prevent" the baby, Mrs. Rosenblum was sure her Uncle Joe—

At which, Callie, more out of fear than moral dismay (Marjorie had smoked out for weeks on grisly accounts of her ordeal) set up such a lamentation that Mrs. Rosenblum said hastily, "I was only suggesting it for your own sake, dear. Naturally Dr. Rosen-blum and I are delighted. . . ." Then she burst into tears herself. A very painful scene.

All this, of course, before the elder Fillmores and Rosenblums had met and, to their offspring's disgust, fallen in love at first sight. Incidentally, Mrs. Rosenblum had been a terrible disappoint-ment to Callie. Instead of a willowy statuesque goddess, she was a small, pert, not-really-pretty creature who dressed like a teenager and almost got away with it. Callie's father wasn't at all disap-pointed, but, then of course, Mr. Fillmore'd had no expectations to stack her up against. "Sure is a good-looking woman, isn't she? And so young to be the mother of grown children."

And Mrs. Fillmore, who had eight years on the sunny side of Mrs. Rosenblum and so could afford tolerance, gave a dreamy smild and murmured, "Doesn't Dr. Rosenblum look just like Paul Newman?"

"Looks more like Sam Levene to me," Mr. Fillmore observed without rancor.

Gherkin reported that the Rosenblums had seemed equally appreciative. "Sidney Poitier was what Mom laid on your father. And Dad asked me man-to-man if it was true black women had more—" he waved his hands "—vibrations than white ones?" He chuckled richly. "He should only know!"

Both sets of parents agreed that although it was a pity the two had to get married at so early an age, kids did marry young these days and it would all work out. So Callie and Gherkin were stuck, but only for the time being. As the era in which they lived was, despite all its drawbacks and hang-ups, still a step from the Victorian, marriage represented a temporary stretch rather than an eternal sentence. At the end of their pearly path of penance there hung the bright beacon of divorce.

Their mothers took hold and organized everything, and it didn't take any super-perception to see how things were trending. Almost inevitable the Rosenblums should feel the Fillmores were the right family for the other duplex, while the little basement apartment would be "just perfect for the kids." The baby could bask in the garden soaking up sunshine and fresh air while Janet did her schoolwork, because, although she would have to take some leave of absence, she must go on to get her degree; even more important these days for a girl to finish college than a boy because of the symbolic values involved. "Talk about the color problem," Mrs. Rosenblum said, "it's *nothing* compared to the sex thing."

And Mrs. Fillmore didn't dare disagree, because it might sound like a betrayal of her female identity. Very hard being a member of two oppressed groups.

While Callie was away at school, Mrs. Rosenblum planned busily, she would look after the baby and her community activities would simply have to be squeezed into odd moments, because she always felt helping the young mind unfold was one of the most important, *rewarding* pursuits in the world. And Mrs. Fillmore, who, after fifteen years in the New York school system, was less starry-eyed about the unfolding young mind, said she would do her part weekdays and evenings so the young couple would be free to pursue their intellectual and social activities unhampered by the ties of premature parenthood.

"But you're going to have to keep away from all those riots and protests, Sanford," Mrs. Rosenblum told her son. "You have a grave responsibility toward your unborn child. It isn't right to have her—or him, I suppose—start life handicapped by a father who's a jailbird."

"I don't think it's right for a father-to-be to have to spend the summer as a counsellor for a bunch of vicious j.d.'s."

"They are not juvenile delinquents, merely disturbed under-privileged inner city boys. And if they do develop antisocial tendencies it will be as the result of intolerant attitudes like yours. No, your father and I don't expect you to go to camp this summer; of course you'll be staying with Janet. Poor little thing, she seems absolutely terrified and of course bearing an interracial child at the age of seventeen is a very difficult thing to have happen to a girl."

"A woman is old enough to be a mother as soon as she reaches the age of puberty," Gherkin declared. "It's the unnatural prolongation of adolescence in this society that's caused so many hang-ups and stuff."

"If you want to quit school and start hustling your own bread, Sanford," Dr. Rosenblum observed, "far be it from me to stop you."

"Shush, Herbert, you know perfectly well these days nobody can get a decent job without having at least a master's, so we owe it to the children to see them both through their doctorates. They must be protected against the future. You never know what might happen—revolution or an atomic war; they should have the best." She also protected them against the present by enrolling them in a Better Parenthood Course, at which Gherkin waxed almost apoplectic. However, Callie accepted the idea of the course with docility. She wanted to be a better parent.

Their intertribal names, inevitably revealed in the course of the family dialogues, caused some surprise. The Rosenblums were primarily amused. "Gherkin's certainly no worse than Sanford," Dr. Rosenblum said, Sanford being a name on Mrs. Rosenblum's side of the family, descended from Samuel, and Dr. Rosenblum had taken exception to it from the start. However, to Mrs. Fillmore, Calliope's sobriquet was a personal insult. "My mother never had the opportunity to get an education. She worked as a domestic and didn't know any better than to name me Lobelia. But you've had every advantage, Janet, including the name of Janet, and I'll thank you to ask your friends—and relations—to call you that." For a while she had strong hostility feelings toward Mrs. Rosenblum for having laughed at the names, but later she forgave her, knowing that she might be able to understand she couldn't possibly identify.

The wedding was scheduled for as soon as possible, before Calliope started showing. "Okay, marriage," Gherkin said, when it finally got through what he was in for. "For the kid's sake, for Call—Janet's sake. But why the whole barbaric ritual of the so-called white wedding? In the first place, according to the ceremony's own symbolism, it would be downright dishonest of her to wear white—"

Here Calliope burst into tears and accused him of wanting her to wear black on black; and Mrs. Fillmore burst into tears and said she was afraid it would never work out—at the heart of every white man, no matter how well-intentioned, there was a racist. Then it was Mrs. Rosenblum's turn to burst into tears, saying Sanford was not a racist, just a rotten kid who'd never brought anything but aggravation to his parents; it ended with their all (except Gherkin) agreeing tearfully that the whole trouble wasn't color, it was man's inhumanity to man (or, specifically, man's inhumanity to woman).

The wedding turned out to be a Social Event, so much so even Callie who had been beginning to look forward to the festivities with some pleasure—she almost *died* when she heard the wedding dress was to cost three hundred dollars wholesale—came round to Gherkin's way of thinking and wanted just a private ceremony. But too late, the invitations were all out. The guest list was pretty impressive—name people from the letterheads of the causes on both sides of the family attended, people who wouldn't have dreamed of coming if the wedding had been either all black or all white. A non-sectarian clergyman made a beautiful speech about the whole thing a step in the direction of universal brotherhood.

"If we're all sistren and brethren," Aunt Ada could be heard bellowing, "how come all the black folks is on one side of whatever you call this place—it sure ain't my idea of a church—and

the white folks on t'other?" Finally she was drowned out by a
soprano singing "Oh Promise Me" or "We Shall Overcome"—
hard to tell over Aunt Ada's counterpoint. Then they all left
the whatever it was to find a JAM picket line outside, led by
Dave Kikipu, very handsome in his dashiki, carrying signs like
"Black Women for Black Men." "A White Wedding Is An Af-
front to Black Manhood," and worse. The wedding party was
driven in Cadillacs and the demonstrators drove themselves in
Chevies and Volkswagens to an elegant catered reception (the
usual non-dairy creamed chicken but with watermelon coupe for
dessert), where Mrs. Rosenblum introduced Callie to all her rela-
tives as "My brilliant daughter-in-law—imagine, not quite seventeen and already a sophomore. A scholarship student too and you
know the University doesn't give out scholarships unless you're
really tops."

"Yes," Callie said, anxious to please, "they don't have a mini-
mum black quota yet; that's one of the things the demonstrations
are about, I think."

An elderly lady with blue hair said, very quick, Sanford was
lucky to have such a beautiful bride and didn't Janet look like
a young Lena Horne?

"How come Lena Horne ain't here?" Aunt Ada demanded.
"Looks like everybody else is. How come they done left her out?
And where's Sammy Davis, Jr.? Where's George Wallace?"

To which Gherkin's great-uncle Milton, a skeleton on the groom's
side, over eighty with dyed hair and still fancying himself a blade,
retorted, "Look, I don't like the idea of my nephew marrying a
schiksa any more than you like the idea of her tying the knot
with a honky, but that's the way the world is blowing; you gotta
swing with the times, baby." Then he and Aunt Ada went off
and killed a magnum of champagne together—"Now this is what
I call real soul food!" she approved—and subsequently were discovered by Mrs. Rosenblum in a pantry, behaving in what she
would only describe as "a very disgusting way." Everybody else
was more admiring than shocked at this triumph of sexuality over
senility and would have liked to press for details.

Later when Aunt Ada had passed out, Great-Uncle Milton told

Gherkin, "I don't care what color the kid turns out—if it's a boy and I kick the bucket before it's born, you name it after me." Gherkin explained to Callie that according to Jewish belief you didn't name a baby after anybody living because it meant one or the other would die.

"But that's a primitive superstition!" she cried.

"Well, there's nobody living I'd want to name the kid after, anyhow."

The rice that was thrown after them when they left was colored; nothing personal, Gherkin assured his bristling bride, pastel-tinted rice was just an in frill these days, like the little pieces of celery in the celery tonic. Among the rice-throwers were the JAM pickets, zestfully entering into the spirit of the occasion. They had been itching to throw something, but rocks and bottles hadn't seemed nice at a wedding. Still, Gherkin was glad when the limousine got out of range. Their families had laid three weeks at a resort in the Catskills on them and no way of getting out of it because the apartment still wasn't ready. Callie fell off a horse and Gherkin nearly drowned in the lake. At that they seemed to be having as good a time as anybody else.

When they got back, the apartment was more or less finished, but Callie didn't have a chance to pick her wallpaper; her mother and mother-in-law had already decided paint would be more practical. As for furniture, the Rosenblums were getting all new antiques, so they bestowed as many of their old but still good pieces as could be crammed into the tiny basement upon the young people. "You should be grateful," Mrs. Fillmore said sternly. "They have some very nice things."

"Why don't you take some of them, Mama?"

"Edythe would think you didn't appreciate all she's doing for you if you gave away her beautiful things. Besides, she's got a cousin in furniture who can give us a very good buy in distressed Spanish."

Both Callie and Gherkin graduated from the Better Parenthood class with honors and learned much, including the fact that there was another side to Dr. Spock. People started giving them so many things for the baby they had to be stowed in one of the empty rooms upstairs—which was still being nerve-wrackingly renovated. "Be sure to keep the door locked." Mrs. Rosenblum advised, "you know what these workmen are like."

"Yeh," Gherkin agreed, "when they see a pile of baby bootees and hand-knitted sweaters, like something inside snaps and they *steal!*" In spite of the lock, two sacques and a receiving blanket printed with a gay Donald Duck motif disappeared.

When classes started in the fall, after violent clashes among student, faculty, police, and a number of people whose identity was never made clear, Gherkin resumed his studies while Callie spent a wretched, boring season, growing bigger and bigger and feeling more and more uncomfortable, without really getting sick enough for constant fussing. Both her mother and mother-in-law looked after her physical well-being and all that. They made her chicken soup and accompanied her to the doctor's office and told her to think uplifting thoughts, but what they were mostly interested in was the house. The Rosenblums' duplex became habitable first and they insisted the Fillmores move in with them until alterations on the top floors were complete. As for the staircase leading up from the garden, this seemed unnecessary now that they were all "one big happy family" (the phrase made Gherkin grit his teeth, at which his father told him to watch out, he was spoiling his bite; but he couldn't help it—they were taking the noble concept of the group, the tribe, and turning it into something sordid). Besides, Mrs. Rosenblum now said, the garden really should go with the basement apartment. "But you won't mind if we old folks use it once in a while?" she asked, all rougish.

Gherkin grimaced but Callie eagerly hoped they would use it often. She wanted everybody she could get to surround her. She would even have liked Aunt Ada to be on hand but that indefatigable octogenarian had run off to Florida and points south with Great-Uncle Milton. At intervals impudent postcards arrived.

The first year nobody used the garden, or as it was more accurately described by the Fillmores, the "backyard." It really was an eyesore—just weeds and a dead ailanthus tree. "And it takes a lot to kill one of those," Callie said. "I wonder if this really is a healthy situation."

Gherkin shrugged. "This is an unhealthy society." By this time they were already both very deep into malaise. It had dawned on them that when the baby was born they were going to be parents.

Mrs. Rosenblum was afraid people looking at the garden out of the back windows of the houses behind might get the wrong idea about their status, think they were on welfare or something. "I'd nag Sanford into doing some work on it, except he's so busy with his schoolwork . . . and Janet says she isn't feeling up to it, although Uncle Joe says she could use some exercise." This was Uncle Joe the obstetrician, as distinguished from Uncle Joe the analyst. He was one of the fanciest obstetricians in town and he was giving Callie a very special rate. "You ought to be grateful," Mrs. Fillmore said again.

All six of them ate dinner together every night upstairs when the elders didn't go out, but afterward Gherkin and Calliope would become uncomfortably aware that six was a crowd and, though politely beseeched to stay, go back down. Sitting there in their low-ceilinged, mouldy-smelling quarters, they would listen to the stamps and squeals of their parents frolicking overhead and feel the generation gap. Alcohol didn't have any effect on them any more than drugs, and they were intolerant of those on whom it did. Such a squalid way of freaking out, with no transcendental hook-ups to make it an enriching experience. "Do you suppose they have communal orgies or just swap?" Gherkin asked.

"Now, Sanford, don't be nasty." And Callie refused to believe it when he told her about the night he'd gone upstairs to borrow some Sucaryl and seen Dr. Rosenblum chasing Mrs. Fillmore through the hall, both stark naked and somewhat overweight, while from the next landing out of sight came giggles and gasps from their lither spouses. It wasn't, he supposed, the kind of thing a girl, no matter how liberally-oriented, wanted to know about her parents.

The only thing from which Calliope and Gherkin could get any kind of pleasure, morbid, of course, was reliving what they still thought had been their drug experience. And the more they interchanged ideas the more similar those ideas became until it seemed almost as if they really had visited another space, another dimension, another world. They kept saying "Do you remember . . . ?" Like old people reliving a past instead of young people whose future had hardly started. That was why they hadn't felt like doing anything about the garden. Even if you took away the weeds and planted all the shrubs dictated by the *Times'* knowledgeable garden editor, the greens, the colors, would be all wrong.

The baby was supposed to be a Christmas baby, but Christmas and New Year's and then Epiphany came and went without his putting in an appearance . . . to everyone's relief because it would have been symbolic to the point of vulgarity to have him arrive just then. "Nothing to worry about," Uncle Joe said, "sometimes the first pregnancy is delayed a little. Very often the young couple are too—uh—preoccupied to keep an accurate record of when—uh—the happy moment actually occurred. Let me see, exactly when did you two kids get spliced?"

"You know it happened before we were married," Callie said bluntly.

His beam remained fixed. "Either you were mistaken or you had a miscarriage so early in the pregnancy you didn't even know it happened; then you conceived again. There was an episode with a horse, as I remember?"

How could she tell him it couldn't have happened like that because she and Gherkin hadn't had any sex together at all after they were married? Even if Uncle Joe hadn't been an in-law it made the whole thing seem so sleazy. So she kept quiet, let the horse take the blame.

Valentine's Day passed, likewise Washington's Birthday, St. Patrick's Day, and Easter. Around Mother's Day Uncle Joe finally did admit he was worried. "It's somewhat incredible," he told the family, whom he'd called in for a caucus. "I've never heard of such a prolonged pregnancy in my life. And yet the mother appears to be in excellent health." Already Calliope had become "the mother," the name under which she was to figure in all the medical journals; futile device because afterward the muck-raking press vultures splashed her real name all over the papers; some with pictures.

And the baby, the anxious grandparents-to-be asked. Was it, too, in excellent health?"

After a pause, Uncle Joe said it was. But that was as far as he would commit himself. He had already heard eerie things in his stethoscope, and finally, even though it was currently unfashionable to expose expectant mothers to radiation, he'd X-rayed her. He took one look at the plates and called Uncle Joe the analyst for an immediate appointment. Uncle Joe the analyst did his thing but the only solace the obfuscated obstetrician derived was from the schnapps that was served afterward (not to all patients, just connections).

No, Uncle Joe the obstetrician told the family, he didn't think a Caesarean was advisable. The baby appeared to be—he shuddered —developing normally. In its own way. It's my opinion he'd seen —sensed—enough not to be anxious to meet the little bundle from heaven any sooner than he had to; and although I—you must have guessed by now that I was that aforementioned bundle— by no means had achieved cognition in even the crude terrestrial sense, still my survival instincts must have already been functioning, for a Caesarian at that time would either have killed me entirely or made me so defective I might as well have been human.

On the Fourth of July, almost fifteen months after her impregnation, Calliope was delivered of a bouncing baby thing . . . later to be called by the newspapers "The Yankee Doodle Monster." Male, yes, emphatically, but a boy only if you conceded that a boy could be covered with green down and have a tail and fangs (baby teeth which would drop out later). Anyone above the level of a primitive would have seen I was as cute as a cometoid; however, you couldn't expect my charm to get through to those clods.

The Rosenblums and the Fillmores gathered outside Calliope's hospital room (private, thank God, even if He had let them down in all else) and wept, while inside Calliope and Gherkin gazed at each other with wonder and gladness. "Golly gee, it was real," she whispered. "All of it was real. He was real."

"She was real," Gherkin murmured.

"Both shes were real," Calliope said unkindly before they freaked out on the operetta bit. Then she added (why shouldn't he be happy, too?), "I'll bet that first chick wanted to be with you on the second round, but it was against the rules. Because all the chicks had to have a chance. Which is only fair, really." She smiled down at the baby, whom she was allowed, *required* to keep with her all the time because none of the nurses would touch him and, seeing his father's face, murmured, "I think he's beautiful."

And Gherkin, looking down and seeing the likeness of the girl whom he loved and who might even now somewhere, some place be bearing his child (and conveniently forgetting the equal similarity to the girl whom he had not loved but who might also be spawning) vowed, "He's the grooviest kid ever, and I'm proud to be his foster father." He and Callie looked at each other with a love whose origin was not in sex but in the sharing of a truly mind-expanding experience that linked them together more meaningfully than any physical interaction . . . thrust them up the evolutionary scale, in awareness at least, centuries before a time that might never come to pass for their self-destructive race. It was thus that I made my entrance into that world, although, since I did not spring into being with fully developed mental faculties (though aeons beyond a comparable smelly Earth infant), the rest of this tale will continue to be based on hearsay.

Calliope and Gherkin tried to tell the truth about the way it all had been, knowing it wouldn't be believed but feeling it should be put on record. Their parents were simply uncomprehending, but Uncle Joe the obstetrician was furious, yet also relieved because this was something he understood. Or thought he did. "We've warned our young people over and over again of the dangers of LSD and its ilk but they wouldn't believe us. They laughed at us when we told them of the harm these hallucinogenic horrors could wreak. Older people with their stultified brains didn't know anything, they said. Well, now that the full horror has been exposed, they'll know better, but why—" his voice broke into a wail—"why did that horror have to be born into *my* family?"

When the Rosenblums and the Fillmores got over their initial grief, shock, consternation, and everything else you might expect, they were simply livid. "If you didn't think of us at least you should have had more consideration for Bill and Lobelia. They've had to live with the color problem all their lives and now—a hairy green grandchild . . . !" Mrs. Rosenblum choked with wrath and self pity. Because not only had the newspapers made much of "Black+White=Green," but some militant segrationists of both persuasions were trying to make out that this was what often happened as the result of interracial breeding.

"I just plain don't know how we're going to live down the disgrace," Mrs. Fillmore said. "What's the point of our giving you a college education if you're only going to use it to take drugs and give birth to monsters?"

"Exactly how I feel!" Mrs. Rosenblum wailed. "How could you have done such a thing to us? And, to top it all, talking to the media!"

"But we didn't," Gherkin insisted. "Take drugs, I mean, at least not until later. This happened on a *real* trip. We went to another . . . planet, I guess. I mean, they know now there are other worlds; scientists keep getting signals, pulsars and stuff. . . ."

"The *National Inquirer* may believe a story like that," Mrs. Rosenblum said coldly, "or pretend to because it makes good copy—I don't for a moment think they swallow it in their hearts —but you can't expect *us* to accept these mad little psychedelic fairy tales of yours. No, might as well face up to the truth and since you seem so anxious for publicity at least seek it with some idealistic purpose, like warning other young people not to follow your tragic example."

"We could form an association," Mrs. Fillmore suggested, "with seals and all. Nobody else has the Fourth of July. We'd have a clear field."

Mrs. Rosenblum hesitated, tempted, then shook her head. "It just doesn't seem right. For one thing, what would you call it?"

"The Teratology Foundation," Gherkin proposed. "Incorporated."

His mother stared right through him. "As for your offspring, whatever you plan to call him—"

"Call him Ishmael," Dr. Rosenblum suggested, was also ignored.

"We will provide for his support until Sanford has his B.A. and can assume his responsibilities as a husband and father, but—" her voice rose "—I beg of you to keep it out of my way. I refuse to consider it as any grandson of mine." With good reason, Callie thought, a little remorsefully. And she and Gherkin named the baby Milton after Gherkin's late Great-Uncle, who had expired in Acapulco in Aunt Ada's arms, because it seemed as good a name as any. Besides, they thought Uncle Milton would have dug the kid.

It was more shocking than surprising when it oozed out that both Mrs. Rosenblum and Mrs. Fillmore by a coincidence, not very strange, were also pregnant, although this was being kept very quiet because it would be embarrassing under any circumstances. "Thanks to you, Uncle Joe refuses to have anything to do with me," Mrs. Rosenblum said bitterly. "I'll have to go to someone outside the family." She blushed. Although she had frequently been unfaithful to Dr. Rosenblum (dentists keep long hours), she had never used a strange obstetrician. It seemed indecent.

"Guess what, Milton, honey," Calliope said to me as I lay in my crib, still stunned by the shock of having been born into this world, "you're going to have two uncles or aunts even younger than you are!" She tickled my feet. "Listen to the precious gurgle," she said as I uttered incoherent sounds of protest. "How could anyone not see how utterly adorable he is?"

How indeed! But Gherkin eyed me uneasily. Already he and I had developed areas of strong non-rapport.

"The new babies'll take their minds off us when we go," she went on. "Not that I think they'll miss us too much, probably be glad to get rid of us, especially Milton, know what I mean?"

"We never really were a part of this lousy world," Gherkin agreed. "Alienated from the start." Alienation! They didn't begin to understand the meaning of the word. "Only," he added hesitatingly, "are you sure they—the Scouts—will come back for us?"

"They'll come back for Milton because they couldn't have carried too many of us up there on fertility field trips; what's more, chances are it wouldn't take every time. So this baby's got to be important to them."

If she had realized just how important, there would have been more confidence in her voice, more apprehension in her heart.

"But how will they know he exists?"

"By reading the papers. That's why I talked you into letting me give all those interviews. Those Scouts stay on top of things. Sooner or later they're bound to get the word." Besides, she didn't tell him, she prayed every night for them to come back, so she was advertising in two different media. Surely the power of public relations couldn't be limited to one measly planet.

"But they seemed—the second girl anyway—such mandarin types. Maybe they won't want us. Maybe they'll just want the baby."

"They can't take the baby without taking me," she said, confident that her own simplistic view of the Universe obtained universally. "I'm his mother. And you're my husband. I'll *insist* they take you."

And, she thought, we can get divorced up there and marry the green people and live happily ever after because, in spite of everything, in her heart she believed in the good old American dream. "Everything's going to be groovy," she told him.

Here is a stunning story that begins with a painful dialogue between a horseplayer and a tout during the second race at Aqueduct, a track in southern Queens, New York. That is where it begins; you may need a few moments of reflection to decide where it ends.

NOTES JUST PRIOR TO THE FALL

by Barry N. Malzberg

Simmons. Simmons the horseplayer. That horseplayer, Simmons. Let us consider him for the moment if we might: he is leaning against the rail at Aqueduct surrounded (he feels) by wheeling birds and doom, clutching a handful of losing pari-mutuel tickets in his left hand. His right hand is occupied with his hair; he is trying ceaselessly to comb it into place, a nervous gesture which caused one of his drinking companions (he has no friends) to call him years ago "Simmons the Dresser," a nickname which, unfortunately, never stuck since his other drinking companions knew his habits too well. It is 1:43 now, some twelve minutes before scheduled post-time for the second race, and Simmons is desperately seeking information from the tote board. He has already lost the first race. The results posted indicate that the horse on which he bet finished third. Simmons did not have the horse to show or across the board. He is a win bettor only, some years ago having read in a handicapping book that only the win bettor has a chance to retain an edge and that place and show were for amateurs and old ladies. He does not know who wrote this book or where it is today, but ever since he read this information he has never bet other than to win. He is not sure whether or not this has made much difference but intends to draw up some statistics, sooner or later. He keeps a careful record of his struggles; the fact is that he never totals. (For those who are interested I say that Simmons has lost slightly less than he might have otherwise lost had he bet place and show, but the difference in percentage terms is infinitesimal and the psychological benefits of having more tickets to cash would have well outweighed the minor additional losses.)

Simmons has, then, blown the first race. He has, for that matter, lost seven races in a row, going back to his score on the second race yesterday, a dash for two-year-maiden fillies that produced a seven-length victory for an odds-on favorite. Simmons collected $7.50 for his $5.00 ticket on that one; before then there is also a succession of losing races, although here, perhaps, Simmons loses his sense of precision. He is not exactly sure how many races he has lost recently or how long the losing streak has gone on. All that he can suggest at this moment is that he is deeply into what he has popularly termed a Blue Period and that his situation will have to markedly change for the better shortly or he will be forced to the most serious and investigatory questions about his life and career. Such as, what is he doing here? And what did he hope to gain? And why did he make the famous decision some months ago to have it over and done with the horses once and for all and to make them pay for his psychological investments? And so on. Simmons will phrase these questions to himself in a low, frenetic mumble, somewhere midway between sotto voce and a sustained shriek, and those people in his presence at the time the inquiries begin will look at him peculiarly or not at all, depending upon custom or interest. If he chooses to ask them of himself at the track, he will incite no response at all. There are, after all, so many questioners at the track. The churches—and I know a little bit about this subject—have nothing to compare with the track in the metaphysical area.

"Sons of bitches," Simmons says, but he says this without conviction or hope; it is merely a transitional statement, in the category of throat-clearing or manipulation of the genitals, and means, hence, absolutely nothing. The fact is that Simmons is not clear as to the identity of the sons of bitches, and if he were confronted by them incontrovertibly now or several races in the future, he would not quite know what to say. Manners would overcome reason. "You could have helped me a little with that four horse in the first," he would probably point out mildly, or, "Gee, I wish that the kid on my eight horse in yesterday's starter-handicap had tried to stay out of the switches." Overall, an apologetic tone would certainly extrude. The fact is—and it is important that we understand our focus at the outset—that Simmons is both mild and polite, also that he expects little beyond what he has already received and that when he is talking about the sons of bitches . . . well, it would be naive and simplistic to say that he refers mainly to himself; but as one who is extremely close to the situation, I can suggest that part of this is valid. (Part of it is not. Everything is irretrievably complex. This must be kept carefully in mind. The distance between a winning and tail-end horse in a field, any kind of field, is at the most ten seconds. Ten seconds upon which rests the ascription of all hope and, in certain cases, human lives. One must be respectful of any institution which can so carefully narrow the gap between intimation and disaster.)

"Sons of bitches," Simmons says again and opens the copy of the *Morning Telegraph* which he is holding to full arm's length and begins to look, with neither anticipation nor intensity, at the experts' selections for the second race. Because this is both a Tuesday and cloudy, Simmons is able to perform this gesture, articulate his feelings in isolation and quiet. There is no one within several yards of him in any direction, and Simmons', in addition, having long staked out exactly this spot at the upper stretch, feels that he can conduct himself here exactly as he would in his own home. The fact is, although he would find it painful to admit this, that Simmons despises company for private reasons and is able to find his fullest sense of identity at the racetrack precisely because it both heightens and renders somehow sinister his sense of isolation. He knows that he would never be able to get away with his rhetoric in a social or subway situation, and he would not dare to do it at home because he has long been conditioned to the belief —alas—that any man who talks sprightly to himself in his own quarters is probably insane.

"Ah, God, there's no percentage," Simmons now mutters, a favorite expression, as he looks at the selection pages of the *Telegraph*. As always, this ominous newspaper renders him little comfort, since its selectors, like all selectors everywhere, are oriented toward favorites or logical choices and tell him only what a sane, conservative advisor (Simmons envisions him as a portly, rather puffy man who inhabits the clubhouse, has a mild cardiac condition, and calls all trainers "Willie") would offer if this advisor were, for some reason, to take an interest in Simmons and his plight and attempt to turn the situation around. Simmons, who once wanted exactly such a friend, now hates the specter of the Advisor, feels that the Advisor—like Clocker Lawton, Clocker Rowe and Clocker Powell—simultaneously embodies and parodies everything about successful followers of racing that he has come to hate and feels that he might as well kill him on sight. He has, therefore, transferred his revulsion to the selector pages, which he now turns away from with a moan. He goes instead to the past performances which he regards with a glazed and horrified expression as he comes slowly to realize that he has seen them all before, most of the night in fact, and that he knows less about differentiating the horses than he did at the beginning.

For the first time this afternoon, it occurs to Simmons that he might be losing his mind. Meanwhile, the bugler walks to the front of the paddock a hundred yards down the track and blows that call to indicate that the jockeys are to mount their horses. It is almost time for the field in the second race to come out.

Simmons has lost twenty dollars on the first race. He has lost two hundred and sixty dollars during his most recent losing streak. He has lost fifteen hundred and eighty dollars and forty cents (plus expenses) since he made his Career Decision some three months and sixteen days ago. I offer these statistics without prejudice, and only because, unlike Simmons, I am in a position to amass them, reconcile them with a larger scheme of possibilities, and see them in what might be tastefully called a metaphysical perspective. They cause me neither pain nor pleasure to recite: fifteen hundred, eighty dollars and forty cents is, after all, less than the total war budget for some sixtieths of a second, and can be considered in a relativistic sense (by which I do not strictly abide) to be an insubstantial amount. Simmons, on the other hand, confronted by these figures, would be unable to speak them distinctly. It all depends, as you see, although I am not saying that my position is necessarily superior to that of Simmons. Unlike him, I take no emotions from event, this being, I am led to understand by the philosophy I have studied, a serious defect. I hold my own judgment in abeyance; certainly, over the past few months, Simmons has taught me a great deal.

Now he sighs, mutters, stretches, curses. He wishes, of course, to make a bet on the second race (he always bets on every race, being unable to cope with the fear that he would otherwise know of missing out on the Ultimate Coup) but has no firm choice, cannot, pity him, arrive at that careful, judicious balance of speed, windage, condition, manipulation, desire, weight, and intrinsic class which is the key to approaching the variables of even the cheapest claiming sprint. Or, as he would put it, he cannot seem to find an angle. It is at this moment, therefore, that I decide to make my entrance, seeing little enough profit in delay and realizing that the Simmons who needs my help at 1:46 may have a definite superiority over the Simmons who could reject it at 3:10. For the fact is that I see already the pattern of the afternoon, and it is not pleasant. (Which is not to say that it is unmanageable. Only Simmons would think that the unpleasant is necessarily disastrous.)

"Look," I say without introduction. "Do you want a play in this race? Because I think I can give you something interesting."

"Oh, boy," Simmons says, looking up and then rapidly down toward his newspaper. (I should point out that this is not the first time I have approached him so abruptly.) "Oh, God, it isn't you again, is it?" Simmons's initial resistance toward my appearance has been somewhat blunted, but the fact remains that he finds me almost unacceptable. While his hold on sanity (I can attest) has never been in the least precarious, Simmons thinks that it is and that I am a manifestation of his breakdown. I have made progress in this area but not quite enough, and now, of course, there is not enough time. "I just don't want to listen," he says and covers his ears. Perhaps he is thinking of blinkers. "I don't want to hear any more of it. Losing is one thing, but this is another."

"Nonsense," I say and then address him with enormous tact and personal force. The covering of the ears means nothing. "We don't

have time for overlong discussions and besides that I must warn
you that unless you take some good advice quickly you will be
verging on a truly massive disaster, one with overtones of violence
and a sense of intrinsic loss more acute than any you have ever
known. I am afraid that I must get to the simple gist of this.
Bet the seven horse, win and place."

"Oh, God," Simmons says again, but obediently—there is an
enormous and satisfying submission to all horseplayers because the
fact is that they need to be told exactly what to do—he opens
the newspaper to the past performances and looks at the horse in
question. "Salem? The number seven horse, Salem?"

"That's the one," I say and let my finger join his against the
newsprint. The faint impression of the type slides against skin with
an almost erotic smoothness. I can understand what is erroneously
called the power of the printed word. "Win and place. Place and
win." I try to speak distinctly. My time, after all, is not unlimited.

"But that's ridiculous," Simmons says. "This horse is already
thirty-five to one on the board. He's the only maiden in the race,
he hasn't shown anything since February at Tropical, and that
was in a claimer two thousand dollars cheaper than this one. The
jockey is a bad apprentice, the trainer is a known stiff, and the
weight is the heaviest in the race. I don't see it. I just don't see
it." It is well known that with such rationalizations about his
marriage, Simmons walked out of his home four years ago and
never returned. For this reason and others, I do not take his
rationalizations seriously.

"Reason enough," I say. "He doesn't figure. That's the point I
am trying to develop. It wouldn't be a good tip if it were logical,
would it?"

At this moment, the bugler blows the second call and our conversation is halted. We stand in almost companionable quiet then
while the announcement is made (I have always been suspicious
of the involvement of the track announcer in the events he is
describing, but that is another issue altogether), and the horses
come onto the track, some of them with a curious skipping gait
which indicates incipient lameness, others with a somnolent prance
which might indicate either good spirits or the presence of un-

detectable drugs. The seven horse, a brown six-year-old gelding, moves somewhat ahead of the field and comes toward us, turns at a point in front of our section of the rail, and then, with some encouragement from outrider and jockey, both of whom are singing, breaks into a sidewise gallop which quickly carries him past the finish line and out of sight along the backstretch. The other horses follow less eagerly and at a cautious distance.

"Front bandages," Simmons says. "Front *and* rear. And he seemed a little rank, too. I don't know. I just don't know. Look, look, he's fifty to one." In his rising excitement—this is, to be sure, the very first tip I have given him, although on previous occasions I have sometimes gone so far as to offer advanced-handicapping advice—his hostility has vanished and his very disbelief seems to wave like a sheet between us punched with enough holes for random communication. "Ah, it's crazy, it's crazy," he says. "I mean, I'm willing to listen to anyone, but I just don't see it. Fifty to one, though." The tote board winks. "*Sixty* to one. Do you think?"

"I do not think," I say. "By the way, I can't stay any longer," and add something about probability currents and cross-angles of time which Simmons is expected to find obscure and to ignore. I leave him rapidly and in such a state of elemental self-absorption that I know he will hardly detect my absence and then only with an abstracted glare. For the fact is that I have put Simmons on to something.

I know that: I see all of the signs. As the horses gather in the upper stretch to talk things over a bit before getting into the dreaded starting gate (I am also privy to the emotions of horses, limited creatures but none the less poignant, at least to themselves), Simmons turns and begins to move at his own sidewise canter toward the pari-mutuel windows. Gasping slightly in my hurry to keep up—I am in rather poor physical condition as a result of my contemplative existence—I follow him, managing to join him only at the window itself, where Simmons joins a short line of ragged men, most of them pallid, who shuffle their feet and clutch their wallets while their twins ahead pass the window and scurry by, looking at the tickets they have bought with wonder. It is the ten-dollar win window, an excellent sign, because Simmons does almost all of his business at the two- and five-dollar shots. He does this, as he once explained to me, not because he wagers little but because he simply feels more comfortable at these more modest windows. Perhaps it is a question of his heritage or only the class system at work. In any event it is a fact—and I have witnessed this—that once Simmons bet fifty dollars on a horse to win and did so at the two dollar window in the form of twenty-five tickets. He simply feels more in place there, the clerk's glare to the contrary. In that case, incidentally, the horse won, profiting Simmons fifty-five dollars, something which he considered an excellent omen as well as a sign that his humility had been observed and respected in Higher Quarters. Nevertheless, he is now on the ten-dollar line.

"Got anything?" the man behind him asks. He does so in response to a certain stimulus which I have implanted midway between the medulla oblongata and the vas deferens, since I am curious about the confidentiality which Simmons feels in our relationship. But I have not been cautious technically, and there is a terrifying moment during which I fear the questioner might faint. Fortunately he does not, but the reasons he has worked out for betting his selection are now and will be irrevocably wiped from his mind.

"Nothing," Simons mutters. "Oh, all right, the six, the six," he adds, "just got a tip out of the infield, but I don't know if it's worth a damn. I'll stab, though." For an instant, I feel a jolt of horror. Has Simmons misunderstood me? Or already forgotten the advice? But then as he comes to the window, I understand that he is only being what he takes to be very cunning, and as he leans over, he makes the clerk lip-read the word *seven*. He has decided then to posture as a deaf-mute in order to protect his information, and this is safe since no ten-dollar clerk at this track has ever before seen him. As he now mouthes *seven ten times*, the clerk returns that timeless, embracing nod of one who has seen everything—this look is also available in whore houses but then only on reservation and for special customers—and punches out ten tickets. Simmons, the new deaf-mute, puts down a hundred-dollar bill (leaving him with only a few dollars and change) and takes the tickets, cupping them so that the man behind can only see his

fine backhand, and then moves to the rear of the line. Pausing
there, he verifies the number (something he always does, although
his losing streak has now reached such proportions that when races
are over he finds himself reaching for his tickets and praying that
the clerk has made a mistake or that he, Simmons, has begun
to lose his vision and did not verify properly) and then returns
slowly toward his place on the rail, pausing for a brief cup of
coffee, which he does not taste, although he can distinctly hear
the clerk cursing him for not leaving the change from a quarter.
I understand with disgust that Simmons will not visit the place
windows, preferring to back up his bet with insistence rather than
circumspection. It is an old failing.

He then goes on to his place on the rail, slightly more crowded
now with only two minutes to post, but sufficiently uninhabited
at the edges that he is able, without difficulty, to cleave out the
yardage which he feels he needs as he prepares himself for the
running. As he curls his hair, wipes his forehead (it is a cool day),
runs a left hand absently over his genitals (his inner wrist catching
the comforting bulge of the tickets in his trouser pocket), he begins
a thin, shrieking monologue which he believes to be private although, of course, I am privy to every word. I listen to it with
relish, delighted as always to see that my effects upon Simmons
have not been imperceptible and that now, as in the past, I have
the capacity to move him. Of course I have had to change many
of my devices and manipulations in order to do so, but I have
never lost that path of connection, and it is this, along with a
few other things, that gives me hope. If I have not lost Simmons,
then there is absolutely no saying what I might not someday gain,
and in the bargain I have been able to keep abreast of his
development. This is no mean accomplishment since Simmons has
been even more variable within the last couple of years than in
the past.

"Oh, you bastards," Simmons is saying, "oh, you bastards, *please*,
please give me this one; it's so little to ask, so little to ask. A hundred dollars, seventy-one now, that's seven thousand, seven thousand
dollars, what's the difference? Who cares? What difference would
it make? Favorites can win, longshots lose, longshots win, favorites

lose, everyone gets out sooner or later. Oh God, give me just
this one and never again. The seven, the seven, just once the
seven, what difference does it make to you, you dirty sons of bitches?
But think of the difference it makes to *me*; a new chance, a new
life, well, maybe the old life but certainly a lot better, a *lot* better,
I deserve it. Oh, give this one to me now. *Eighty* to one now, oh,
God, eight thousand dollars, maybe more, never less. Oh, please,
please, it won't cost you a thing but think of what it means to
me."

(There are two aspects to this monologue which I find objection-
able. The first is that the main thrust of Simmon's appeal is to
the sons of bitches rather than to the one who gave him the tip—
that is to say me—and the second is that Simmons knows as
well as I that were he to win eight thousand dollars, he would
have no more idea of what to do with it than as to what to do
with the hundred he has just bet. It is various and peculiar, peculiar
and various, as they say, but it is the very *perversity* of Simmons
and, by inference, humanity itself, which has always so involved
me and, yes, made them lovable in my eyes. Who, other than
themselves, would have ever conceived them?)

In any event, Simmons is now barely coherent. "Oh, I picked
him, for God's sake, let me know that I still have my wits about
me!" he moans and this, as everything else, I find amusing . . . it
is not the fact that my tip has so rapidly been transmuted into
judgment that titillates me. No, it is something else; it has to do
with the certainty of Simmons's conviction that, large or largest,
massive things now work in the balance. This is an emotion only
fully apprehensible at the racetrack, although other situations occasionally come close. None of those situations are, however, at
all accessible to what Simmons or I would think of as the "working
class."

It is now post-time. Post-time. It is, in fact, some seconds after
post-time, one of the horses in the gate having clearly, to Simmons's anguished but far-sighted gaze, unseated his jockey. "Oh,
God, not the seven, not the number seven," Simmons says, and
the announcer says, "That's number one, Cinnamon Roll, unseating
the rider," and Simmons gives a gasp of relief as the announcer

adds, "that's Cinnamon Roll now running off from the gate." "Oh, boy," he says again (actually the acoustics are quite poor, and for an instant he had thought that the announcer was talking about *Simmons* unseating his jockey and not the crazed horse) as several patrons to his right and left begin to spew curses, at the same time extracting tickets which they regard with loathing. Cinnamon Roll is the 7–5 favorite, as one glance at the tote quickly affirms. "I really can't stand this," Simmons says to no one in particular and bangs an elbow into the mesh, giving him enough distracting pain to keep him functioning while the outriders meanwhile recover number one, gently urge her toward the gate, stand guard while the jockey remounts, and then tenderly pat the horse into position. The grandstand mutters angrily. The horse is the favorite and they feel (*they* is a generalization, but I can do a great deal of research very quickly) that it should have been scratched for medical reasons. But Simmons himself is beyond judgments; he has moved into an abyss of feeling so profound that only the announcer's statement that the horses are out of the gate is able to move him to passion.

The effect of this is, however, galvanic and would surprise anyone in the vicinity of the ten-dollar window who had decided to take a tip from the mute. "Oh, you bastards, here you come!" he says with conviction, a sidewise glance at the board now informing him that the horse is at least ninety to one. "Oh, boy," he says, "come on, come on, get me out of this, come *on*, please," his voice winding its way from a low rumble to a whining shriek during the final words and impressing me, as it always has, with Simmons's utter lack of obscenity under stress situations. It all falls away in the same fashion, I understand, that soldiers in mortal danger of their lives or with broken morale, are apt to curse somewhat less than a cross-section of the Mothers Superior. Obscenity, according to those studies with which I am familiar, occurs only during the relative contentment of hope and tends to vanish when the stresses become evident. "Oh, please," says Simmons and clasps his hands prettily. "Oh, please."

(Once Simmons had made a resolve not to address horses or jockeys during the running of races. He came to this decision on the basis that he was trying to be businesslike and participating in an investment program not dissimilar to stocks and bonds. Did brokers or customers, he wondered, scream curses at the ticker and shake their fists when old IBM went up two in the middle of the track? Of course they did not, and he made no fewer demands of himself than he would if he had been in a more favored position. This resolve had lasted four races, until Cruguet had done something really disastrous with a longshot who was caused to bear in on the rail, and from that time on Simmons has comforted himself with the belief that without air-conditioning, all brokers would work in their undershirts.)

The horses come toward the stretch turn. It is difficult to pick up the call in the midst of the shouting and difficult as well to see the numbers of the leading horses as flashed on the tote board because of the angle. It is for this very reason—a sense of rising mystery during a race, all possibilities enacted until the deadly, final knowledge—that Simmons has elected this for his vantage point, but now, past all shrieking, his voice is only a terrified whisper as he says, "What's going on? What's going on?" Hurling himself half over the rail, he is able to see the race for the first time; he cannot spot the seven horse. Four is on the lead and two outside of it is coming on. The seven must be behind another horse on the rail; either that or it has adjourned from the gate because, as the horses pass, he is unable to see it. "Please," Simmons says as he watches the field scuttle from him, "oh, please." There are diminishing shrieks in the distance and then a silence so deep and white that it could be laid over acres of glowing bone.

Numbers come up on the tote which Simmons is unable to see. After a time—and it is a considerable time, for first all of the horses must return to the paddock to be unsaddled and the jockeys to weigh in, but for Simmons there is no sense of chronology whatsoever—the announcer says that the race is official and reads off the money horses.

The seven finishes third, which is, in my estimation and possibly the announcer's, a remarkable showing for a ninety-to-one shot. Only one ninety-to-one shot out of ten beats even a third of its field; this one has beaten fully three-quarters. I point this out to Simmons in a mild, apologetic tone. "It was rather remarkable, you've got to admit that," I say. "And you could have had the show bet, which incidentally paid only eight sixty due to the two favorites running in."

Simmons says nothing. He is beyond modest mathematical remonstrances or calculation. Instead he is shaking his head, up and down alternately, his neck constricting, his ears bulging, his eyes fluttering. He appears to be entering a period of sea change, or at any rate, it seems to be Simmons Transmuted which I see before me, an older, wiser, infinitely altered Simmons who looks at me with compassion and loathing intermingled as, palms spread before me, I back away, apologizing for my faulty information, my old impulsiveness, my overextended and familiar desire to please. My suspicion is that I too have become a compulsive gambler.

But after a long time, Simmons does say something. He says it in a low voice, and it is difficult for me to distinguish it for a moment. Then, the words seem to explode through me with the force of a grenade, or perhaps I am thinking of a waterfall, my taste for metaphor being as faulty as my way with horses. Nevertheless, I find that I am drenched in knowledge, swaying, gasping, so moved that I am virtually inarticulate, and the silence deepens further as we plunge into the True and Final Disaster and the epochal and grim events of the deservedly famous Last Descent truly begin.

"You can't win 'em all," Simmons says.

"Best damn special effects man in the business."

Regular readers of the magazine and of this series know that Ron Goulart writes funny stories. This is one of his funniest. It is about mechanical dogs, Woodstock, an airborne house called Blackhawk Manor, Military Pills, Spiro Agnew, naked bicycling, and a giant, shaggy Commando Killer, among many other things.

CONFESSIONS

by Ron Goulart

The stubby man pounded his fist on the patio table. He then looked hopefully across at Jose Silvera. "That's about how I've been doing it."

"Basically," said the tall, wide-shouldered Silvera, "your table pounding is okay."

Hugo Kohinoor brought his still-fisted hand up and rubbed his outspread stomach. "Not a great table thump, though, is it, Joe?"

Silvera studied the clear blue afternoon sky. He stroked his chin with the chill rim of his ale mug. "When I suggested you had a problem, I meant not with *how* you pound the table but *when*. The point being that the fault isn't really in those speeches I wrote for you."

A waiter in a white flannel surcoat came trotting over. "You don't have to hammer on your table, I was coming."

"We don't want you," Kohinoor told him. "I was only practicing."

The waiter bent and scrutinized the pudgy man. "Ah," he said. "You're Hugo Kohinoor, head of the Cultural Surveillance Agency for our entire planet of Murdstone." From a flap pocket of his surcoat he took a pair of lemon-yellow spectacles and clamped them on. "You don't look as squabbish in person as you do on the lecture platform."

"Thank you," said the CSA head.

"Another ale," mentioned Silvera. Rose-tinted gulls were spiraling down through the sky to skim the calm waters of the bay.

"I must tell you, Mr. Kohinoor," continued the waiter, "I was deeply moved by your recent speech at our Melazo Territory Citizens Club. Usually I don't pay much attention to a squatty man. You, however, have something to say and you say it well."

"How about when I pounded my fist on the lectern. Was that attention-getting?"

"It was the day I heard you," replied the waiter, "because you knocked over the water carafe." He bowed. "I'll fetch your order now. One ale? Good. Keep up your fine work, Mr. Kohinoor."

Kohinoor smiled at Silvera. "He seemed sincere in his appreciation."

"The speeches are fine," said Silvera. "So pay me the rest of the money."

Kohinoor said, "At first I thought $1500 for only three speeches attacking the . . . what was it you called them?"

"Lords of the press. You still owe me $750."

"Freedom of the press is a flaming sword. That's how it goes, right? Freedom of the press is a flaming sword, and I am here to tell you that the lords of the press have turned that sword into a lawnmower which is nipping in the bud the free flow of thought. Yes, that's nicely put."

Silvera nodded and picked up the fresh ale the waiter had brought. "When you recited it just now, you hit the table on *here* and *lawnmower*."

"Not effective?"

Silvera said, "On *flaming sword* you ought to wave your hand in the air. Then after *free flow* you let it fall with a thud and smash into the table. You'll get applause."

"They have been applauding on lawnmower and I was wondering why," admitted Kohinoor. "Traveling around the planet a lot you sometimes get confused. Melazo Territory is mostly resort country and there's nothing like a lawnmower industry here. Now I understand."

"Cash if you have it."

Kohinoor reached into his knickers and pulled out his wallet. "I'm sorry I criticized the speeches, Joe. Actually you did a fine job. Is one 50 and seven 100s okay?"

"Yes." Silvera took the cash, folded his hand over it. He was reaching for his own wallet when a three-story wooden house flew over. He jumped up and ran to the marble rail of the resort hotel patio. The black house was flying over at about two thousand feet. Silvera shook his head and returned to the statesman's table. "Those bastards," he said, sitting again.

"Who? The Blackhawk Group?"

"Yes. You know them?"

"I'm a close friend of Professor Burton Prester-Johns," said Kohinoor. "McLew Scribbeley, who, as I understand, is the legal owner of Blackhawk Manor, I've had a few conflicts with. Because of that Scribbeley Press of his. Basically, though, I'm fond of all the writers in the Blackhawk Group."

Silvera said, "McLew Scribbeley owes me $2000."

"I thought it was part of your code as a freelance writer, Joe, to always collect your fees."

"I do," said Silvera, "usually. These Blackhawk people keep moving their house."

"A delightful novelty, I think, Flying mobile homes. I'd like to settle down like that someday."

"I've tracked McLew Scribbeley to three different territories on Murdstone so far," said Silvera.

"Did you write something for that vile Scribbeley Press of his?"

"Yes, three confessions," said Silvera. "I did *Confessions of a Robust Man*, *My Disgusting Sex Life* and *I, a Rascal*."

Kohinoor blinked his little blue eyes. "You mean you're A Man Of High Station, Dr. X, and Anonymous? I had them down in my Cultural Surveillance files as three separate authors."

"I can write in different styles."

"That one, that *My Disgusting Sex Life*," said Kohinoor. "I found it to be . . . disgusting."

Silvera asked, "Do you know where he's going to land that damn house this time?"

"Yes, on Post Road Hill," said Kohinoor. "As a matter of fact, I'm invited there to dinner tonight."

Silvera frowned. "I'll come along."

Two hundred bicycles came clattering down over the crest of the hill, each ridden by a shouting adolescent. Silvera caught the squat Kohinoor by the fur collar of his formal doublet and hauled him back against their just-landed cruiser. Even so, a passing handlebar whacked the surveillance chief in the elbow.

"Long live Prester-Johns!" cried the cycling youths as they rattled by Blackhawk Manor and on downhill.

Kohinoor said, "Cyclemania has caught up with the youth of Murdstone."

"Yes, I saw your friend Prester-Johns talking about it on television last night."

"Old P-J relates to youth in ways some of us can't, and he's nearly sixty," said Kohinoor. "Of course, he's a tall man. It's easier to radiate charisma when you've got height."

After the last cyclist had passed, Silvera and Kohinoor crossed the wide dirt roadway and walked to the iron gate that stood at the edge of the wooded acres the Blackhawk mansion now occupied. A frail man in an ironmonger's tunic peered up over a hedge. "Don't use the gate yet, gentlemen."

"Why?"

"It's not screwed to the fence," explained the workman. "I only now got the thing uncrated. See, one of the delays was the box with the razor-sharp fence spikes got misplaced. What is more, the nitwit movers threw out the ground glass I'm supposed to sprinkle atop the stone wall out back. See, they opened the box and saw all that broken glass and felt responsible. So they ditched the glass, box and all. Well, come around through here."

"Thank you," said the stubby Kohinoor.

Silvera helped him get over the hedges onto the path.

"Oh, sirs," called the ironmonger as they started up the winding gravel pathway to the house. "You're the final guests of the evening. So you can tell them to turn on the watch dogs in another fifteen minutes. I'll be finished by then."

"Scribbeley and P-J have a dozen robot hounds," said Kohinoor.

"I've encountered them," said Silvera.

"Did you notice that some of those young girls on the bicycles weren't wearing much, Joe?"

"A few of them were naked."

"Should I be for or against that, I wonder," reflected the stumpy man. "The kids are holding their big annual Bike-in some three miles from here all this week. Perhaps I should issue a position paper. You could write one up for me. Do you know anything about naked bicycle-riding?"

"I've done it." They climbed up the red stone steps of the dark wood mansion.

"Oh, really? I guess when you freelance you have more spare time for fooling around." Kohinoor used the golden hawk's-head knocker on the door.

The butler was pale, dressed in shades of grey. "Good evening, Mr. Kohinoor." He glanced then at Silvera. "Yipes." He backed and ran off along the flowered hall carpeting.

"I've encountered him before, too." Silvera walked into the house.

In a huge oak-paneled room at the hall's end were gathered several people. The butler had not gone there, but up a curving staircase to the second floor. In the paneled room a piano stopped playing and then a muscular man in a tweed oversuit leaped out into the hall. He had an upthrust jaw, square teeth and shaggy blond hair. "Well, well, Kohinoor, you old bastard. Was it you spooked Dwiggins?"

"No, Henry." He pointed a thumb at Silvera. "This is my friend, Jose Silvera. The sight of him startled poor Dwiggins."

"Silvera, Silvera," said the tweedy man. "You write, don't you?"

"That's right, Dobbs."

Henry Verner Dobbs nodded, his chin bobbed. "Know me, know me, do you? Or more likely my work. I'm Henry Verner Dobbs, the author. My specialty is deluxe war books. You probably encountered my photo on the back of my latest hit, *The Coffee Table Book of Hand Grenades*. Big mother of a book, weighs eleven pounds. We, my publishers and I, had it printed on the planet Tarragon by zombies. Those little zombie bastards do lovely color plates, and cheap."

Silvera circled around Dobbs and went into the living room. Scribbeley, the publisher who owed him $2000, wasn't there. Seated at the grand piano was a lovely girl of twenty-six, a tall, coltish brunette with deeply tanned skin and a slight feverish flush.

"Why, it's Jose Silvera," said this lovely girl now. Her voice had a gentle throaty sound. "I've been an admirer of yours since I was a convent girl."

"You've read the fellow's work?" asked the thin, white-haired man standing near the piano.

"I've never read his books, no," said the girl. "I never read other writers. But I saw a picture of Mr. Silvera on a book jacket and I swiped the book. Clipped the photo and kept it pasted inside the cover of my breviary. A good many authors are so unauspicious looking. Mr. Silvera is, on the other hand, big and cute. I am Willa de Aragon, Mr. Silvera." She left the tufted piano bench and came over to him. She touched his hand with her very warm fingers, smiling.

"Do you have a fever?" asked Silvera.

"No, I'm naturally very intense and it seems to heat my body up," she answered. "What brings you to Blackhawk Manor, Mr. Silvera? My invitation didn't mention you."

"Aren't you the fellow?" asked the thin old man.

"Kohinoor came hurrying over. "This is Jose Silvera, P-J. Joe, this is Burton Prester-Johns, one of our leading philosophers."

"Aren't you the fellow who threw Dwiggins out of the greenhouse?"

"Into," said Silvera.

"Whichever direction, it played havoc with the glass panels. We had to abandon the greenhouse, in fact. It's grounded, won't fly. Yes, you're that fellow."

"Joe is a very talented and affable person." Kohinoor reached over and pounded on the piano top. "I brought him along tonight, P-J, so he and McLew Scribbeley can settle their differences for good and all."

"Kind of fellow who throws butlers through greenhouse walls," said Prester-Johns. "Not the kind of fellow one can trust. Yes, it's no small wonder our young people have more faith in bicycles than in their elders." He rubbed a sharp forefinger in the opposite palm. "As I summed up the situation in *Bikocracy*, the responsibility for . . ."

"Shall I give, shall I give him the heave-ho?" Dobbs had leaped back into the room.

"Well, he isn't the kind of fellow one wants to get cozy with."

Kohinoor hit the piano again. "You have to be less suspicious, P-J. Just because the Commando Killer is still loose, you don't have to be so cautious."

Prester-Johns inhaled so deeply he tipped over slightly. He touched his lined cheek with one thin hand.

Dobbs said, "Uh."

Her breath warm, Willa whispered to Silvera, "They have a rule never to talk about the Commando Killer within these walls."

"Why?"

"Apparently, Mr. Silvera, this fiend who has been roaming Murdstone for nearly a year now, claiming a score of victims," said the warm girl. "Apparently this fiend has struck several times in the vicinity of Blackhawk Manor. If you are aware how mobile Blackhawk is, you'll know this involved several separate vicinities."

Through the arched entranceway came a fat man in a white suit. He had a bristling red moustache and a ribbed bald head. "Throw out that wop," he said, pointing at Silvera. "Hello, wop." He chuckled. "Only kidding, Joe. Who cares if you're a dago." He came closer to Silvera. "The throw-you-out-on-your-keaster part is true. Dwiggins just went to get a couple of my hunky retainers. Just kidding. I don't hold their race against them." He shot out his hand suddenly and pinched Willa's left buttock. "Hi, there, you sex-crazed little wench. Just kidding, Willa."

Silvera noticed Scribbeley's suit was one that had the currently fashionable lapels. He grabbed these and wrenched the publisher up off the floor. "$2000."

"Joe, what did I tell your agent, that sweet little Jenny Jennings?"

"Nothing. You pinched her ankle and that was it."

"I was aiming for her left buttock," said the fat publisher. "Look, Joe, I confess I have a compulsive desire to pinch girls. I swear to you that is my only fault. I told your agent and now I tell you, I never got paid by my distributor. Take that one title you did. *My Disgusting Sex Life.* We got a lot of negative mail from people saying it wasn't disgusting. Incidents like that can make people lose faith in Scribbeley Press."

"$2000," repeated Silvera, dropping Scribbeley.

"I could let you have eighty-six thousand unbound copies of *I, a Rascal*, Joe. You could maybe bind them in a nice, sensual cloth and make a fortune selling them mail order."

"Cash, now," said Silvera. Then something came down and hit his head. It hit him hard and several times and he fell down.

Silvera awoke in midair. He hit on his side in among piles of fresh-cut shrub, some hundred yards from Blackhawk Manor. He saw, by squinting through the branches and leaves his head was lodged among, three of Scribbeley's henchmen strutting back toward the turreted mansion.

Extracting his left arm from thorned branches, Silvera knifed his hand in alongside his stuck head and got the thorns away from his cheek. He gave a grunt and pulled back and out free. He stood up and a black dog bounded over and bit him in the leg. Its teeth were stainless steel and penetrated quite deep. Silvera took a small tool kit out of an inside pocket, and recalling a diagram he'd consulted at the Melazo Territory Free Library that afternoon, he deactivated and then dismantled the mechanical dog.

He dropped the dog components in with the shrub and brush that had been cleared away to make landing room for the mansion. Silvera nodded, looked at the newly arrived moon, stepped into the pine woods that surrounded the mansion site. He worked his way quietly back toward the house, favoring his injured leg.

Silvera worked slowly through the woods and emerged at the rear of the mansion. Through the lighted windows of the kitchen, he saw a robot pastry chef filling cream puffs. Crouched low, Silvera approached the twenty wooden steps leading up to the pantry door.

Three more mechanical dogs came around a black edge of the house. They didn't bark, giving out instead a beeping siren sound. One of them had eyes that flashed a bile yellow.

Silvera ran. They pursued him twice around a sundial and once through the still-empty fishpond.

"Do come in, Mr. Silvera," called a sweet voice from a quickly opened door below the pantry stairs.

He obliged. Silvera ducked through the storeroom doorway, and Willa de Aragon slammed the thick door against the vinyl muzzle of the yellow-eyed hound. "Thanks," said Silvera.

The slim, glowing girl held her hand torch toward his injured leg. "You've sustained a wound, Mr. Silvera. You're lucky they haven't had time to unpack the rabies and other poisons for the fangs."

"You were coming out to look for me?"

"I was concerned and I thought I might be able to help out. I believe your friend, Mr. Kohinoor, was talking about going to bring you back, but he hasn't as yet." She touched one warm hand to his cheek. "Whenever I'm a houseguest at Blackhawk Manor, I insist on a room with a secret passage." She gracefully crossed the musty room and pointed at a slid open portion of the raw wood wall. "By going up a little narrow stairway you're in my bedchamber. There's an adjoining bath and I'll be able to minister to your wounds."

"Okay," said Silvera. The girl smiled and stepped into the dark hole. He followed, asking, "Won't they miss you?"

"I can join them for dinner later perhaps," said the warm girl.

Her bedroom was large, with flocked rosebuds on the walls and a pastoral scene painted on the slightly domed ceiling. There were thick rugs, thick tapestries, thick draperies, and a huge hand-carved bed. A six-prong candelabra stood on a marble table near the bed.

As Silvera stepped out of the wall, he heard an odd clattering down on the grounds. He pulled aside a wine-colored drape at the nearest window and looked out. A tall young man was walking a bicycle into the pine woods. A moment later, without the cycle, he came walking by the sundial and then was out of sight. The dogs didn't bother him.

"Would you mind taking off your pants?" asked Willa. "Before I turned to authorship I worked as a practical nurse in a satellite gambling-hell orbiting Tarragon. I can treat your injuries quite professionally, you'll find, Mr. Silvera."

He left the window and moved toward the pale-blue bathroom that the lovely girl was stepping into. He stopped at the threshold, unseamed his trousers, and after getting out of his boots, dropped the trousers. "What sort of writing do you do, Willa?"

She nudged a knee-high white wicker hamper toward him. "Sit on that," she said. "Well, Mr. Silvera, there is a genre of novels which is quite popular here on Murdstone at the moment. They're known as Gothics, though I'm not sure why. All about sensitive young girls who are put upon by strange dark men in sinister old houses in out of the way places."

"Yes, I wrote a dozen of them when there was a Gothic craze on Barnum five years ago," he said, sitting. The mechanical dog bite didn't look too bad.

"Under your own name?" She cleansed the wound.

"No, I was," said Silvera, remembering, "Anna Mary Windmiller."

Willa stopped applying a bandage. "My goodness, Mr. Silvera. You don't mean to tell me you are Anna Mary Windmiller?"

"A dozen times I was anyway," he said. "They were paying $1500 per book."

"You've been an inspiration to me, those books have been. Why, I carry tattered, much-read copies with me still," said Willa. "I am particularly fond of *The Crumbling Chateau on Grave Spawn Hill*. Though, *Return to the Crumbling Chateau on Grave Spawn Hill* is nearly as moving. The opening lines of the former, I think, are excellent and exemplary. 'I confess a sense of dark chagrin flowed through my young, recently graduated from a quiet girls' school, frame when I first opened the door of that crumbling house and tripped over the lifeless body of the local vicar.' A brilliant piece of writing, I think. Oh, I only wish I could write my own Gothics half as well." She finished the bandage and stepped back. "Are you violently anxious to rush down and collect your money?"

"Not violently. Eventually I'm going to get the $2000 from Scribbeley, though. Why?"

"It seems a shame, since you already have your trousers off, not to go to bed together, don't you think?"

Silvera rose from the wicker hamper. "You're pretty aggressive for a writer of polite ladies' fiction."

"Yes," admitted Willa, "and I fear it shows in my work at times."

Silvera smiled, picked her up off the blue tiles and carried her into the bedroom.

It wasn't until the next morning that Silvera left Willa. When he tried to get downstairs by way of the hall, he was stopped by a uniformed police captain.

The policeman, who'd appeared around a turn in the broad, curved stairway, said, "You might as well join the suspects, sir. Do you happen to know where Miss de Aragon is at the moment?"

"Putting on her shoes," said Silvera. "Suspects for what?"

"The murder, sir," said the man in the sea-green uniform. "The inspector is waiting in the living room. Don't try to escape, by the way, as there are vicious dogs outside."

"I know about the dogs."

"Not those robot mutts. We brought our own."

Silvera shrugged his broad shoulders slightly and descended. As he stepped into the living room, McLew Scribbeley called out, "Hello, killer."

Silvera stopped beside a marble statue of a fawn.

"The man who jumps to conclusions often lands on unfirm ground," said a round-headed man in a plaid greatcoat.

"Just kidding," said Scribbeley.

"I am Inspector Ludd," said the round-headed man. "I would like to know who you are."

"He's the fellow who brought the victim," put in Prester-Johns, who was dressed in a paisley lounging robe this morning.

"I'm Jose Silvera. Kohinoor's beeen killed?"

"Death is like a loose shingle," said the inspector, "that falls on whoever is passing beneath. Yes, Hugo Kohinoor is dead, the victim, so it appears, of the Commando Killer." He had a sliding walk and he made a sort of skating motion approaching Silvera. "Sometimes memory is like a garbage truck with some valuable object thrown away by mistake and lost among coffee grounds and watermelon rinds. Forgive me for not recognizing you sooner, Silvera."

"Since we've never met, it's okay."

"You are the same Jose Silvera who has done such excellent articles for the *Interplanetary Real Crime* magazine?"

"I did a series on pattern killers for them once, yes."

"Modesty here is of no more use than a bunch of bananas in a lion's den," said Inspector Ludd. "I'll appreciate your help on this investigation, Silvera."

Dobbs leaped in, eating a square waffle. "He's probably the murderer. I doubt he'll be much help," said the war book author.

"Please accompany me to the site of the crime, Silvera," suggested the inspector. "I'll continue this series of interviews later."

"I have an autographing party at a book shop this noon," said Dobbs. "They're going to unload a hundred remaindered copies of my *Picture History of Poison Gas*."

"Murder, though he often arrives late, takes the best seat in the house," said Inspector Ludd with a half-round smile.

"What does that mean?"

"It means, Mr. Dobbs, no one can leave Blackhawk Manor until this investigation has been concluded," said the inspector. To Scribbeley he added, "It means, too, the scene of the crime cannot leave either. Don't go flying off in this mobile home of yours."

"We're renting this location for a month," said Prester-Johns. "I'm to lecture at the Bike-in all this week, and then I'll be doing a little tramp-cycling act for the young people on the weekend."

"Perhaps," said the Inspector. He led Silvera outside.

Standing on the fresh earth at the edge of the woods, Inspector Ludd said, "You can see why this murderer has earned the name of Commando Killer, Silvera. Notice the use of the bayonet, plus the garrote. There are several other little military touches as well. You were here all night, Silvera?"

"Yes. When was Kohinoor killed?"

"Probably between three AM and dawn," said Ludd. "Did you notice anything unusual?"

"I must have slept through the murder." Silvera knelt down beside the body of Kohinoor. "Little scrap of paper between this thumb and forefinger."

"Yes, it is the corner of a $100 Murdstone currency bill. We are hopeful of finding the rest of it."

"What do they say in the house?" Silvera got to his feet.

"Kohinoor stayed to dinner, though angry because you'd been roughly handled," said the round-headed inspector. "Most everyone retired at midnight or thereabouts. No one admits to being out here at all. Kohinoor was not supposed to have stayed overnight. One of the men coming to finish the new greenhouse found his body here before breakfast. You spent the night with Miss de Aragon?"

"Yes."

"I deduced as much from her reported absence at dinner last evening and from what I've heard of you," said Inspector Ludd. "Added to the fact you are still here many hours after you were ejected. I don't think, though, you would have killed Kohinoor over a fee."

"I never do that, no," said Silvera. "I either collect my money or I don't. Most often I do."

"The freelance life," said the inspector with a sigh. "I chose the security of a civil job rather than attempt it. You may have noted my speech is frequently spiced with aphorisms."

"Yes, I noticed."

"The remnants of an ambition to be a lyric poet," said Inspector Ludd. "Did you know that when the Commando Killer struck two months ago in Esfola Territory he was seen and they got a description plus composite sketches?"

"No, it hasn't been in the news."

"Not as yet," said the inspector. "In a way it is disappointing. This Blackhawk house has been in the vicinity of almost all the attacks by the Commando Killer, and neither I nor any of the other investigators across Murdstone can link anyone in Blackhawk Manor with these crimes."

"Fingerprints, footprints?"

"No fingerprints and the only footprint we've found this time is that one there. We've made a cast of it."

"Belongs to nobody at the house?"

"It was made by an old commando boot of extremely large size. We haven't as yet located one inside, though my men are still searching," said the inspector. "The description and the eye-witness sketches I've gone over, and the brute looks like no one here."

"A disguise maybe."

"No," said Ludd. "Look at that footprint. The fellow is a giant and a brutal-looking shaggy fellow." He sighed again. "We rounded up all the giant brutal shaggy fellows in our files and got nothing. So I think . . ."

"What?"

"You no doubt recall the famous Nolan and Anmar case on Venus a generation ago."

"Double personality. Nolan turned himself into Anmar with a pill he'd invented."

"Exactly," said Ludd. "I have the feeling something similar may be involved here. Though there is no proof of any such thing."

Silvera scratched at the back of his neck. "The kid on the bicycle," he said.

"We found cycle tracks in the woods, yes. But no bike and no cyclist on the premises. No one admits having had such a visitor either. What do you know?"

"Something about that kid," said Silvera. "I saw him get here about nine last night, park his bicycle in the woods, and sneak into Blackhawk Manor through the back way. Yes, and he was one of the kids who came by earlier on the way to the Bike-in."

"You could recognize him?"

"Sure."

"We'll go looking at the Bike-in," the inspector said. "Sometimes the slenderest thread unravels the most of the sweater." He smiled at Silvera. "A sample of my aphoristic style."

Silvera smiled briefly.

Silvera walked among hundreds of parked cycles and around groups singing bicycle songs and groups taking off each other's clothes and groups dismantling and rebuilding bikes. All on a rolling grassy plain with a wide roadway bordering part of it.

"You look awfully old to be a bike person," said a half-dressed girl who was leaning against a unicycle.

"I thought so, too," answered Silvera, "until I fell under the spell of Burton Prester-Johns."

"That old twit," said the girl, rubbing her bare, freckled stomach. "He's disgusting. Whenever I see someone over thirty riding a bicycle, it makes me retch and gag."

"Those are interesting symptoms." Silvera glanced away from the girl and spotted Inspector Ludd wandering down through the crowds from the opposite side of the plain. "I'm looking for a guy who rides a 10-speed black Martian Wollter-brand bike. Lean guy, sandy hair, little moustache."

"Are you a law person? Law people make me have severe pains in the lower abdomen."

"I'm a freelance journalist, researching an in-depth story on the bicycle culture."

"That's repellent," said the girl. "Old gents way up in their thirties trying to understand youth. That makes me writhe and have severe chills."

"Maybe you ought to be home in bed."

"That's all you old boys think of."

Silvera walked on. Then, over in the afternoon shade of a refreshment stand, he saw the sandy-haired boy. He caught the inspector's eye and nodded toward the stand.

The two of them began working through the crowd and toward the boy, who had one elbow against the yellow wall of the stand and was drinking a mug of May wine.

The boy sensed Silvera while he was still two hundred feet from him. He recognized the inspector apparently, turned on his left toes and ran off.

Silvera began to run, too, shouldering through cyclists. A plump albino boy took offense and threw his May wine in Silvera's face. Silvera kept running, wiping strawberries off his coat. He dashed around the refreshment stand, saw the boy starting up the plain toward the roadway, riding now on his black 10-speed bike.

Silvera stopped and grabbed up a parked 3-speed local bike. He only covered twenty feet before a girl cried out, "Aged bicycle thief!"

Three cycle singers leaped up, swinging lutes and mandolins.

Silvera pedaled hard. Four more boys came after him. They tackled both Silvera and the borrowed bike.

Leaving the bike seat, Silvera was carried ten feet and then dumped on the short grass. Before any of the four boys could jump on him he rolled, bowling over a picnic lunch for three. At the far zig-zagging, after the escaping boy.

side of the picnic drop cloth Silvera regained his feet. He ran,

He was tackled again, by three chunky girls in blue leather jerkins this time, a few yards short of the roadway. "Nasty old man," said one girl, hitting him up beside the ear with a bicycle pump.

"I'm only thirty-three," explained Silvera, ducking away from a second swing of the hard metal pump.

"Well, that's plenty old."

"Stop! The hand that takes up the sword against another often unsheaths more than it bargains for."

"What?" asked the girl who was jumping on Silvera's stomach with her bent knees.

Inspector Ludd, panting, said, "I mean he who would wear the judge's wig must first be abundantly certain he has the right-sized head."

"Drop the aphorisms," said Silvera, "and tell them you're a cop."

The three blocky girls stopped attacking Silvera. "You're a cop, granpappy?"

"Inspector Ludd of the Municipal Police, yes," said Ludd. "I have been trying to suggest that you ought to leave law enforcement to me."

As the girls drifted away, Silvera got himself up off the grass. "That was the kid I saw last night. He seems to have gotten away from us."

"I know who he is," said Inspector Ludd. "Which puts us one step closer to the solution."

Silvera decided to sit down again for a moment. "The greatest journeys often begin with a single step," he said and began dusting himself off.

The day ended and rain began to fall with the darkness. A rough wind came blowing through the pine woods and rattled the spires and shutters and dark carved wood of Blackhawk Manor. In the living room a fire was starting to take hold in the deep tile-bordered fireplace.

Inspector Ludd had taken off his plaid greatcoat and was in his dark two-piece civilian suit, pacing.

Dobbs said, "How can we reenact the crime, inspector?" He sipped at the glass of wine that had been passed to him a moment before by Dwiggins. "We are fairly certain, aren't we, this Commando Killer is someone from the outside, who more or less by coincidence, by repeated coincidence, happens to commit his crimes around our house. I'm no crime expert, like you and your boy Silvera. No, since my time is given over to the study of somewhat more important matters. Military matters. Such as the new book I'm putting together, *The Picture History of Trenches*."

When everyone had been served a drink, the inspector said, "First, Silvera, tell them what we have found out."

Silvera was on the piano bench next to Willa. He lifted his hand from the small of her back and said, "A young guy named Roberto Koop came here on his bicycle last evening."

"Friend of yours, isn't he?" McLew Scribbeley asked his philosopher housemate.

"I'm not intimate with everyone who rides a bike," said Prester-Johns. "Possibly I met the young fellow during one of my encounters with our new bikocracy. What does he say?"

"The young man is being sought at the moment," said Inspector Ludd.

"The point is," said Silvera, "Koop has an uncle, Professor LeRoy Koop. Professor Koop has been doing some military research for the Murdstone Combined Armed Forces."

"Wait, now," Dobbs interrupted. "That CAF stuff is all very secret."

"Inspector Ludd has been allowed to sit in on some of the briefings," said Silvera. "So he knows young Koop's uncle has developed a new drug, and it's known as Military Pills."

"These Military Pills," explained the inspector, "can turn any average recruit into a giant vicious fighting man."

"I've never heard of them," said Dobbs.

"The Military Pills have been developed and completely tested. They were ready for extended use over three years ago," continued the inspector. "That they have not been widely used as yet is due to the fact the Combined Armed Forces have been tangled up in an ethical debate."

"We contacted Professor Koop late this afternoon," said Silvera. He hadn't touched his wine as yet. Setting the glass on the piano, he stood. "Koop eventually admitted young Roberto Koop had swiped several hundred Military Pills from him over a year ago and gone into hiding. He's apparently learned how to make the stuff and has been selling Military Pills through the underside of the territories. Some of his customers are probably higher priced. One of them, someone who has found the pills to be addictive, is in the house here."

Inspector Ludd said, "We were able to borrow some sample pills from Professor Koop." He smiled his half-round smile at them all. "A little earlier Silvera discovered an important clue. Because of his particular orientation he figured out where the Commando Killer had hidden his boots. We now have them."

"Where does that get you?" asked Prester-Johns."

"The Commando Killer," said Silvera, "is one of you. He takes the Military Pills and changes into a giant shaggy killer. All we have to do now is see who fits into the boots."

"They won't fit anybody," said Willa. "If this killer is a dual personality. I mean, it's his alter feet you want."

"Exactly," said the inspector. "Which is why we dissolved several of the tasteless Military Pills in your wine. Our discussion has gone on until everyone has finished his first glass. The drug, for those of you who aren't familiar with it, takes roughly fifteen minutes to take effect and lasts for two to three hours."

All the lights went out.

Silvera, as he'd rehearsed earlier, ran across the room and through a side door. He sprinted down a dark hallway and through another doorway. In this new dark room he got behind a full-length drape and waited.

In less than a minute a panel in the wall slid open and McLew Scribbeley stepped into the room. He turned on a desk lamp and got down on his hands and knees in front of a globe of the planet mounted on a tripod. He spun the Murdstone globe three times to the left, three to the right, once to the left. Then he pressed his fingers on five separate cities. The large globe clicked open, one quarter of it swinging out. Scribbeley thrust a hand inside. He raked out packets of paper money first, bags of coin next. Then he yanked out a giant pair of muddy commando boots. "That's odd," he muttered. "They're still here."

"We were just kidding." Silvera was out from behind the drapes, a small hand-blaster aimed at the kneeling publisher. "I'd figured it was you and we wanted to see where you had the damn shoes hidden. So we told you we'd already found them and you couldn't keep yourself from coming here to see if it was so."

"What do you know?" said Scribbeley. "How'd you decide it was me?"

"Most of the murders have been motiveless," said Silvera. "Something you couldn't help once the Military Pills got hold of you. You probably tried the stuff in the first place to boost your virility, but it didn't work out that way. Last night, though, you had a real reason for the killing. Kohinoor, I figure, came to you and pressured you. He was angry about the way you'd handled my complaints. He probably threatened to crack down on your book enterprises if you didn't settle. So you told him you'd pay him the $2000 you owed me. You told him to meet you outside after everybody'd turned in. You gave him the cash, and while he was still in the woods, you turned into your killer side."

"Son of a gun," said Scribbeley, standing by pressing on his knees. "You sure are a smart one, you dago rascal. Well, I confess you're absolutely correct. The thing you've overlooked is that I'm going to change into the Commando Killer. When I do, your little gun won't stop me." He paused, then roared and came at Silvera. He ran halfway to the window and then stopped, frowning at his hands. "That's odd, I'm not changing. Even though you put the stuff in the drinks."

"We were kidding about that, too," Silvera said.

Inspector Ludd came in with one of his captains. "A shot fired while blindfolded still sometimes finds a worthwhile target." They took Scribbeley from the room.

When Willa came to find Silvera a few moments later, he was at the globe. "Are you all right, Mr. Silvera?"

"Wait until I count out two thousand of this."

"All that cash and you're only taking two thousand?"

"That's all he owed me," said Silvera.

Of all the younger writers who have made a name for themselves in the last half-dozen years, Larry Niven is certainly one of the best—perhaps the best—practitioners of the short story, whether hard sf or fantasy. Mr. Niven calls this story fantasy ("I regard time travel as fantasy, not sf."). Its hero is sent back in time to get a horse, which is not your usual portentous time-travel itinerary, but under Mr. Niven's sure hand, it turns into a most surprising story.

GET A HORSE!

by Larry Niven

The year was 750 AA (Ante Atomic) or 1200 AD (Anno Domini), approximately. Hanville Svetz stepped out of the extension cage and looked about him.

To Svetz the atomic bomb was eleven hundred years old and the horse was a thousand years dead. It was his first trip into the past. His training didn't count; it had not included actual time-travel, which cost several million commercials a shot. Svetz was groggy from the peculiar gravitational side-effects of time-travel. He was high on pre-industrial-age air, and drunk on his own sense of destiny; while at the same time he was not really convinced that he had *gone* anywhere. Or anywhen. Trade joke.

He was not carrying the anesthetic rifle. He had come to get a horse; he had not expected to meet one at the door. How big was a horse? Where were horses found? Consider what the institute had had to go on: a few pictures in a salvaged children's book, and an old legend, not to be trusted, that the horse had once been used as a kind of animated vehicle!

In an empty land beneath an overcast sky, Svetz braced himself with one hand on the curved flank of the extension cage. His head was spinning. It took him several seconds to realize that he was looking at a horse.

It stood fifteen yards away, regarding Svetz with large intelligent brown eyes. It was much larger than he had expected. Further, the horse in the picture book had had a glossy brown pelt with a short mane, while the beast now facing Svetz was pure white, with a mane that flowed like a woman's long hair. There were other differences . . . but no matter, the beast matched the book too well to be anything but a horse.

To Svetz it seemed that the horse watched him, waited for him to realize what was happening. Then, while Svetz wasted more time wondering why he wasn't holding a rifle, the horse laughed, turned and departed. It disappeared with astonishing speed.

Svetz began to shiver. Nobody had warned him that the horse might have been sentient! Yet the beast's mocking laugh had sounded far too human.

Now he knew. He was deep, deep in the past.

Not even the horse was as convincing as the emptiness the horse had left behind. No reaching apartment towers clawed the horizon. No contrails scratched the sky. The world was trees and flowers and rolling grassland, innocent of men.

The silence— It was as if Svetz had gone deaf. He had heard no sound since the laughter of the horse. In the year 1100, Post Atomic, such silence could have been found nowhere on Earth. Listening, Svetz knew at last that he had reached the British Isles before the coming of civilization. He had traveled in time.

The extension cage was the part of the time machine that did the traveling. It had its own air supply, and needed it while being pushed through time. But not here. Not before civilization's dawn; not when the air had never been polluted by fission wastes and the combustion of coal, hydrocarbons, tobaccos, wood, et al.

Now, retreating in panic from that world of the past to the world of the extension cage, Svetz nonetheless left the door open behind him.

He felt better inside the cage. Outside was an unexplored planet, made dangerous by ignorance. Inside the cage it was no different from a training mission. Svetz had spent hundreds of hours in a detailed mock-up of this cage, with a computer running the dials. There had even been artificial gravity to simulate the peculiar side-effects of motion in time.

By now the horse would have escaped. But he now knew its size, and he knew there were horses in the area. To business, then . . .

Svetz took the anesthetic rifle from where it was clamped to the wall. He loaded it with what he guessed was the right size of soluble crystalline anesthetic needle. The box held several different sizes, the smallest of which would knock a shrew harmlessly unconscious, the largest of which would do the same for an elephant. He slung the rifle and stood up.

The world turned grey. Svetz caught a wall clamp to stop himself from falling.

The cage had stopped moving twenty minutes ago. He shouldn't still be dizzy!—But it had been a long trip. Never before had the Institute for Temporal Research pushed a cage beyond zero PA. A long trip and a strange one, with gravity pulling Svetz's mass uniformly toward Svetz's navel . . .

When his head cleared, he turned to where other equipment was clamped to a wall.

The flight stick was a lift-field generator and power source built into five feet of pole, with a control ring at one end, a brush discharge at the other, and a bucket seat and seat belt in the middle. Compact even for Svetz's age, the flight stick was spin-off from the spaceflight industries.

But it still weighed thirty pounds with the motor off. Getting it out of the clamps took all his strength. Svetz felt queasy, very queasy.

He bent to pick up the flight stick, and abruptly realized that he was about to faint.

He hit the door button and fainted.

"We don't know where on Earth you'll wind up," Ra Chen had told him. Ra Chen was the Director of the Institute for Temporal Research, a large round man with gross, exaggerated features and a permanent air of disapproval. "That's because we can't focus on a particular time of day—or on a particular year, for that matter. You won't appear underground or inside anything because of energy considerations. If you come out a thousand feet in the air, the cage won't fall; it'll settle slowly, using up energy with a profligate disregard for our budget . . ."

And Svetz had dreamed that night, vividly. Over and over his extension cage appeared inside solid rock, exploded with a roar and a blinding flash.

"Officially, the horse is for the Bureau of History," Ra Chen had said. "In practice it's for the Secretary-General, for his twenty-eighth birthday. Mentally he's about six years old, you know. The royal family's getting a bit inbred these days. We managed to send him a picture book we picked up in 130 PA, and now the lad wants a horse . . ."

Svetz had seen himself being shot for treason, for the crime of listening to such talk.

". . . Otherwise we'd never have gotten the appropriation for this trip. It's in a good cause. We'll do some cloning from the horse before we send the original to the UN. Then—well, genes are a code, and codes can be broken. Get us a male, and we'll make all the horses anyone could want."

But why would anyone want even one horse? Svetz had studied a computer duplicate of the child's picture book that an agent had pulled from a ruined house a thousand years ago. The horse did not impress him.

Ra Chen, however, terrified him.

"We've never sent anyone this far back," Ra Chen had told him the night before the mission, when it was too late to back out with honor. "Keep that in mind. If something goes wrong, don't count on the rule book. Don't count on your instruments. Use your head. Your head, Svetz. God knows it's little enough to depend on . . ."

Svetz had not slept in the hours before departure.

"You're scared stiff," Ra Chen commented just before Svetz entered the extension cage. "And you can hide it, Svetz. I think I'm the only one who's noticed. That's why I picked you, because you can be terrified and go ahead anyway. Don't come back without a horse . . ."

The director's voice grew louder. "Not without a horse, Svetz. Your *head*, Svetz, your HEAD . . ."

Svetz sat up convulsively. The air! Slow death if he didn't close the door! But the door was closed, and Svetz was sitting on the floor holding his head, which hurt.

The air system had been transplanted, complete with dials, intact from a Martian sandboat. The dials read normally, of course, since the cage was sealed.

Svetz nerved himself to open the door. As the sweet, rich air of twelfth-century Britain rushed in, Svetz held his breath and watched the dials change. Presently he closed the door and waited, sweating, while the air system replaced the heady poison with its own safe, breathable mixture.

When next he left the extension cage, carrying the flight stick, Svetz was wearing another spin-off from the interstellar-exploration industries. It was a balloon, and he wore it over his head. It was also a selectively permeable membrane, intended to pass certain gasses in and others out, to make a breathing-air mixture inside.

It was nearly invisible except at the rim. There, where light was refracted most severely, the balloon showed as a narrow golden circle enclosing Svetz's head. The effect was not unlike a halo as shown in medieval paintings. But Svetz didn't know about medieval paintings.

He wore also a simple white robe, undecorated, constricted at the waist, otherwise falling in loose folds. The institute thought that such a garment was least likely to violate taboos of sex or custom. The trade kit dangled loose from his sash: a heat-and-pressure gadget, a pouch of corundum, small phials of additives for color.

Lastly he wore a hurt and baffled look. How was it that he could not breath the clean air of his own past?

The air of the cage was the air of Svetz's own time, and was nearly four percent carbon dioxide. The air of 750 Ante Atomic held barely a tenth of that. Man was a rare animal here and now. He had breathed little air, he had destroyed few forests, he had burnt scant fuel since the dawn of time.

But industrial civilization meant combustion. Combustion meant carbon dioxide thickening in the atmosphere many times faster than the green plants could turn it back to oxygen. Svetz was at the far end of two thousand years of adaptation to air rich in CO_2.

It takes a concentration of carbon dioxide to trigger the autonomic nerves in the lymph glands in a man's left armpit. Svetz had fainted because he wasn't breathing.

So now he wore a balloon, and felt rejected.

He straddled the flight stick and twisted the control knob on the fore end. The stick lifted under him, and he wriggled into place on the bucket seat. He twisted the knob further.

He drifted upward like a toy balloon.

He floated over a lovely land, green and untenanted, beneath a pearl-grey sky empty of contrails. Presently he found a crumbling wall. He turned to follow it.

He would follow the wall until he found a settlement. If the old legend was true—and, Svetz reflected, the horse had certainly been *big* enough to drag a vehicle—then he would find horses wherever he found men.

Presently it became obvious that a road ran along the wall. There the dirt was flat and bare and consistently wide enough for a walking man; whereas elsewhere the land rose and dipped and tilted. Hard dirt did not a freeway make; but Svetz got the point.

He followed the road, floating at a height of ten meters.

There was a man in worn brown garments. Hooded and barefoot, he walked the road with patient exhaustion, propping himself with a staff. His back was to Svetz.

Svetz thought to dip toward him to ask concerning horses. He refrained. With no way to know where the cage would alight, he had learned no ancient languages at all.

He thought of the trade kit he carried, intended not for communication, but instead of communication. It had never been field-tested. In any case it was not for casual encounters. The pouch of corundum was too small.

Svetz heard a yell from below. He looked down in time to see the man in brown running like the wind, his staff forgotten, his fatigue likewise.

"Something scared him," Svetz decided. But he could see nothing fearful. Something small but deadly, then.

The institute estimated that man had exterminated more than a thousand species of mammal and bird and insect—some casually, some with malice—between now and the distant present. In this time and place there was no telling what might be a threat. Svetz shuddered. The brown man with the hairy face might well have run from a stinging thing destined to kill Hanville Svetz.

Impatiently Svetz upped the speed of his flight stick. The mission was taking far too long. Who would have guessed that centers of population would have been so far apart?

Half an hour later, shielded from the wind by a paraboloid force-field, Svetz was streaking down the road at sixty miles per hour.

His luck had been incredibly bad. Wherever he had chanced across a human being, that person had been just leaving the vicinity. And he had found no centers of population.

Once he had noticed an unnatural stone outcropping high on a hill. No law of geology known to Svetz could have produced such an angular, flat-sided monstrosity. Curious, he had circled above it—and had abruptly realized that the thing was hollow, riddled with rectangular holes.

A dwelling for men? He didn't want to believe it. Living within the hollows of such a thing would be like living underground. But men tend to build at right angles, and this thing was *all* right angles.

Below the hollowed stone structure were rounded, hairy-looking hummocks of dried grass, each with a man-sized door. Obviously they must be nests for very large insects. Svetz had left that place quickly.

The road rounded a swelling green hill ahead of him. Svetz followed, slowing.

A hilltop spring sent a stream bubbling down hill to break the road. Something large was drinking at the stream.

Svetz jerked to a stop in midair. *Open water: deadly poison.* He would have been hard put to say which had startled him more: the horse, or the fact that it had just committed suicide.

The horse looked up and saw him.

It was the same horse. White as milk, with a flowing abundance of snowy mane and tail, it almost had to be the horse that had laughed at Svetz and run. Svetz recognized the malignance in its eyes, in the moment before it turned its back.

But how could it have arrived so fast?

Svetz was reaching for the gun when the situation turned upside down.

The girl was young, surely no more than sixteen. Her hair was long and dark and plaited in complex fashion. Her dress, of strangely stiff blue fabric, reached from her neck to her ankles. She was seated in the shadow of a tree, on dark cloth spread over the dark earth. Svetz had not noticed her, might never have noticed her . . .

But the horse walked up to her, folded its legs in alternate pairs, and laid its ferocious head in her lap.

The girl had not yet seen Svetz.

"Xenophilia!" Svetz snarled the worst word he could think of. Svetz hated aliens.

The horse obviously belonged to the girl. He could not simply shoot it and take it. It would have to be purchased . . . somehow.

He needed time to think! And there was no time, for the girl might look up at any moment. Baleful brown eyes watched him as he dithered . . .

He dared waste no more time searching the countryside for a wild horse. There was an uncertainty, a Finagle factor in the math of time-travel. It manifested itself as an uncertainty in the energy of a returning extension cage, and it increased with time. Let Svetz linger too long, and he could be roasted alive in the returning cage.

Moreover, the horse had drunk open water. It would die, and soon, unless Svetz could return it to 1100 Post Atomic. Thus the beast's removal from this time could not change the history of Svetz's own world. It was a good choice . . . if he could conquer his fear of the beast.

The horse was tame. Young and slight as she was, the girl had no trouble controlling it. What was there to fear?

But there was its natural weaponry . . . of which Ra Chen's treacherous picture book had shown no sign. Svetz surmised that

later generations routinely removed it before the animals were
old enough to be dangerous. He should have come a few centuries later . . .

And there was the look in its eye. The horse hated Svetz,
and it knew Svetz was afraid.

Could he shoot it from ambush?

No. The girl would worry if her pet collapsed without reason.
She would be unable to concentrate on what Svetz was trying
to tell her.

He would have to work with the animal watching him. If the
girl couldn't control it—or if he lost her trust—Svetz had little
doubt that the horse would kill him.

The horse looked up as Svetz approached, but made no other
move. The girl watched too, her eyes round with wonder. She
called something that must have been a question.

Svetz smiled back and continued his approach. He was a foot
above the ground, and gliding at dead slow. Riding the world's
only flying machine, he looked impressive as all hell, and knew it.

The girl did not smile back. She watched warily. Svetz was
within yards of her when she scrambled to her feet.

He stopped the flight stick at once and let it settle. Smiling
placatorially, he removed the heat-and-pressure device from his
sash. He moved with care. The girl was on the verge of running.

The trade kit was a pouch of corundum, Al_2O_3, several phials
of additives, and the heat-and-pressure gadget. Svetz poured corundum into the chamber, added a dash of chromic oxide, and
used the plunger. The cylinder grew warm. Presently Svetz dropped
a pigeon's-blood star ruby into his hand, rolled it in his fingers,
held it to the sun. It was red as dark blood, with a blazing white
six-pointed star.

It was almost too hot to hold.

Stupid! Svetz held his smile rigid. Ra Chen should have warned
him! What would she think when she felt the gem's unnatural
heat? What trickery would she suspect?

But he had to chance it. The trade kit was all he had.

He bent and rolled the gem to her across the damp ground.

She stooped to pick it up. One hand remained on the horse's neck, calming it. Svetz noticed the rings of yellow metal around her wrist, and he also noticed the dirt.

She held the gem high, looked into its deep red fire.

"Ooooh," she breathed. She smiled at Svetz in wonder and delight. Svetz smiled back, moved two steps nearer, and rolled her a yellow sapphire.

How had he twice chanced on the same horse? Svetz never knew. But he soon knew how it had arrived before him . . .

He had given the girl three gems. He held three more in his hand while he beckoned her onto the flight stick. She shook her head; she would not go. Instead she mounted the animal.

She and the horse, they watched Svetz for his next move.

Svetz capitulated. He had expected the horse to follow the girl while the girl rode behind him on the flight stick. But if they both followed Svetz, it would be the same.

The horse stayed to one side and a little behind Svetz's flight stick. It did not seem inconvenienced by the girl's weight. Why should it be? It must have been bred for the task. Svetz notched his speed higher, to find how fast he could conveniently move.

Faster he flew, and faster. The horse must have a limit . . .

He was up to eight before he quit. The girl lay flat along the animal's back, hugging its neck to protect her face from the wind. But the horse ran on, daring Svetz with its eyes.

How to describe such motion? Svetz had never seen ballet. He knew how machinery moved, and this wasn't it. All he could think of was a man and a woman making love. Slippery-smooth rhythmic motion, absolute single-minded purpose, motion for the pleasure of motion. It was terrible in its beauty, the flight of the horse.

The word for such running must have died with the horse itself.

The horse would never have tired, but the girl did. She tugged on the animal's mane, and it stopped. Svetz gave her the jewels he held, made four more and gave her one.

She was crying from the wind, crying and smiling as she took the jewels. Was she smiling for the jewels, or for the joy of the ride? Exhausted, panting, she lay with her back against the warm, pulsing flank of the resting animal. Only her hand moved, as she ran her fingers repeatedly through its silver mane. The horse watched Svetz with malevolent brown eyes.

The girl was homely. It wasn't just the jarring lack of make-up. There was evidence of vitamin starvation. She was short, less than five feet in height, and thin. There were marks of childhood disease. But happiness glowed behind her homely face, and it make her almost passable, as she clutched the corundum stones.

When she seemed rested, Svetz remounted. They went on.

He was almost out of corundum when they reached the extension cage. There it was that he ran into trouble.

The girl had been awed by Svetz's jewels, and by Svetz himself, possibly because of his height or his ability to fly. But the extension cage scared her. Svetz couldn't blame her. The side with the door in it was no trouble: just a seamless spherical mirror. But the other side blurred away in a direction men could not visualize. It had scared Svetz spitless the first time he saw the time machine in action.

He could buy the horse from her, shoot it here and pull it inside, using the flight stick to float it. But it would be so much easier if . . .

It was worth a try. Svetz used the rest of his corundum. Then he walked into the extension cage, leaving a trail of colored corundum beads behind him.

He had worried because the heat-and-pressure device would not produce facets. The stones all came out shaped like miniature hen's eggs. But he was able to vary the color, using chromic oxide for red and ferric oxide for yellow and titanium for blue; and he could vary the pressure planes, to produce cat's eyes or star gems at will. He left a trail of small stones, red and yellow and blue. . .

And the girl followed, frightened, but unable to resist the bait. By now she had nearly filled a handkerchief with the stones. The horse followed her into the extension cage.

Inside, she looked at the four stones in Svetz's hand: one of each color, red and yellow and light blue and black, the largest he could make. He pointed to the horse, then to the stones.

The girl agonized. Svetz perspired. She didn't want to give up the horse . . . and Svetz was out of corundum . . .

She nodded, one swift jerk of her chin. Quickly, before she could change her mind, Svetz poured the stones into her hand. She clutched the hoard to her bosom and ran out of the cage, sobbing.

The horse stood up to follow.

Svetz swung the rifle and shot it. A bead of blood appeared on the animal's neck. It shied back, then sighted on Svetz along its natural bayonet.

Poor kid, Svetz thought as he turned to the door. But she'd have lost the horse anyway. It had sucked polluted water from an open stream. Now he need only load the flight stick aboard.

Motion caught his eye.

A false assumption can be deadly. Svetz had not waited for the horse to fall. It was with something of a shock that he realized the truth. The beast wasn't about to fall. It was about to spear him like a cocktail shrimp.

He hit the door button and dodged.

Exquisitely graceful, exquisitely sharp, the spiral horn slammed into the closing door. The animal turned like white lightning in the confines of the cage, and again Svetz leapt for his life.

The point missed him by half an inch. It plunged past him and into the control board, through the plastic panel and into the wiring beneath.

Something sparkled and something sputtered.

The horse was taking careful aim, sighting along the spear in its forehead. Svetz did the only thing he could think of. He pulled the home-again lever.

The horse screamed as it went into free fall. The horn, intended for Svetz's navel, ripped past his ear and tore his breathing-balloon wide open.

Then gravity returned; but it was the peculiar gravity of an extension cage moving forward through time. Svetz and the horse were pulled against the padded walls. Svetz sighed in relief.

He sniffed again in disbelief. The smell was strong and strange, like nothing Svetz had ever smelled before. The animal's terrible horn must have damaged the air plant. Very likely he was breathing poison. If the cage didn't return in time . . .

But would it return at all? It might be going anywhere, anywhen, the way that ivory horn had smashed through anonymous wiring. They might come out at the end of time, when even the black infrasuns gave not enough heat to sustain life.

There might not even be a future to return to. He had left the flight stick. How would it be used? What would they make of it, with its control handle at one end and the brush-style static discharge at the other and the saddle in the middle? Perhaps the girl would try to use it. He could visualize her against the night sky, in the light of a full moon . . . and how would that change history?

The horse seemed on the verge of apoplexy. Its sides heaved, its eyes rolled wildly. Probably it was the cabin air, thick with carbon dioxide. Again, it might be the poison the horse had sucked from an open stream.

Gravity died. Svetz and the horse tumbled in free fall, and the horse queasily tried to gore him.

Gravity returned, and Svetz, who was ready for it, landed on top. Someone was already opening the door.

Svetz took the distance in one bound. The horse followed, screaming with rage, intent on murder. Two men went flying as it charged out into the institute control center.

"It doesn't take anesthetics!" Svetz shouted over his shoulder. The animal's agility was hampered here among the desks and lighted screens, and it was probably drunk on hyperventilation. It kept stumbling into desks and men. Svetz easily stayed ahead of the slashing horn.

A full panic was developing.

"We couldn't have done it without Zeera," Ra Chen told him much later. "Your idiot tanj horse had the whole center terrorized.

All of a sudden it went completely tame, walked up to that frigid bitch Zeera and let her lead it away."

"Did you get it to the hospital in time?"

Ra Chen nodded gloomily. Gloom was his favorite expression and was no indication of his true feelings. "We found over fifty unknown varieties of bacteria in the beast's bloodstream. Yet it hardly looked sick! It looked healthy as a, healthy as a . . . it must have tremendous stamina. We managed to save not only the horse, but most of the bacteria too, for the Zoo."

Svetz was sitting up in a hospital bed, with his arm up to the elbow in a diagnostician. There was always the chance that he too had located some long-extinct bacterium. He shifted uncomfortably, being careful not to move the wrong arm, and asked, "Did you ever find an anesthetic that worked?"

"Nope. Sorry about that, Svetz. We still don't know why your needles didn't work. The tanj horse is simply immune to tranks of any kind.

"Incidentally, there was nothing wrong with your air plant. You were smelling the horse."

"I wish I'd known that. I thought I was dying."

"It's driving the internes crazy, that smell. And we can't seem to get it out of the center." Ra Chen sat down on the edge of the bed. "What bothers me is the horn on its forehead. The horse in the picture book had no horns."

"No, sir."

"Then it must be a different species. It's not really a horse, Svetz. We'll have to send you back. It'll break our budget, Svetz."

"I disagree, sir—"

"Don't be so tanj polite."

"Then don't be so tanj stupid, sir." Svetz was *not* going back for another horse. "People who kept tame horses must have developed the habit of cutting off the horn when the animal was a pup. Why not? We all saw how dangerous that horn is. Much too dangerous for a domestic animal."

"Then why does our horse have a horn?"

"That's why I thought it was wild, the first time I saw it. I suppose they didn't start cutting off horns until later in history."

Ra Chen nodded in gloomy satisfaction. "I thought so too. Our problem is that the Secretary-General is just barely bright enough to notice that his horse has a horn, and the picture book horse doesn't. He's bound to blame me."

"Mmm." Svetz wasn't sure what was expected of him.

"I'll have to have the horn amputated."

"Somebody's bound to notice the scar," said Svetz.

"Tanj it, you're right. I've got enemies at court. They'd be only too happy to claim I'd mutilated the Secretary-General's pet." Ra Chen glared at Svetz. "All right, let's hear *your* idea."

Svetz was busy regretting. Why had he spoken? His vicious, beautiful horse, tamely docked of its killer horn . . . he had found the thought repulsive. His impulse had betrayed him. What could they do but remove the horn?

He had it, "Change the picture book, not the horse. A computer could duplicate the book in detail, but with a horn on every horse. Use the center computer, then wipe the tape afterward."

Morosely thoughtful, Ra Chen said, "That might work. I know someone who could switch the books." He looked up from under bushy black brows. "Of course, you'd have to keep quiet."

"Yes, sir."

"Don't forget." Ra Chen got up. "When you get out of the diagnostician, you start a four weeks vacation."

"I'm sending you back for one of these," Ra Chen told him four weeks later. He opened the bestiary. "We picked up the book in a public park around ten Post Atomic; left the kid who was holding it playing with a carborundum egg."

Svetz examined the picture. "That's *ugly*. That's really ugly. You're trying to balance the horse, right? The horse was so beautiful, you've got to have one of these or the universe goes off balance."

Ra Chen closed his eyes in pain. "Just go get us the Gila monster, Svetz. The Secretary-General wants a Gila monster."

"How big is it?"

They both looked at the illustration. There was no way to tell. "From the looks of it, we'd better use the *big* extension cage."

Svetz barely made it back that time. He was suffering from total exhaustion and extensive second-degree burns. The thing he brought back was thirty feet long, had vestigial bat-like wings, breathed fire, and didn't look very much like the illustration; but it was as close as anything he'd found.

The Secretary-General loved it.

"The sandwich man killer has struck again!"

*It is not going out on any limb to call Theodore Sturgeon the finest
artist science fiction has ever had. Others have said it before, notably
the respected sf critic James Blish. Sturgeon appeared in the very first
issue of F & SF (with a story called "The Hurkle Is a Happy Beast").
The story you are about to read was probably the most eagerly received
piece in our twentieth anniversary issue (October 1969).*

THE MAN WHO LEARNED LOVING

by Theodore Sturgeon

His name was Mensch; it once was a small joke between them,
and then it became a bitterness. "I wish to God I could have you
now the way you were," she said, "moaning at night and jumping up and walking around in the dark and never saying why, and
letting us go hungry and not caring how we lived or how we
looked. I used to bitch at you for it, but I never minded, not really.
I held still for it. I would've, just for always, because with it all you
did your own thing, you were a free soul."

"I've always done my own thing," said Mensch, "and I did so
tell you why."

She made a disgusted sound. "Who could understand all that?"
It was dismissal, an old one; something she had recalled and worked
over and failed to understand for years, a thing that made tiredness.
"And you used to love people—really love them. Like the time
that kid wiped out the fire hydrant and the street-light in front of
the house and you fought off the fuzz and the schlock lawyer and
the ambulance and everybody, and got him to the hospital and
wouldn't let him sign the papers because he was dazed. And turning
that cheap hotel upside down to find Victor's false teeth and
bring them to him after they put him in jail. And sitting all day in
the waiting room the time Mrs. What's-her-name went for her first
throat cancer treatment, so you could take her home, you didn't

even know her. There wasn't anything you wouldn't do for people."

"I've always done what I could. I didn't stop."

Scorn. "So did Henry Ford. Andrew Carnegie. The Krupp family. Thousands of jobs, billions in taxes for everybody. I know the stories."

"My story's not quite the same," he said mildly.

Then she said it all, without hate or passion or even much emphasis; she said in a burnt-out voice, "we loved each other and you walked out."

They loved each other. Her name was Fauna; it once was a small joke between them. Fauna the Animal and Mensch the Man, and the thing they had between them. "Sodom is a-cumen in," he misquoted Chaucer. "Lewd sing cuckold," (because she had a husband back there somewhere amongst the harpsichord lessons and the mildewed unfinished hooked rugs and the skeleton of a play and all the other abandoned projects in the attic of her life). She didn't get the reference. She wasn't bright—just loving. She was one of those people who waits for the right thing to come along and drops all others as soon as she finds out they aren't the main one. When someone like that gets the right thing, it's forever, and everyone says, my how you've changed. She hasn't changed.

But then when the right thing comes along, it doesn't work out, she'll never finish anything again. Never.

They were both very young when they met and she had a little house back in the woods near one of those resort towns that has a reputation for being touristy-artsy-craftsy and actually does have a sprinkling of real artists in and around it. Kooky people are more than tolerated in places like that providing only that a) they attract, or at least do not repel, the tourists and b) they never make any important money. She was a slender pretty girl who liked to be naked under loose floor-length gowns and take care of sick things as long as they couldn't talk—broken-wing birds and philodendrons and the like—and lots of music—lots of *kinds* of music; and cleverly doing things she wouldn't finish until the real thing came along. She had a solid title to the little house and a part-time job in the local frame shop; she was picturesque and undemanding and never got involved in marches and petitions and the like. She just believed in being kind to everyone around her and thought . . . well, that's not quite right. She hadn't ever thought it out all the way, but she *felt* that if you're kind to everyone the kindness will somehow spread over the world like a healing stain, and that's what you do about wars and greed and injustice. So she was an acceptable, almost approved fixture in the town even when they paved her dirt road and put the lamp-post and fire-hydrant in front of it.

Mensch came into this with long hair and a guitar strapped to his back, a head full of good books and a lot of very serious restlessness. He knew nothing about loving and Fauna taught him better than she knew. He moved in with Fauna the day after she discovered his guitar was tuned like a lute. He had busy hands too, and a way of finishing what he started, yes, and making a dozen more like them —beautifully designed kitchen pads for shopping lists made out of hand-rubbed local woods, which used adding-machine rolls and had a hunk of hacksaw-blade down at the bottom so you could neatly tear off a little or a lot, and authentic reproductions of fireplace bellows and apple-peelers and stuff like that which could be displayed in the shoppes (not stores, they were shoppes) on the village green, and bring in his share. Also he knew about transistors and double-helical gears and eccentric linkages and things like Wankels and fuel-cells. He fiddled around a lot in the back room with magnets and axles and colored fluids of various kinds, and one day he had an idea and began fooling with scissors and cardboard and some metal parts. It was mostly frame and a rotor, but it was made of certain things in a certain way. When he put it together the rotor began to spin, and he suddenly understood it. He made a very slight adjustment and the rotor, which was mostly cardboard, uttered a shrill rising sound and spun so fast that the axle, a ten-penny nail, chewed right through the cardboard bearings and the rotor took off and flew across the room, showering little unglued metal bits. He made no effort to collect the parts, but stood up blindly and walked into the other room. Fauna took one look at him and ran to him and held him: what is it? what's the matter? but he just stood there looking stricken until the tears began rolling down his cheeks. He didn't seem to know it.

That was when he began moaning suddenly in the middle of the night, jumping up and walking around in the dark. When she said years later that he would never tell her why, it was true, and it wasn't, because what he told her was that he had something in his head so important that certain people would kill him to get it, and certain other people would kill him to suppress it, and that he wouldn't tell her what it was because he loved her and didn't want her in danger. She cried a lot and said he didn't trust her, and he said he did, but he wanted to take care of her, not throw her to the wolves. He also said—and this is what the moaning and night-walking was all about—that the thing in his head could make the deserts bloom and could feed hungry people all over the world, but that if he let it loose it could be like a plague too, not because of what it was but because of what people would do with it; and the very first person who died because of it would die because of him, and he couldn't bear the idea of that. He really had a choice to make, but before he could make it he had to decide whether the death of one person was too great a price to pay for the happiness and security of millions, and then if the deaths of a thousand would be justified if it meant the end of poverty for all. He knew history and psychology and he had a mathematician's head as well as those cobbler's hands, and he knew damned well what would happen if he took this way or that. For example, he knew where he could unload the idea and all responsibility for it for enough money to keep him and Fauna—and a couple hundred close friends, if it came to that—in total luxury for the rest of their lives; all he would have to do would be to sign it away and see it buried forever in a corporate vault, for there were at least three industrial giants which would urgently bid against one another for the privilege.

Or kill him.

He also thought of making blueprints and scattering millions of copies over cities all over the world, and of finding good ethical scientists and engineers and banding them together into a firm which would manufacture and license the device and use it only for good things. Well you can do that with a new kind of rat-killer or sewing machine, but not with something so potent that it will change the face of the earth, eliminate hunger, smog, and the rape of raw materials—not when it will also eliminate the petro-chemical industry (except for dyes and plastics), the electric power companies, the internal combustion engine and everything involved in making it and fuelling it, and even atomic energy for most of its purposes.

Mensch tried his very best to decide not to do anything at all about it, which was the moaning and night-walking interval, and that just wouldn't work—the thing would not let him go. Then he decided what to do, and what he must do in order to do it. His first stop was at the town barbershop.

Fauna held still for this and for his getting a job at Flextronics, the town's light industry, which had Government contracts for small computer parts and which was scorned by the town's art, literary and library segment. The regular hours appalled her, and although he acted the same (he certainly didn't look the same) around the house, she became deeply troubled. She had never seen so much money as he brought in every payday, and didn't want to, and for the first time in her life had to get stubborn about patching and improvising and doing without instead of being able to blame poverty for it. The reasons she found now for living that way seemed specious even to her, which only made her stubborn about it, and more of a kook than ever. Then he bought a car, which seemed to her an immorality of sorts.

What tore it was when somebody told her he had gone to the town board meeting, which she had never done, and had proposed that the town pass ordinances against sitting on the grass on the village green, playing musical instruments on town thoroughfares, swimming at the town swimming hole after sundown, and finally, hiring more police. When she demanded an explanation he looked at her sadly for a long time, then would not deny it, would not discuss it, and moved out.

He got a clean room in a very square boarding house near the factory, worked like hell until he got his college credits straightened out, went to night school until he had another degree. He took to hanging around the Legion post on Saturday nights and drank a little beer and bought a lot of whiskey for other people. He learned a whole portfolio of dirty jokes and dispensed them carefully, two-thirds sex, one-third bathroom. Finally he took a leave of absence from his job, which was, by this time, section manager, and moved down the river to a college town where he worked full time on a post-graduate engineering degree while going to night school to study law. The going was very tough around then because he had to pinch every nickel to be able to make it and still keep his pants creased and his brown shoes shiny, which he did. He still found time to join the local church and became a member of the vestry board and a lay preacher, taking as his text the homilies from *Poor Richard's Almanac* and delivering them (as did their author) as if he believed every word.

When it was time he redesigned his device, not with cardboard and glue, but with machined parts that were 70% monkey-puzzle—mechanical motions that cancelled each other, and wiring which energized coils which shorted themselves out. He patented parts and certain groupings of parts, and finally the whole contraption. He then took his degrees and graduate degrees, his published scholarly papers, his patents and his short hair-cut, together with a letter of introduction from his pastor, to a bank, and borrowed enough to buy into a failing company which made portable conveyor belts. His device was built into the drive segment, and he went on the road to sell the thing. It sold very well. It should. A six-volt automobile battery would load coal with that thing for a year without needing replacement or recharging, and no wonder, because the loading was being powered by that little black lump in the drive segment, which, though no bigger than a breadbox, and requiring no fuel, would silently and powerfully spin a shaft until the bearings wore out.

It wasn't too long before the competition was buying Mensch's loaders and tearing them down to see where all that obscene efficiency was coming from. The monkey-puzzle was enough to defeat most of them, but one or two bright young men, and a grizzled oldster or so were able to realize that they were looking at something no bigger than a breadbox which would turn a shaft indefinitely without fuel, and to wonder what things would be likely with this gadget under the hood of a car or in the nacelles of aircraft, or pumping water in the desert, or generating light and power 'way back in the hills and jungles without having to build roads or railways or to string powerlines. Some of these men found their way to Mensch. Either he hired them and tied them up tight with ropes of gold and fringe benefits, or had them watched and dissuaded, or discredited, or, if need be, ruined.

Inevitably someone was able to duplicate the Mensch effect, but by that time Mensch had a whole office building full of lawyers with their pencils sharpened and their instructions ready. The shrewd operator who had duplicated the effect, and who had sunk everything he had and could borrow into retooling an engine factory for it, found himself in such a snarl of infringement, torts, ceases-and-desists, and prepaid royalty demands that he sold his plant at cost to Mensch and gratefully accepted a job managing it. And he was only the first.

The military moved in at about this point, but Mensch was ready for them and their plans to take over his patents and holdings as a national resource. He let himself be bunted higher and higher in the chain of command, while his refusals grew stronger and stronger and the threats greater and greater, until he emerged at the top of the company of the civilian who commanded them all. This meeting was brought about by a bishop, for never in all these busy years did Mensch overlook his weekly duty at the church of his choice, nor his tithes, nor his donations of time for an occasional Vacation Bible School or picnic or bazaar. And Mensch, on this pinnacle of wealth, power and respectability, was able to show the President the duplicate set of documents he had placed in a Swiss bank, which, on the day his patents were pre-empted by the military, would donate them to research institutes in Albania and points north and east. That was the end of that.

The following year a Mensch-powered car won the Indy. It wasn't as fast as the Granatelli entry; it just voomed around and around the brickyard without making any stops at all. There was, of course, a certain amount of static for a while, but the inevitable end was that the automobile industry capitulated, and

with it the fossil-fuel people. Electric light and power had to follow and, as the gas and steam and diesel power sources obsolesce
and are replaced by Mensch prime-movers, the atomic plants await
their turn.

It was right after the Indianapolis victory that Mensch donated
his blueprints to Albania anyway—after all, he had never said he
wouldn't—and they showed up about the same time in Hong Kong
and quickly reached the mainland. There was a shrill claim from the
Soviet Union that the Mensch Effect had been discovered in the
19th century by Siolkovsky, who had set it aside because he was
more interested in rockets, but even the Russians couldn't keep that
up for long without laughing along with the audience, and they fell
to outstripping all other nations in development work. No monkey-
puzzle on earth can survive this kind of effort—monkey-puzzles
need jungles of patent law to live and thrive—and it was not long
before the Soviets (actually, it was a Czech scientist, which is the
same thing, isn't it? Well, the Soviets said it was) were able to pro-
claim that they had improved and refined the device to a simple
frame supporting one moving part, the rotor, each made, of course,
of certain simple substances which, when assembled, began to work.
It was, of course, the same frame and rotor with which Mensch, in
terror and tears, had begun his long career, and the Czech, that is,
Soviet "refinement" was, like all else, what he had predicted and
aimed himself toward.

For now there wasn't a mechanics magazine in the world, nor
hardly a tinkerer's workshop anywhere, that didn't begin turning
out Mensch rotors. Infringements occurred so widely that even
Mensch's skyscraper-full of legal-eagles couldn't have begun to stem
the flood. And indeed they did not try, because—

For the second time in modern history (the first was an extraor-
dinary man named Kemal Ataturk) a man of true national-dicta-
tor stature set his goal, achieved it, and abdicated. It didn't matter
one bit to Mensch that the wiser editorialists, with their knowledgeable index fingers placed alongside their noses, were pointing out
that he had defeated himself, shattered his own empire by extending its borders, and that by releasing his patents into the public
domain he was making an empty gesture to the inevitable. Mensch

knew what he had done, and why, and what other people thought
of it just did not matter.

"What does matter," he said to Fauna in her little house by the
old fire hydrant and the quaint street-lamp, "is that there isn't a
kraal in Africa or a hamlet in Asia that can't pump water and plow
land and heat and light its houses by using a power plant simple
enough to be built by any competent mechanic anywhere. There
are little ones to rock cradles and power toys and big ones to light
whole cities. They pull trains and sharpen pencils, and they need
no fuel. Already desalted Mediterranean water is pouring into the
northern Sahara; there'll be whole new cities there, just as there were
five thousand years ago. In ten years the air all over the earth will
be measurably cleaner, and already the demand for oil is down so
much that offshore drilling is almost completely stopped. 'Have'
and 'have-not' no longer means what it once meant, because everyone has access to cheap power. And that's why I did it, don't you
see?" He really wanted very much to make her understand.

"You cut your hair," she said bitterly. "You wore those awful
shoes and went to church and got college degrees and turned into a
—a typhoon."

"Tycoon," he corrected absently. "Ah, but Fauna, listen: I
wanted to be listened to. The way to get what I wanted was short
hair, was brown shoes, was published post-graduate papers, was the
banks and businesses and government and all of those things that
were already there for me to use."

"You didn't need all that. I think you just wanted to move
things and shake things and be in the newspapers and history
books. You could've made your old motor right here in this house
and showed to people and sold it and stayed here and played the
lute, and it would have been the same thing."

"No, there you're wrong," said Mensch. "Do you know what kind
of a world we live in? We live in a world where, if a man came up
with a sure cure for cancer, and if that man were found to be married to his sister, his neighbors would righteously burn down his
house and all his notes. If a man built the most beautiful tower in
the country, and that man later begins to believe that Satan should

be worshipped, they'll blow up his tower. I know a great and moving book written by a woman who later went quite crazy and wrote crazy books, and nobody will read her great one any more. I can name three kinds of mental therapy that could have changed the face of the earth, and in each one the men who found it went on to insane Institutes and so-called religions and made fools of themselves—dangerous fools at that—and now no one will look at their really great early discoveries. Great politicians have been prevented from being great statesmen because they were divorced. And I wasn't going to have the Mensch machine stolen or buried or laughed at and forgotten just because I had long hair and played the lute. You know, it's easy to have long hair and play the lute and be kind to people when everyone else around you is doing it. It's a much harder thing to be one who does something first, because then you have to pay a price, you get jeered at and they shut you out."

"So you joined them," she accused.

"I used them," he said flatly. "I used every road and path that led to where I was going, no matter who built it or what it was built for."

"And you paid your price," she all but snarled. "Millions in the bank, thousands of people ready to fall on their knees if you snap your fingers. Some price. You could have had love."

He stood up then and looked at her. Her hair was much thinner now, but still long and fine. He reached for it, lifted some. It was white. He let it go.

He thought of fat Biafran babies and clean air and un-polluted beaches, cheaper food, cheaper transportation, cheaper manufacturing and maintenance, more land to lessen the pressures and hysteria during the long slow process of population control. What had moved him to deny himself so much, to rebel, to move and shake and shatter the status quo the way he had, rather than conforming—conforming!—to long hair and a lute? *You could have had love.*

"But I did," he said; and then, knowing she would never, could never understand, he got in his silent fuelless car and left.

Tony Morphett has written a story about garbage disposal, dead cats, a hard nosed and amiable engineer named Rafferty, a planet orbiting Vega; and it is one of the funniest stories of first contact with aliens that we've ever read.

LITTERBUG

by Tony Morphett

Rafferty stood six foot two, was built like a fullback and had a reputation for gentleness except on certain specific occasions. This was one of those occasions. He had got home, thumbed the lock on his front door, and from a habit dating back to less civilized periods in his life, he had gone inside without turning the light on.

And had known that in the dark house he wasn't alone.

It could have been smell, it could have been sound, it could have been that other thing which was just *the feel*, and which had saved his life on occasion. But he knew they were there, and he moved fast, he moved silent from the front door. They must have heard the lock, so the area of the lock was somewhere not to be.

"That you, Joe?"

A voice from the laboratory. It must have been his not turning on the light. A man coming through his own front door turns the light on. Therefore the voice thought that the noise had been made by another of the intruders. Rafferty smiled. The intruders were fortunate that they didn't see that smile. It was not at all a nice smile.

Now he knew there were two of them, otherwise the one who had spoken would not have pinned the noise source to one name. Now, at the laboratory door, he could see one of them, partly silhouetted by a torch held in the left hand while the right hand moved across the face of a control panel.

Rafferty had a reputation for gentleness, but under some circumstances he had no social graces whatsoever, and when he saw someone else's hand on his laboratory pet, Emily Post went out the window and Rafferty turned from an engineer into a hunting primate. A very fast-moving hunting primate.

It is not true that the man didn't know what hit him. He said later that he *did* know what had hit him. He said it was the roof. It was actually the edge of Rafferty's hand. Rafferty had tackled him, they had gone down together, Rafferty's right hand had moved twice. Once up, once down. Then *the feel* had taken over, and Rafferty had rolled away just fast enough for the second man's blackjack to strike his shoulder, not the base of his skull. Every man got one chance with Rafferty, and that had been Joe's. Still lying on the floor, he scooped the man's feet from under him, then realized he had caught himself a pro. The man struck at him again on the way down. Rafferty blocked with his left forearm, had to block again as the man's bladed left hand came into action, and then felt an increased respect as his opponent flicked away the blackjack and struck for Rafferty's solar plexus with a right forearm-hand-extended-finger assembly as straight and solid as a quarterstaff. What Rafferty thought had saved him was his own right hook which laid his opponent out at the same time as Rafferty started to concentrate on unknotting his stomach. At least, he thought, he'd be on his feet before they were conscious.

And then the light went on. For an engineer, he had made one assumption too many.

There had been three of them.

It was infuriating. He could have taken the third one, gun and all, if there'd been anything in his belly except a black gaping pain which would not let him stand. The slight, grey-haired man with glasses didn't look as if he knew one end of his 44 magnum from the other. Which worried Rafferty more than if he'd looked like a killer who wouldn't let it go off by accident.

"Mr. Rafferty, I must ask you to abstain from further violence. I realize that, as a citizen, you have a perfect right to be irritated at this intrusion on your privacy. But please do not be violent."

Rafferty swallowed so hard it straightened out most of the knots. "That is the craziest speech I've ever heard a burglar make."

"Unfortunately," the little grey man with the big gun continued, "we felt it necessary to have a little more information before we approached you more . . ." he cleared his throat, "ah, formally."

"We haven't," said Rafferty, "even been introduced."

"Since, however, you returned as you did . . . somewhat prematurely Mr. Rafferty . . ."

"Next time I come through my own door I'll knock."

"I think we had better come into the open. I'd like you to accompany us if you would."

Rafferty's deep breath straightened out the rest of the knots. "Look, you're holding the gun, and that makes me very polite. But may I put it this way? You break into my house, you tamper with expensive lab equipment, one of your men turns my solar plexus into a disaster area, and *then* you ask ever so politely for me to accompany you. Who the hell are you? And apart from the gun, why should I go anywhere?"

"We all work for the government. My department . . . well it doesn't really *have* a name. These two gentlemen," he nodded to his now-conscious companions, "work for a rather better-known bureau. Perhaps you could . . . ?"

The two men produced leather cases. Flipped them open. Rafferty looked at the metal shields. He must, he decided, be in better fighting trim than he had thought. "All right, I'll come along."

The little man handed the gun to the operative called Joe. "I'll have to telephone. There are two people who'll want to meet you."

Rafferty lowered himself into the chair. The office was comfortable, but there was nothing soft about it. The little grey man sat at the desk. He had introduced himself as Watson. The other two men in the room he knew from reputation, technical journals and television: Professor Clemens, a Nobel prize winner in physics, and Dr. Simpson Navarre, one of the government's chief scientific advisers. Watson looked up from a slim file on his desk. "Now, Mr. Rafferty, what we wish to talk to you about is your, ah, matter transmitter."

"I don't have one. I make garbage disposal units."

Professor Clemens leaned forward. "Mr. Rafferty, let's save a bit of time. You *call* them garbage disposal units. Now, as I understand it, a conventional garbage disposal unit is like a mincing machine.

You put matter in one end and it comes out the other end ground
up fine enough to be washed away."

"Do you know," said Rafferty, "I don't believe I've ever dis-
cussed garbage with a Nobel prize winner before?"

"That'll be enough, Rafferty! You're in trouble enough without
impudence!" Watson sounded angry. Rafferty diagnosed a chronic
case of lack of sense of humor.

Rafferty stood up. "Good evening."

"You'll . . ."

Navarre turned on the grey government man. "Be quiet, Watson!"
Navarre went on more quietly. "We wish to talk to Mr. Rafferty
about garbage."

Clemens joined in the smile. "Garbage *disposal*. In a conventional
unit you put matter in the form of, say, orange peel in one end,
and you get matter in the form of slush out the other. In your unit,
Mr. Rafferty, you put matter in one end, and *nothing* comes out the
other end. In fact there would appear to *be* no other end."

"Well that seems to me to be an advantage," Rafferty said. "It
saves water, prevents clogging . . ."

"Mr. Rafferty," Navarre broke in, "please don't play the hillbilly.
You know exactly what we mean. *Where does the garbage go?*"

Rafferty smiled. "I don't know."

"You don't know?" Clemens was out of his chair. "You must
know! You built it. You manufacture it. You must know where it
goes!"

"Does it work?" Rafferty said.

"Yes," Clemens said tightly, "it works."

"Is it a good garbage disposal unit?"

"Yes. It is a good garbage disposal unit. Which is like opening
a bottle on a metal edge in a Polaris sub, and calling the submarine
a good bottle opener."

"I asked is it a good garbage disposal unit?"

"All right, I agree it's a good garbage disposal unit."

"And I," Rafferty said, "am an engineer. It works."

Watson leaned forward. "Mr. Rafferty, I think you should be
informed of a few things. For a start, if we want to, we can lock
you up and throw away the key."

"You're the one who threatened me before." Rafferty sounded quiet and unamused.

"You have endangered the security of this country and the security of the Free World by applying for a patent on a device which has immense military potential. When your patent application was rejected because you couldn't explain the principle, you went ahead anyway, manufactured your device, and now you're selling it to anyone with the money to pay for it. That means anyone in a number of embassies which even *you* ought to be able to name. In short, Mr. Rafferty, you are a traitor."

Rafferty's chair was empty and Rafferty was leaning across the government man's desk. Rafferty took Watson by the shoulders and squeezed in a way which Rafferty thought was gentle. "Mr. Watson," he crooned, "you are no longer holding a gun. Unless you are, never say that again. Understand?" He let go. He walked back to his chair. Watson tried to get his shoulders back into place.

Navarre cloaked his smile. "I can understand your resentment, Mr. Rafferty, but what Mr. Watson meant was that you might have new ideas . . ."

"I did."

Navarre put his head in his hands like a man who had heard it before. "Go on."

"I tried it on the army, navy and air force and a set of very well-qualified young men told me my math wasn't as good as it might be, and anyway the effect was theoretically impossible."

"But didn't you show them a working model?"

"Have you ever tried to demonstrate a perpetual motion machine to a government physicist? Or a mermaid to a government marine biologist? Or telekinesis to a government psychologist? The majority of scientists want to ask only those questions they can answer. The fact that they could throw my math was enough. The fact that I didn't have even a bachelor's degree didn't help much."

"You don't have a degree?" Watson's spectacles were twin barrels. "You mean you were lying to us when you called yourself an engineer?"

Clemens smiled. "I shouldn't worry too much about degrees, Mr.

Watson. Thomas Alva Edison didn't have one either, and it was probably the saving of him."

Rafferty looked across at Clemens. He decided he could possibly warm to this man.

Navarre, the government adviser, was still looking unhappy. Rafferty guessed that other people in the army, navy and air force would be looking even more unhappy the next day. Navarre spoke. "So we've done it again. We'll just have to see what we can salvage. Presumably, Mr. Rafferty, you weren't trying to make a garbage disposal unit when you started?"

"No. I was trying to do what the burglar over there suggested," he said, nodding at Watson. "I was trying to push matter from one place to another without actually carrying it. A man paddling a log and a man riding a rocket, they're not different in *kind*, you're only talking about an improvement in technique. I was looking for a difference in *kind*."

"I've got scientists who say it's impossible," Watson said.

Rafferty didn't look very nice when his eyes narrowed. "Mr. Watson, in my lab I've got a unit just big enough for a man your size. Would you like to try it out and then talk about possibilities and impossibilities?"

"So you started out to make a matter transmitter," Navarre said. "How did it turn into a garbage disposal unit?"

"Money. As you can probably read in that file there, my factory's for repetition engineering, and this thing's just a hobby of mine. The firm makes enough so it can be a high-priced hobby, and there have been economic by-products in the past, but still, so far it's been a hobby. Well, I ran into a deadend. The transmitter, the matter transmitter works fine. It's, uh, the *receiver* end that still has some bugs to iron out."

"What bugs?" Clemens said.

"One very simple one. It doesn't work. The transmitter's fine. You put something in, you throw the power, it goes away. It doesn't disintegrate, burn, atomize, or get washed down a drain. It just goes away. Now it ought to be going into the receiver. But it doesn't. It goes somewhere else."

"Where?"

"I don't know. It must be going somewhere. I used to watch the newspapers. I used to have this nightmare that an explorer was going to come back and say that he'd found the Lost Valley of the Incas and it was filled to the brim with orange peel and beer cans and coffee grounds. Now I think the stuff's not ending up on this planet at all. The odds are it's in deep space somewhere. It's going somewhere in space-time, anyway. I'm conventional enough not to believe that all that matter's just being destroyed. So I had a matter transmitter but no matter receiver. I needed development money, a lot of it, so I went to the government. Whose representatives, Dr. Navarre, told me very politely that I had shot my lid." Rafferty lit a cigarette. "Now that didn't alter the fact I still needed money for development, and the thing it worked best at was getting rid of things. Which to me said garbage disposal. So I put in about a dozen fail-safe devices to stop tampering idiots from losing arms, and I got it on the market this week, and the orders look very nice indeed. No status-home is going to be without one."

"The government will recompense you, but we've got to get every single one back." Watson winced at Navarre's use of the word "recompense," but nodded.

Rafferty smiled. "I wish you luck then. They're already distributed coast-to-coast, and our sales are running into thousands."

It wasn't until a week later that the garbage started coming back.

Rafferty always ate breakfast in his laboratory, because that was the place in the house the best morning sun got to. It was also the place in the house where he felt most comfortable.

He finished eating, put a toast crust and two egg shells into the rind of a grapefruit, and threw the lot into the maw of his big experimental Watson-sized disposal unit. He switched the power on and turned away to pour himself some coffee.

Sproiiing.

Rafferty looked back. His unit had never said *sproiiing* before. He was in time to see the grapefruit rind, the two egg shells and the toast crust come flying through the opening. Something else followed them.

On the domestic models there were spring-loaded doors and an automatic shut-off if they were opened. Rafferty's lab model ran to power rather than to refinements like doors and idiot-proofing.

Rafferty went to the machine. The power was still on. The grey vortex in the transmission area was as it should have been. Rafferty had a peach left over from his breakfast. He put it on the conveyor belt. The conveyor belt bore the peach into the grey vortex, where it disappeared. Rafferty waited.

Squelch!

Rafferty straightened up, wiping peach out of his eyes. Rafferty was a gentle man and would never have laid hands on his own invention, and besides there wasn't an axe in the laboratory. He left the machine for the moment, and looked at what had come out the first time. He seemed to remember seeing something fly out that he hadn't thrown in.

He picked it up. It resembled a cat and it resembled a four-legged bunch of broccoli, and it wasn't either. It was dead, and among the things it *didn't* resemble was a bunch of violets. Rafferty got a towel and a carving knife. The towel he tied round his mouth and nose. His past included being a slaughterman and skin-diving for a marine biologist, so he didn't think anyone would mind if he had a first, semi-professional cut.

He had made three cuts and decided it wasn't cat or broccoli, fish or steer, when the phone rang.

"Rafferty."

"Jim here, from the factory. Two of the units on the test bench. Garbage is coming *back* through them."

"Other stuff as well? Stuff that doesn't look like . . . well normal sorts of garbage?"

"Well, I don't know, what some people throw out, others'd live on for a week. I mean, what's *normal* garbage?"

"But you're just getting back what you're putting in?"

"Yeah."

"How fast?"

"Some oozes back, some flies back."

"Any pattern?"

"Not yet."

"I'll keep in touch."

He hung up. Looked at the broccoli cat again. No pattern. At least he'd have something to throw at the first biologist who told him that a broccoli cat was theoretically impossible and that his DNA spelling grades were on the other side of illiterate.

Then he took an apple, and tossed it into the grey vortex. Then instantly switched off the power. And waited. Nothing. So when he switched off, the stuff couldn't get back. Logical, except that it was illogical for it to come back at all.

He sat on the stool at his drawing board, and he cracked his scarred knuckles for a while and stared at the wall like he was going to take it apart. Then he swung on the stool, and leaned back, and took a piece of paper tape in his right hand. Put one twist into it, and held the two ends between finger and thumb, making a Moebius strip. He knew that the pad of his finger and the pad of his thumb were touching different parts of the same side of the strip. That they were both twelve inches and one millimeter apart. He threw the tape away. Somewhere . . .

Where?

He looked out the laboratory window. Then he whistled as he went to the lab unit, turned it on, then went to the bookshelves on the wall and selected a volume. Then watched as the grey vortex of the unit slowly enveloped the book of maps of the night sky as seen from earth.

The phone rang.

"Rafferty?"

"Yes. That's Watson, is it?"

"We want to see you, Rafferty. There's been a complication."

"You mean the garbage is coming back through *your* test units too?"

"Not on the phone, Rafferty, not on the phone. You'll be picked up in five minutes."

"I've things to do at the factory."

"Five minutes, Rafferty."

Rafferty hung up, and then phoned his factory, and made a priority order for delivery to him that afternoon.

The biologist looked up from his examination of the broccoli cat. He smiled. "It's an extremely convincing fake, gentlemen."

"Fake?" Navarre's hands were tightening.

"Well, of course, nothing like this exists."

"Thank you, Professor." After the man had gone, Navarre used the telephone. "Send me a *real* biologist. If the ancestors of that one had been as adaptable as he is, he would now be a sea squirt which knew that free oxygen was a poison and that mobility and limbs were something an adult grew out of." He sat down.

Rafferty grinned at him. "Any other . . . fakes coming back through the units?"

"We're sifting the material as fast as we can. It appears that there's some vegetable material that's . . . well, unknown, but that . . . thing of yours is the first . . . is it an animal?"

"Roughly speaking, yes. Can you find out for me what it breathes and eats?"

Watson cleared his throat. "Now your theory, Rafferty, is that you've somehow . . . punched I think was your word, punched a hole in space-time, and the other end of the hole is on some planet circling another star."

"Yes, I think so."

"But even if we accept the principle of punching holes in space-time," Clemens said, "the odds against finding the other ends of those holes on another planet in another solar system, well, the odds are, if you'll pardon the expression, astronomical."

"I shan't pardon the expression," Rafferty said, "but odds like that have come off before. And if you don't believe they've come off this time, then tell me where on this planet the broccoli cat comes from."

"But why should the thing come back through the machine at all?" Watson couldn't bring himself to call it a broccoli cat.

"You ever live in a slum, Mr. Watson? I guess not." Rafferty had his grin tucked down at the corners. "Well you throw garbage onto someone else's back landing, they'll throw it back, uh? And some people, they get mad, they'll throw a dead cat with it." Rafferty's hands were palms up, and more pious than his eyes. "It's terrible what some people'll do when they get mad."

Navarre had a grin of his own. "Well, I've had the problem of First Contact on my hands for three years now, and I never thought it'd be garbage over the fence."

"And that, Mr. Navarre, is because you've never lived in a slum either. But where you can put a dead cat, you can put other things. And I thought even a cat thrower's not going to throw back something that looks important. So that's why I sent him the star maps."

"What star maps?" Navarre was quiet, cold.

"You know the sort of book. Amateur astronomers use them. They show the night sky, northern and southern skies as they are at the various months of the year. I sent it through my lab unit this morning. Nearest thing I could give them to an address."

The way Watson looked, Rafferty should have had a snakebite kit on him. "You're under arrest, Rafferty. Last week I called you a traitor. Today you proved it. Gave them our address, did you? Do you expect them to pay you?"

"Pay me, Watson?"

"When they invade."

"No one's going to be invading, Mr. Watson. They can't be closer than four light-years. They're probably further."

"They can get a dead cat here. They can get an army here in the same way."

"But, Watson," and Rafferty smiled, "how do you know the cat was dead when it left there?"

"What do you mean?"

"Maybe it was alive, and got killed on the trip through."

"But who'd throw a live animal into a thing like that? Why, it'd be . . ."

"Please don't say *inhuman*, Watson, I don't think I could bear it." Navarre turned to Rafferty. "You mean you don't think someone could go through there alive?"

"I don't know. Until I knew there was something at the other end, I wasn't very keen about trying it. Couldn't see myself making a laughing exit into hard vacuum and absolute zero. Or into the center of a sun. But now? Well the odds are better. But I still say that there's tourism and tourism."

Watson was putting down his phone. "The general will be here in one monent."

"General?"

"Rafferty's action has made this a military matter."

The general heard them through and then refilled his corncob pipe. "Should have been in on this at the jump. But it's not irretrievable. One thing, we've got no problem delivering the bombs."

"The bombs!" Rafferty stood up.

"Of course. Now they know where we are, we'll have to exterminate them. You say a grapefruit rind came back through your unit. Could just as easily have been a grenade. Or an H-bomb. We have to hit them first. Before they hit us."

"But they've shown no signs . . ."

"Can you assure me they won't?"

"I don't know them!"

"Neither do I, Mr. Rafferty, neither do I." He turned to Watson. "I'll be recommending a simultaneous, all-out attack. Enough to take an earth-size planet apart."

Professor Clemens leaned forward. "General, I must protest! This is our first chance to contact what might be an intelligent alien species, and . . ."

"You're not a military man, Professor. You wouldn't understand."

Rafferty was sitting again, and looking relaxed. Which was a danger sign. "General, I'm not a military man either, but I guess it'd take a lot of power to smash an earth-size planet."

"An immense amount," Clemens said before the general could answer.

"And we know these units provide a two-way tunnel," Rafferty continued. "Now Watson, how many units have you got back so far?"

"Fifteen hundred, give or take twenty. As at close of business yesterday."

"Leaves about four thousand still in the field. Now supposing you used about a thousand in your attack . . ."

"I'm afraid that's classified . . ."

"Just supposing. Now these four thousand you haven't got back yet, if any were open, that is, switched on, during the attack, it'd be just like pumping high pressure steam into a sieve. You would literally be getting your own back. You were talking about assurances, General. Can you assure me they'd all be closed? Even if you made it an order? Can you assure me that among four thousand human beings there wouldn't be some who'd forget to turn off, or who wouldn't hear the radio and TV announcements, or some who wouldn't see it as a way to buck authority, or some who'd just think it would be a good idea to blow this planet at the same time? I think until you get all the sets back, General, and I'll make damn sure you don't, I think until then we'd better try talking to them. So I'd like to see my laboratory unit. I left it on. I just wonder whether the postman's been there."

"But you're under arrest," Watson said.

"Watson," said Navarre, "he's released into my custody. And if you want to find out if I have the authority, I suggest you check higher up. Now, Mr. Rafferty, we'll go check that letter box."

The sheets were probably synthetic, but they had the feel of an extremely thin leather. The markings on them were obviously writing, but which way it ran was by no means obvious. Rafferty revised his original thought. Was it so obvious that it was writing? At least they had shut Watson up for a while. He seemed hypnotized by the pale grey sheets with their black markings.

Clemens looked at Navarre. "Black on grey? Implies brighter light on their world?"

Navarre shrugged. "Could be. I wouldn't be in a hurry to assume anything. They may not see in the same range we do. Do we know that it's writing? Do we even know whether the information is in the black marks or in what we'd call the background?"

Watson came out of his trance. "But you notice one thing. You sent them star maps. They've sent back something which could easily be the equivalent of the *Daily News*. Hardly, Mr. Rafferty, a fair exchange."

Rafferty shrugged. "You're all educated men. Which of you has a book of star charts in your home?" Only Navarre nodded. "One in three. And you three are scarcely representative of humanity in general. My guess is that he's sent through what he figures is a similar artifact as a sign of good faith. I think we can expect some more." The four of them looked at the machine. Nothing happened.

Nothing happened for another three quarters of an hour. Then the grey vortex at the back of the machine changed. Clemens was watching at the time, and he called the others over. They gathered, and watched as the sheets emerged from the vortex and piled in the transmission area of the machine. Rafferty switched off, reached in and got them, and then switched on again. He spread the sheets on the bench. They were star maps.

Rafferty looked at Watson. "Looks like someone with common sense got to their soldiers and bureaucrats, Mr. Watson. It seems they've sent us their address." He turned to Navarre. "How much astronomy do your computers know, Dr. Navarre?"

"Enough." Navarre grinned. "I'll get the boys working on it. By the way, you can stay here if you like. I don't think we'll lock you up just yet."

Rafferty smiled, and stretched. "Guess I could use a little lab-time anyway. Might even be able to get the bugs out of it. Seems the transmitter's a mite overpowered."

"There'll be a guard round your house," Navarre said. "They won't bother you. Some of our technical people will be over later. We might have to move you out of the house altogether in the next week or so, but we can leave that until later."

They left Rafferty alone with his machine. As soon as they were gone, he rang his factory. "That set-up I asked for this morning. Send it over."

Then he fed some picture magazines into the unit, and was busy at his bench until the arrival of some crates from the factory.

He opened them, and from the contents quickly assembled a disposal unit. From the last box he took the Ni-Cad batteries he had ordered. If you couldn't expect the same power supply in different countries on your own planet, to be optimistic about standard power on someone else's wasn't optimism, it was idiocy. When he finished, he had a self-powered unit big enough to send a book or a cat, but not big enough for a saber-toothed tiger. And the whole thing was small enough to put through the feed jaw of his big laboratory unit.

And it was too heavy to lift. Rafferty's prodigies of Anglo-Saxon four-letter expression should by rights have produced the smell of ozone. Then he stopped talking, and smiled. Outside his house, he approached one of his guards.

"Can you help me with something?"

The guard raised a hand to one of his colleagues to cover for him. "Sure. What?"

"Just something I want to lift."

The guard followed him inside. Together they manhandled the small unit into the lab machine. They watched, Rafferty with satisfaction, the guard with awe, as it disappeared into the grey vortex.

"Never seen the inside of one of those things before. Kinda pretty, isn't it?"

"It works," Rafferty said. Then he smiled his gentle smile. "Which means I think it's kinda pretty."

"Where's it go?"

"I'll tell you when I find out," Rafferty said.

"Vega," Navarre said. "A planet orbiting round Vega."

"Vega," Rafferty repeated. "How far's that?"

"Twenty-six and a half light-years."

"A long way." It was a very rare thing for Rafferty to feel small. And even when he did feel small, Rafferty never said so. "It makes me feel small," Rafferty said.

"It's a long way to throw a dead cat."

Rafferty joined in the smile. "Broccoli cat. Do we know what it breathes and eats yet?"

"Breathes an oxygen-nitrogen mixture. Slightly richer in oxygen, they think. Food? The planet's got a carbon-hydrogen cycle, but they suggest you don't try eating his brother if you find him. Apparently there's a metal distribution on the planet that . . ."

And he stopped, because at that moment the window opened in the air.

Watson hurriedly backed behind the laboratory's central bench. Clemens walked closer to it like a man mesmerized.

Navarre stared.

Rafferty smiled the smile that Watson had grown to know and loathe.

It was a grey, shimmering window in the air, big enough for a book, too small for a saber-toothed tiger. And out of it things started to flow. Sheets of what they thought was writing, small objects which could have been cups, toys, anything at all, and finally what looked like a magazine. The flow stopped, the window irised in on itself, and vanished. Rafferty picked up the thing that looked like a magazine. Every page was devoted to a single picture. What was pictured was a . . . creature. Humanoid enough if you didn't define the term too closely, residual feathery scales, and nothing else. Rafferty turned from the magazine to one of the other sheets, where there was a picture of a similar creature, except that this one was wearing what could have been called clothes. Rafferty grinned and turned to Watson, handing him the magazine. "I think you should have this for your files. It's the first known example of the interstellar delivery of a . . . girlie magazine."

Watson looked at three of the pictures, snapped the magazine shut and then in a way which Rafferty found disconcerting, blushed. "It appears," Watson said, "that at the other end we have a Vegan version of Mr. Rafferty."

Navarre's voice was cold. "At the other end of *what*, Rafferty?"

"How do you mean?"

"These things didn't come out of *your* machine, Rafferty. What was that we saw in the air?"

"Oh, that? I sent 'em through a small unit."

"You what!" Watson came round the bench to Navarre. There were tears in his eyes. "Please, Dr. Navarre, you must let me have him. Just a simple firing squad, nothing elaborate, nothing elaborate, just a simple, simple, simple . . ." He wandered away into a corner.

"Why did you do it, Rafferty?" Navarre was beginning to sound old.

"He'd been polite enough to send his address. Figured I'd send him something so he could get in touch when he wanted, instead of having to wait for me to open the tunnel."

"Rafferty, you're going to come with us."

"Sure, but can I send him a copy of *Playboy* first?"

"If you must."

Two days later they came to him in his cell. It looked like a comfortably furnished hotel room, but as far as Rafferty was concerned, anything he couldn't get out of was a cell.

Navarre opened the conversation. "Rafferty, you're coming back home."

"I'm quite comfortable here, thanks."

"Nevertheless, you're coming home."

Rafferty detected a hardening of Navarre's attitude. It was an effect he had had the opportunity of studying in many other people he had come into contact with. "Why?"

"Because it appears you're the only man who has more than a mechanic's knowledge of these things. On your feet."

Rafferty shrugged. Navarre had disappointed him. The only point on which Rafferty's knowledge of his device was wider than that of his highly prized mechanics was that Rafferty knew that by guess and by the seat of his faded levis and by fiddling and by *the feel,* he had made the thing work. He had tried to explain to Navarre that this didn't mean theoretical knowledge. He had told Navarre that Edison hadn't known what electricity was. Navarre still wouldn't believe that Rafferty was simply what he said he was: an engineer.

So Rafferty shrugged, and followed Navarre out of his comfortable cell.

Now his home itself was a cell, but Rafferty found he didn't mind much. He was getting to know his Vegan neighbor, and the anthropologists who came round to exchange artifacts with the Vegans were good company.

The next three months were busy. Although the air was right and the temperatures and gravities matched closely enough to be tolerable, small animals sent through the machines died quickly of sicknesses from which they had no immunities. So far, neither side was willing to send through an ambassador, only to have him die of a xeno-analogue to a cold in the nose or a splinter under the nail. Fortunately, something in the matter-shift prevented an exchange of atmospheres, but after the first experimental animal died, they took to freezing and sealing off the carcasses.

In his time, Rafferty had made many strange friendships, and now he was getting on passably well with the Vegan whose home contained the other end of the tunnel created by the lab unit. Rafferty called the Vegan Kelly because he couldn't manage the

mixture of clicks, groans and diphthongs that the Vegan had put
onto tape on the tape recorder they had sent him. In the three
months, he and Kelly had established a kind of basic picture and
written form of communication, and they used it to send messages
back and forth after hours, like two rather unskilled radio hams.

So he half suspected he knew what Navarre was talking about
when the government scientific adviser arrived, almost choking on
his anger.

"Rafferty! What have you done to us now?"

"What do you mean?"

"We've got reports of three more windows. That means the Vegans have got three more machines. Did you make them and send
them through this?"

"I'm a lot of things, Dr. Navarre," Rafferty said with some dignity,
"but I am not a goddamn altruist! And as long as you're impound-
ing everything that comes through, there's no way of their paying.
So of course I didn't send them any."

"Well, they've got them. How?"

"I admit I sent them the plans," said Rafferty. "Much more sensible than sending them the units, anyway. They pay me a royalty, and
I collect when trade gets easier." He lit a cigarette. "Did you know
Kelly tried to tell me he'd never heard of compound interest? I just
pointed out that since he had worked out how to use the unit I'd
sent him, he belonged to a technological civilization, and that I
couldn't conceive of technology without compound interest. Then
he broke down and admitted he was a trader himself."

"How in the . . . how did you express the concept of compound
interest in sign language?"

"I'm just a simple engineer, but the day I can't explain compound
interest to a Vegan is the day I go out of business."

Suddenly, Navarre began to sob. This embarrassed Rafferty, who
hated having men cry in public. Navarre looked up, and out of his
tear-stained face shone what they used to call a look of indescribable
horror. "Watson was right," Navarre muttered. "Poor Watson, he
was right. They should have used a firing squad."

Rafferty wanted to change the subject. "Whatever happened to
Watson?"

"Transfer. He's doing accounts in the naval dockyards now. Poor fellow. He was right all along." With an effort, Navarre steadied his voice. "So they've got the plans now and they're manufacturing."

"Well, of course."

"Of course. Of course." Navarre tottered out. Rafferty wondered whether there was any room left in the accounts branch of the naval dockyards.

The next day, Navarre was back. "Can I have a drink?"

Rafferty got him a drink.

Navarre took it in one. "The Soviet Union is calling it a gross imperialist provocation. The French have mobilized and are on the point of declaring war on every other member of the United Nations. The British are calling it an attack on the Monarchy, and the Chinese are rattling rockets and talking about running-dog revisionist stooges of fascist Wall Street imperialism." He reached out his glass and Rafferty filled it again. Navarre emptied it without seeming to notice. "Something like vegetable peel falling out of the air in Lenin's tomb. Dead Vegan cats in the Louvre. The Royal Coach covered with something which I hope is indescribable. The Majority Leader was talking in the House when a grey shimmering window opened in front of him and he was hit in the face with the Vegan equivalent of a pail of wash water. And the Chinese say that their Great Helmsman was on his fifteenth lap of the Yangtze when he was sunk and nearly drowned by a barrage of strangely shaped soft-drink bottles. Apparently he was only saved by remembering his own thoughts."

Rafferty poured him another drink, and then poured one for himself. "I knew I'd forgotten to tell you something yesterday."

"What was that?"

"I forgot to tell you Kelly was selling them as garbage disposal units."

Six months later, Navarre was looking a lot better. The Earth-Vegan trade treaty had been signed, and wholesale garbage disposal was a thing of the past. Rafferty was doing well. Kelly, as head of Vegan Export, was also doing well.

Then one day Rafferty got a phone call from the office. It was his business manager. "Mr. Rafferty, Vegan Export has just made an announcement about its new transmission unit."

"Oh?"

"They're taking advantage of a clause in the trade treaty to sell them on the Earth market," the manager continued.

"Oh?"

"And they're undercutting us seven and a half percent."

"Seven and a . . . thanks."

Rafferty drove around looking for a vacant lot. When he got back to his laboratory, he turned on his unit, and sent through a message for Kelly to come to the end of the tunnel.

When the acknowledgment came that Kelly was there, Rafferty shaped up like a pitcher and let fly.

At speed, the very dead cat hurtled into the grey vortex.

Rapidly, Rafferty switched off.

Slowly, Rafferty smiled.

As a grey, shimmering window appeared in the air and a bucket of Vegan wash water swept his bench clear.

Rafferty still smiled. After all, it wasn't every day that a man could trade with a nice, quiet, sensible friend like Kelly.

A blurb is supposed to act sort of like the label and bouquet of a bottle of wine, but this story is so good and so different that it does not respond to that formula. Rather than trying to give you a hint of what's going to happen below—an almost impossible task—we will simply say that we've published many fine stories by Vance Aandahl over the years and this, we think, is the finest.

AN ADVENTURE IN THE YOLLA BOLLY MIDDLE EEL WILDERNESS

by Vance Aandahl

Bigfoot had gone without food for three days when she finally strode over the top of a ridge and saw a long, arm-shaped meadow in the valley just below her.

As she crouched against a hemlock and pushed aside the tangle of brush blocking her view, Bigfoot's nose told her that there was no danger in the valley—no predator large enough to hurt her, and nothing made of metal—and her eyes told her that here at last she could pause to eat: tumbling from the forest's edge, a brook meandered across the elbow of the meadow, and both of its banks were thick with the light-green grasses whose roots bore tubers she could eat.

Rising to her full height, she bounded over the fallen bole of a spruce and padded down the slope of the ridge. Her stomach ached with hunger, but she took the time to find a path around a snarl of upturned roots and strawberry bushes that she might have trampled straight through were it not for the thin, sweet odor of copperheads; and she also paused, at the bottom of the slope, to check once again for enemies in the valley. Finally, assured that she was safe, she moved out of the forest and trotted through the waist-deep chaparral of manzanita and buckbrush that led into the meadow.

The stream was only an icy trickle at the bottom of its bed, but lush patches of grass grew from the sand on both sides. Slapping her cheeks with excitement, Bigfoot leaped back and forth from one bank to the other. Stooping, she yanked two handsful of grass and tossed them high in the air: a snatch of green blades spun up past the morning sun, then fluttered back to settle lightly on her up-turned face. Clucking joyously, she brushed the gravel and grass from her crest and then fell to her knees to dig and clean and eat.

Each tuber was no larger than the nail of her little finger, and a long time passed before her stomach was full.

When at last she had gorged herself, Bigfoot saw that the sun was high in the sky. She yawned and knuckled her eyes, then lum-bered across the meadow, through the chaparral, and back into the forest. A short time later, just after crossing the next ridge into the next valley, she found a natural lean-to of dwarf junipers; and though she would have much preferred the greater comfort and safety of a birch-leaf bed in a cave, she crawled under the thick thatch of dark green needles, camouflaged herself with a row of broken branches, and then fell instantly asleep.

Bigfoot knew that she needed as much rest as possible before nightfall.

For then she would rise again to continue the desperate search that now had taken her far from her home in the northern moun-tains—the search for a mate.

Andy Skaarhaug was driving north on a winding dirt road through the Yolla Bolly Middle Eel Wilderness when his blue 1960 microbus began to choke and sputter and lose power.

He pulled to the side of the road and looked at the engine. Out of the darkness the hot, sullen steel dared him to touch its skin. From his high school physics class he remembered a movie about the four stages of combustion, but he couldn't say now what the four stages were, and he certainly didn't know anything else about a car's motor. At least nothing looked broken.

The microbus started again. As it putt-putt-putted down the gravel road, Andy hoped that nothing was really wrong. Maybe his mind had been fooled by the sinister-looking pills the doctor had given him. But the bus lost all its power at once, and after it had coasted to another stop, it wouldn't start again.

Andy suddenly realized that he was alone in a great forest. An unseen vise tightened on his chest.

Hugging the wheel, letting his forehead rest against the windshield, he whispered a long wordless incantation against the fear rising in his throat and wondered at the irony of it all: his father, who had never dared to own or drive a car, had managed to warn him against nearly every hazard in a hazardous world except the danger of running out of gas on a deserted mountain road.

A man of many maxims, his father had twice or thrice daily announced that "life is what you make it," apparently meaning that Andy had better dig in deep or run like hell. His father had lovingly and repeatedly taught him to look out for lightbulb sockets, icy sidewalks, scissors, toadstools, liars, TB, railroad tracks, gasoline fumes, fallen power lines, dope fiends, unlabeled bottles, masturbation, dynamite caps, crazy drivers, drunk drivers, careless drivers, reckless drivers, truck drivers, motorcyclists, pool halls, oversimplifications, radicals, reactionaries, polio, colds, tree houses, razor blades, knives, guns, horror comics, botulism, unsupervised swimming, winos, bums, beggars, roughhousing, falling branches, dirty books, dirty pictures, heavy machinery, sunburn, eyestrain, hail storms, rusty nails, flu bugs, sore throats, syphilis germs, black widow spiders, mad dogs, rattlesnakes, broken glass, child molesters, pimps, prostitutes, rape artists, homos, sex maniacs, lightning, daydreaming, hot bacon grease, bicycles, swings, slides, roller coasters, aerosol cans, snowball fights, fistfights, fireworks, public toilets, electricity, idleness in school, frozen lakes, insecticides, matches, sneezers, coughers, hangnails, mosquitoes, bumblebees, wasps, hornets, hotplates, tight shoes, angry mobs, horse racing, dog racing, poison ivy, mine shafts, old refrigerators, plastic bags, card games, dice, bigots, bohemians, bars, boiling water, busy intersections, bullies, blisters, bad habits, boils, smoking, drinking, caves, gas leaks, earaches, religious fanatics, rafts, mumps, con men, pickpockets, lunatics, flash floods, violent movies, vitamin deficiency, sadists, homicidal maniacs, oddballs, hitch-hikers, political nuts, juvenile delinquents, cavities, measles, sunstroke, frostbite, splinters, firetraps, dangerous sports, carbon monoxide, and slippery bathtubs. To name a few of the prevalent dangers. But he had never told Andy about running out of gas.

Andy scrubbed his scalp with both hands and stared up through the windshield at the sun burning like magnesium against the cloudless azure. As a child, he had always been able to escape from the drab, relentless terrors of his father's world, had always fled into a clear and certain universe of his own invention. But now he was beyond the safety of invention. He was alone—alone with the buzzing terror deep in his brain—alone beneath the darkening pines of the Yolla Bolly Middle Eel Wilderness. And he was defenseless.

He stepped out of the car. His body felt stiff and unreal.

He knew he had to wait for a passing car, but somehow he also knew that no car would come.

For he had been alone on the road for over an hour before the bus had run out of gas, and by now he was sure of what he had only suspected before: he had wandered in his daze onto a forbidden, derelict road that no one ever used anymore.

In her sleep beneath the junipers, Bigfoot dreamed of her childhood.

In her dream she touched her father's chest and felt the strength of his cradling arms, arms that could toss her in the air and catch her again as though the earth itself were rising and falling beneath her. She tittered at the boom of his laughter. And she looked into his black eyes: sometimes they were flat and hard; but now as he held her in his arms, she could see all the way into them, could see within them depths quick with swarming glints of colored light— apples and violets, slates and indigos.

He dropped her in the grass, stepped back to beckon her with a swing of his hand, then ran away from her down a curving slope of sorrel and heather. She shrilled and chased him. She stalked him up and down the slope, round and round a knobcone pine, then back and forth across a boulder field until at last she cornered him at the edge of an emptiness—a deep gorge boiling with water spray and mist; and then, as she stared up at the hulk of his body silhouetted against the moist white clouds, she realized fully the immensity of his power in an immense universe, the potency of the muscles swollen tight across his shoulders.

Suddenly the light dimmed: the sky of her dream rolled with thunderheads, the wind cut through her coat, and with a single signal of forked lightning the rain fell in a downpour. She stretched out her arms, but her father floated away from her, floated into the mist, floated and grew like a cloud in the mist, grew and faded until at last he seemed to cover the entire storming sky . . . and to lose himself in it. She turned and ran.

Elsewhere she found sunlight and a lake.

She lay on her stomach in the grass and drove her chin into the lion-colored loam until her lips touched and took the moist sand. She gazed down through the reeds and rocks into the waters floating with weed and hailstones. Fish moved in their dark channels beneath the air—fish with salt-gray faces, gnarled mouths, and yellow lidless eyes fixed on the unchanging pathways. Ouzels and water shrews and a single mink splashed past the fish at the lake's edge, and then, when they had gone, the fish, too, were gone.

Bigfoot tumbled across the dark red heather of her dream. She crawled through a patch of huckleberries, sat against a stump to crush asters between her blue and petaled palms, heaved rocks and clods at a kingbird's nest, licked up the dab of taste from the egg that fell, then stood and turned and saw her father and the grizzly.

Her father waited in a crouch, his fingers opening and closing in front of his face.

Sniffing the air, the grizzly shuffled forward a step or two and paused. A thick blue scar ran through its empty right eyesocket and across its damp snout. Its left eye burned into her father's face. Slowly, the hair from its head to its tail bristled up. With a hissing snarl it swung up to its full height and rushed forward.

Bigfoot's father drove upward from his crouch to catch and hold the full impact of the charging bear: against the rainbowed sky their two straining bodies shook in a perfect balance of rage. Her father's hands locked around the bear's throat at the same instant that its claws sank into his back to rake the flesh, and then they bellowed death across the shrieking inch between their teeth. Each held ground and would not fall. The bear lifted pawsful of hair and muscle from her father's back, but her father tightened his black sinew-bursting hands until the bear's eye bulged and its tongue swelled from its mouth and its nostrils flared and bubbled with red foam and at last its gory paws slid from their claw-work. Finally, as the dead grizzly sank against his chest to the grass wet with their mingling blood, Bigfoot's father roared and roared again.

But did he roar in exultation or pain?

As he sank to his knees, the bright lifeblood streamed from the furrows in his back.

Bigfoot stared harder and harder . . .

And then she fell into a darker, dreamless sleep.

Two hours had passed, and no car had come to rescue Andy.

His head felt light. The muscles in his chest tightened painfully around his ribs. He wondered whether or not he should take another pill.

He leaned against the car and closed his eyes, trying to slide his mind back three days to when it had happened.

Presently, in his mind, he was there again.

He was standing behind a podium.

As he shuffled his notes, he imagined himself as a white-robed prophet bleeding poetry from a cross of stone. Then he moved into the conclusion of his lecture:

"The striking parallels between Jake Barnes and Hemingway himself should be evident by now. As we have seen, Hemingway was wounded on the Italian front while bicycling chocolate and postcards to the soldiers in the trenches; Jake is wounded while *flying* on the same front—surely an attempt by Hemingway to glamorize a reality which may . . . which may have embarrassed him . . ."

He paused to lift a forefinger to his upper lip.

He didn't bother at first to consider why he was touching himself; but then, as he prodded and poked and pinched, he began to realize that the entire region where his mustache would have been had he dared to grow a mustache was now numb and tingling—buzzing the way a foot buzzes when it goes to sleep—and had been for some five or ten seconds.

Abashed, he pulled his hand away from his mouth, hesitated for a moment, lifted his fingers to touch the lip again, then looked up from the podium to glance shyly at his pupils. Two girls in the front row cocked their heads to eye him, but the rest of the class dozed on, waiting in their mighty patience for the bell.

"We also know that Hemingway recovered from his wounds under the care of an American Red Cross nurse named Agnes von Kurowsky."

Andy gripped the podium and tried to will the spreading numbness out of his lip.

"Similarly, Jake recovered under the care of Lady Brett Ashley."

It was getting worse, much worse.

"And just as Hemingway fell hopelessly in love with Agnes . . . so too . . . does Jake . . . fall . . ."

By now the numbness had spread to his cheeks and was beginning to creep down into his lower lip, his chin, his jaw. Andy gulped and lifted both of his hands to his face, then panicked when he suddenly realized that his fingers too were growing numb. Terror pushed up through his throat like a metal fist.

"I'm . . . going . . . to . . . lie . . . down . . ."

Trying to see clearly the faces of his students now half lost in a diamond shimmer of light, he forced each word separately out of the tightening sphincter of his mouth, then sat down on the floor behind the podium. He lay back and stared up at the white checkerboard ceiling. The ocean roared in his ears.

"Mr. Skaarhaug! Do you want us to do something?" Faces hovered over him in the dazzling light.

"Esh . . ." Desperate, he pushed the word through his lips.

"What do you want us to do?"

"Hosh . . . pittle . . ."

His entire face was paralyzed now, and his hands were curling into claws on his chest. The light brightened in his eyes until he could not see, the roar loudened in his ears until it seemed he was lost in the heaving seas, lost and drowning in the timeless white scud of a sea storm; and then he began slowly to realize that he was in a car—that he was lying on his side in the back seat of a moving car, that he was staring at an old, bent, half-smoked cigarette bouncing up and down in the car's ashtray.

He tried to move, but could not: he was paralyzed from the waist up, and now his feet were beginning to buzz and tingle too.

His chest was locked in a vise of its own panicking muscle, and in a moment he grew terribly afraid that he would soon be unable to breathe.

"Hur . . . ree . . . peash . . . hur . . . ree . . ."

My goodness, he thought. *I am dying. My goodness, my goodness.* The light in his eyes and the roar in his ears were drowning him again, and this time he was terribly sure he would not be able to surface. A five-foot sea spider hung on the crest of a wave above his face, waiting to drop . . . he remembered then for the first time in twenty-two years that the spider had come to him once before, once when he was three and in his crib and close to dying from pneumonia, that the spider had hung above him then as now, waiting, silent, invisible, ready to drop on the crest of the blinding light and the deafening roar . . . *Am I really dying? My goodness, my goodness, my goodness, my goodness, my goodness* . . . he remembered clearly for the first time in twenty-two years that then, as now, there had been a frantic rush to the hospital in a strange car, his father holding him then and screeching at the cabby, though now there was no one to hold him and no cabby, only a girl whose name he hadn't yet memorized, a nameless female student who was asking him something, shouting some question at him through the spray of foam . . .

"Mr. Skaarhaug! *What* hospital?"

"Peash . . . hur . . . ree . . . peash . . ."

"I'll head for Mercy! It's closest!"

He tried once to open his hands, but his fingers wouldn't move; then the white storm blew in upon him again, and the last thing he saw before it closed around him and swept him under was the butt of a cigarette vibrating in the burnt chrome jaws of the spider . . .

Suddenly Andy realized where he actually was.

He was standing next to his car on a deserted road in the heart of the Yolla Bolly Middle Eel Wilderness. And as he had reminisced, the afternoon had darkened imperceptibly into twilight.

The pressure in his chest was worse. Though he hadn't eaten for hours, something leaden and heavy sat on the left side of his stomach. He burped acid. His head buzzed.

"Help." He practiced the word in a stage whisper. His lips made a tiny popping noise each time he said it, and he repeated it again and again as a charm against the growing darkness.

Night fell.

Around him he could imagine the wilderness listening. Then he thought he heard a human cry, far in the distance.

"Help!" he shouted.

No answer.

He ran twice around the microbus, then crouched by the front door and stroked its pocked and peeling paint with the side of his face.

"HELP!"

The night air swallowed his shriek.

He jumped into the bus, locked all of its doors, and curled into a tight fetal ball on the floor beneath the back seat.

Bigfoot awoke to the chill of an evening breeze: it was still autumn, but winter was in the air.

She lay quietly for a moment, sniffing the wind and listening for prowlers. Assured, she lifted herself with her hands and knees to scratch her back against the roof of juniper, then stood straight up in a shower of needles, twigs, and branches.

Stepping free of the junipers, she shuffled into a shaft of light that rose like a solitary luminous column in the darkness of the forest: above her, impaled on the jagged edge of a single rent in the conifer ceiling, the moon shone brilliantly. She stretched in its false warmth and then sank into a squat.

While her bladder and bowels emptied, Bigfoot combed her fingers through her coat to shake loose the insects, needles, and bits of bark that had gathered there in her sleep. Her hands paused beneath her breasts, and she looked down at the moonlight glowing in the black fur.

For a long time those breasts had ached to give suck.

She tipped back her head and stared directly at the moon and then closed her eyes and then moaned softly deep in her throat.

It frightened her to be compelled and driven—frightened her to remember how far south she had traveled in her search.

Four nights ago the itch for a mate had finally overwhelmed her, and she had run from the box canyon that she had lived in alone since her mother's death ten seasons before. She had torn her way through the tangle of rhododendron and madrona trees at the canyon's mouth, had run until she stood at last on a ridge—breathless and ecstatic above the waves of timber and rock stretching as far as she could see in all directions, and then in her ignorance she had gone south only because the writhing spine of the ridge had pointed her in that direction.

Before the sun had risen, she had trotted farther from her home than she had ever gone before.

And now, four nights later, she was still alone—alone in a strange land whose mountainsides were too gently sloped and too thinly forested, a land where food grass was scarce, an open land she could not trust, a land which twice had carried to her the distant bitter smell of metal.

She opened her eyes to the moon and moaned again, much deeper and louder this time.

Far away, across the farthest ridge, tiny but distinct in the evening stillness, a voice seemed to challenge her anguish with its own strange cry.

It was a cry much weaker, though shriller, than hers . . . yet somehow just as human . . .

Curled up on the cold metal floor of the bus, Andy tried to pass the terrifying minutes by remembering how he had awakened, three days ago, from the ocean that had drowned him.

He had awakened beneath a pea-green ceiling.

There had been only one noise: the heavy panting of a wounded animal.

As his vision had cleared and focused on the tiny ridges and craters of the ceiling above him, he had suddenly remembered the car ride and had first thought that he had been left in some lonely place to die. Panic had surged through his chest.

But then a face had quietly entered his field of vision and hovered over him—a face composed of curves, a face wrought of smooth brown eggshell modeled into flesh, a face with lemon rosettes fixed around eyes as black and quick as oil under glass.

"Dr. Sumitomo," he had said. "Hi."

"Try to relax, now . . ." Smiling, the doctor's face had moved back an inch: bits of yellow had glistened in the pores; among the white, one gold tooth had caught an arc of saffron light and then had been lost in moving shadow. "Breathe as slowly and shallowly as possible, and just try to relax . . ."

Realizing then that the heavy panting was his own breath, Andy had closed his eyes and pitched his will against the terror in his chest.

As he had struggled against himself in the darkness, his fingers had moved idly across the surface beneath him: it had felt like leather; and at the same time that he had realized that he was no longer paralyzed, that the buzzing, tingling numbness had drained from his body, he also had guessed that he must be lying on the examination table in the emergency ward of Mercy Hospital.

"I have a pill that the doctor wants you to take."

Andy had opened his eyes and lifted his head. While the nurse had first filliped a tablet onto his tongue and then had thrust a cup against his chin, he had gazed through the orange haze of down on the back of her arm and wished only that he might be made well enough to touch someday her flesh with his lips; but then he had lifted his eyes and seen that her face was the face of a bloodhound—soft, wrinkled, sagging with sorrow—and he had felt again that he was going to die.

Above him, pea green and menacing, the ceiling had threatened to descend with its weight of deaths: how many others, panting in their extremity, had perished on the same leather table beneath the same green ceiling?

"Just relax . . ." Dr. Sumitomo's face had appeared again.

"I was paralyzed from the waist up." Andy had licked his lips and tried to smile. "Did I have a stroke?"

"No, no. No." The doctor's eyes had glittered. "No. No."

"What happened to me then? I don't understand."

"You just had a little collapse—a spasm. How much sleep did you get last night?"

Andy had had to swallow. "I didn't go to bed until two. And then I woke up at five and couldn't get back to sleep."

The doctor had smiled. "You were drinking last night, weren't you?"

"I had a few beers." Andy had swallowed again and looked away. "But lots of times I've stayed out all night long, drinking *hard* liquor, and nothing like this ever happened before. Is something wrong with my heart?"

"Relax. Nothing's wrong with your heart. The nurse just took your blood pressure, and it's perfectly normal. Just relax and try to breathe slowly and shallowly."

"What *is* wrong with me?"

"Chances are you're developing an allergy to alcohol."

"An *allergy?*"

"Liquor's bad for you—very bad."

"Okay." Andy had looked squarely into the doctor's eyes. "I'll quit. I'll quit drinking."

"There's something else. You have to start taking it easy. You've been working too hard. You've been worrying too much about your job. Hmm?"

Bewildered, too ashamed to confess his laziness, his long hours of sloth and ennui, Andy had shook his head back and forth without answering.

"I want you to take a vacation." The doctor had patted his shoulder. "I want you to rest in bed for at least two days—I'll give you a prescription for some pills that'll help you to relax and sleep—and then I want you to drive down to the seashore or up to the mountains and take a nice long holiday. You've been pushing yourself much too hard, but three or four weeks of relaxation should make you feel like a new man. You'll see."

"But what about my *job?*"

"Forget it for a while. Your health is more important."

"Well . . . I guess . . ."

"Of course." The doctor had leaned closer until the smooth bistre surfaces of his face were Andy's only heaven. "The most important thing now is *taking it easy*. You have to learn how to *relax and enjoy life. Life is what you make it . . .*"

The doctor had withdrawn, and Andy had been left alone—alone beneath the dark green ceiling, alone with its history of deaths: black coin-shaped cancers had grown beneath the skin of his neck; both kidneys had withered and shriveled into useless white pods; an artery had exploded somewhere deep in his brain.

Why had the doctor hid the truth? What really had shattered in his body? And how long would it be before he died?

Later, much later, after the doctor had spoken to him twice more and then had finally left, the nurse had lifted Andy into a sitting position and had smiled at him from the sad pouches of her jowls. "Your breathing seems much better. I think we'll have your wife drive you home now. It'll be easier for you to rest in your own bed."

"Not my wife . . ." Andy had wondered who she meant.

"Oh." The nurse had chuckled deep in her throat. "Your girl friend."

"No." Looking past her into the darkening pea ceiling, innocent and virginal Andy had suddenly understood. "My student."

After two days of fitful sleep, Andy had risen from the limp and faintly malodorous sheets of his bed and gone to the telephone, and then it had taken a nerve-shredding hour to con four graduate assistants into teaching his classes for the next month. He hadn't dared to phone the department chairman, had gone instead to the kitchen window to stare from the darkness of his dingy apartment at the bright autumn sunshine glinting off the lid of the trashcan, had stood there in indecision for nearly an hour, had finally sat at his typewriter to prepare an explanation for his forthcoming absence.

As he huddled shivering against the back seat of the microbus, he remembered how he had mailed the letter in the morning, just before leaving on this, his vacation trip to the mountains.

He had dropped it into the mailbox.

And then he had glanced guiltily behind him and slunk into the bus.

Bigfoot rose out of her crouch and stood still. The cry she had heard was gone. The only sounds now were the hoot of an owl sweeping through the night sky and the susurrus of the quickening breeze.

But then she heard it again: a tiny shout beyond the farthest ridge.

The hair on her back tingled, and without understanding she began to feel the old fear that had driven her ancestors thousands of years before her to hide in the deep and inaccessible recesses of the high mountain forests, to sleep by day and go about by night, to live always alone or in small families so as never to leave lasting evidence of their existence. She felt that ancient fear, and though she did not understand it, her whole body shivered once.

And then, for the third time in as many nights, her nose caught the acrid odor of metal.

Bigfoot had seen metal only once in her short life.

It had happened ten seasons before.

Bigfoot's mother had left her alone in their canyon, had not come back for two nights and days; and in her happy innocence Bigfoot had awakened from sleep on the third evening to romp after mice and voles in the tall alpine grass, to splash herself with water until her fur was soaked and sleek, and only casually to wonder why her mother had not yet returned with mountain raspberries and softer bedding.

As she played, the evening had darkened into night. Joyous beneath the stars, wrestling with countless imaginary bears on the sandy porch of their cave, Bigfoot had lifted her head to sing and cluck, but instead she had seen in the moonlight at the mouth of the canyon her second terrible vision of personal and immediate death: her mother dragging herself through the grass, pushing herself forward with one straining leg while the other—a swollen mass of raw meat—caught in the underbrush and held her back.

All through the night Bigfoot had wailed over the dying body—

had wailed and bawled until at last beneath a sky brightening into morning she had seen the pain in her mother's eyes darken into jelly. Only then, in the glare of the rising sun, had she seen clearly the metal jaws locked in the swollen ankle.

And now, ten seasons later, alone in a strange land, Bigfoot knew that she was close to the same death. The breeze which had brought her a strange but human voice was bringing her now from the same ridge the sharp reek of metal.

For a long moment she hesitated.

Then she rolled her enormous black shoulders and strode out of the moonlight into the darkness; and as her pace quickened to a trot, she moved not away from the distant ridge, but toward it . . .

Andy first knew something was wrong by the stink.

Wrapped now in the two blankets he had brought, he was hunkering on the floor of the microbus, wondering what the trappers would say when they found his heart-failed body in the morning ("Look here, Lucas . . . some damfool flatlander got hisself lost on the ol' Yolla Bolly Middle Eel Wilderness Road 'n' ran outta gas 'n' cashed in his chips . . ."), when a tangible stench rolled across his face like a stream of liquid garbage. He choked and opened his eyes. The reek of decaying filth thickened around him. For the first time in nearly three hours he forgot the horror in his chest.

He lifted his head an inch to stare up through a window: stars shone in the night sky.

But the nauseating fetor was growing richer and stronger: his stomach moved and he gagged.

Then he heard a noise.

Someone . . . or something . . . was walking around the bus.

His body froze. Inside his chest he could feel the blood-muscle exploding. His eyes locked on the window above him.

For the stars were slowly disappearing: a great black presence slowly rose against the sky, slowly pressed forward against the fragile, meaningless glass. At first it was nothing less than the horror in his chest come alive and huge to rend and gnaw his parts; but then he saw that it was a face. Bars of moonlight glowed across its nose and cheekbones, and Andy could see the indigo glister of its eyes as they moved to meet his, the yellow gleam of its teeth as the lips parted in what could only be a smile. It *was* a face—a *human* face, a human face half again as large as any face he'd ever seen before. And it was covered with fur. And it was smiling—smiling down at *him*.

Andy stiffened.

His arms and legs were paralyzed. He tried to move his fingers, but they stayed where they were, clamped to his genitals. He could feel only the racing of his heart, hear only the buzzing roar of blood pounding through his brain. He was lost again in the heaving ocean that had swept him under four days before, but this time he saw something more than an imaginary sea spider hanging over him—he saw something else, something impossibly real. As the storming darkness closed around him, he saw the great loving smile of a human giant.

He fainted so quickly that he didn't even hear the first crunch of metal folding under enormous hands.

Branch by branch and leaf by leaf, Bigfoot loped through the pathless forest with her mate slung across her shoulder.

He was only a child, half her weight.

He was pink and hairless.

And he was wrapped in a clinging stuff she'd never seen before. But he was a man.

Tittering, chortling, clucking gleefully, Bigfoot swung her way beneath the conifers. She had ripped the big metal bear to pieces. She had taken her mate from its belly, and then she had torn out its entrails and strewn them up and down the bear's path to frighten other bears, to tell them that she, Bigfoot, was their terrible enemy.

She stopped beneath a giant tongue of rock and lifted her lips to the light streaming down through the pines and firs. Pied luminous, glossy and vibrant, her face shone back at the moon.

First she would take her mate back to the valley where she had found food grass growing. She would strip away the stuff clinging to his skin and clasp his pink, hairless body to her warm fur until he awoke. She would feed him, and then the two of them would travel north to her home in the high mountains. There she would care for him until he grew into manhood. Someday he would stand as tall and strong as her father, and someday she would bear many children by him.

Bigfoot crooned up at the moon. Then she leaped up from one ledge to the next until she stood on the roll of the forest's huge stone tongue. She let her mate slide from her shoulder into her arms, and she gazed down at his delicate face.

He stirred once. He opened his eyes and looked up at her face. His mouth opened. His mouth opened wider and wider until the lips seemed ready to split. Then his eyelids drooped again; his head rolled back against her arm; and presently his gaping mouth closed into a thin, tight line.

Bigfoot caressed his forehead with the downy fur on the back of her thumb. Then she hugged him to her breasts. Spinning from one foot to the other, she danced with her mate across the smooth bright stone.

Andy was wakened by the cold wind against his back and legs. But his naked front was warm.

He moved his face against fur. Its living stench was all around him. He pushed feebly away, met no resistance, tumbled. Then he was lying face down on the ground: rough sand, the prod of a weed, rocks cutting into his thigh. He did not look up.

Something touched his back. He stiffened and ground his face into the sand. It was unmistakably a hand—an enormous hand covered his back from one side to the other. The only thing then that amazed him was the thought that caught in his mind and would not leave: *I feel good: nothing's wrong with me.* The muscles of his chest had relaxed; his face and hands no longer buzzed with terror; his once-boiling blood moved smoothly now through its channels; his heart, he knew, would never burst. And as the huge and loving hand gentled his flesh, something from the primitive callus of its palm curled through nerve and bone and blood to twine itself in his brain: *I feel good: nothing's wrong with me. I feel good: nothing's wrong with me.*

He lifted his face from the earth and brushed the sand from his cheeks. He rolled slowly onto his back and looked calmly up at her.

Nothing about her surprised him, not now, not with the immaculate certainty of well-being and goodness rolling through his mind like a warm liquid: *I feel good: nothing's wrong with me. I feel good: nothing's wrong with me. I feel good: nothing's wrong with me.*

She was kneeling over him, looking down at him as she stroked his stomach and chest.

Her face was twice as large and twice as hard as Dr. Crashi Sumitomo's had been that other time—not limp morocco polished with earwax, but the black and uncured hide of a jungle buffalo. Her features were sharply defined: a high forehead, large intelligent eyes, an arched nose, prominent ears, chiseled lips, and a strong chin. Except for the nose, the cheeks, and the ears, her entire face was covered with black hair rising to a bushy crest of tufts at the top of her brow.

The muscles of her shoulders curved directly up to her ears, as though she had no neck at all; but even while he watched, she turned her head to question something beyond them in the darkness. He saw then the huge jut of her breasts in profile, saw also that her arms and legs were straight and well proportioned in length to the bulk of her torso. Except for the palms of her hands and the soles of her feet, her entire body was furred with black hair. But she was no animal: she was a human giant.

It occurred to Andy that he was no longer offended by the stink of her body. As he lay beneath her, he smiled.

Anyone else would be frightened and would try to break away and run. He wondered why. His head felt remarkably clear—clear and clean and empty of even the slightest fear. *I feel good: nothing's wrong with me. I feel good: nothing's wrong with me. I feel good: nothing's wrong with me. I feel good: nothing's wrong with me.* The words flowed smoothly through his mind, washing it, flushing from it the toxic wastes of twenty-five years.

It didn't matter that he was lost and naked somewhere in the Yolla Bolly Middle Eel Wilderness. It didn't matter where he was or what he had. It only mattered that she was lifting him again to the warmth of her bosom—the warmth that would protect him from the cold wind. He muzzled his face between her breasts, closed his eyes, and slept.

Bigfoot knew now that her mate was not merely a sick child. He was different altogether. Yet he was still somehow human.

Just moments before, when he had opened his eyes to look at her, she had seen him smile. And as he smiled, the odor of fear had finally stopped oozing from his soft pink skin.

She patted the tiny body dozing between her breasts. Shifting back and forth from one buttock to the other, she rocked the burden of love in her arms. She clucked melodies in his ear. She crooned the chill from his hairless flesh.

Then she lifted her eyes to the crystalline skies and prayed.

She had no language. She prayed only in pictures and sounds, not in words:

Beneath the pure and frosted light, she saw her mate: grown large and strong, he stood at the mouth of their canyon like a birch tree in the wind.

Beneath the pure and glittering light, she saw her mate: leaping, he side-stepped the grizzly's first lunge and pounced onto its back; he locked his knees against its ribs and sank his fingers into its neck; the grizzly screamed; its claws thrashed behind its head; then its whole weight sank slowly beneath the grip of her mate's hands.

Beneath the pure and dazzling light, she saw her mate: he moved through the shadows of their cave, lowered himself to his knees between her legs, waited for a moment above her, then met the rising arch of her body with the sudden forward-rolling mystery of his male strength, then breathed deeply into her mouth, just—she remembered—as her father had panted against her mother's lips in the dim caves of earliest childhood.

Beneath the pure and streaming light, she saw her mate: he flexed his shoulders now great with muscle and hair, laughed once, then ran easily across the meadow as their daughter shrilled with joy and romped after him; and at the edge of the creek, Bigfoot herself looked up from the piles of food grass she had collected to watch and smile in sweet reminiscence.

Beneath the pure and never-ending light, she saw her mate . . .

Sleeping in Bigfoot's arms, Andy dreamed, as he often had, of a dormitory.

He was sitting with a black man and a yellow man on the bed in one of the rooms of the dormitory. All three of them were wearing pajamas. Andy's were purple with green rings. The black man's were green with yellow rings. The yellow man's were yellow with blue rings.

"Let's write poems," said the black man.

Andy braced a Big Chief tablet against his knees and began to print with a ballpoint pen in very fine lettering as clean and neat as type:

> How do I love thee? Let me count the aberrations.

But before he could write a second line, he was disturbed by a sifting noise from the ceiling, as though the whole room were being powdered with flour.

He looked up from his poem just in time to see that the yellow man was disappearing into a painting on the wall. It was, in fact, a painting of Dr. Crashi Sumitomo. He was wearing a black ten-gallon hat, a red and black kerchief tied around his neck, a blue denim shirt, a white and brown cowhide vest, wind-whitened levis, a pair of furry gray sheepskin chaps, black boots with silver spurs, and a big gunbelt slung low across his hips. One foot in the stirrup, he was just preparing to mount his horse, a golden palomino. A single red mesa stood in the distance.

So Andy was left alone on the bed with the black man.

"Let's trade," said the black man.

They traded.

Andy read the black man's poem:

> Because you fed me hellebore
> I now must eat your flesh and skin
> And drink your dappled clotted gore
> That you may come to me within.

When he looked up, the black man was gone. He was alone in the room. He looked at the painting on the wall. It had changed into a pin-up.

The pin-up girl was a strawberry blonde with hazel eyes. She was wearing a black ten-gallon hat, a red and black kerchief tied around her neck, a white and brown cowhide vest, black boots with silver spurs, and a big gunbelt slung across her hips. She was standing next to her horse, an appaloosa. Her fingers were twined in its mane.

Andy slipped off the bed and walked across the cold tile floor for a closer look.

The cowhide vest was thrown open by the thrust of the girl's plum-nippled breasts. Her dimpled white buttock stood clearly against the pied flank of the horse.

Andy sighed.

While his left hand rose to idly trace the full curve of her breast, his right hand fell to fret at the buttons of his fly. The purple cotton parted. At length the stiffened flesh emerged. He gripped it and squeezed it gently—once, twice. He moved the skin against the shaft—back and forth, back and forth—slowly at first, then faster, then frantically.

And then he awoke . . .

As her mate's body stirred and squirmed against her belly, Bigfoot rolled back in the sand and smacked her lips at the moon.

But then, when he squirmed again, something small and hard touched her groin. She lifted her head to stare at his face in the thicket of fur between her breasts.

His eyes opened. In the moonlight they burned as red as the fire that had run through the forest once when she was a child. His mouth was sealed in a hard line, but a froth of bubbles foamed from one nostril. His hands crawled over her breasts. She saw his buttocks lift and fall, and once again she felt something prod the soft flesh between her thighs.

She stared in amazement. His lips opened, and he groaned. His teeth ground through the hair, and she suddenly felt his tongue against her chest.

His buttocks lifted again. His whole body bucked down. For the third time a tiny hardness butted futilely against her. She heard him moan through his foaming nose. She felt one of his hands leave the swollen nipple it had been squeezing and work its way down between their bodies until the fingers were groping into her damp tissues. He arched his back again; and when she pushed down this time, she felt his thrust move all the way into her body.

In her abdomen she felt a strange vibrant warmth. She let her head roll back: above her, the moon seemed to swell and the stars to spin. She lifted her hands to her mouth and bit into the knuckles. She heard him moan again, and then she heard another, deeper moan from her own lips.

Something wonderful was moving in her body, but somehow it was not enough—it was not, for her, the thing itself. She lifted her back from the sand to meet it, but it was still too small, too gentle. Her mate was shrieking now on the bridge of her body, his frail arms locked around her sides, his little knees churning frantically against her thighs, but even the extremity of his lust was only a suggestion, for her, of what the thing itself might be.

Suddenly she felt his tiny seed pulse into her body. For one tantalizing moment his hardness seemed to grow within her, but in the next moment it softened and shriveled away.

And then her frustration overwhelmed her: agonized, she lifted her arms and brought down her fists in one convulsion of blind rage.

Something snapped.

Lifting her fists from his back, she stared down in horror at his eyes. They looked closely at her . . . through her . . . beyond her . . . and then they closed. A sigh that might have been a laugh escaped from his mouth. The froth bubbles shivered and hung unmoving from his nose.

Hugging his body to her bosom, Bigfoot staggered to her feet. His head fell back, and she saw the hairless pink flesh of his face withering and hardening in the light of the moon.

And then she felt the pygmy seed dribbling down her thigh. A great coldness filled her womb.

Later that same night she began the long trip north to the canyon where she would live out the rest of her life . . . alone and childless in the darkness.

Robert Sheckley's short-short is, in one sense, a very funny spoof of the perceptions obtained under the influence of "mind expanding" drugs. In another sense, it is about a time of chaos and disaster among a very ancient race, and you should not scratch anywhere until you finish the story.

STARTING FROM SCRATCH

by Robert Sheckley

Last night I had a very strange dream. I dreamed that a voice said to me, "Excuse me for interrupting your previous dream, but I have an urgent problem and only you can help me with it."

I dreamed that I replied, "No apologies are necessary, it wasn't that good a dream, and if I can help you in any way—"

"*Only* you can help," the voice said. "Otherwise I and all my people are doomed."

"Christ," I said.

His name was Froka and he was a member of a very ancient race. They had lived since time immemorial in a broad valley surrounded by gigantic mountains. They were a peaceable people, and they had, in the course of time, produced some outstanding artists. Their laws were exemplary, and they brought up their children in a loving and permissive manner. Though a few of them tended to indulge in drunkenness, and they had even known an occasional murderer, they considered themselves good and respectable sentient beings, who—

I interrupted. "Look here, can't you get straight to the urgent problem?"

Froka apologized for being long-winded, but explained that on his world the standard form for supplications included a lengthy statement about the moral righteousness of the supplicant.

"Okay," I told him. "Let's get to the problem."

Froka took a deep breath and began. He told me that about one hundred years ago (as they reckon time), an enormous reddish-yellow shaft had descended from the skies, landing close to the statue to the Unknown God in front of the city hall of their third largest city.

The shaft was imperfectly cylindrical and about two miles in diameter. It ascended upward beyond the reach of their instruments and in defiance of all natural laws. They tested and found that the shaft was impervious to cold, heat, bacteria, proton bombardment, and, in fact, everything else they could think of. It stood there, motionless and incredible, for precisely five months, nineteen hours and six minutes.

Then, for no reason at all, the shaft began to move in a north-northwesterly direction. Its mean speed was 78.881 miles per hour (as they reckon speed). It cut a gash 183.223 miles long by 2.011 miles wide, and then disappeared.

A symposium of scientific authorities could reach no conclusion about this event. They finally declared that it was inexplicable, unique, and unlikely ever to be duplicated.

But it did happen again, a month later, and this time in the capital. This time the clyinder moved a total of 820.331 miles, in seemingly erratic patterns. Property damage was incalculable, and several thousand lives were lost.

Two months and a day after that the shaft returned again, affecting all three major cities.

By this time everyone was aware that not only their individual lives but their entire civilization, their very existence as a race, was threatened by some unknown and perhaps unknowable phenomenon.

This knowledge resulted in a widespread despair among the general population. There was a rapid alternation between hysteria and apathy.

The fourth assault took place in the wastelands to the east of the capital. Real damage was minimal. Nevertheless, this time there was mass panic, which resulted in a frightening number of deaths by suicide.

The situation was desperate. Now the pseudo-sciences were brought into the struggle alongside the sciences. No help was disdained, no theory was discounted, whether it be by biochemist, palmist, or astronomer. Not even the most outlandish conception could be disregarded, especially after the terrible summer night in which the beautiful ancient city of Raz and its two suburbs were completely annihilated.

"Excuse me," I said, "I'm sorry to hear that you've had all this trouble, but I don't see what it has to do with me."

"I was just coming to that," the voice said.

"Then continue," I said. "But I would advise you to hurry up, because I think I'm going to wake up soon."

"My own part in this is rather difficult to explain," Froka continued. "I am by profession a certified public accountant. But as a hobby I dabble in various techniques for expanding mental perception. Recently I have been experimenting with a chemical compound which we call *kola,* and which frequently causes states of deep illumination—"

"We have similar compounds," I told him.

"Then you understand! Well, while voyaging—do you use that term? While under the influence, so to speak, I obtained the knowledge, a completely far-out understanding . . . But it's so difficult to explain."

"Go on," I broke in impatiently. "Get to the heart of it."

"Well," the voice said, "I realized that my world existed upon many levels—atomic, subatomic, vibrationary planes, an infinity of levels of reality, all of which are also parts of other levels of existence."

"I know about that," I said excitedly. "I recently realized the same thing about my world."

"So it was apparent to me," Froka went on, "that one of our levels was being disturbed."

"Could you be a little more specific?" I asked.

"My own feeling is that my world is experiencing an intrusion on a molecular level."

"Wild," I told him. "But have you been able to trace down the intrusion?"

"I think that I have," the voice said. "But I have no proof. All of this is pure intuition."

"I believe in intuition myself," I told him. "Tell me what you've found out."

"Well, sir," the voice said hesitantly, "I have come to realize—intuitively—that my world is a microscopic parasite of you."

"Say it straight!"

"All right! I have discovered that in one aspect, in one plane of reality, my world exists between the second and third knuckles of your left hand. It has existed there for millions of our years, which are minutes to you. I cannot prove this, of course, and I am certainly not accusing you—"

"That's okay," I told him. "You say that your world is located between the second and third knuckles of my left hand. All right. What can I do about it?"

"Well, sir, my guess is that recently you have begun scratching in the area of my world."

"*Scratching?*"

"I think so."

"And you think that the great destructive reddish shaft is one of my fingers?"

"Precisely."

"And you want me to stop scratching."

"Only near that spot," the voice said hastily. "It is an embarrassing request to make, I make it only to save my world from utter destruction. And I apologize—"

"Don't bother apologizing," I said. "Sentient creatures should be ashamed of nothing."

"It's kind of you to say so," the voice said. "We are nonhuman, you know, and parasites, and we have no claims on you."

"All sentient creatures should stick together," I told him. "You have my word that I will never ever again, so long as I live, scratch between the first and second knuckles of my left hand."

"The second and third knuckles," he reminded me.

"I'll never again scratch between *any* of the knuckles of my—left hand! That is a solemn pledge and a promise which I will keep as long as I have breath."

"Sir," the voice said, "you have saved my world. No thanks could be sufficient. But I thank you nevertheless."

"Don't mention it," I said.

Then the voice went away and I woke up.

As soon as I remembered the dream, I put a Band-Aid across the knuckles of my left hand. I have ignored various itches in that area, have not even washed my left hand. I have worn this Band-Aid all day.

At the end of next week I am going to take off the Band-Aid. I figure that should give them twenty or thirty billion years as they reckon time, which ought to be long enough for any race.

But that isn't my problem. My problem is that lately I have begun to have some unpleasant intuitions about the earthquakes along the San Andreas Fault, and the renewed volcanic activity in central Mexico. I mean it's all coming together, and I'm scared.

So look, excuse me for interrupting your previous dream, but I have this urgent problem that only you can help me with. . . .

This story is about a man who awakens after 200-plus years of frozen sleep. Much has been said lately about Change in the arts and in communication, and we are not sure whether we are more impressed by this story's poignant narrative or its refreshing statement: that things may change more readily than ways of saying things . . .

BENJI'S PENCIL

by Bruce McAllister

George Maxwell suddenly felt a web of warmth on his skin, then the burn of his heart's fresh beating, then the first flutterings of sound in his ears. He awoke to focus his eyes weakly on a bare ceiling. His eyes rolled once like oiled agates, then clung securely to the clarity of the white surface above him.

He was beginning to feel the warm crescendoing tones of his muscles when a voice near him said, "George Maxwell, welcome to life."

The muscles sputtered hotly in his neck, but Maxwell turned his head and found the face that belonged to the voice. A pale man smiled back at him, his shiny shaven head contrasted like a wrinkled egg on the thick weave of his white robe.

Maxwell tried his lips, but they sputtered as all of his muscles seemed to be doing.

"George Maxwell, please try to say something."

"Fihnlegh," Maxwell tried. "Finlehrg . . . Finahlrg . . . Finalih . . . Finally."

The other man laughed kindly. "A most appropriate choice of your first word. It makes me want to start off my talk with an apology for the institute's tardiness in reviving you. Do you mind if I talk while you regain your lips?"

Maxwell shook his head.

"The Institute for Revivication wants to apologize for taking so long in unfreezing you. Your records were misplaced for five years and—"

"Ahm," Maxwell interrupted.

"Yes?"

"Ahm ah curd?"

"Pardon me? Please try again."

"Am ah cured?"

"Oh. Of course you're cured." The man smiled, almost laughing. "All you needed was a new heart. I hope this won't bother you, considering what you were accustomed to in your time as far as heart transplants go, but we put a synthetic heart in your chest."

Maxwell jerked and emitted a feeble "Argh."

"I am sorry. In your time that would have seemed terrible, I'm sure. Something inorganic within you. But let me assure you, you'll be fine. We've been giving people synthetic hearts for a long time, and the psychs always report that there is negligible personality change as a result. Okay?"

Maxwell nodded, a little relieved. His mind was shouting, "Now I'll be able to see the green!"

"Let me finish your formal introduction first. By law I must give you this intro speech, then we'll have some minutes to talk about anything you'd like. Your grandson—rather one of your multi-great-grandsons—will be here soon to pick you up."

Maxwell jerked again, but tried a smile with his limp lips. Relaxing, he waited for the soothing voice of the first man he'd heard in a terribly cold long time.

"Fine? As I was saying, your records were misplaced, so we had no way of finding any relative of yours. By law a relative must be willing to house and feed you for the remainder of your life. You were lucky. One of your multi-great-grandsons is an assistant food-distributor and can afford to support you. But I won't say more—you'll be talking to him soon enough . . . and that's another problem. The language. The written language of this time is not very different from yours. Inflections and sectional dialects often make it hard for a 'new' person to understand. I happen to be an Introducer, so I've had to study tapes of past spoken language in order to communicate with people like yourself."

"Lingige hahd?" Maxwell asked. "Linguage hahd?"

"No, it's not hard at all. You'll be able to pick it up in a week or so. I just wanted to prepare you for it. Now, there's one other matter for intro—"

"Ah git wrkuh? Kin ah get wrkh?"

"Get work? No, I'm sorry. That's one of our problems. Not many jobs, so that's why we had to find a relative to support you. I know you'll feel bad about that, being a burden and all, but that's *modus vitae* these days."

"How longh will ah liv?"

"Ah, yes. Technically we could keep you alive and in very good health for over a hundred years. But mandatory death, I'm afraid, is at seventy years of age. Population control, you understand. Family planning and euthanasia. According to our records, you have ten years left. That's quite a while, you must realize. And it will be ten years of life in a time that's new to you." The man smiled again.

Maxwell remembered his sleep, and said, "Ohnly a momenth. A breifh momenth."

"Pardon me?"

Maxwell shook his head to say "nothing," but he was thinking, "He wouldn't understand at all."

"One last bit of intro information. The reason you were revived so late was not because of your need for a synthetic heart. We've been installing hearts for a long time. The problem was the process for unfreezing all of the cases like yours. It's a delicate operation, and we only developed it ten years ago."

"How longh hav ah bin asleep?"

The Introducer opened his mouth to answer, but a door snapped open suddenly behind him. By raising himself on one elbow, Maxwell tried to look past the man to the doorway, but fell back when his strength failed. The weakness scared him. His eyes wanted to close, but his mind's hatred of the thought of sleep pricked them open and kept them quivering.

"I want you to meet," the Introducer said, "one of your multi-great-grandsons." A green-eyed boy in a soft loincloth and baggy shirt appeared by the side of Maxwell's bed. "His name is Benji-tom Saphim. His father will be your guardian."

Maxwell's mind raced into happiness. This boy, his mind

shouted, will show me the green of a hundred hills and the warm palette of all the flowers I've missed for so long.

The Introducer said something garbled to the boy. It sounded to Maxwell like nasalized English, chopped but softer than German. The boy said something equally strange to Maxwell, and smiled.

I don't understand their language, Maxwell thought, and there is so little time.

The boy took Maxwell's hand as they left the cottony white corridors of the hospital. It had taken the old man three hours to learn to walk again, but now his legs flowed under him as if the long sleep had only been a dream, and the desire to see green things had not waned at all.

I was an English teacher, Maxwell was thinking, but this drive in me to see the green of grasses and the ripples of ponds and the lace of pastel flowers seems more poetic than academic. Perhaps the long sleep did this to me, or perhaps I should have been a poet back then. Maybe Lana would have been happier with me, had I been a poet.

They took a vast empty elevator down to the ground level and stepped out into the quiet city, the boy still holding his hand. Perhaps, Maxwell thought, his father told him to hold my hand—"Take the old man's hand and be careful with him."

The streets were like clean gutters, rendered Lilliputian by the towering cement walls on either side. Maxwell was afraid to look up, afraid that the buildings pierced the clouds; so he kept his eyes at street level, and the boy was silent, a flicker of smile playing across his lips when the old man looked at him.

Something seemed dead. A color was missing. Maxwell stopped suddenly and looked around him. The color green was absent. Maxwell laughed at himself and resumed walking. On many streets of the New York of his time there had been no green at all. He should expect even less green in a time when population increases would have spawned miles and miles of cement structures for housing and business.

At the end of an hour's walk nothing had changed. The same buildings and streets seemed to jump from block to block, keeping up with Maxwell, making the walk monotonous. Still no green. And soon an irrational fear popped into existence in Maxwell's chest, making his synthetic heart beat faster. Was there any green anywhere? Even the green of a man's shirt or the green paint of an automobile would have helped, but the few people on the street wore only drab cloth, and the only traffic was the intermittent passing of gigantic trucks.

Another empty elevator let Maxwell and the boy out on the dark fortieth floor of an apartment building. Maxwell still only understood a word or two when Benji-tom's father and the fifteen members of his family—parents, sisters, brothers, infants and aged—greeted him with the pale smiles of people who were never touched by a sun that had been exiled past towering cement walls.

Maxwell sat on his blanket, the squall of babies to his left, and to his right the rustle of Benji-tom's mother in the kitchen-bedroom. After a week of learning to understand the sectional dialect of Benji-tom's family, Maxwell's heart had begun beating even faster from his one fear. In the language of these people never once did he hear the words "green," "flower," "hill" or "grass."

Benji killed a cockroach that had just flashed across his floorblanket. Maxwell watched him, thinking, "God, poetry is dead. There is no green." He had asked Benji a month before to take him to the nearest park, and Benji hadn't understood him. Maxwell had then asked Benji's father, who said that he didn't understand either, that buildings and streets and food-trucks were the only things in the city. And the city, Maxwell realized with a sick thumping in his chest, consisted of seventy-five regions; a region meant one hundred sectors; a sector was one hundred sections, and a section, as Maxwell understood it, was about twenty miles square. "What is a 'park'?" Benji's father had asked, and Maxwell was now afraid to mention the words "tree," "grass," or "flower."

The absence of green was one part of Maxwell's agony. The first two nights with Benji's family, he had screamed. The pull of fatigue had advised him to sleep, and his mind had bellowed in revolt. He

had slept too long and too cold, and he remembered the acid of
that sleep. The colorless, dreamless, icy sleep. And the three apartment rooms containing Benji's family were crowded, stuffy and light-
less at night. The cockroaches scuttled, the babies whimpered, and
the only clear sound was the buzzing that issued briefly in the morning from a black knob on the wall, meant to waken Benji's father in
time for his job at the market. Maxwell knew the market, too, and
he hated it. He had visited the market once while Benji's father,
hoping to find green vegetables for sale. Something green to look
at. But there was never any sale. There were only government cou-
pons that allowed husbands and wives to obtain boxes of yellowish
biscuits, dried fish, sometimes dried meat. The market was housed
on two floors of an apartment building where the walls had been
ripped out to permit the flood of sweating individuals flowing in
with the food supplies from the massive food-trucks—those lone
members of street traffic.

Compared to the masses, Benji's father was well-off. He could
afford to house and feed his wife's mother, father, brothers and
sisters, in addition to his own. As Maxwell had discovered the day
before, two of the old people in Benji's family were sixty-nine and
would be put to sleep like animals in a year.

In the dim room, where Maxwell slept on a blanket beside
Benji, Maxwell watched the boy pick up the cockroach carcass and
play with it, pretending it was alive, pushing it across the floor,
flicking it with his finger to make it slide away "in escape." Maxwell
had watched the boy's play before, and the loneliness of the vision
made the loss of nature's green things even worse. Mother Nature,
Maxwell thought to himself, reached the magic age of seventy and
was then put to sleep—by cement rivers of human fish.

Maxwell tried not to think of his own son. Many people had
died during his long sleep, and he knew that, were he to think of all
of them, of his sixty years of life with them, he would fail to live in
this new present. Maxwell said, "Benji-tom?"

The boy looked around, his pale face the only clear light in the
room. The cockroach dropped from his fingers and lay still by his
blanket.

"Yes, great-father?"

"Are you ever sad?"

"Yes. Sometimes."

"When?"

"When the food-trucks break down."

"No, I mean sad about living here."

"I don't understand." The boy was smiling, but confused. But he wasn't dumb at all, Maxwell knew, and that made everything a little sadder.

"I mean, what do you do to be happy here?"

"Lots of things, great-father."

"Does it make you happy to play with that roach?"

"Uh-huh." The boy poked at the insect and smiled more surely.

Maxwell was silent. Something that felt like optimism was suddenly nagging at him, asking him to talk to the boy. "What do you do with the roach, to be happy."

The boy looked embarrassed, confused again, but he said, "I think that the roach is like a food-truck. I push it around. M'father says that food-trucks can run even faster than roaches. He likes food-trucks, and I've seen a lot of them when I go down on the street."

Something in the boy's words sounded familiar to Maxwell. A vague memory of his own youth flickered at the back of his mind. Maxwell persisted, "Do you ever dream about food-trucks?"

"Dream?"

"Do you ever see pictures in your head at night? Pictures of food-trucks."

"Oh! Sometimes, yes." The boy was happy with this. "I once saw a picture of myself, and I was a food-truck running down the streets taking food to everybody. I never broke down because . . . because . . . I just never broke down."

My God, Maxwell thought with excitement. Sitting down quickly beside the boy, he said, "What do you like as much as the food-trucks? Anything else?"

"I like the elevators. When they don't have to stop on a lot of floors, then they go fast. They go fast like food-trucks go fast. M'father says they do. Just *like* food-trucks go fast."

Maxwell's heart stopped. The word "like" pounded in his mind, and he remembered happily that "like" was one of the two key words of a simile, and that a simile was the most common sign of poetic thought. Maxwell thought to himself with growing content- ment: "Grass is like a blanket . . . an elevator is like a food-truck." It wasn't the poetry Maxwell was used to, but it was poetry. Poetry, he realized, is not at all dead here.

Maxwell wanted to hug the boy, but Benji had picked up the cockroach again by its legs and was staring at it closely as it dan- gled from his fingers.

"And dead cockroaches," Maxwell said anxiously, "are they like broken-down food-trucks?"

The answer was slow in coming, but the boy said "yes" and smiled.

With the aftertaste of dinner biscuits in his mouth, Maxwell lay still on his blanket, hoping that Benji-tom was still awake. The dark- ness and threat of sleep was much less fearful these days, and the compulsion for seeing green things had been supplanted by a desire to know the poetry of Benji's world. Maxwell remembered his long cold sleep, and that naked memory told him again: There is little time, just a brief moment; the night is coming.

Benji stirred beside him and Maxwell wanted to begin another murmured night conversation with the boy. The daylight hours were always occupied with Benji-tom, but Maxwell didn't want to stop there. He wanted to speak to the boy now, but thoughts stilled his lips for a moment.

"How easy it is," Maxwell thought to himself, "to forget the real persons of a past time when you are busy with the present." He had often thought of his wife and son, wondering how they finally died, but those reflections were rarely heavy with sadness. How much does one pine for a far historical past, was the question.

Maxwell was busy in this world. There was no green poetry to know in this world—no flowers or grass. But what mattered was that poetry did exist, and Benji's mind held it. Maxwell was busy—and he knew it—trying to capture the poetry of this time; and as he thought about it, he remembered a prediction made by a great Romantic poet of the distant past.

"Benji-tom?"

Calm silence. Breeze-less air. Then: "Great-father?"

"Before you go to sleep, I want to tell you something. Sometime soon I want to read you some words written a long time ago. I'll have to find a library first. Do you—"

"A 'library'?"

Maxwell sighed. There must be libraries, he thought, filled with books or tapes or whatever would fill libraries in these times. Someone would know. Perhaps the hospital.

The nearest library had been five sections away, packed with microfilm and tapes, and the search for the piece of writing Maxwell wanted had taken a year and a half. Seated now on his blanket, Maxwell began reading to the boy, with a hand-copied version of the poet Wordsworth's words rattling nervously in his hands. He knew that an explanation of the poet's prediction might take months, considering Benji's mind; and, even though time was so short, Maxwell knew that the explanation would be the main thing to be accomplished.

"Poetry is the first and last of all knowledge—it is as immortal as the heart of man. If the labors of men and science should ever create any material revolution in our condition, and in the impressions we habitually receive, the poet will sleep then no more than at present . . ."

Maxwell had left Benji crying in his room two sections away, and the tears had been the first Maxwell had ever seen on the boy. Escaping from their presence, the old man hurried from the apartment on his own, and faced the long street walk to the "chamber." He was exactly seventy years old now, and the brief moment for finding poetry was over. But things were fine.

When he arrived on the twentieth floor and passed through the blank door that opened onto the waiting room of the chamber, Maxwell saw a cushion on the floor and sat down beside another old man. In all, there were five old people in the room, draped in off-white cloth. They remained quiet, eyes on their hands or on the floor, allowing Maxwell to think proudly of the past ten years with his grandson.

He had taught Benji to write, had taught him archaic words like "tree" and "grass," and had discovered for himself that for Benji the dirty wall of a room could be as kind as the sweaty face of his mother, that an old woman's cough in the night could be as assuring as a box of dried fish. "As" was the other key word for similes, for the poetry of similes.

He had also explained Wordsworth's words to the boy. Actually it had taken almost eight years for that explanation—all that talking about everything Maxwell could think of. More than the brief discussion of word-meanings that had followed the first reading of the poet's prediction, what had been the real explanation of meaning was Maxwell's persistent teaching. The fruit: the growth of Benji's mind's eye.

He had also made a present of twenty pencils to Benji. The Introducer had granted Maxwell the instruments as a last request before the old man's visit to the perfumed chamber where he would "sleep," but not have to face the agony of waiting for sleep to end and warmth to begin again.

Maxwell had worried for a long time about paper for the boy's pencils, until he found that there were other things Benji could write on. More permanent things.

A man who looked a little like the Introducer opened the door to the chamber and motioned to Maxwell. The old man rose and entered the death-room, only to smile when the perfume—meant to disguise the odors of gas and human sweat—made Maxwell think of flowers, perfumed petals stretching along the green hills of a river region where frogs sang of green water-lillies and green and green and green . . .

Benji-tom's father returned to the market, leaving the boy happy to know that the Super at the market would be willing to hire him the next year. A job was very important. There were fifteen people to feed; and soon Benji would have a wife.

Benji sat down on his blanket in the room and took a pencil out from under it. Staring at the wall, pencil raised in his hand, the boy remembered what the Introducer had told him that morning. The boy had made the long walk to the hospital only for an answer to a question, but a question that had been voicing itself in his mind every day since his great-father's visit to the chamber. The Introducer had answered the question well.

"I don't understand," Benji had whispered, "why my great-father always said that he had only a little time left to live and do things. He lived ten years, and that's a long time."

"It's only a minute, really," the Introducer said, "for a man who slept two hundred and twenty-three years."

Benji raised his pencil to the wall, and began slowly to write large printed letters. When he finished one line, he cocked his head and smiled, then read aloud to himself: "Walking and walking on the streets down there is like half-sleeping on my blanket with the running of cockroaches across my legs."

The words would remain on the wall, the boy knew. His mother didn't care if there was writing on the walls. The walls were as dirty as rat-tails anyway.

AFTERWORD

I have edited five anthologies in this series, and this one has been, without question, the hardest one to compile. The reason is that the series, for the time being at least, has turned from an annual into a biennial affair, meaning that I have twice as many stories to choose from.

I normally begin work on the anthology by compiling a short list of "must" stories that form the core of the book and a longer list of other favorites. I keep the latter list in sight for a few weeks, letting the "least favorite" stories settle out; and, from the remainder, I choose a group that, when combined with the core, forms a reasonably balanced collection. Eliminating stories is a painful process, sort of like extracting perfectly good teeth. Since this year there were so many perfectly good stories that, for various reasons, did not get included, I would like to mention some here.

The following were a bit easier to omit because they have appeared in other, recently published collections, and hopefully you will see them elsewhere if you missed them in the magazine:

NOT LONG BEFORE THE END	Larry Niven
COME TO ME NOT IN WINTER'S WHITE	Harlan Ellison
	and Roger Zelazny
CAR SINISTER	Gene Wolfe
THE FATAL FULFILLMENT	Poul Anderson
THE MAYDAY	Keith Roberts

The remainder are not necessarily relegated to limbo, since science fiction is a well-indexed and anthologized field; so if this list is helpful to some future anthologist, fine:

DEEPER THAN THE DARKNESS	Greg Benford
FOR THE SAKE OF GRACE	Suzette Haden Elgin
SHIP OF SHADOWS	Fritz Leiber
MUSE	Dean R. Koontz
THE SOFT PREDICAMENT	Brian W. Aldiss
THE FINAL QUARRY	Eric Norden
TOMCAT	Gary Jennings
OUT OF CONTROL	Raylyn Moore
LONDON MELANCHOLY	M. John Harrison
A MEETING OF MINDS	Anne McCaffrey
BYE, BYE, BANANA BIRD	Sonya Dorman
FROM THE MOON, WITH LOVE	Neil Shapiro
NIGHT OF THE EYE	Dennis Etchison
INITIATION	Joanna Russ

—*Edward L. Ferman*